Praise for LIVE A LITTLE

"A sparky, gutsy story about how an unintentional lie sends one woman's life spinning out of control. Raquel Rose is a charismatic heroine who will have you rooting for her from the first page."

—Whitney Gaskell, author of *Good Luck* and *Mommy Tracked*

"Green's effervescent prose and pitch-perfect humor will surely charm readers. Her deeply imagined characters seem like old friends as their story unfolds with effortless grace."

—Jody Gehrman, author of *Notes from the Backseat*

"Kim Green is a must-read! LIVE A LITTLE is wise, winning, and funny, with engaging characters that pull you in and pages that crackle with wit and insight."

—Veronica Wolff, author of *Master of the Highlands*

Praise for previous novels by Kim Green

"Kim Green is an exceptionally talented writer who explores love, life, and friendships with wit and honesty. In *Paging Aphrodite*, she creates a world you will love to lose yourself in."

—Theresa Alan, author of *Who You Know* and *Spur of the Moment*

"I loved it!"

—Melissa Senate, author of *See Jane Date* on *Is That a Moose in Your Pocket?*

Previous Titles by Kim Green

Is That a Moose in Your Pocket?

Paging Aphrodite

Live a Little

A Novel

KIM GREEN

5 SPOT

NEW YORK   BOSTON

5 Spot
Hachette Book Group USA
237 Park Avenue
New York, NY 10017

Visit our Web site at www.5-spot.com.

5 Spot is an imprint of Grand Central Publishing.
The 5 Spot name and logo are trademarks of Hachette Book Group USA, Inc.

Printed in the United States of America

First Edition: August 2008
10 9 8 7 6 5 4 3 2 1

Library of Congress Cataloging-in-Publication Data

Green, Kim, 1969–
    Live a little / Kim Green.—1st ed.
        p. cm.
    ISBN-13: 978-0-446-69793-4
    ISBN-10: 0-446-69793-1
    1. Motherhood—Fiction.   2. Self-actualization (Psychology)—
Fiction.   3. Life change events—Fiction.   4. Problem families—
Fiction.   5. Domestic fiction.   I. Title.
    PS3607.R433L58 2008
    813'.6—dc22

                                                    2007043730

Book design by Stratford, a TexTech Business

For Lucca and Zev

ACKNOWLEDGMENTS

Some books emerge from the author's mind shimmering with wit and clarity. Then there's the other kind. I owe a great deal to the editing talents and fortitude of Amy Einhorn and Caryn Karmatz Rudy, without whom this book would be an anemic version of itself. Thanks again to Victoria Sanders and her associates, for finding such a good home for *Live a Little*. Beth Thomas is a brilliant copy editor, and Brigid Pearson's jacket design thrills me every time I see it. Dierdre Gilmore's insights into breast-cancer culture and the psychology of the disease were invaluable. Heather Hughes gave me perceptive feedback when I needed it most. It seems like my family is always stepping up to offer support, child care, and the occasional cocktail in times of need: the Wassermans in Nashville, the Gibrats in Antibes, and the Greens in San Francisco, New York, and Montana. Thank you, all. Also: Many thanks to my readers, especially those of you who have taken the time to write to me over the years. And, finally, to Gabe, Lulu, and Zev; I love you. If you didn't make the house so lively, I wouldn't have found so many charming cafés in which to work.

There are a thousand small ways in which friends and family help me push a book along, foremost among them continuing to believe that I can do it. If I have forgotten to mention you here, know that I appreciate everything you do, from the impromptu brainstorms to the unscheduled pep talks.

Please visit the following organizations and others like them and get involved in beating this disease; their work is *our* work.

Breast Cancer Fund
http://www.breastcancerfund.org/

National Breast Cancer Coalition
http://www.natlbcc.org/

Avon's Breast Cancer Awareness Crusade
http://www.avoncompany.com/women/avoncrusade/

Y-Me National Breast Cancer Organization
http://www.y-me.org/

National Breast Cancer Foundation
http://www.nationalbreastcancer.org/

Susan G. Komen for the Cure
http://www.komen.org/home/

Young Survival Coalition
http://www.youngsurvival.org/

The Mautner Project
http://www.mautnerproject.org/home/index.cfm

Living Beyond Breast Cancer
http://www.lbbc.org/

Celebrating Life Foundation
http://www.celebratinglife.org/

National Alliance of Breast Cancer Organizations
http://www.nabco.org/

Live a Little

CHAPTER 1

We Interrupt This Broadcast...

Have you ever wondered what you'd do if they told you that you were dying? Not like, someday you're going to die. Imminently. As in three months.

I used to think about it periodically. But when they tell me, my reaction is nothing like what I'd imagined: the raw terror, tingling in the spinal region, crying ranging from dignified sobbing to Irish wake–style caterwauling. Perhaps a swoon. No. What I actually do is thank the doctor—*thank* him, for God's sake—proceed to have a calm, rational conversation with him about my prognosis, then—"sexual fantasy starring the middle-aged" alert!—hypothesize doing him. Yeah, him. *Il dottor.* The guy nervously plucking at his white sleeve, exposing a swatch of swarthy ethnic wrist.

As soon as the words leave his mouth, I wonder opportunistically if his dismay can be leveraged somehow. Sexually, that is. I guess when you're going to die and you can count the number of orgasms you've enjoyed in low double digits, it suddenly seems absolutely essential to cram in as many as you humanly can. The doctor is young, divinely average-looking, and terrifically bad at it. Delivering grim news, I mean.

"But I'm only forty-three," I say. That part goes as rehearsed.

"I know. Sadly, it's not as rare as you'd—"

"But surely there's some treatment, some operation..."

"We'll operate, of course, but it's not statistically likely to work against this type at this advanced stage, Mrs. Rose—"

"But they cure people, like, all the time! I read something about a new drug from Norway...or was it Denmark?"

Meissner's eyes flick to the desk clock, which he has cleverly attempted to conceal behind a trophy topped by a golf club–wielding bald man. He nods sagely. "Cyclopaclizole. FDA pulled it. Too many myoclonic seizures," he says with a trace of regret, as if we are discussing a very effective flea collar.

At the word "seizure," my shattered brain does a clumsy swan dive, landing in the convivial pool that is carnal escapism.

"Oh, can it, will you? Look," I say, leaning over slightly so he can get an eyeful of cleavage, which I know is Grade A prime in spite of being riddled with tumors. "Will you have sex with me?"

Then we fuck like demented bunnies on the oversize big-dick-substitute oak desk, right on top of the dreaded biopsy results.

Okay, a girl can dream, can't she?

Somehow I manage to stagger out of the office without collapsing on or molesting anyone. I slide into the car and burn myself on the sunbaked seat-belt buckle. Something perverse makes me press my hand hard against it, conjuring a sizzle. Chemo terrifies me. I wonder if it will hurt ten times as much as the burn. A hundred times as much? Five hundred?

The minivan skews to a stop in front of our mailbox. For a millisecond, I contemplate moving it to make way for the postman. Then it dawns on me that I no longer have to care what he thinks of me. I don't realize I've left my purse and keys in the car until I'm at the front door.

I ring my own doorbell.

Taylor swings the door open. "Yeah?" Her cell is rammed in her ear. She's wearing a triangle bikini top, and her boobs are insanely perky. It is hard to believe we emanate from the same gene pool.

"Did you look in the peephole? What if I was a rapist?" I am nearly shouting.

"Then I'd kick you in the nuts and shut the door."

I push past her, pausing in the guest bath to gulp water directly from the faucet. My throat hurts. Suddenly, everything wrong in the universe seems like a symptom instead of just garden-variety Jewish hypochondria.

Taylor blocks the way to my bedroom and holds up a scrap of cloth. "Mom, can you go to Urban Outfitters tomorrow and get me some more of these tanks? Not the girls' ones, they're in the guys' section. Get me blue, green, and black. And orange! But not the gross traffic-cone one, the cool one."

Too wasted to counter the assault with an inspired lecture on the perils of not appreciating your parents properly in case they die prematurely, I ball the shirt in my hand and fall into the pile of murky bedsheets. I close my eyes and pray in what I imagine is a semi-authentic manner. I whisper "amen" and "hallelujah" several dozen times before giving up on sleep and scouring the bathroom cabinet for drugs.

The toilet seat stands at attention, the rim festooned with dabs of pee and hair. For some reason, this detail, this mundane particle of injustice, sends me over the edge.

"Goddammit!"

I slam the seat down, my hand protected by Taylor's shirt. A puny scream erupts from the now-cracked seat joint, which, like my mind, has never been completely stable. "Fuck!" I yell into the bone-dry hand towels (Phil always wipes his hands on my bath sheet).

Afternoon blurs into evening while I toss and turn, willing the catastrophe on a better-equipped individual. Once every 2.5 seconds, I actually forget I have it. My thoughts are weird. For example: *What's better for the kids, preserving my posthumous reputation by delivering the news with grace and decorum, or maintaining a consistent familial environment by crying and cussing?*

At one point I smell my son and open my eyes. Micah is leaning over me, in the process of stealing my cherished heating pad from the opposite nightstand.

"Why are you wearing cleats in the house?" I croak.

Micah kicks a clod of soggy turf off his soccer shoe, which, for the price, should not only have David Beckham's signature on it but also include a charity fuck for the wearer's mother.

"See ya later, Mom. I'm taking the car." He waggles a set of keys.

My keys.

I roll out of bed, stomp across the house, and lock myself in the off-garage toilet, shaking, until I hear the garage door open and my husband's evening sacraments begin. In preparation for what lies ahead, I try to do the sort of deep breathing they teach you at yoga, in which you're supposed to cram healing breaths into every possible orifice of your body until you are at peace.

Finally, I go in search of my forever-in-wasted-motion partner in life.

Phil goes utterly still when I corner him in the living room and deliver the news. Then, true to form, he goes on the attack.

"What are you talking about?" he says irritably. His fingers twitch. I can tell he wants to flick the volume button and return to his life's work: wallowing in flatscreen, high-definition television.

With what I believe any reasonably dignified person would call great dignity, I walk calmly toward the father of my children, plant myself in the path of the TV, and obstruct his view of Barry Bonds, my arms crossed just like Barry's (except that his are big, black, and muscular, and mine are big, white, and flabby). Then I leap on Phil and wrestle the remote clumsily from his hands. I brandish this electronic sliver of power triumphantly as I crawl toward the couch.

This part I accomplish sans dignity.

"What the hell are you doing?" Phil says. We are both panting.

"I have cancer," I say, experimenting with the pronunciation a bit. This time, I emphasize the "I."

"How can you have cancer? You haven't even been to the doctor." Phil's green eyes, which I'd once found feline and mysterious, now exude a grim haze as predictable as the sky over L.A. They flicker back to the screen: Giants, 11; Dodgers, 3.

"We need to make the necessary arrangements."

I finally have my husband's attention. "What arrangements? Raquel? What are you saying?"

"I'm saying I have cancer of the breast. The doctor says it's stage four, maybe inoperable. Twelve lymph nodes, Philly! Twelve!" Through the window, I watch as Ronnie Greenblatt strips off his soccer jersey and pulls the lawn mower out of the shed. At seventeen and nine months, my son's best friend has the kind of cobbled abs that could make a nun weep.

"I thought breast cancer was hereditary. Your mom doesn't have it. Lauren doesn't have it."

"Well, apparently, I have it." I bank the factoid that only 5 percent of breast cancers are inherited for future use.

"Do you have"—a maroon flush of shame saturates Phil's cheeks—"a lump?"

"Of course I have a lump. That's why I went for a mammogram and then the biopsy." I envision myself through my husband's eyes at this moment: the picture of pale goddesslike piety and patience in the face of doom. Lumpy doom.

"Good God." I can tell Phil thinks he should have found it himself. My husband is nothing if not dutiful. If someone had slipped it into our marriage contract—*Responsibility number three: Perform breast lump exam on [blank's] tits bimonthly*—he would have kneaded me like bread dough every other Wednesday without fail. Also, he was probably wondering, as was I, when was the last time he actually touched my breasts. Strangely, it was one of the first thoughts that curdled in my head after my visit with Meissner: *Did Phil touch it?*

Telling the kids afterward is worse.

"Oh my God, Mommy!" Taylor screeches, lunging into my arms in a manner she abandoned at eight.

"It's okay, honey. I know it's hard. I know," I say, rubbing her back, which is bare where her baby tee cowers above her low-slung jeans.

"But Mom, aren't they even going to try chemo?" Micah, whom I'd considered the smart one until he smoked the joint with Ronnie and plowed the Accord into the side of the Circle K last spring, defaults to calm interrogation. He takes after Phil that way.

"The doctor says we'll do chemo, radiation, even stem-cell replacement if we have to. After the surgery to remove as much of the cancer as they can, of course." That's something I hadn't understood at the time and had been too addled to ask: How can inoperable cancer be operated on?

"What about Tamoxifen? Ronnie's grandma had breast cancer, and she did chemo and took Tamoxifen for five years, and now she's fine." My son's denim-blue eyes are wide and panicked.

"I can't believe you remember that," I say, impressed.

The blue eyes snap. "Don't treat me like a fucking idiot!"

"Mike, calm down." But I don't really want my boy to calm down. In fact, I don't want anyone to calm down, anywhere, ever again. My family least of all; as far as I'm concerned, they should start building the shrine now. I can already imagine it: my best photos (all taken in the early eighties and slightly pixilated), my favorite scented candles from Tocca, sympathy cards, a lock of hair, smooth stones to facilitate my journey to the other side—all of it with the faint whiff of idolatry and Catholicism about it. With a dash of Eastern mysticism thrown in. This is de rigueur among the coolest dead young mothers.

"How am I supposed to calm down?" Micah yells. My son goes from zero to sixty in a heartbeat. He takes after me that way.

Taylor lifts her tear-stained face from my soon-to-be ravaged bosom. "Shut up, you douche! Mom's dying, and you're making it worse! You're such an asshole!"

"Kids! Let's give it a rest, okay? I'm really tired," I lie. Actually, the conversation has left me weirdly energized. The kids are being so damn attentive, so nice.

"Mom, I love you! You can't die!" Taylor snuggles against me; it seems I'm now her preferred parenting resource. The runner-up slumps against the couch, his head in his hands.

Micah pushes Taylor aside and folds his five feet eleven inches into the crook of my arm. I am fairly sure that the last time my offspring hugged me willingly was 2001, when our first family dog, Pickle, was laid to rest in a patch of rosemary. Nearly purring, I inhale my children's gamey teen scent, stroke their silky skin, lap up their delicious need. It is pure bliss.

And that's when it comes to me: Maybe, now that I am dying, it is time to live a little.

CHAPTER 2

Waiting to Expire

"Mom!"

The cry cuts through my calm, the cloud of misty heat billowing around me, three handfuls of bath salts and a really good life escape plan featuring me, Viggo Mortensen, and a catastrophic earthquake that wipes out three quarters of the population, forcing all—even the perimenopausal—to wildly attempt procreation for the cause.

Mom.

How such a simple, monosyllabic word can be stretched to three parts, I don't know; its unique, eardrum-piercing delivery is one of the unexplained gifts of childhood. What I do know: Whatever semblance of peace I manage to achieve through sensory or narcotic means, a good strong *"Mom!"* is guaranteed to destroy it with the exuberant finality of a SCUD missile. It's like the pool guy said when I suggested that, in the future, he leave his stash of weed at home instead of enjoying it on my front porch: *Dude, don't harsh my mellow.*

Reluctantly, I raise myself out of the tub, one of those boxy numbers from the sixties that lacks both neck rest and overflow drain. I hate it; it's number 531 on my list of domestic insults. A river of water surges over the side, gathering in the grout-filled moat between bath and floor. I should soak it up immediately, before it turns into green mold. Then again, green mold is number 847, so I wouldn't classify the issue as pressing.

"I'm coming!" I yell.

"Mah-ah-ahm!" Taylor bellows as if she did not hear my piteous response.

I grab a bath sheet—fluffy! still sort of white!—off the rack and towel off vigorously. I should probably aim for vigor while I can, before death—preceded by chemo, social isolation, mastectomy bathing suits—claims me.

Robe on, slippers AWOL, I wander in search of the summons. It doesn't pay to dawdle; they get antsy when you take too long. Once I overheard a woman at the dry cleaner's liken her family dynamic to sled dogs jostling for raw meat. I can relate.

Micah is in the kitchen. In front of him, on the counter, is a row of whole-wheat tortillas, fanned out neatly, like crop circles. He is busy scooping refried beans out of a can and piling shredded cheese on top. Afterward, he will roll them up with a squirt of habanero. It is his favorite midmorning snack: the fart rocket.

"Have you seen Taylor?" I ask him.

"She went out to the garage." Micah stops midwrap and turns to me as if just remembering I have an oft-terminal disease. Absorbing the ferocity in his eyes, I think, not for the first time, *I can't believe Philly and I made this.*

"Mom, I'm quitting golf," he adds.

"Why would you do that?" True, it's not his main sport—that's soccer—but the dream of Tigerish endorsements and a job that justifies sunscreen dies hard.

Micah grimaces. "So I can take care of you. You're going to need help after the operation…and, you know, the other stuff."

This is unprecedented. Three days ago Micah agreed to help me wash the garbage cans—after I threw the spaghetti dinner I was making against the wall, cried, and threatened to revoke his driving privileges.

"Mike, that's sweet of you to offer," I manage to say, "but you don't have to start changing your life around for me. I *want* things to stay the same as before. I'm sure things are going to be just like they were before. I mean, after I get better."

But what if I don't?

A finger of unease trails down my neck.

Willing myself not to scream, I shakily fill a mug with coffee and add a dollop of whipped cream and six or seven sugars and carcinogenic sugar substitutes. It occurs to me that I no longer have a need to fear them, so I throw in a couple more.

I set the mug on the counter next to a fart rocket. "I suppose I could use a little help around the house and stuff, but it's not your job to take care of me anyway, it's—"

Phil walks in. His tie is broad and rumpled, with a stain in the middle like a third eye. The patch of eczema on his knuckles is raw and red. It gets worse when he's stressed or annoyed with me. The last time his hands looked normal was August 2004, when he returned from a three-day fishing trip with the neighborhood husband posse. Whatever the skin-care benefits, there is nothing sadder than a paunchy middle-aged man with a beer cozy and a half-empty cooler of dead spawning salmon.

Panic clutches my throat. *With Mr. Primetime in charge of things, we'd better order that tombstone now.*

"How are you feeling?" Phil sounds uncharacteristically syrupy, oversolicitous, maybe even guilty. Perhaps it has also crossed his mind that the source of my sickness is his beloved toxic weed killer, though I expect he is too callow to admit it.

He and Micah are both looking at me. There is something almost reverent in their expressions. It's as if I have, by getting sick, become more important, more commanding, more *present,* than I was yesterday. I can see that they are really surprised by this development. Like, with another whole person in the room, they are fretting over how they are going to get enough air to breathe, enough space to occupy, enough room to navigate their lives.

"I'm fine," I snap. Through the laundry room, the door to the garage is ajar. I can hear rummaging that is presumably Taylor making more work for someone—me—to clean up at an unspecified time. After a nice round of radiation, perhaps.

I tug my robe tighter around my waist and storm out of the room before fury executes a bloody coup on my emotional state. Taylor is indeed in the garage. She has managed to unshelve six boxes and rifle through all of them. The floor is littered with old paper, bedraggled Halloween costumes, mismatched gym socks Phil won't let me throw away, a plaque with the gold leaf flaking off. Last year, when I finally tackled the garage, I'd indulged the bright idea of organizing our lives alphabetically: "H" is for Health Insurance, Holidays, Honors. I was proud of the scheme at the time. It seemed so rational, so clearheaded. That changed. Names of things, I came to realize later, are oblique, subjective, elusive. Who the hell knows if something is called a bank statement ("B") or a monthly balance ("M")?

Now nobody can find anything, even me. I see that I should have sorted our mess by emotional state. It's always easier to remember how something made you feel than the actual fact of it. Thus, I'd have slotted the Lake Tahoe vacation photos into a "Happy" folder, while Phil's abandoned dissertation would be filed under "Grim" and the 2003 taxes tucked neatly into "Suicidal."

"Mom, where'd you put my junior high yearbooks?" Taylor's forehead has a dewy sheen. Even for an athlete, undermining your mother is hard work.

Hmm. Try "I" for "Ingrate."

"I think they're over there, in that white bin," I say instead. "What do you need them for, anyway?"

"Linds and I are trying to figure out if Quinn got a nose job the summer after eighth grade. She says she didn't, but I remember it being bigger."

Supposedly, Taylor, Lindsay, and Quinn, along with three or four other girls who attend the H. Arnold Tater Academy, where Phil teaches with skill but without political aptitude, are best friends. The horror of Taylor's statement tells you something about the state of comradeship in suburban America and why raising a daughter in today's world is a thankless job.

I nudge the holey socks into a pile. "Well, maybe Quinnie's self-conscious about it. If you're going to tease her about it or judge her, why should she tell you? She's probably afraid you're going to act like little bitches and sell her out to the whole school for a few laughs."

Taylor's eyes widen. Her lips are parted slightly, like a transfixed toddler's. Before I can backpedal—*"I don't know what got into me, honey. I'm sure you'd never act like a little bitch, nor would any of your darling friends. Plus, it's not really a very nice way to describe someone, is it? Even if she is a little bitch, I mean"*—Taylor's shoulders jerk slightly, and she starts burbling.

"Oh, Mom," she says. Tears pool, making her look even younger than her fifteen years.

"Oh my God. I can't believe I was going to do that. I'm a *total* bee-atch. It's just—Linds and Quinn were ragging on me about spring break, and I couldn't stand it anymore"—her eyes dart toward the washer, where a tangle of jockstraps and sports jerseys circles—"I know it sounds bad, but I just wanted them to stop picking on me. They treat me like shit."

"Don't say 'shit.' "

Taylor nods. "I can't believe you're really sick, Mom. You seem so normal."

"I am normal, Tay," I say calmly.

Raquel, don't be a shit.

"Dad said—"

"What did Dad say?" I suppose the discreet meetings—the ones about how to carry on after I dissolve into a husk of my former strapping self and, eventually, join Pickle under the rosemary—have already begun. I wonder if Phil has surveyed the range of available divorcées and widows and chosen a replacement yet.

Taylor nervously flicks her ponytail. "He said it doesn't make sense to talk about it until you get a second opinion."

"You're getting a second opinion, right?"

"Meissner's the best, Laurie. It *is* Stanford, you know." I say it a little proudly, as if I'd gained admittance to graduate school instead of chemo.

"You said he was young."

I shrug. "I think he was second in his class at Harvard Medical School." The diploma hung, crooked and dusty, over the big-ass oak desk, broadcasting that Meissner was too busy fighting the crime of cancer to bother with ambience.

My sister leans forward on her Laura Ashley–style floral lounge, radiating the slightly manic style of caring that has made her a local celebrity. "Rachel," she says in her classic compassionate purr, "you need to cover all the bases. You need to mount the fight of your life. I think you should see another oncologist, and a naturopath, and an O.M.D."

"Raquel." I know it seems petty, but why can't a family chock-full of brainy lawyers, doctors, and CEOs remember that I changed my name legally back when I still had a waist?

"Quel, I think you should see an oncologist, a naturopath, and an O.M.D." she repeats, her voice even.

"What's an O.M.D.?"

"Doctor of Oriental medicine."

"Oh, like an acupuncturist."

"Eastern medicine has been healing people for literally thousands of years, when our people were still running around in loincloths and slapping on leeches. When I was studying with Xia Chi-Hong at the Center, I personally witnessed him cure several terminal cases who'd been written off by Western doctors."

When I was studying at the Center . . .

Spare me.

My sister is one of those insufferable people whose lives sprout magic the way the rest of ours breed boredom and regret. Lingerie model (okay, so it was just catalogs, but still), chief executive officer of her holistic fitness video empire, personal coach, successful guru on local television . . .

The list goes on. If that weren't enough to screw up the most secure, accomplished sibling—and we all know I'm far from that—it gets worse.

She married my guy.

With the ironic timing of those who deserve to be entitled, the onetime love of my life, Loren "Ren" White, glides into his family room right after I drop the bomb. Polite skeins of gray have just begun gilding his wavy mass of golden hair. Aristocratic bearing. No paunch to speak of. Real life-size muscles.

Warm hazel eyes. Full lips ready with a tension-shattering quip.

God, how I'd loved him.

"Jesus, Quel," he says, and then I am folded into my brother-in-law's embrace. His chest, gift-wrapped in tennis whites, feels like a premium extra-firm mattress, sans pillow-top. After a respectable ten seconds, he releases me and enfolds Laurie, who tilts her highlighted head aside so he won't muss her hair. I watch them, not twins, exactly, but indisputably complementary, what with their blond manes; lithe, naturally toned physiques; and born-to-the-manor carriage. They even have matching names (Lauren and Loren), which is why we call one Laurie and the other Ren.

I don't hold this against them. Much.

Laurie frees herself. Ren's beautiful hazel eyes are gratifyingly damp.

"I'm calling Xia in Beijing," my sister says, brushing aside my reluctance, as per usual. I can see gears meshing in her head, transforming her from the host of the Bay Area's leading healthy lifestyle show, *Living with Lauren!*, into the humble integrative health-care student who mastered Mandarin while becoming Xia's star pupil, beating out hordes of native Chinese and a handful of hairy-armpitted Europeans in the process.

"Okay." I have to give in. I have twenty minutes to get to the school to pick up Taylor from cheerleading practice. It's funny how these types of mundane duties continue in the face of my impending demise.

Ren grasps my hand in both of his. Compared to his lean, smooth, manicured ones, mine looks like a fifteenth-century washerwoman's, chapped and broad and designed to withstand prolonged contact with lye and the rigors of crude sex acts performed under less than luxurious circumstances.

"You're going to beat this thing, Quel," he says.

Not sure if this statement requires a response, I mumble something unintelligible and discreetly check out Laurie's new red-lacquer Chinese butterfly cabinet, which must have set them back a pretty penny. Ren's hands are warm. If I concentrate—which I do—I can almost remember the feeling of them cupping my nineteen-year-old ass. As a matter of fact, I recall it better than the feeling of owning a teenage ass, which tells you something about the flame in my torch. . . .

"If there's anything we can do—taking the kids, driving you to the doctor, hiring someone to make dinner and do the cleaning—just let me know. I'll take care of it. Christ, I can't believe this is happening. . ." Ren's voice trails off, empathy filling the silence.

Ren White is the only man I've ever met who can say these types of things without sounding like a secretly gay soap-opera hero. He even makes *me* want to be a better person.

Laurie smiles at him in sympathetic synchronicity. Better person or not, I want to kill them both.

I swing the Sienna into the parking lot at the north end of Big Basin Redwoods State Park at 5:46 P.M. I'd dropped Taylor off at Lindsay's, where the girls were ostensibly going to study for their trig exam. Mikey had called after soccer practice to say he'd grab dinner at Ronnie's. And I'd fulfilled my sole culinary responsibility already—scribbling "fettuccine alfredo, add peas" on a Post-it and slapping it on the fridge so Phil would be sure to open the correct bags of frozen foodstuffs.

I slide out of the car and inhale the brisk damp scent of California redwoods and shaded water. It is the sort of bright, cool light the Bay Area is famous for, igniting everything green and wet into pearly iridescence.

Based on what I've read, I should want to be alone right now. Alone with my thoughts. Which are (presumably) deep because I've just been leveled by The Diagnosis. Given free tickets to the exclusive yet undesirable cancer club.

The problem is, being alone is making me nervous. No, wait: *panicked*. Untangled even briefly from the threads of mutual need and ridicule that comprise Rose family relations, I feel ephemeral and temporal, a substance that dissolves quickly under threat of space and quiet. These days, those feelings are too close to nonexistence for comfort. It's ironic, really, because if someone had told me three days ago that a one-hour solitary walk would provoke anything but the most delicious flush of liberation, I would have called her nuts.

Swallowing dread, I lock the car and strike out blindly for the trail. My plan is to walk the challenging three-mile loop around the reservoir. The one I'd sworn I'd circle daily the last time I flunked out of Jenny Craig with an extra fifteen pounds buttressing my waist. My current goal is not thinness, exactly, but the glory of a thin epitaph: *May God grant you eternal rest, dear (skinny) Raquel.*

"Raquel! Raquel, is that you?"

I lift my head and stare into the horizontal sun, tipping my navy old-lady visor to shield my eyes. I am enveloped by a cloud of noxious, lollipop-scented after-bath spray. A millisecond later, a tangerine helmet head and white sweat suit with gold lamé stripes assaults my field of vision.

"How you doing, sweetie?"

Rochelle Schitzfelder grabs my shoulders and pulls me against her ample bosom briefly. Rochelle is sixty if she's a day, can pass for fifty-nine after dusk in heavy fog, and runs the local JCC board like a cavalry platoon. I know it is infantile, but every time I see her, I issue a quick, silent prayer of thanks that I'm not one of those unfortunate Jews forced to bear a name with "shit," "fish," or "wiener" in it.

We deliver the usual platitudes about how great the other looks, how thin the other is, how busy and exhausted we are, how challenging it is to meet the needs of our genius-athlete offspring, and what a pain in the ass our husbands have become.

"Did Micah get his acceptance letters yet?" Rochelle says.

I nod. "A couple of UCs, Michigan"—I tweak an imaginary piece of lint from my jacket in an attempt to play down my (almost tacky) level of satisfaction—"and Princeton." I happen to know Rochelle's youngest, Larry, is, at twenty-four, in his (second) final year at a small state school up north known mainly for its alcoholic recidivism rate. Thankfully, Micah has delivered the goods.

Rochelle frowns. "You're coming to the party on Saturday night, right?" She folds her hand around my arm. Her nails look like calcified slabs of lox.

"What is it again?"

Rochelle fixes me with an I-can-get-your-kid-bounced-from-varsity stare. For a swollen second, I am tempted to blurt out my bad news; it's a ready-made excuse for every failure to execute I've ever had. Some wise kernel of self-preservation stops me. Telling Rochelle Schitzfelder before the two or three hundred people I like better than Rochelle, just because I'm too wimpy to just say no to her (endless) requests for slave labor, would hammer the final nail into the coffin of my self-respect. Also, I don't think I can deal with Rochelle staring at my breasts.

"I'm sorry, Rochelle," I say instead. "I've had a really rough week, and things are sort of slipping."

"The fund-raiser? For the library? The expanded tolerance section?"

"Oh! Yeah, I was going to call you...Phil double-booked us. I was so pissed at him. But it's work-related, so we kind of have to go. His boss's birthday or something."

Thankfully, Rochelle Schitzfelder's gossip meter is set higher than her pique gauge. She leans in so close I can see her sherbert-colored lipstick bleed into the cracks of her upper lip.

"Did you hear about the Welch-Yens?" she whispers, as if Wendy Yen, a dermatologist who gave up her practice to raise her Silicon Valley CTO husband's two hellions from his first marriage plus their own Clomid-generated twins, is going to spring out from behind a rock and rain staccato Chinese curses down on Rochelle's hennaed head. I am fairly sure I met the woman only once, but, lacking a proper creative outlet, I pride myself on my meaningless-fact retention skills.

"Splitsville," Rochelle goes on before I can reply. "Annunciata knows the receptionist at Blakely and Chao. Wendy's already signed on with them to fight the terms of the prenup. She'll get a nice package, that's for sure. Connor's rolling in it. I just feel sorry for the kids." She shakes her big Hobbit head. "Wendy was just starting to get somewhere with the little shits. God knows Sylvia never managed to control them. Annunciata says Wendy's going for the house. With the Bay Area real estate market like it is, I say more power to her! The girl can sell it and get something precious in Carmel or Laguna and still have a lot to live on. She'll marry again, mark my words. Doesn't have an ounce of fat on her!"

If I cut her off at five minutes, I'll still have time to hit Starbucks on the way home for a green tea Frappuccino. Green tea...it must be healthy, right? That will definitely balance out the lemon bar.

"...not even the worst part..." Rochelle is saying as I tune back in to the stream of words. "The worst part is the"—gulping intake of breath that always indicates an incoming bomb—"the *cancer.*"

Initially, I assume she is talking about, well, me. It takes me a full five seconds to wrestle my throat open again. You know that weird piece of dangling flesh in your throat, that hangy thing? Mine is abruptly way too big. Perhaps a side effect Meissner forgot to mention?

"Cancer? Who has cancer?" I manage.

"*Wendy* does. Uh-huh. Hardly anybody knows. Only her closest friends—Annunciata, me, Mimi LeMaitre, maybe Robin Golden."

"What kind?" I can't believe that fucker Connor Welch is divorcing his beleaguered, if well-tended, wife right when the Big C hits. Fucker.

"Ovarian. Wendy thinks it was all those fertility drugs she had to take to get the twins." Rochelle pauses to pluck a loose gold thread from her lamé fanny pack. "They already did the surgery. She starts chemo next week. That's why she had to resign from the committee."

"That's terrible. What an asshole! How is Wendy doing?" I say rather oversolicitously, to mollify Rochelle for my earlier transgression.

Rochelle draws her lox fingers across my arm. "Oh, Raquel, sweetie, you got it backward. It's not Con who's leaving Wendy. *She's* leaving *him.* She's been sleeping with a doctor over at Stanford for over a year. Her own doctor, can you believe it? The boy's barely legal, even if he is an oncologist! Messner, I think his name is. No, wait a minute. Meissner. Sam Meissner. That's it. That's the one. I'm pretty sure he went to Harvard," she adds.

Yep, Class of '95.

This is the moment when I begin to suspect that justice

post-cancer-diagnosis is not qualitatively different from justice before the bomb. That Wendy Welch-Yen should get a side of sex with her sickness courtesy of *my* Meissner while I satisfy myself with *Sex and the City* reruns and the occasional brother-in-law fantasy must be the universe's idea of a practical joke. I'm not laughing.

CHAPTER 3

Lifestyles of the Ditched and Nameless

"Three, two, one...we're live!"

The young girl with the enviably shiny ponytail and the clipboard waves her hands at the cameras, which are trained on my sister up on the dais. Laurie smiles at the audience in a way that emanates both accessibility and superiority. Where did my little sister learn that? It certainly wasn't from Dad, whose idea of torture was being the center of attention for longer than the ten seconds it takes to sing happy birthday to a person. And it wasn't from Ma, whose shtick is founded on a hybrid of suffering and exclusion plucked directly from the biblical Hebrews. And it definitely wasn't from me: The only thing I can credit myself with bestowing upon Laurie—with the obvious exception of her husband—is the art of how *not* to balance career, family, and a persistent cream-cheese addiction.

There is something unnerving about watching a loved one perform for television. For this reason, I have seldom visited my sister's South of Market San Francisco set. (This is the reason I tell myself. Other explanations, among them laziness, chronic brother-in-law avoidance, and garden-variety envy, I would rather not consider.) Today, however, my back is to the wall: The combined hard sell of Ma the do-gooder and Laurie the flinty-eyed ratings queen convinced me that the world needs another voice broadcasting breast-cancer awareness. They caught me in a weak moment.

"When do you see the doctor again?" Ma asked last week. She and Laurie had come over to double-team—er, help—me in my hour of need. This consisted of lots of vigorous grout-scrubbing and duster-wielding interspersed with disgusted clucking over my lack of domestic prowess.

"Two weeks."

Ma grimaced. "What are those *mamzers* waiting for, the grass to grow?"

I couldn't argue with her. Frankly, I'd been a little shocked myself. For me, the earth had tilted on its axis, the trains of normalcy, of reality and decency, ground to a creaking halt. It seemed obscene, criminal even, that people were still shopping for underwear and jogging around the reservoir complaining about their lives while I was catapulting toward death, appointmentless and unsure how Viggo really felt about our future together.

"Dr. Meissner says that was the first opening he could get for me in surgery. He even bumped me up ahead of a whole bunch of people." *I bet he always manages to fit Wendy in, the jerk.*

"Give it a rest, Ma." Laurie gave Ma the hand and turned to me. "Rach, I want to talk to you about something. Hear me out before you say no, okay? I've been thinking about a way for you to direct your energies right now. Something that may make you feel better. Would you be willing to come on *Living with Lauren!* and talk about everything? Like, what you're going through? How you're coping. What you're *feeling.*"

"Uh..." Image of me, face slick with flop sweat, staring into the camera with all the charisma of a doped cow, intruded. Charming.

Laurie went on, "Listen. I've talked to some local breast-cancer groups who are interested, and better yet—keep this on the QT—my producer is *this close* to inking a deal with the Sharks organization to raise money for breast-cancer research."

I literally didn't know what Laurie was talking about. Me? Breasts? Carnivorous fish? Then awareness kicked in. "A professional hockey team wants to sponsor *me*?"

"They want to match pledges. We'll hold a telethon. You'll be the featured guest speaker." Laurie was very patient.

"What do I have to do?"

"Nothing too onerous, I promise. You'll just come on and tell your story. Be yourself. Take audience questions. We'll have a phone bank all set up to take calls. Someone from San Jose representing professional hockey will be there." Laurie leaned forward, her face lit with a grin that was somewhat—I kid you not—sharkish. "I'm thinking 'Pink in the Rink.' Get it? Or do you like 'Rink, Pink, Think' better?"

Ma nodded. "Just make sure the money goes to the research and not some cockamamie PR firm. I heard one of the cosmetics companies was scamming us with those walks, and most of the funds were going to..."

I floated to my safe place—a sort of high-end version of an IKEA showroom with me and a *Walk on the Moon*–era Viggo tucked into a perfectly dressed Scandinavian bed—while Ma and Laurie launched into a discussion of Laurie's latest brilliant idea and how nonstarter Raquel could be micromanaged into furthering the cause without messing things up too badly.

"Mrs. Rose? Can you come with me, please? We need you

in makeup now." Shiny Pony still has the high, optimistic intonation of a college coed, even though she is, reputedly, the show's associate producer.

The image of me, Ma, Laurie, and a latent Viggo dissolves, and I follow Shiny into a small, brightly lit room. Nervousness has gelled inside my veins so that my limbs bear the thick spasticity of recent spinal injury. All I can think about is sitting next to Laurie under the klieg-light glow. There is no doubt: I *will* look fat. Also, there is not enough spackle in the world to tamp the shine from my Roman nose.

"This is Cleo. She'll be doing your face today. And this is Jonesie. He's hair." Shiny Pony lopes away, leaving me in the hands of Cleo and Jonesie, who are examining me the way one might an insect skewered on Styrofoam. I am especially intimidated by Jonesie, one of those sylphlike gay Asian boys who has never had a zit and wears chartreuse blouses with composure.

"Not much you can do with this," I say, running a hand over my bun, which resembles a day-old cinnamon roll that has been run over by a backhoe.

"Are you really Lauren's sister?" Cleo says, not hiding her incredulity. She is heavily tattooed, chubby, smooth-skinned, a study in black, white, and red.

"Yes," I say, anxiety ratcheting up a notch. "But she's adopted. Her birth mother was a lesser member of the Norwegian royal family who got knocked up by the stable boy at fourteen. She—I mean Lauren—was found in the mailbox by Carmelite nuns. Her birth name was Helga," I add, proud of that last embellishment.

Cleo and Jonesie stare at me in a kind of mute horror. Then Cleo laughs, her black-lipsticked mouth opening like a tunnel. I can sort of relate to her look, which I interpret as passive insubordination.

"You're funny," she says, already whipping out a box of brushes and pots.

"You're tall," says Jonesie. Then: "Do you want to wear a wig?"

"Do you have one of those Jewfro ones, like Barbra Streisand in *The Main Event*?"

He frowns. "Um, no, but maybe a bob or something."

"Jonesie, she's kidding." I can see that Cleo, goddess of some dark art or another, is on my side.

In minutes Cleo and Jonesie turn me into, if not a different person, an infinitely more colorful, mattified one. My white blouse is deemed a disaster—"You want them to think you have cirrhosis instead of breast cancer?" Cleo says, prompting an elbow from Jonesie—and is replaced with a crisp wrap shirt in a flattering sapphire blue. Cleo pauses when she sees the bandage around my bosom, a relic of biopsy. "Does it hurt?" Her voice is husky with respect.

The glass of Chardonnay Shiny Pony slipped me a few minutes ago is starting to work its magic.

"Not anymore," I say.

If I'd known how well groomed and, quite frankly, *petite* I'd look next to a professional hockey player, I'd have hired one to stalk me a long time ago.

Jean-Baptiste Lebecq sits with his ham-hock thighs spread and a cheerful grin splitting his doughy face. His right lateral incisor is missing, through which I can see a wad of chewing tobacco that, thankfully, shows no sign of imminent ejection. He sports the type of bilevel hairdo that is, in the words of my friend Sue, "business in the front, party in the back." Perhaps cancer has affected my vision, but I'm finding John the Baptist attractive, in a fifth-century-Gaul sort of way.

"Miz White, I speak for the San Jose Sharks about how I am happy we will match twice the pledge of the callers." Mr. Lebecq cheerfully mangles his point in Pepé Le Pew Canadian French.

Fortunately, Laurie is able to pluck references of money and fame from nowhere. I guess that's why she gets paid the big bucks. "Did you hear that, folks? Our corporate sponsor is going to not just match but *double* any pledge you call in. Now's the time to call! Remember, we're aiming to challenge the scourge of breast cancer for all of us: you, your mother, your wife"—she grips my hand—"your sister. Call us now. In the meantime, while our volunteers are taking your calls, let's hear from Raquel." She turns to me. "Raquel, how does it make you feel to know that so many people are behind you in your battle against cancer?"

If I squint, the banner with pucks at either end that reads PINK + RINK = DO MORE THAN THINK . . . ABOUT BREAST CANCER looks sort of like a baby announcement—of the grandchildren I'll never meet.

How does having people throw money at cancer make me feel?

"Good," I say firmly. I think it's a pretty diplomatic answer, considering my real mental state falls somewhere between shitty and clinically insane. The lights are unexpectedly hot on my cheeks. Oh my God, could I be having a hot flash? Are my ovaries closing up shop just because things are shaky in the boob department?

I don't realize my foot is jiggling until Laurie's decidedly unsensible Louboutin heel skewers my toe.

"Can you elaborate, Raquel? I'm sure some of the other women out there facing the same challenges would welcome your point of view." Laurie's face is open and guileless, but she doesn't have cancer, so I sort of hate her anyway.

The strange sort-of-hate sensation clogs my throat. "Well, you want to know the truth? I'm scared shitless," I blurt out. The words stream out of me, not from the new, shocked I-have-cancer place, but from some deeper inferno that, I realize, has been brewing for years. I go on, "I hate that this happened, and I don't know why it did. I hate that I have to keep it together. I hate that I got it instead of somebody else. I do! I'm sorry, but it's true! I hate that I'm supposed to smile when I buy groceries, and for that matter, why do I even have to go shopping anymore? Like, can't somebody else get off their ass and do it? I keep having crazy thoughts, like maybe I shouldn't have bought all that regular milk with bovine-growth hormone or whatever in it instead of the organic stuff, because it's so friggin' expensive, and would it be inappropriate to ask for a breast lift when they cut me open to do the mastectomy"—surprisingly, a few audience members laugh at this—"and I'm so angry. Like, crazy angry."

Breathing hard, I let my hair, which Jonesie blow-dried into fleeting submission, fall over my face. It feels cool, soothing, like a school nurse's palm.

"I think I want to kill something," I announce loudly and clearly to Laurie's studio audience.

Fuck. Am Hannibal Lecter of breast-cancer victims.

Before I can attempt to repair the damage caused by my anger-management problem—*Congratulations, Raquel Rose! You have just cost breast-cancer research half a million dollars!*—a weird alarm peals through the studio. Only the fact that I have sweated through my underwear and slacks keeps me from jumping under the table.

One of Laurie's minions trots out and hands her a piece of paper. Laurie's face brightens. It must be my commitment papers.

"We have just topped a hundred thousand in matched

pledges, a show record, people!" Laurie says. "I want to personally thank every one of you, and of course our corporate partner, and the Bay Area Breast Cancer Alliance for providing the resource materials, and also my sister, Raquel, who is, in the words of one of our callers"—she flicks open the note—"'a breath of fresh air and an honest voice representing real women who don't take'—well, I think we know what she said, but I'll substitute 'guff'—'from anybody'!"

The audience cheers. I wonder if this means I will get a mountain-facing room at Casa Loca.

"Raquel, would you like to take the audience through the pamphlet the BABCA so generously provided?" Laurie says.

The pamphlet is in my hand. It is pink except where my palm has perspired through the paper and turned it the arterial purple of an internal organ.

"Um, okay. It's called 'What Every Newly Diagnosed Woman Needs to Know.'" Above me, the page's contents appear on a gigantic screen—the one that formerly featured my hot-tub-size pores.

"'Number one, don't go to the doctor by yourself,'" I read. *Hmm. Unless your husband is one of those guys who thinks a Pap smear is a topping at Noah's bagels.* "Uh, 'number two, get informed before you go on doctors' visits. Number three, make a list of what you want from your doctor.'" Babyface Meissner's luscious brown eyes fill my mind, and I feel a creepy, inappropriate grin start to spread over my face. *Get a grip, Quel.* "'Four, get a second opinion. Five, journal on what it means to you to potentially lose a breast to the disease.'" I glance into the wall of lights with facial silhouettes behind them and lean in to my microphone. "Can someone please tell me when 'journal' became a verb? When I first met with my counselor, I read that one and was, like, what does losing a breast mean to me? And I said the first thing that popped into my head: at least five pounds!" Big laughs. "Which was sort of embarrassing. For the counselor, I mean." Bigger laughs, which has the unexpected effect of making me feel sort of, well, good. "And '*numero seis,* develop a plan for talking to your kids about cancer.'" I glance up. "If any of you are able to do this without feeling like a complete failure as a mother, let me know, because I haven't quite managed to pull this off. Where was I? 'Number seven, be on alert for signs of depression following treatment,' because, hey, what's depressing about cancer, right?"

The audience laughs. Hard.

Am not Hannibal Lecter. Am irresistibly winsome comedienne.

Laurie straightens her already straight mauve cashmere cardigan. "I have just been told that, thanks to Raquel and all of our generous callers and our sponsor, the BABCA is going to be able to fund a campaign to provide health-care advocacy for low-income women!"

This announcement is met with a round of applause.

"And a new Web site directed at women under thirty who are fighting breast cancer!"

The audience goes a little crazy.

"And launch a child-care program so that Bay Area women can get the help they need when they're sick or have appointments!"

Off to the side, I see Shiny Pony hold up a sign that says SHUSH. The audience complies. Sort of.

"Thank you all for your support," Laurie says. "Now I'd like to go back to what Raquel said earlier. What we're hearing here is that women feel *angry* about their diagnoses. And that this anger has no place constructive to flow. That we're letting our women, our*selves,* down, people." Laurie turns to me. "Raquel, what do you think we could do, as a society and a community, to help women through the diagnostic stage of dealing with breast cancer?"

Gawd, pull off one half-assed joke and they think you're Dr. Friggin' Laura.

I try to think of something helpful and sage to say. Really. Contrary to family opinion, I hate disappointing people. I just happen to be really good at it.

I stare into Laurie's clear eyes and think: *Lucidity.* "Well, don't expect her to get used to the idea right away. I mean, here I am on TV, pretending I know something about, well, *anything,* and I'm still in shock. Things are moving too fast. That's what people who don't have it don't understand— everyone wants to rush us toward some positive outcome, but we haven't even had time to process things, to accept it yet. A part of me still believes it's all a dream, honest to God"—my throat clogs again—"I feel so normal. Wouldn't I *know* if I had it? Wouldn't I have known something was wrong? How did this happen, for chrissake? I almost feel like I did some-thing wrong, like it's my fault."

Did I just say that? Did I answer the question? Once, in college, an essay exam came back to me with the words WELL-CONSTRUCTED ARGUMENT; EXACTLY WHAT QUESTION WERE YOU ANSWER-ING? scrawled at the top next to an inky C+. Plowing a hundred miles per hour toward the wrong objective: story of my life.

Laurie grasps my hand. The word pops into my head: "sis-ter." It is startling, the feeling of comfort and succor that comes with it. When we were kids, we'd sometimes lie together in bed, the other's hair tickling our cheeks, flannel nightgowns tangled around our legs. We'd playact *Lassie* and *Charlie's Angels* with gusto, serenaded by the distant hum of the down-stairs television. With an older sibling's sense of entitlement, I always made Laurie be Kate Jackson, reserving sexpots Jaclyn and Farrah for myself.

"And now we'll take questions from the studio audience," Laurie says, her voice naturally bright as she lets my latest ill-advised comment float, mostly harmlessly, in space.

Last night I had my first death dream.

I know, I know, *so* cliché. But here's the thing: It was so real, so *ordinary*. You know that ethereal, cinematic quality dreams have? The wishful note that takes the edge off the scare factor, that tells some subconscious monkey part of our brains, *Hey, this isn't real, so why* don't *you take twenty pounds off our plucky heroine and upgrade Ren to Viggo. Aim high, girlfriend, 'cause you're going to wake up sooner or later!*

This dream wasn't like that at all.

It starts out okay. I am walking the halls of my high school, not my teenage self, but me now. I'm wearing a backpack slung over one shoulder the way only too-cool sixteen-year-olds can, heavy with books but without visible back pain. The distinct chorus of several thousand hormonal teenagers teeming in an enclosed space, of lockers slamming, of scudding sneakers and screechy stabs at popularity, fills my ears. The smell—bubble gum and sweat and testosterone with a whisper of pot—froths in my senses. It makes that detached monkey part of my grown-up brain pipe up: *Remember this?*

Slut queen Christie Mueller and her minions are gathered around their locker mirrors, applying Lip Smackers and lasagna-like layers of eye shadow. Back then the favored color was an unreasonable blue, the exact shade of Robby Benson's eyes (I should know, having seen *Ice Castles* fifteen times). I hunch by them in full Quasimodo mode, mindful to avert my eyes lest they accuse me of trying to initiate contact with my betters. Christie's birdcall laugh seems to chase me down the corridor. I am borne into Mrs. Rossi's conversational-Spanish class by the bell, my heart pounding out a stuttering flamenco along with this thought: *Congratulations on surviving one more day without being humiliated.*

A scene change: The asbestos-tiled walls of the classroom morph into our house in Palo Alto. Well, sort of our house. The basics are the same, but it seems to me like other people live there, because the lawn is freshly mowed and someone has finally reinforced the saggy rain gutter I was nagging Phil about for at least three years. It doesn't smell like our house, either, the usual perfume of molting teen, dog, and interior paint replaced by a suspiciously pleasant lavenderish concoction.

I take a quick peek in the living room. The Bonafacios from next door are perched stiffly on kitchen chairs, their identical turkey-gobbler necks quivering. Phil's boss, Ross Trimble, checks out Robin Golden's rack while pretending to focus on a loosely rolled deli slice. Friends and family mill about, whispering. Nobody laughs. The dining room table is buried under an avalanche of casseroles, triangular sandwiches, and that to-die-for mayonnaise-artichoke dip that I have always secretly wished to bathe in.

A restless blonde with jiggly buns whom I vaguely recognize as a volleyball parent corners Phil. "I'm so sorry. If there's anything I can do, *anything,* you call me, okay? I'm *so* sorry, hon. Call me." She hands Phil a card. Phil—the traitor—slips it into his jacket pocket and nods. His green eyes are either pinched with fatigue, or he has been on one of his TV marathons; his face is the definition of haggard.

I float into the bedroom wing. One of the basset hounds has dragged a platter of tuna casserole into the hall and is hastily slurping it down. Nobody intervenes. Music flows under the closed door to Taylor's room. Inside, a circle of teenagers cling and sway together, as if at a rock concert stoked up on Ecstasy. My daughter and son are enfolded in a nest of kids. Taylor has a cup of punch in her hand. Instinctively, I know it is 64 percent vodka, 36 percent Crystal Light. Don't ask me how; it's just one of those dream things. Micah's head rests in his hands. A skinny girl with a sheet of glossy black hair runs her hand along his back. My dream mind calculates an 89 percent probability they will have sex tonight (72 percent likelihood of using a condom; 3.4 percent chance the condom will break).

This is when it hits me: I am dead.

My dream self reels at this sorry revelation. Although I cannot see her hand, I know it is there, against the wall, propping up the ghostly soul of Raquel Rose in her own dog-hair-strewn hallway. I stagger around a bit before going on—okay, this is morbid—a search for my casket. Finally, wending my way around friends, neighbors, and more than a few annoying people I am surprised to see there at all, I realize there is no body. I, the special guest, am AWOL at my own wake. Typical! This could be because (a) my will explicitly requested cremation as the preferred mode of corporal disposal, and I am already occupying mantel space in a pretty vase; (b) nobody but the Bedouin really lays out the dead anymore; or (c) my body was stolen by grave robbers, and everybody's too embarrassed to mention it.

Panic engulfs me.

At this point I basically wake up. My mouth is dry and vile with a cheesy coating of sleep. I can feel blood rushing around my body without a plan, ending up in weird places, broadcasting the spastic rhythm of my heart to the outer reaches of the faltering kingdom.

Like everyone else, I have heard that if you see yourself dead in a dream, you will really die. Soon. I wonder if the fact that I couldn't find the body is at all germane, or if praying for a technicality is just the futile yearning of a middle-aged woman who has witnessed the crooked finger of the Reaper before her time.

Extricating myself carefully from the blankets so as not to wake Phil—if we ever divorce, it will not be because of our sleep habits, which are civilized to the point of real refinement—I pad to the kitchen to comfort myself.

I shove aside the New Agey collection of colon-cleansing teas I habitually buy and allow to molder. Instead, I grab one of the juvenile brands of cookies featuring drawings of smiling dinosaurs and monsters, and arrange several—okay, several dozen—on a plate.

The source of the dream is as obvious as the furrow on my brow. Earlier today I'd had a call from Laurie's associate producer, Shiny. She wanted to know when I could come back to the *Living with Lauren!* set.

"Did I leave something there?"

"Leave something?"

"Was it my cell? Oh no, did I leave my purse? I must have left my purse."

I could almost see Shiny's untarnished face pucker up. "Not at all. I'm talking about having you back as a guest. Raquel, do you realize how successful your first appearance was? We're still getting calls and e-mails about it."

"Laurie wants me to come back?" *Why didn't dear sister call herself?*

Shiny had been briefed on the Schultz talent discrepancy. "She was the first to suggest it!"

Hmm.

"We were thinking of doing another fund-raiser. Maybe something on location. Something adventurous. Something that hasn't been done before. There's a brainstorming session on Tuesday."

Brainstorm?

"We have a real opportunity here to make a difference!" Even Shiny's voice was, well, shiny.

"If I die, do you still get the money?" Where this came from, I don't know. Probably the heinous well of morbid thoughts that had been brewing since I first sat across from Babyface Meissner stiff with fright and pondered his hairy, steepled knuckles.

"Uh, I don't—" Shiny had momentarily lost her patina.

"It's okay. I don't know why I said that." *Because I so, so don't want to. Die I mean.*

"Well, there are strict regulations governing fund-raising and philanthropy. I don't know the details—we have lawyers and tax people for that stuff—but I do know that everything goes directly to the Breast Cancer Alliance. We aren't even taking a share for operating costs. Laurie's rules." Shiny's admiration of my sister nearly shimmered across the phone lines.

"I'm glad." I was. Really. Gladness personified.

Shiny's squeaky falsetto dropped to a conspiratorial whisper. "You didn't hear this from me, but this couldn't come at a better time for the show. Our ratings have been slipping a little. Alicia—that's the station director—isn't happy, Laurie's nervous, and our biggest competitor is gaining on us. That's why we need a win right now, something we can spin but really *matters,* you know? But we have to dot every 'I' and cross every 'T', too. Otherwise they'll find some reason to can us, and…let's just say I think it would be, like, a *travesty* if the world lost a visionary like Lauren White to the ratings wars, you know?"

She had me convinced.

"Look, Raquel, I'm glad to have this chance to talk with you, because I just want to say you're really making a difference.

I, like, totally respect you for putting yourself out there while you're going through this, and trying to help other women. Nobody would blame you if you didn't, but the way you think of others before yourself, is, well, it's awesome. And the fact that you speak your mind instead of sugarcoating everything. You may not realize it, but you've just become an icon to the breast-cancer community."

Raquel Rose, icon.

Like all thoughts that brew in the cavernous pit of self-doubt and wishful thinking that is midnight ponderings, this one stinks of delusion. I lick my finger and dab at the potpourri of crumbs on my plate. Being a pillar of iconlike strength sounds like hard work. All the more reason to keep my strength up.

CHAPTER 4

Confucius Wish You Double Happiness

"I don't understand. How can you possibly make a mistake like this?" I wail.

Samuel Meissner, M.D., sighs and rakes his hand through his Harvard-approved mop of chestnut hair. It is hard to look straight at him, now that I know where that hand passes the time when it isn't palpating my breasts.

"Mrs. Rose, I'm sure you can appreciate the unlikelihood of two women named Raquel Rose getting breast biopsies the same week at the same hospital."

"Not really. I mean, don't you use computers to keep track of this stuff?"

Meissner leans back and studies me. He looks unhappy. I wonder if he gives Wendy Yen that look when she does something that pisses him off, like rushing back to San Carlos to make sure the housekeeper has finished making Connor Welch's brats' dinner or not letting Meissner come in her mouth.

"Mrs. Rose, you've just had a death sentence revoked. I would think you'd be thrilled."

"I am. Of course I am." *Am I?*

"You don't have cancer. The lump's benign. You'll live a long, full life." He checks his watch, a fancy gold cuff that shouts Shiksa Goddess, There's More Where This Came From.

"But how can I trust anything you people tell me after this? What if I *do* have it?"

"I promise, you don't. The biopsy, remember?"

Oh yeah. "But..." *But what?* "I don't *feel* right. I feel sick."

Annoyance flashes, quickly veiled. "Mrs. Rose, I have a hundred percent confidence that at this moment you are suffering nothing more than an attack of nerves. You've had a trauma, but you'll recover. If you want, I can refer you to a qualified therapist." His hand dangles threateningly over his Rolodex.

"I already have one, thanks." *And she's going to get an earful this week!*

He is halfway out the door. "Now you just skedaddle on home and tell your family the great news."

"Skedaddle." I hate that word, even when children use it.

I tuck the sunflower with the snapped stalk between two of its sisters to prop it up, careful to maintain the upturned motion of its face. Wouldn't do to have a party pooper spoiling it for everyone, now, would it?

I drove home from Meissner's office in a daze. "Reeling" would be too scrawny a word to describe my state of shock. Once you've had someone point the finger at you and pronounce the "C" word, it's pretty much incomprehensible that God is going to amble on down the mountain and revise His handiwork. I'd even demanded to see the biopsies side by side. Meissner had humored me with a shrug and a sigh, but by that time the characters had blurred into a morass of ink and I'd stumbled out of the office into the sunlit, alien-looking parking lot. During the forty-nine minutes it took to locate the car, I had plenty of time to ponder the latest development.

On the one hand: *This is great, right? I won't have to delegate the preservation of Taylor's virginity to Phil after all.*

On the other: *Several thousand people just wrote fat checks to the Bay Area Breast Cancer Alliance because I spilled my sob story.*

That said: *It's not my fault the hospital data-entry people suck.*

Still: *The Alliance cashed them.*

And: *You did go on TV...with a blow-out, no less.*

But: *They told me I had to! Mom and Laurie railroaded me! I was scared!*

Not to mention: *Nobody will believe you.*

Hey: *It's true!*

So: *Pathological liar spins better than data-entry victim.*

But: *Duh ...*

Plus: *And let's not forget, you've been...different since this happened.*

So: *Different how?*

Well: *Different good.*

Okay: *Whatever. Do you ever think about, you know, the other Raquel Rose?*

'Nuff said.

The most pressing issue: how to break the news to my family for the second time. It seemed wrong to deliver the good—awesome? apocalyptic? weird?—news without ceremony, so I buckled down and cleaned the house, undoing some of the damage I'd done when I'd thought no one would hold it against me (salad spinner put away unwashed, household receipts plopped in art-supply drawer, wine bottle opener put back with cork rammed on). I put on a festive garment—red knit tunic and matching palazzo pants—and dabbed Chanel number something behind each ear and in the furrow of my (happy again) cleavage. My beloved tunic is, in Sue's opinion, one small step above Jaclyn Smith for Kmart, but it does have the magical redeeming quality of expanding to accommodate whatever I care to put in my stomach. I go out and shop for foods that occupy the bottom portion of the pyramid at the snooty organic store, come home and crack my mother's *Joy of Cooking,* and sweat my way through a four-course meal.

At the last second, I light a stick of tangerine–butternut squash incense I got free for participating in a focus group ("Mrs. Rose, on a scale of one to five, how likely would you be to buy peanut butter with fish oil in it?"). Now Phil, Micah, and Taylor will associate my second lease on life with the restorative scent of citrus and root vegetable instead of the stench of anxiety perspiration.

Sounds of teenagers and husband and canines mingling at the front door.

"Mom! We're home!"

It's funny how it takes a cancer diagnosis to rouse a civilized greeting. Maybe they're afraid I'm dead?

"I'm in here!" I call gaily, Doris Day with a tumor (or not, as the case may be).

They explode into the room. I watch, amused, as the kids go through the usual ritual of dropping their backpacks on the floor then, shamefaced, pick them up unsolicited and deposit them on the countertop in a semblance of order. Taylor pauses to sniff the table bouquet, as if verifying that it is indeed real.

"Hi, all. Hungry?" I say.

Micah and Taylor nod, suspicious. I crack the oven; eau de pot roast wafts out. My kids look at each other, then at Phil, who still has a sheaf of exam papers clutched to his chest.

"I also made Micah's favorite mashed potatoes with the baked garlic and chives. And green beans with those little bacon bits. See?" The pot lid comes off, enveloping us in a pork sauna. I wink at Tay. "I got *green tea ice cream!*" I hear myself singsong, vaguely aware that there is something frightening about my behavior but powerless to stop it.

"Mom, shouldn't you be resting?" Micah seals the pot. Bye-bye, bacon.

I shrug. "I just felt like making dinner. I have something to tell you guys. Something great."

"It's just...We didn't expect you to be, uh, cooking and stuff," Taylor says.

"Why don't you all sit down and get comfortable?" Before they can argue, I strip Phil of his papers, briefcase, and jacket and give him a wifely peck on the cheek. He leans over. I swear I hear him sniff my breath.

"Are you all right?" he whispers.

"Hon, I couldn't be better."

I steer the three of them into their seats and proffer the platters I created. Between the giant sunflowers, their faces peek at me, creased with worry. Oh well, that'll change when I drop my bombshell.

Back to biz as usual.

"Isn't this nice?" A droplet of sweat tickles the trough between my breasts, itching against the synthetic fabric of my minimizer bra.

Raquel, don't be a freak. Just get on with it.

"Guys, you're not going to believe this, but..." Why is Micah looking at Phil like that, like there's a feral bobcat loose in the house and nobody else has spotted it yet? "I don't have, you know, um, cancer."

Silence.

"They mixed up the test results. It was all a big mistake."

I smile, expecting glad cheers, backslaps, relieved tears. Something...considerable.

Nothing.

"They mixed them up with somebody else's. I know, I know...it's hard to imagine, but I guess even computer networks aren't perfect. Dr. Meissner told me today. Isn't it terrific?" I stab my fork into a pile of green beans with a satisfying crunch. A weird giggle escapes me, as disconcerting as a public fart.

Taylor gets up, crosses the room, and kneels beside me. She grabs my hand and stares into my eyes. "Stop it, Mom. Just stop it!" Her whole body issues a rolling but subtle spasm, as if it's coming from so deep inside her, it's emerging diminished.

Huh?

"Dad, I think Mom needs to go to bed," Micah says. He says it almost leisurely, as if he needs time in between words to locate the stun gun.

Phil stands up. The logo on his white T-shirt, advertising some off-Strip hotel in Vegas, filters through his gray dress shirt. What does he do with the dozens—hundreds—of plain white undershirts I buy him? Why does he think it's okay for the world to know he's too cheap to spring for the Bellagio or Mandalay Bay?

"I don't need to go to bed! Why aren't you listening to me?" I don't mean to cry out, but nonetheless, green-bean paste dribbles from my lips. Embarrassed, I wipe it away, which only results in the formation of a big veggie mouth booger that I am forced to deposit on the tablecloth because I have forgotten the napkins. "I'm trying to tell you something important! Something important to me! You never listen! You just. Never. Listen." I realize I am whining.

"Quel, come on. You're tired. You've worked so hard on all

this. And it's great, it really is. But you just want to go to bed, right?"

I feel myself nodding. They're right, of course. I do want to go to bed. Who doesn't? Who doesn't want to go to bed after slaving over a hot stove and, like, arranging flowers for four fucking hours? That doesn't mean I have cancer. Or that I'm crazy.

Does it?

I let them lead me to my fluffy cell of a room because, truth be told, a goodly part of me does not believe what Meissner said or what I'm saying, either. Who ever heard of someone getting cancer—then ungetting it? Perhaps I imagined the conversation, or maybe this is all another dream, my version of *Dallas* and the Sue Ellen yearlong nightmare that won't end until somebody important gets shot for ratings.

When I wake up, there is breakfast on a tray on my bed-side table, and the room is ruddy with morning sun. My neck feels stiff, as if I dreamed too deeply to make the usual night-time movements. I lift the platter lid, which some resource-ful person has created out of an only slightly dingy hatbox, and sniff: steaming eggs crisscrossed with shredded cheddar and chives, chubby strawberries, and a fragrant sprinkling of bacon over the eggs that was probably rescued from last night's green beans. Still, I have to give it an A for effort. I lean over the accompanying pink and yellow mottled rose and inhale deeply before drifting back into the mound of pil-lows. Delicious. A rose! A freakin' rose!

Shit, I'm dead.

I have entered the hereafter. I must have. How else to explain the otherworldliness of my current circumstances? Breakfast in bed. Uninterrupted sleep. Absence of needy humans. Starched sheets. Quiet. Good smells. These are not things that happen to me on a regular basis.

I wiggle my toes, wondering at the authenticity of sensation, the clarity of sight. I'd envisioned something more ephemeral, gauzy, a simulation of real life, minus the bad parts, of course. Breezy islands and starlit nights. Gentle slap of angels' wings. Skinny jeans. Sweeping flights over the unknowing heads of my loved ones, me impishly dropping hints of my presence—a whiff of perfume here, a ghostly reflection there. Piles of M&M's. Good books. Viggo.

"Mom?"

Taylor pokes her head into my afterlife bedroom. The living spend so much time enticing the dead to return to the corporeal world; nobody warns you (the dead) about them (the living) dropping by.

"You were a wonderful daughter," I say. I want her to think of me fondly after Phil remarries.

"Uh, thanks, Mom. Do you need me to feed you the eggs now?"

I breathe in the unmistakable aroma of laundry detergent, which seems to be emanating from the basket in Taylor's arms.

Laundry. Basket. Taylor?

Yep. Definitely dead.

"Everything smells so *real*," I whisper.

Taylor drops the basket and kneels next to me. "Mom, Dad and Micah and I talked after you went to bed, and we want you to know we're going to do everything we can to help out right now. You have to rest, you know? You're, like, the most important thing to us. We know you're going to get better." Her pretty brow puckers. "Mom, where do you keep those little bags that make the clothes smell good? I couldn't find any, so I squeezed in just the littlest bit of that Tom's toothpaste. It smells, like, almost the same."

Toothpaste. In the dryer.

Alive. Fuuuuuck.

I sit up. Then I instruct my daughter on the particulars of all things domestic, laundry-compliant, and lavender-scented. I eat my eggs, which have cooled under the hatbox and taste somewhat of cardboard. I read the style section in the newspaper. I worry. I try to decide if I really do have cancer after all, or if I am insane, or something infinitely worse.

CHAPTER 5

Night of the Living Dead

Later, I attribute it to being one of those hell-bent days. Every mom has them. The kind of days when you're in and out of the minivan a dozen times before noon, strangling on the seat belt, racing from school to market to soccer field, flinging a batch of snickerdoodles in the oven, forgetting to set the timer, burning the batch and (unsuccessfully) substituting corn syrup for the goddamn depleted sugar when you have to mix a second batch, dropping the dog off at the vet and discovering it's the wrong dog, returning home to find you left the garage door open and the tandem bike's gone, stolen by some neglected neighborhood rich kid or flinty-eyed gardener, forgetting you told Carla Bonafacio you'd water her hydrangeas while they were in Puerto Vallarta, discovering said hydrangeas lifeless with heat, accidentally taping over Phil's 'Niners match, thereby giving weight to his argument that we need TiVo, screening your mother's calls so ruthlessly that she shows up at your door at 3:35 P.M., just when you're supposed to leave to pick up the (cone-wearing, drugged, bladder-control-impaired) dog.

You know the kind of day.

I guess what I'm trying to explain is, I didn't set out *not* to correct their mistaken notion that I was sick. Certainly not. How maladjusted would that be? It's just...the opportunity didn't present itself. Nor had I managed to clarify things on the committing-fraud-on-live-TV or causing-the-financial-ruin-of-a-do-gooder-organization fronts. For all I know, I could be disowned by my family. I could go to jail and serve hard time without a single visit from a loving family member, with nary a care package to ease the journey between crime and a San Quentin–cured complexion. Clearly, I mishandled things the last time I tried to break through. Clearly, you can't rush into this sort of thing. You could give someone a shock.

"Hey, Ma," I call when my mother's shouts that she knows I'm in there watching *Maury* can no longer be ignored. A little guiltily, I turn off the TV—which I'm using only to keep me company while I chop beets for tonight's salad—and check my eyes for latent mascara circles while I trot to the door.

My mother, Minna Louise Schultz Abramson, peers at me over the waning moons of her reading glasses, which hang around her neck on a beaded string embellished by slack-breasted fertility goddesses. Ma is old-country short but has a tall voice, like Bea Arthur in *The Golden Girls*.

"What is it today?" she rasps.

"High school teachers who married their students."

Ma wrinkles her small, straight nose. "You would have been lucky to marry what's-his-name, that chemistry fellow, Mr. Profitt?"

"Why would I have been lucky to marry him?" I say, barely recalling a balding, rotund, Socratic type with a disobedient walleye that constantly slid toward the girls' chests.

"He won the lotto a few years ago. Used his cats' birthdays or some foolishness. Came in and quit his job the next day." Ma nods approvingly. "Married some little Oriental girl,

I think. Hair down to her tushie. They bought a place in Los Altos Hills." She names a tony community slightly south of our own Palo Alto digs.

"Asian, Ma."

"Okay, Asian."

"Oriental is for carpets," I add. "Or food."

Ma flings her hands up in supplication. "I come over to check you're alive, and this is the thanks I get? A language lesson?"

Ma enjoys playing the role of long-suffering mother and has been performing it off-off-Broadway to great acclaim since about the time Dad's sperm wiggled its way toward the plump, too-tall ovum that would become me, Raquel Rose, née Rachel Schultz. It is a testament to Ma's commitment that her enthusiasm has not diminished in the wake of my diagnosis.

Okay, misdiagnosis.

I slide the puddle of bloody-looking vegetables off the wooden cutting board into the salad bowl and try to think tactically while I hack at a stinky block of feta. Phil will be home by eight P.M., assuming he hasn't already switched his racquetball game to Wednesdays to accommodate Ren's latest goodwill project—performing life-or-death surgeries on needy women who, like the rest of us, suffer the scourges of saggy eyelids, collapsing jawlines, earthbound tits, and laissez-faire stomachs. Micah promised nine P.M., which really means ten P.M. Taylor...I realize with a hot, fleeting spark of guilt that I have no idea where my daughter is, whom she is with, or if she plans to consume an item from the vegetable food group for dinner.

I am indeed slipping.

"So, how are you feeling, kitten?" Ma says, stroking my back.

"Pretty shitty," I say. It does not feel like a lie.

Ma takes off her glasses. Without them, squinting, she looks older, more vulnerable. She is so small, it is a miracle I baked to ripeness in her womb, all future five-ten of me curled inside her like escargot on the shell. Laurie, at a reasonable five-seven, is less of a surprise, her height the natural progression from the unwholesome Warsaw ghetto to California's hearty breadbasket. Our mismatched heights and bodies are a symbol of the fundamental ill fit that has plagued my family since I was born, the surface sign of a schism that flows deep and decaying through our bones.

Ma withdraws her hand, frowns. "If they let you on Laurie's show again, make sure you remind the audience to get their mammograms." She shifts her Raisinet eyes toward the heavens, which, in my world, masquerades as a greige, lumpy ceiling shot through with *très* eighties gold sparkles. "She's on television like a movie star, and she forgets the mammograms! *Oy, gevalt.*"

With that, the confession bubbling on my lips, the one that would have given my mother the quick, sharp, narcotic shot of relief she needs, bursts and dies, unspoken. An idea blossoms in its place: *Raquel, honey, Laurie ain't the only one who can do Mama proud.*

Good Raquel: *Excuse me?*

Naughty Raquel: *Do I need to spell it out? You raised* bank *for cancer research, girl. Not Laurie.* You.

Good: *I suppose that's true, but . . .*

Naughty: *But nothing. You want to talk truth? How about Mama Schultz always treating Laurie like the cat's meow and you like the dog's dinner?*

I couldn't argue with that. It's almost as if Ma doesn't know I'm a breast-cancer-community *icon,* able to leap enormous budget shortfalls in a single telethon.

I also noted that Ma's perennial pride in Laurie, golden of touch and fair of head, has even managed to cut through any despair she might have had over my death notice.

Naughty Raquel: *Stop feeling sorry for yourself and slice me a hunk of that cheese. You'll see, Ma's gonna be impressed.*

Ma hands me the olive oil. I pour it on and toss the salad. Rice vinegar. Lemon squirt. Dash of salt to provoke Ma. I am sealing it in Saran Wrap when Naughty Raquel pipes up again.

Glad that's settled. Let the games begin!

"Get you something else to drink, hon?" Phil grasps my jersey-covered elbow lightly and dusts off the secret Phil-and-Quel smile that had been pulled from rotation these last few years, until the (mis)diagnosis. He is being so solicitous. Tonight. After the party, I'll tell him with a flourish, like a general returning victorious from battle. I'll share the astounding Wendy Yen–Jailbait Meissner love story as background, and we'll laugh together. Then we'll have delicious, dirty, celebratory sex. Relief sex. "Thank God I'm Not Going to Be a Widower and Have to Do My Own Laundry" sex.

I tilt my head to say no to his offer of a drink and try to remember not to slump. In heels, at parties, I tower over all the women and many of the men. Supermodel mystique to the contrary, my height, swarthy coloring, and ampleness have always made me feel awkward and mannish, a Valkyrie among Tinker Bells.

"Raquel, you're looking lovely tonight."

I lean over and accept Ross Trimble's dry kiss. With what I am realizing is a side effect of being diagnosed with cancer— obviously not contingent on *having* cancer—I sense that my husband's boss knows about my diagnosis. The extra-intense eye contact, the sympathetic just-longer-than-normal brush of hand on upper arm, the ember of interest burning behind heavy-lidded, pale brown eyes that has never been there before, as if I've acquired a patina of charm that was lacking before my cells ran hopelessly amok.

"Happy birthday, Ross," I say.

He shrugs. "Come with me a moment. I need your artistic opinion of something."

I acquiesce and let Phil's slim, distinguished-looking, slightly older, and filthy-rich employer lead me down a sleekly modern hallway barely lit with wall sconces.

In my experience, private high school staffs are populated with two types: wealthy trust-funders who fancy their teaching or administrative duties a natural and pleasurable extension of a privileged life; and idealists or lapsed idealists who can't hack it in the loftier, crueler pool that is university-level academy.

Ross Trimble is the former. Phil is the latter.

Ross stops in a small room lined with books and a discreet computer system. Two prints have been tacked to the wall over the daybed, which is, to my surprise and slight embarrassment, rumpled and emanating a distinct air of debauchery.

"I'm thinking of acquiring a Miró. I can't decide between these two. What do you think?"

In my postgraduate days, before Micah came along, I briefly curated a small surrealist collection to underwrite my sculpting. I distinctly remember imagining future versions of my life, which typically featured me, an enormous studio filled with ground-breaking conceptual pieces, and lots of sycophantic admirers. What they did not include: mommy-and-me mall walks, gassy husbands, and mothers who accuse their daughters of being quitters when life gets in the way of career brilliance.

The two paintings—prints, actually—are of nudes, one standing, a jumble of curvy, slightly anatomical-looking limbs topped by a brunette bun. The other is seated, holding a mirror, slouched and plump. Something about the way her knees come together seems inhibited and relatable.

"This one," I say, pointing at the seated nude. "She's softer, more real, more accessible...see how her shoulders hunch over? She's trying to shield her breasts—" I realize I am speaking too personally and abruptly cut myself off.

Ross gazes at me warmly. "That's what I was thinking, too." Then he does that thing with his eyes, the one where you can tell someone wants to touch you but is heroically restraining himself. "Raquel, I hope Philip knows what a lucky man he is."

Death has made me a winner like nothing else I ever did prior.

Over the years I have jettisoned all but a few house rules, freeing myself of ballast so that I might float, unconstrained, into the expected delights of the empty-nest years. One of my few requirements is that everybody appear for Sunday-night dinner. A proper dinner, with the TV off, music—Bud Powell or Charlie Mingus or, if we are feeling racy, something Latin— seeping gently through the speakers, loving communication flowing between parents and offspring in which the pertinent details of our busy lives are exchanged and contemplated.

Taylor pouts. "Lindsay, Madison, Quinn, Savannah, and Lisa's parents all said they could go!"

My sixteen-year-old daughter's standard MO: relentless wheedling.

"That doesn't mean going alone to surf camp in Mexico is an appropriate spring-break activity for you, Tay," I say. Before the (mis)diagnosis, we talked about taking the kids backpacking in the lake-dotted Desolation Wilderness, one of my and Phil's favorite places. Back in the day. Apparently, like the two of us having sex under the stars, family vacations are a thing of the past, consigned to dusty photo albums tucked into the far reaches of the hall closet.

"Daddy!" Taylor shrieks.

Phil rouses himself from his pot roast. "Your mother needs us around right now, honey. Did you think about that before you promised the girls?"

Our eyes meet over the spray of gerbera daisies, and I feel something tranquilizing and hopeful stroke my thoughts. This hopefulness, it's...new. I have an idea.

"Tay, you going alone with your friends is out of the question. Lindsay just got her license. I think driving in Mexico's a bit much. Frankly, I don't know what Ann and Rich are thinking"—Taylor's green eyes shimmer with teen angst— "but maybe I could, you know, go with you." The shimmering angst morphs into equal parts hope and suspicion. "I just don't think six sixteen-year-olds should be gallivanting around third-world countries by themselves. Did you even think about transportation and hotels? You aren't even old enough to rent a car." I'm building a case for Raquel Rose's unobtrusive style of chaperoning. I am already picturing it: me on the beach, a delicious new Anne Rivers Siddons or Marian Keyes in hand, sarong tucked strategically around all offending parts while my long, naturally tan legs scissor out into the silken sand, Corona standing sentry beside me, fresh lime wedge bobbing in time to the soft kick of waves at my feet.

Oh yes.

"Are you sure you're, you know, feeling well enough to go?" I can see that Tay has (correctly) deduced that my attendance at the Mexico surf-camp extravaganza represents her only chance of going and decided to roll with it.

"I think so," I answer, somewhat truthfully.

"Sweet! I'm going to call Lindsay!" Taylor says, already half-way out of her chair.

"After dinner," Phil says. Tay falls back like a lanky deer and resumes picking at her baked potato.

"Actually, I'm glad we're all together, because there's something I have to tell you," I say. This is it. The time is right. I'm going to tell them. So what if it means the end of Phil defending me against the succubae and the cancer people issue a fatwa on my ass.

The phone rings.

"Let it go," I say.

Micah jumps up. "Can't, Mom. It could be Ronnie. My cell's dead." My son leans over and grabs the phone, listens for a moment, then hands it to me.

"It's Aunt Laurie."

"Laur, can I call you back?" I say.

"Quel?"

"We're in the middle of dinner."

"Well, I hope you're eating broccoli. It's the most powerful anticancer food around."

"What's up?" I say. Of course we're eating broccoli. I mean, I'm sure it's in there somewhere. See? There's a sprig of it right there, sticking out of my potato, under a nice warm blanket of melted cheddar.

"I made an appointment for you to see Dr. Minh tomorrow afternoon in San Francisco. Minh's a disciple of Xia's, very knowledgeable, very respected, an amazing healer. I'll e-mail you the address, okay?"

Disciple? What is this, modern medicine or the Moonies?

"Oh, Laur, really, I don't think it's necessary." Little does my sister know how unnecessary it is. I'll call her after dinner to explain, after I tell Phil and the kids.

"Quel, people wait months to see Minh," Laurie says.

I rack my brain for a legitimate out. "I have to go to Costco. We need toilet paper."

"I don't think you understand. The only reason I was able to get you in is because I dropped Xia's name." Laurie's normally calm voice turns shrill. "You know, if I didn't know better, I'd think you want to be sick. You're being so...defeatist about it all."

"That's ridiculous! I can't believe you said that!" Out of the corner of my eye, I see Phil shake his head, get up, and start clearing the table. The kids bring their plates to the sink and dematerialize, beaming back into their social whirl like passengers on the starship *Enterprise*. Shit.

"Ma was right," Laurie says.

My ever primed competitive-sister demon bares her fangs. "What?"

"Oh, never mind."

"No, you can't just say that, Laur! What did Ma say?"

"Forget it. I'm sorry I pressured you. I was just trying to help. You're a stubborn ass sometimes, you know that?"

You don't know the half of it, Mrs. White. "What did Ma say?" I say forcefully.

"Well, she said she hoped you'd, you know, use this as an opportunity...oh, I can't remember what she said. It was nothing, just one of those stupid things people say. Frankly, I think it was a little insensitive. I'm sorry I mentioned it. You know how Ma gets when she's upset. She says things she doesn't mean. We all do."

"What. Did. She. Say," I growl.

"She said she hopes you don't quit fighting the cancer like you quit everything else," Laurie says softly. I have to turn off the sinuous murmur of Bebel Gilberto to hear her.

Silence thickens between us. I hear Phil rooting around, molelike, in the living room before the TV kicks in.

"She didn't mean it, Quel. She's terrified of losing you. Especially after Dad—Quel? Are you there? You know how Ma is, she's just venting. You're not a quitter, you're just…in transition."

"Lost in transition." I try to sound jokey, but my voice is shaking.

"Hey, Moose. We've all been there." Instead of stinging, the old, despised nickname feels unexpectedly cozy.

"Thanks, Laur," I say, meaning it.

"Will you go, then?"

Oh God. The homeopath. Sociopath. Whatever.

Stewing over my mother's jagged words, then, I know.

I can't tell them.

I have been (mis)diagnosed for a reason. My diagnosis means—and I got this straight from Shiny, so it must be right—$245,325 for breast cancer. It means babysitting services for some poor woman who would otherwise have to drag her kids to chemo with her. It means somebody's mother or grandmother, who hasn't had a manicure or a doctor's appointment or a day off in years, will be more likely to keep that follow-up appointment after that soul-killing mammogram because somebody, somewhere, is getting paid to harangue her about it. It means somebody who should live is going to live.

It's not all about "them." I can be honest with myself. I can! I am being given a chance to reinvent myself, a rare opportunity for change, extended into my life like an olive branch for the soul. I will fight this thing. Even if it isn't real, I will fight it. I will show Ma, show all of them, that I'm not the quitter, the forever-in-transition mediocre artist/half-assed mother/feeble wife they think I am. I'll show Laurie she isn't the only Schultz sister who can make Ma proud. I'll show my kids their mom can bring it on with the best of them. I'll show them how to rise up when life bites you in the butt. I'll show Phil I am more than the slightly chunkier, infinitely less sparkly, version of the girl he married. I'll show him I *deserve* to be cherished. I'll show Ren he chose the wrong sister.

I'll show them all.

"Send me the directions," I tell Laurie.

CHAPTER 6

This Is Your Colon on Meat

I feel the minivan shudder as its transmission registers the sharp incline and drops to a lower gear. For one startling moment I see nothing through the windshield but stark blue sky, then the grade levels slightly and neat rows of Victorian cottages appear, spliced by blossoming cherry trees.

Dr. Minh of the eight-month waiting list practices out of his home, a low-lying Buddhist-shrinish collection of buildings hidden behind a high fence crawling with bougainvillea. I find a parking spot and ease the Sienna into it, mindful to turn the wheels toward the curb so the car doesn't hurtle down the steep San Francisco hill if the brake fails.

Walking up to the house, my heart beating wildly from a combination of generalized anxiety and deception, I find myself wondering about the other Raquel Rose. Did she change her name, too, or was she actually born with the sparklier Raquel? Were her kids nicer to her now that they knew she had cancer? Did her husband's boss take her into private bedrooms at company parties and flirt with her under surrealist artwork? How did Meissner break the news to my less fortunate alter ego? Did he have sex with her on the biopsy results, or just tell her to skedaddle on over to radiation for a few UVBs?

I ring the bell. The intercom crackles to life.

"This is Raquel Rose. I have a two o'clock with Dr. Minh," I say, as if I am getting my hair done instead of attempting to deceive a master diagnostician.

"Come through the red door at the back. Please leave your shoes in the entryway. I'll be out to get you shortly," a woman says.

I follow her instructions and plant myself next to a Zen fountain and a framed diagram of the body's major systems. The room is peaceful and faintly scented by flowers, almost like a spa. I close my eyes and fantasize that I am about to get naked and kneaded by a hulking Nordic type with huge hands and Arnold-esque English. *Hasta la vista, stress-induced belly fat.*

"Mrs. Rose?"

The young woman in front of me has a light brown snarl of dreadlocks, and tattoos of Asian characters drip out from under her white tank top. Her arms are lean and brown and sexy, like Gina Gershon's in that lesbian movie that lurks in every straight man's Netflix queue.

"You haven't eaten today, right?" she says, after introducing herself as Karen.

I shake my head. "After this, I'm heading straight to the taqueria to get a burrito." I smile, expecting commiseration— I am, after all, a frail cancer patient who has been forced to starve through two meals—but rat-nest-head Karen just takes my personal belongings and guides me to a room that looks like a massage studio, with a sheet-draped table in the center and various bottles of oils and unguents.

"Dr. Minh will be with you in a few minutes. Please disrobe and put this on." She hands me a waffle-weave robe.

My mood lifts slightly; it really is like a spa! I thank her and undress, enjoying the slightly flatter feel of my empty stomach even though it is somersaulting with hunger.

My cell phone bleeps. Quickly, I rifle through my purse and grab it.

Susan.

I flip open the phone. "Can I call you back later? I'm at the doctor," I whisper to my best friend.

Sue manages to warble a line of "Nothing's Gonna Change My Love for You" before I snap the phone shut. A snort of laughter escapes against my will.

Karen sticks her thatch of knots through the door. "Mrs. Rose, didn't you see the sign? We don't allow cell phones here. You have to turn that off. The waves!" She gestures an imaginary halo with her beringed hands, apparently one of those people who believes cell phones induce brain cancer and flaxseeds must be sprinkled on everything from breakfast cereal to toothpaste.

"Sorry, sorry!" I put it back in the bag.

After a few minutes, I hear a gentle swish enter the room. I sit up halfway on the table, feeling awkward in my gown, which gapes around my big breasts and splits up to the crotch.

Dr. Minh shakes my hand. *"Hola."*

To profoundly understate it, Minh is not what I expected. I suppose I imagined a stringy Confucian, robed and wrinkled, wise almond eyes peering at me from under graying brows, Fu Manchu beard offsetting the long ponytail held with a leather thong, slim hands primed to fondle my chakras and flip through ancient volumes of Chinese medicine for the right cure.

I got the ponytail right.

Dr. Minh is about my age, clad in designer jeans and a

leather vest with nothing under it save an expanse of smooth brown chest. His neck is wrapped in leather amulets and beads, and his tattoos look more S&M than M.D. Excuse me, O.M.D.

"Your sister told me you've just been diagnosed with breast cancer," he says.

"Yes."

He picks up my hand in a loose grip and presses his fingers against my wrist. The man's eyes, I notice, are a liquid gold, startling in the Chinese face.

Dr. Minh offers neither encouragement nor condolences. I stare at the V of sparse chest hair six inches from my nose and try to still my thoughts, which are centered on whether he can tell that I do not, in fact, have cancer and am merely overweight and neurotic.

He lets my hand drop. "I can feel the imbalance."

Guess not.

"Do you eat meat?" he says, easing me to a supine position.

"Yes, but not very often." I've been waiting for this, the part where the experts—medical, holistic, psychological—start picking apart my life, examining my eating, health, lifestyle, and exercise habits with a magnifying glass, looking for transgressions to pin the cancer on.

Dr. Minh digs both hands into the ring of flesh around my belly. Before I can squeeze out a protest, he literally scoops both sets of erect fingers deep into my internal organs, as if I am dead and he is conducting an autopsy without the appropriate excavation tools.

"Stop it!" I cry out involuntarily.

He lessens the pressure slightly. "Mrs. Rose, you have a severe vata imbalance. I'm just trying to assess the state of your intestines and upper colon. Relax. I know it's uncomfortable, but most of my patients start enjoying the release after a while."

Release? Enjoy? While?

Cowed beyond speech, I lie back and try not to groan while horrible Dr. Minh tugs and pulls at my flesh and everything vital underneath. I try to maintain an open mind about the wonders of Eastern medicine but cannot imagine what medical benefit this torture is bestowing on me, the victim. Tears slide down my cheeks. All in all, I feel my performance is befitting an inoperable cancer patient who is having her internal organs pummeled and being denied a burrito.

"Okay, all done. You can sit up now."

Shakily, I raise myself. To my embarrassment, the thick roll of flesh around my middle has jumped my underwear like an Olympic hurdler and spilled over, revealing the hated ridges of pale stretch marks and the thick coffee-colored line from navel to pubic bone that has lightened but not disappeared in the fifteen years since I last gave birth. For some reason I find it tolerable to be accused of carnivorous behavior but not to be visibly overweight. I can handle cancer and even Dr. Minh's idea of restorative massage, but I cannot handle this hippie-biker-doctor person charging me with overeating my way to breast cancer.

"It's interesting," he says, those amber eyes weighing mine. "Your pulses are fine. Your chi's a little off, but that's to be expected. I do have some suggestions for you. And a treatment regimen. I think we can do a lot for you. Are you going to be seeing an oncologist?" Minh must be the new kind of Chinese doctor: savvy, reimbursed by the HMOs, and ready to copilot with a cutter.

"Yes. Meissner over at Stanford," I say faintly. Thoughts of burritos have flown out the window along with my spleen.

"Mrs. Rose, why don't you get dressed, and Karen will show you to my office." He slips away. I hear him conferring with beastly Karen, who has probably donned a Darth Vader helmet against my toxic incursion into her habitat.

I jump off the table and quickly throw my clothes on. Karen comes back and leads me to a beautiful room with French doors off the garden. Dr. Minh is pouring himself a cup of tea. His desk is just as big as Meissner's. On it are two photos: one of him with Xia Chi-Hong outside a pagoda, and another of him with a petite Chinese woman with a punk haircut and a baby in a papoose.

"Green tea?" he says.

"Please." Predictably, even though the man just finished torturing me in the name of integrative health care, I want to please him.

We sit down. Karen hands him a few messages. I see her finger, blunt of nail and too dirty for a respectable health-care professional, slide against his neck for a second.

"Mrs. Rose, have you ever seen a picture of a colon?" he says as a way of segueing into my treatment plan. Frankly, I think it needs improvement.

"Um, no."

Lo and behold, Dr. Minh has one on hand! He whips it out and lays it on the desk. It isn't a real photo, thank God, just a series of illustrations.

"This is what a carnivore's colon looks like." The organ in question is rotund and engorged, like a boa constrictor that has ingested a rat.

"And this is a typical herbivore's gastric system." The slimmed-down version fits comfortably among its friends, some of which I can identify as gallbladder, stomach, and rectum.

"Look at this." Dr. Minh moves his finger over the third drawing. The figure is trim and content-looking, considering that he is sliced in half crosswise. "Have you ever considered giving up food?" he says.

"Actually, I was a vegetarian for years," I say, proud of my veggie cred. "All through college, until I got married. It's hard when you have to cook for a husband and kids, though. Who has time to make two versions of every meal?" I gloss over the fact that except for Sundays, clan Rose is lucky to get one meal.

Dr. Minh raises his eyebrows at me. They are finely arched and sensitive. I wonder if he has them waxed. I really want to know; I don't think I can respect him anymore if he does. It's just so, you know, womanly.

"I don't mean giving up meat," he says, cringing, as if the very word could cause a slice of pastrami to cross his tongue. "Historically, breathivores are almost immune to the heart disease, cancers, diabetes, and other systemic illnesses that plague ingesters."

"Breathivores?"

"Yes," he says patiently. "We drink green tea, a little water-based vegetable, a little seaweed. It's a beautiful, clean way to live. Of course, it takes some getting used to. But it sure beats breast cancer."

"What?" Did he say what I think he said?

"Mrs. Rose, you're going to have to make some lifestyle changes in order to detoxify your body. I don't want to shock you, but the cancer's the least of your problems. It's your body's way of telling you—shouting at you, actually—to wake up and start taking care of it. You should listen."

"What are you saying, that I gave myself breast cancer?" A vision of the other Raquel Rose pops into my head. Is she, in true desperation, also consulting a series of quacks, trying to "cover her bases" with visits to bossy herbalists and deranged chiropractors? Are they insulting her—our—dignity with such misguided accusations?

"We're all responsible for the health of our own bodies," Dr. Minh says.

"So if someone gets beheaded in a car accident, that's their fault?" I can feel heat browning my cheeks.

"Unfortunate, but there are cycles to these things. We'd all benefit from a little consciousness-raising, a little self-reflection."

"That should be challenging without a head."

I stand up. I think Dr. Minh can tell I've had enough without reading my pulses, because he stands up, too. I flex my calves to my full height, which is quite a bit more than his.

"Mrs. Rose, if you change your mind, please feel free to contact me. Given a little time, you might see things differently. I mean, your colon's so blocked right now—"

My latent rage boils up and over. "Shove it up your ass, you vegan freak!" I mutter, the magenta glove of bougainvillea along the path muffling my words as I run.

"You should have seen his face. I thought he was going to plotz."

"What could he plotz, a tea bag?" Sue giggles, her hand coming up in a habitual gesture to hide her teeth.

"What a hypocrite. The prick was lecturing me on healthy living while he practically diddled his assistant." I gave my friend an edited version of why I was at the acupressurist/sadist's in the first place. I was not worried about Sue seeing me on Laurie's show before I could talk to her personally; she turns on her ancient black-and-white television for one purpose only—cooking shows—and that's only when she's depressed.

Sue pads over to the pantry. "Chocolate-chip peanut butter or backpacker?" she calls, naming my two favorites of her restaurant's arsenal of delicious baked goodies.

"What do you think?"

Sue hands me one of each, and I stretch out to full length on one of her Adirondack chairs. Susan Banicek's funky little Victorian on San Francisco's Potrero Hill is my absolute favorite home in the world. She's transformed it from a warren of dim railcar rooms into a loftlike habitat that resembles a cat's dream house, complete with exposed beams, platform nooks, and vast windows.

"Where's Fina?" I ask.

"With Arlo."

"Ooh, I want to see her."

"I know. I called when you pulled up. They're coming home from the park."

"Thanks, Soodle." I lay my hand on my friend's plump arm.

She squeezes it and inspects my nails. "You need a mani." Her gaze drops to my feet, long and battered in old sandals. "And a pedi."

"Yeah."

"How about we go over to Mani/Pedi? My treat. They can meet us over at Klein's after," she says, naming a delicious delicatessen near the neighborhood nail salon.

"Let's go."

I follow my friend out the bright blue door. Sue and I have been friends since college. We met at U.C. Santa Barbara our first day. I knew instantly, taking in the pretty, curvy girl with wild curly hair, retro granny glasses, and Dalmatian-spotted suitcase, that we would be friends for life. Unlike my self-diagnostic romantic forecasts, which have been accurate only in their tendency to culminate in marriage—to somebody else, in every case but Phil—my friendship oracle has remained true.

I've stuck with Sue through thick and thin. Through her parents' divorce in college and the financial disarray that followed. Through her first, unplanned pregnancy and the abortion that ended it. Through the menial jobs and bad relationships with bad men. Through culinary school. Through the commune. Through Sarafina's birth. Through the long drought between her daughter's commune leader–musician father and the gentle motorcycle mechanic Arlo. Through the restaurant's lean early months, before Sue's unique blend of Mediterranean ingenuity and California freshness became the toast of the neighborhood and, later, the town.

She was there for me when Ren broke up with me and pursued Laurie and I could eat nothing but jelly beans and creamy peanut butter for six weeks. When I pounded NoDoz and Diet Coke for five days to finish my thesis project, and when—courtesy of Sue's tenaciousness and contacts—I won my first private commission. When I foundered in creative dry spells. When I married Phil. When we had the kids. When Phil dropped out of the Ph.D program and I went back to work.

When our paths led Sue and me circuitously—me to marriage and stay-at-home motherhood in the suburbs, her to bohemian entrepreneurship and single motherhood in the city—we sought the other out like a tonic, basking in everything our life wasn't.

For the most part, it worked.

"This one or this one?" Sue asks, holding up two bottles: demure pink and vixen red.

"That one." I point to a silver chrome instead.

"Okay, but I get to pick yours." She scans the rows of neat bottles and plucks out an iridescent blue.

"Sue! It'll look like toe fungus!"

"No, it'll look cool. You'll see. It's a good color for you. It matches your eyes and brings out your olive skin."

We sit down for a heavenly interlude of cleansing, exfoliating, massaging, and gabbing.

We are just finishing up when Sue's lover, Arlo, and daughter, Sarafina, come in.

"Quel!" Sarafina flings her lanky six-year-old body into my arms. She smells of that scent unique to small girls, a heady mixture of grape juice, Play-Doh, grass, and string cheese.

"Fina, watch out for Raquel's nails, okay?" Sue admonishes.

"It's okay." I tug on one of Sarafina's tight faun-colored curls and peer into her face. The marriage of her father's bronze skin and regal bearing and her mother's enveloping sweetness produced a beautiful, strong-willed, sweet-spirited child.

"Do you like my bindi?" she says with just the right amount of gravitas.

"Yes. You look very spicy and Indian."

She giggles madly. With her coltish body squirming in my arms, I feel gifted and cool-mom and fantastic, Ellen DeGeneres on a good day.

"Hey, Quel. Nice to see you, baby," Arlo says. We lean over and exchange a quick, fond hug. After I got over the initial surprise of Arlo Murphy's intricately inked arms, grizzly-bear bulk, and grease-monkey dress code, I came to appreciate— love—what he brought to my friend's life: fidelity, devotion, stability, and free oil changes.

"You taking good care of my friend here?" I say.

He chuckles. We go through this every time. "I know she deserves better than this old tomcat. But I do the best I can. The best I can." Arlo is a good ten or twelve years older and served in Vietnam while we were still in kindergarten. He doesn't talk much, but I know he considers himself lucky to have landed in Sue's orbit.

"C'mere, you big Wookie!" Sue says. They kiss passionately. The flock of Korean women around us stops filing toenails and collectively blushes.

"Gross," Sarafina says.

"Yep," I concur.

After our nails dry, we move on to Klein's Deli.

"Don't forget to leave the conditioner on her hair while you pick it out," Sue tells Arlo as he gets ready to leave with Sarafina. "Otherwise it frizzes."

He nods and kisses the top of Sue's head. Something about the way Arlo's rawboned hand, with its row of hieroglyphic-marked knuckles, smoothes Sue's hair makes my breath stumble in my throat.

Sue and I watch them exit, Sarafina skipping alongside Arlo's massive, leather-clad frame. Then Sue turns to me and fixes me with her potent gaze, which has always been as clear and resilient as gray pearls.

"What's going on with you?"

Drat. The woman sees everything. Like a witch.

"Nothing," I say. "This salad is good. I like the cranberries."

The gray pearls glisten faintly, as if lit from within.

"Okay, there is something," I confess.

She waits. Experience has proved that Susan Calliope Banicek can wait a long time for things. I don't bother prevaricating further.

"This is hard to say," I begin, chewing my thumbnail. It already has a ridge in the blue polish, sort of like my life, which is unable to maintain its smooth veneer for longer than a few minutes at a time.

"Jump in fast, like in cold water," Sue suggests. "It's easier."

"Okay. I went to the doctor two weeks ago. I mean, actually, I went earlier than that, but they called me back to get the test results, then..." I see my friend's normally healthy color drain away and feel both sick and foolish at the way I am doing this. "Don't worry! I'm fine. At least now I am."

"Cancer," Sue whispers.

"Yes."

"Oh, my ever-loving goddess—"

"Why are we whispering?" I murmur.

"You better save this woman," Sue goes on in fierce sotto voce as if she hasn't heard me. "Because she's the best god-damn friend in the world, and a loving mother, and a crea-tive…creative, fuck, *spirit*…so if you think you can just do this to her, I'm here to tell you—"

"Sue! Just listen!"

"*I won't stand for it!*" Sue nearly shouts.

"I don't have it," I say.

"What?"

"I said I don't have cancer." The words make me feel a little giddy. And guilty, of course. Super guilty.

"What do you mean?"

"I mean they gave me somebody else's test results. Then they realized the mistake. She has it. I don't. End of story."

"How does *that* happen?" Sue's round, freckled face is stormy. "You should sue their ass! For scaring you!"

"Well, there's more." I wait a moment while two construc-tion workers with hefty guts squeeze past us to a corner table. I lean in close enough to shift Sue's Raphaelite curls with my breath. "I haven't told Phil and the kids yet. Or my mom. Or Laurie and Ren."

As I say this, I feel my face freeze in a weird parody of a smile. It's like I'm talking about somebody else, living out one of those sad-sack stories in the *National Enquirer* where the one-legged guy loses his sprinkler-factory job and doesn't tell his Dairy Queen–clerk wife and seventeen kids until after the bank has foreclosed on the trailer.

"Haven't told them," Sue repeats slowly. Then her face brightens. "Hey, it's okay, since you're fine anyway!"

"It's a little more complicated than that."

I draw a deep breath. Clarity is everything when it comes to deception. "I told them I was *sick*."

The gray pearls cloud over. Sue is looking at me in a way that does not say *friend* or *mutual respect* or *remember that time in Cancún when we screwed the Canadian Football League twins?*

"It's just that...Okay, listen, I tried! I cooked dinner, and we sat down and I tried to tell them the doctors got the results mixed up, and honest to God, Sue, they didn't believe me! They didn't listen!"

Sue's face is still stormy. I see that I am going to have to dig deep.

"Here's the thing: The timing has been off. First Phil and the kids shanghaied me into bed. I was planning to try again last night, but then Laurie called and harangued me for, like, fifteen minutes about God knows what, and then she told me something Ma said about me and the cancer that really pissed me off, and by the time I got back to the table, the kids had taken off for their friends' and Phil was watching the game and it just didn't make sense to tell them then." With great effort, I cut off the flow of word dung and just let it sit there steaming in front of us.

"What complete bullshit," Sue says quietly.

"Sue!"

"Well, it is. You just found out that you *don't* have cancer, and you're letting your family think you do? Quel, I'm worried about you, I really am. I'm more worried than if you had cancer, girl, because this is so not normal, it is scaring the crap out of me. This is *sick*, Quel. Really, really sick."

"I know." I do. I do. I am going to tell them. It is insane

to let this go on just because Laurie will lose her show, Ma's being her usual hard-ass self who needs to remind me on a regular basis what a prototypical fuckup I am, the kids are treating me like a goddamn queen because they think I'm dying, and Phil thinks he owes me because he hasn't fulfilled the feel-up quota since Donohue ruled daytime TV.

I work at the knot in my throat. "Sue, I know it sounds bad, but there's more. I went on Laurie's show last week and talked about my diagnosis. They did a telethon and everything! They had a corporate sponsor! *I* had a corporate sponsor! On TV! And don't ask me why, but the audience loved my ass—like, two hundred thousand dollars' worth of love! So there's a lot of money on the line here, and frankly, I don't know what to do about it. There's this BC support group that's getting all these programs started with the donations, and Laurie could maybe lose her job over this if they thought I faked it, plus her ratings have tanked, and if this comes out now...I guess what I'm saying is, it's complicated."

Sue's eyes narrow to slits. When she does this, she looks like Judi Dench, all stern and Church of England and intimidating. Predictably, I collapse under the pressure.

"I know what I've done is really wrong—yeah, I know, it's unforgivable. It's just...Yeah, okay, I'm going to fix it. Tonight. When I get home. I mean, as soon as Phil gets home from the gym and Micah finishes baseball practice and Taylor is done studying after volleyball. Then I'll tell them."

"You better. Or I'll do it."

"You would," I say sourly. I know she is dead serious. If I don't tell them soon, I'll come home one day and find her sitting at the kitchen table with Phil and the kids, everyone shaking their heads in aggrieved consternation while they plot my stay at Shady Acres and divvy up my miniature Snickers collection.

"Hey, Sue!"

A sleek reed of a woman slides up to our table. She has a cap of dyed apple-red hair and is wearing black from head to toe: black crocheted poncho, black tank top, black studded belt, black skinny jeans tucked into black wedge boots in crinkly, fashionably abused leather. She looks about fifty, her skin and body and voice cigarette-cured down to bone.

"Hey, Saskia. It's been ages," Sue says. The women hug, and I pick at my salad, grateful for the reprieve.

"How's the restaurant?" Saskia says.

"Good. The *Chronicle* updated our review, and it was good. They said the stacked crepes—I love this—'are lighter than freshly fallen snow.' "

"Congratulations."

"Thanks. Oh, Quel, this is Saskia Waxman. She runs a gallery South of Market"—Sue widens her eyes at me, needling me, as always, to promote my dubious (and increasingly untested) talent—"Saskia, this is Raquel Rose. We went to college together a hundred years ago. It's so fortuitous, us running into each other like this, because I was going to introduce you anyway. Raquel's an amazing sculptor and visual artist. She has a studio on the Peninsula and has been talking to some galleries about a show," Sue improvises shamelessly. "You should really see her work."

"Oh, I'm sure Saskia has other projects going on right now," I say quickly. "But thanks for the suggestion, Su*san*." I kicked Sue's shin under the table, wincing as she kicks me back.

"What are you working on?" Saskia Waxman says bluntly. The woman's eyes are hazel and cold, with no buffer between her gaze and the mechanical precision of her thoughts.

I feel my mind—sluggish and atrophied from so many years of nonartistic work that centered on provision of frozen food, cycling of laundry, and minivan travel—contort itself,

grappling for purchase on something compelling and com-
prehensible to say. No thoughts coalesce in the dim space
upstairs, but my mouth moves anyway.

"Right now I'm doing a series of plaster casts of women's
torsos," I hear myself say. "Women with breast cancer. All
the women have had lumpectomies or mastectomies. I use
plaster-of-paris strips for the mold and seal it in gesso, but
they're embellished with mosaics or decoupages that symbol-
ize the, um, identity politics of breast-cancer treatment. I've
done a couple in bronze patina and even one fountain"—the
lies are flowing so freely that I almost believe I have indeed
fashioned a fountain out of some poor woman's papier-mâché
nipples—"my idea is that while society focuses on what these
women—we—have lost, physically, that is, the women have
gained much more in the search for self than they've, as I
said, lost," I finish rather lamely.

Saskia Waxman's feline eyes glow. "This is personal, your
plaster casts," she says with calm assurance. Again, as with
Ross Trimble's awareness of my diagnosis, my not-cancer-
driven sixth sense kicks in, and I know she herself has survived the disease.

In a flash, I see the string of numbers on *Living with
Lauren!*'s computerized pledge tracker, and I know what I
have to do.

"Yes," I whisper. Sue's gray eyes widen further.

What have I done?

My hand comes up involuntarily to stroke my long, thick
wavy hair back from my forehead, as if in anticipation of its
impending absence.

"Yes," Saskia Waxman echoes. We lock eyes like would-
be lovers who once made out briefly and find themselves
together again in another stolen moment. After a second, Saskia manages to snap out of it and pull herself together.

"I'll send a messenger to pick up your portfolio." She hands me her card. "You'll e-mail me your address?"

"Perfect."

"It's been really nice meeting you, Raquel. I can't wait to see your work." She turns to Sue. "Darling, I want to book something for Jacob's birthday."

"Just e-mail me, and I'll talk to the reservationist myself."

"Great. See you."

We watch as Saskia Waxman's trim backside and dark presence disappear behind a wall of matzo boxes and gefilte fish.

"Fuck," I say too loudly. The construction workers look up at me, corned beef stuck in their teeth.

"Double fuck," Sue concurs.

CHAPTER 7

Francis Hale's Manicure

The waiting room is comfortingly bland, wallpapered with smears of asylum-approved salmon and sage that smother dark thoughts, and filled with the sort of nubby-upholstered chairs that never show wear, no matter how much effluvia spills on them. Nice magazines, not random or dog-eared or germy-feeling. Firm yet caring receptionist with subtle, not tacky highlights. Kleenex for the teary. Soothing music.

I am a nervous wreck.

Phil is downstairs somewhere, hopefully prowling the flower shop or watching TV or sipping watery coffee in the hospital cafeteria. At any moment he could show some uncharacteristic initiative and breach the office of Samuel Meissner, M.D.—down the hall and to the left fifty feet—and unearth my moral depravity. Or he could get lucky and stumble into the restful interior of the oncology office I selected at random because I liked the combination on the nameplate: Lourdes Ruiz-Milligan, M.D. This is where I currently wait out my sentence, clenched in terror at my own audacity.

You see, it is one thing to decide you are going to temporarily not correct your family's misapprehension that you have cancer while you swan about raising money for the cause. It is another thing entirely to continue as if the wheels of Western medicine are churning onward with your treatment regimen. *That* is some kind of tricky.

"Is this your first time seeing Dr. Ruiz?"

I put down the *Dwell* magazine I was fiddling with. The woman sitting next to me is about my age, freckled and blowzy in that Shelley Winters way. Her red hair is pulled back in a careless knot. It is flattened on one side. I notice this at the same time I realize that her velour sweatsuit has the pilled, shiny look that comes from sleeping in your clothes.

"Yes," I almost whisper. For some reason, deceiving this woman, a stranger, presumably one with actual cancer, feels worse than lying to Phil, Ma, the kids, or Laurie's old-lady viewers as they scratch out spidery signatures in checkbooks. I want to help this woman somehow, take her home and launder her clothes, or go to a salon for one of those blow-outs so sleek you can't help but feel important and nurtured afterward.

"What are you here for?" the woman asks. She pops open her purse and fondles a king-size bag of nutless M&M's. In stark comparison to all other aspects of her person, her manicure is flawless, her nails long, arched, and coated in coral enamel.

"Sentinel node biopsy." I have done my research. This dye test for lymph node involvement is the latest if not the greatest. It is also the best way to stop Phil from trying to come in with me, since it can be done under local anesthesia and isn't as nauseating as chemotherapy or as momentous as tumor removal. In other words, it is the perfect way to keep Phil out of the doctor's office and roaming the hospital, waiting for me to stumble out, frail and ripe for emotional succor.

The woman nods and gives me her hand. "Frances Hale. Stage three, two-neu-positive, lymph-node-positive." She takes in my wedding band. "Do you have kids, honey?"

"Two." *Hellion One and Tasmanian Devil Two,* I don't say. "You?"

"Five boys." Frances Hale pauses with practiced good humor. "It's not as bad as it sounds. The twins are mama's boys, and the older ones are away at school. And I have some help."

My promise to gallery owner Saskia Waxman to show her my (fictitious) series of plaster casts pops into my mind. A bubble of excitement fizzes in my chest. I recognize the feeling as the one I used to have as an artist when I figured out the missing crucial element in understanding a piece.

Frances Hale's manicure.

Those nails are that single, uncompromising act of resistance that says, *You can attack my body, decimate my blithe sense of normalcy, burgle my will to do laundry, even murder my marriage, but you cannot take away my conviction that I deserve to be adorned.* To be gilded. To be cherished. To be *honored.*

The thoughts swirl around in my head so forcefully they nearly drive my head between my knees. Frances Hale, looking worried, taps the top of my hand with one perfect nail.

"You get through it," she says.

I squint at my notes, trying to mold them into something I can express visually.

Your body betrays you—yet you must nurture it more than ever.

Your loved ones fail you—yet you must rely on them more than ever.

You are a stranger to yourself—yet you prefer what you've turned into.

You are dying—yet you are more aware of being alive than ever before.

Ideas skip through my internal eye. *Pride. Acceptance. Rage... What do they look like?*

I get to work.

Four hours later, I push aside the pile of sketches and glance at the clock, flushed with exhilaration. Dang—two hours left to shower, throw dinner together, pack for Mexico, and make the house presentable so that Phil and Micah have something to destroy while Taylor and I are in Sayulita.

I manage everything but the shower before Phil comes home. It's funny how knowing you'll soon be downing Modelos and waking up at noon makes even vacuuming rewarding.

Phil is sitting on the toilet when I emerge from the shower, his briefcase standing sentry next to his holey tube socks. In most cases, such a picture would prompt one to inquire about a sudden attack of dysentery; Phil, I have learned over the years, simply enjoys spending time here.

Oh, the romance.

"Hey," he says matter-of-factly. While I dry off, he wraps up his little siesta and takes off his shirt, rubbing it across the back of his neck, which tends to sweat. "You packed?" he says, as if the suitcase is not sitting openmouthed on the bed.

"All set. Did you remember to get dog food?"

"Damn." Phil eyes the pile of clothes. "I'm supposed to meet Ren at the club in fifteen minutes."

"Phil, I asked you to do *this one thing*!" My annoyance propels me back into the shower, where I grab a wad of shed hair from the side of the shower stall. "My hair's falling out!" I say triumphantly, nuzzling it like a house pet.

Phil blanches. Then, without speaking, he picks up his keys and walks out. I hear the car rev into gear. It is hard to believe, but I guess he never noticed me painstakingly gathering my fallen hair, post-shower, for the past two decades, so that he wouldn't be grossed out and our marriage would, you know, thrive.

With a little reluctant help from Sue and an amenable Internet, I cooked up a treatment regimen. First chemotherapy. Then surgery. Next radiation. Since I haven't yet conceived a way to fake post-surgical trauma, I'll need to have a tumor big and vile enough to require chemo before surgery. This is called neoadjuvent chemotherapy. It is a horrible thing, but I guess it works.

Wait...the hair. Emboldened by Phil's acquiescence, I pick up his electric razor and tentatively attack a small square near my ear. Nothing happens. After a few hacks with scissors, I am good to go. Giant sheaves fall to the ground, then tufts, then nothing. I look like a kosher chicken.

I have been told more than once that my hair is my best feature. (Let's face it, brawny shoulders don't earn a girl many points in this world.) Vanity must be more than insecurity plus a dash of lipstick, because I shed real tears as I check out my plucked visage in the mirror.

Oh well. As they say south of the border, *Hasta la vista*.

"It's fucking beautiful, isn't it?"

The boyish voice snaps me out of my reverie. The combination of the sun's caress on my bare head and the hypnotic embrace of wave and shore has lulled me into one of those fantastic fugues where the eyes narrow to slits, identity blurs into sea and sand, and crazy stuff seems more than possible.

The person who made the remark is pretty fucking beautiful himself: medium height, lean and muscled, smooth chocolatey skin, gold-tipped silky-shaggy brown hair, and the brightest aquamarine eyes I've seen outside of a mascara ad.

"I'm Duke," the vision says. He shakes my hand.

"I'm your student's mother," I answer in return, anxious to pop the bubble before he does.

Duke smiles. His teeth are—of course—white and enhanced by a slanted bicuspid, which happens to be a particular obsession of mine. "Do you have a name, or should I just call you Mom?"

I cringe. "God, anything but that. It's Raquel. Raquel Rose. Taylor's my daughter. I brought all the girls to the camp." We have been in Mexico for three days, most of the daylight hours spent at the beach under the bright blue/green/brown eyes of the various Apollonic surf gods the school gifts us with like flavors of the day.

"Nice to meet you, Raquel." Duke smiles at me in a decidedly nonpitying way that makes me wonder if he has a sick fetish for geriatrics with thickish waists.

Before I can do something unwise, unseemly, or illegal, I recline in my lounge chair and close my eyes, relishing the soft touch of the late-afternoon sun on my eyelids. Something about having a shaved head makes my skin exquisitely sensitive. Sue once got a Brazilian bikini wax and said the same thing, but I thought the kick only pertained to depilation down there.

"You ever surf?" Duke says.

I open my eyes. The boy—okay, man—no, guy—has stretched his very fine body out beside me on his stomach, clad solely in a pair of ragged blue board shorts that hang from the moon of his butt as if on a coat hook.

"Three times. In college. That was almost twenty-five years ago, in case you're wondering."

"I'm not."

"You should be." Okay, I have officially flirted with my daughter's ten-year-old surfing instructor.

Duke just grins at me in that I-may-be-ridiculously-underage-but-still-possess-the-skills-to-corrupt-you kind of way. Then he tosses his hair back and stares out to sea. It is impossible for me to discern if his gaze is vacant, because of the strong glare. I decide to be optimistic for a change.

"Mom, can I have some money for lunch?" Taylor and two of her girlfriends, Lindsay and Savannah, have beached their boards and blocked our sun, their bodies nubile and tanned in their bikinis and rash guards. Yesterday they had their hair braided into cornrows by an Indian woman on the beach. They look like Bo Derek on Botox.

"Your mom's going to surf with us tomorrow," Duke says.

"Uh, I don't think so." I fish around for my wallet.

"Moms don't surf. Besides, Mom doesn't like getting her hair wet. She always swims like this"—Taylor mimes a clumsy breaststroke with her head sticking up, turtlelike, and her friends laugh overenthusiastically for Duke's benefit. Realizing what she's said, Taylor stutters to a stop.

I squint into the searing Mexican sun. "Maybe I will go surfing tomorrow," I say. The girls don't hear me; they are already heading toward the stand that sells fish tacos and lovely, sweaty bottled beer.

"Go Mom." Duke grins.

"Okay," Duke yells against the roar of the waves. "Paddle! Paddle, paddle, paddle!"

He shoves me forward, and I windmill my arms through the

water as hard as I can. The surfboard rides the crest of the wave for a moment, then slides down the backside, bobbing gently.

"Damn. Missed it," I say as I row my way back to him.

Duke squints into the sun, his legs spread on either side of his shortboard. His chest and shoulders are dotted with salty drops, as if his skin is impervious to damp. My ribs are killing me, knees scraped raw, wax ground into my elbows, arms paralyzed from overwork. I cannot remember the last time I felt so good.

"You need to paddle harder. I'm going to push you again. You'll know when you catch it. It just feels... sweet. Then you stand up. Don't worry about falling. You won't. Don't crouch. Just stand up." Duke slides off his own board and pulls himself onto mine near the nose. He looks like Gael García Bernal, the Mexican actor with a name like a chocolate Kiss and eyes that make you want to purr.

"You know when you've just had sex and everything's all loose and easy and spent-like?" His mouth is four inches from the top of my head.

"Oh... um, sure." I ransack my memory for this sensation and manage to uncover something vaguely reminiscent of it in a compartment marked SPRING BREAK: SOPHOMORE YEAR.

"Just channel that feeling," he says. He scans the horizon. "Okay, here you go. That's your wave, Raquel. You got it. Easy now."

Duke jumps into the water, lines me up, and gives me a monster shove. The wall of water grabs me and then I am a speck, a nothing, merged with it as we hurtle into space. My mind sifts through the possibilities and chooses one. I stand up. No wobbles. I am easy. Spent-like. As if I've just had great sex. I even have the presence of mind to pull my dark blue swim dress out of my crack.

Next thing I know, the sky is gone and I am stuck in the

dishwasher on power cycle. I feel the ocean bottom reach up and scrape my back raw.

Strong fingers clasp my arm and drag me up. I explode out of the water into the light, filling my lungs with sweet air.

"It's a good thing you're bald," Duke says. "You're really easy to spot."

CHAPTER 8

Signs of Good Breeding

I love my kids.

Perhaps this is self-evident. Who doesn't? What kind of egotistical harpy has children and then consigns them to the bitter trough of a loveless rearing? Often just looking at them is enough to send a spurt of adoration through my veins. The curve of their foreheads, the timbre of their laughs, even the shape of their insubordination thrill and mystify me. In their presence, I am no better than a drug addict, intoxicated by some unidentified maternal potion, without judgment or instincts for self-preservation. I am all good intentions and unappeasable need.

Or perhaps I doth protest too much.

There are times—I would not call them rare, perhaps infrequent—when I am convinced that my offspring thrive not because of but at the expense of, well, me. That they are the parasites to my host, feeding on my affection with the canny resoluteness of soul-eating aliens. That their ascent toward greatness fills my own place in the universe, snatches at the space left by my own dissipation, leaving me less and less nourishment as my aspirations wither toward their final puny end. (I always picture myself in a housedress at this point in the dark fantasy. The sort of worn, faded garment whose provenance is known only by Sicilian grandmothers and a few old-fashioned maids.)

Before you have kids, parents, especially mothers, will hasten to disabuse you of your romantic ideals of procreation and especially its compatibility with maintaining some semblance of what you currently refer to as life. They use words like "sacrifice" and "dependence," "surrender" and "spawn." They drone on about the horrors of maternal sacrifice and end with an abrupt "But it's sooooo great" that resonates about as profoundly as the Bradley childbirth instructor's prediction that you will feel no pain.

Nevertheless, there are varying definitions of sacrifice. The divergence on the subject of mom-child love is maddening. Once, when I was discussing this very topic with Ma, she told me without flinching, "You have one kid, you look into that little *punim* and you think, *Okay, this is it. This is the great love. This is where it ends.* What's the husband next to love like that? You think, *God forbid something ever happens to this kid.* God forbid! Then you have the second kid. You're surrounded by kids! Kids all over the place, turning the house into a war zone, playing their cockamamie music and blabbing on the phone. They don't listen, because who listens anymore? Suddenly, the husband's not looking so bad. You're thinking, *As long as he's around, we can always make more.*" Ma smiled as she bestowed this great gift. "*That's* motherhood!"

I'll be honest. My mother? Not always wrong.

Still, I love my kids.

Next: I love my husband.

It is fun, after twenty years of marriage, to try saying this with the appropriate gravity, to imagine yourself choking on the rich bile of spousal passion as you once may have. If it were posed as a question—*Do* you love your husband?—you would feel "yes" bubble up inside your vascular cavity like carbonation in a Diet Coke. The silliness of the question is exceeded only by the pointlessness of the answer. You have kid(s). You have house(s). You have car(s). You have bill(s). You have shit(s) to deal with. The tentacles of partnered life bonding you to your husband are guaranteed to both murder the triumphant passions of early marriage and build, in their place, an infinitely less destructible set of sentiments. The fact that Phil takes me for granted these days and shows me less ardor than he does heated toilet seats does not negate this basic truth.

The impetus for my marriage is as old a story as the love triangle that imprisoned Tristan and Isolde. No, I wasn't knocked up. Nor was my biological clock ticking itself into a time bomb. Nobody arranged it; I wasn't sold to the highest bidder with a chest of baubles and a gaggle of chickens. My beloved didn't croak, leaving his brother no choice but to save me from the dire straits of widowhood. Did I wake up one day and find myself floating solo in a pool of merry marrieds? Nope. At the time most of my friends were in the same boat as me, wedded to nothing more convoluted than pulling off a successful Friday night, obsessed with our careers, warmly embraced by our first post-graduate apartments, our friends, our naked selves stripped of clingy college sweethearts. In fact, the artlessness of it all is almost embarrassing.

I was in love.

Not the fearless, ravenous, consuming, if-I-can't-have-you-I-might-have-to-eat-you variety that had afflicted me with Ren White. I can safely go on record as never wanting to eat Philip Atticus Rose. Kill him, yes. Ingest him, no. Nevertheless, in my twenty-second year, not quite fresh out of college but not yet stinking with inertia, I'd lived and loved enough to know the tart pang of attraction when I felt it.

Attraction.

Isn't it ironic that the crucial ingredient of attraction, mystery, is not only the enemy of marriage, it's the enemy of human relationship? When there's mystery, there's horniness. When there's mystery, there's hope. When there's mystery, he just might turn out to be Viggo Mortensen with a side of monogamy.

Once I was young and Phil was mysterious. And it was good.

But before we get into it, a confession: My sister isn't the only Schultz sister with a celluloid life. It may seem corny, but I tend to see my own existence as a sort of epic blend of *Pollock* and *Love Story.* Okay, actually, it's more like *Charlie's Angels: Full Throttle,* except without the clothes, great bodies, and excitement. Just the mess.

Set the scene: San Francisco. It's 1985, and the city is in the throes of Indian summer...

Sweet curls of pot smoke waft up between the weeping trees in Golden Gate Park. Joggers and Rollerbladers zigzag down the Embarcadero, the city's Goliath bridges rising up around them with utter majesty. That fall, the city simmers with the flavors of love: Chinese, Indian, Italian, El Salvadoran, Thai, the exotic, spicy thrill of it all scenting the skin. Rachel—Raquel—is a young sculptor living the bohemian dream in the Mission District, a squalid, rousing pastiche of artists, Central American immigrants, drug addicts, homeless, hippies, dykes, and urban-minded sorts who prefer the rainbow-colored sunny side of the city to its more rarefied hills and heights (Nob, Russian, Pacific).

Her loft, which she shares with an aspiring chef named Sue Banicek, opens languidly to the city's exquisite light. It sits on top of a taqueria-tamale parlor. The tamales are filled with ropy cheese and succulent chicken, salty carnitas and juicy cactus. The tacos are pliant and plump, bursting with shredded meat and haphazard salsa and fat, meaty pinto beans. Raquel and Sue eat dozens of them each week, washing them down with draft beers from San Francisco's very own Anchor brewery. Sue likes Liberty Ale; Quel prefers the Summer Beer, a paler wheat.

The girls—women—are blooming with youth and beauty. Best of all, after years of self-doubt and real or imagined social ostracization, they know it. Finally removed from the blandly insidious comfort of institutional food, Raquel is sleek and tan, almost firm, she thinks. In fact, sometimes, peering at herself in the cracked full-length mirror that's propped against the loft's exposed brick wall, she almost likes her body. Her breasts are still too full and heavy, her stomach more pillowy than the unyielding flatness required for blithe exposure. But her best features buoy her as never before. At last, she thinks, she looks like someone. Someone with enough exoticism to capture the attention she so desperately craves. Her hair falls, black and shiny, to midback, snaking waves that don't quite break into ringlets but don't frizz, either. That year everybody is cutting their hair short, spiking it out in dyed tufts. Raquel, correctly sensing disaster were she to follow suit, sometimes fastens her thick mane into a ponytail on the side of her head; mostly, she wears it long and loose, contrary to fashion. Against the olive backdrop of her smooth skin, her eyes are slate blue, striking if she wears makeup, unnerving and pale if she doesn't. That year she wears a corset with a miniskirt or Levi's, dark, high-waisted jeans that make her legs look even longer, paisley blouses and flat jeweled slippers she buys in Chinatown. She has three pairs of huaraches. She carries a battered black bag whose decay she takes an inexplicable pride in, which she decorates with buttons proclaiming APARTHEID SUCKS and TRA-VOLTA IS REVOLTA.

One night Sue pokes her curly head into Quel's studio—the part of the loft shielded by a wall of torn Oriental screens—and waves a set of tickets in Quel's face.

"I won!" she yells, knowing Quel will understand. Sue has phoned in to the local new-wave radio station every day for the past five months, hoping to win concert tickets they can't afford. Now they are going to R.E.M.

Quel puts down the chunk of metal she has been blowtorching and wipes her face of the sweat rolling down her forehead, stinging her eyes. The odor of charred steel is bitter, intoxicating, hopeful; years later, she witnesses a fatal car fire from a safe street corner perch and thinks, inexplicably and guiltily, of art and youth.

Together, the girls—women—dance around, reveling in the kiss of pure gladness. Sue's hot-pink prom dress swirls around her small waist, highlighting her plump white arms. She is wearing red Converse high-tops.

"I'm going to marry Michael Stipe," Sue chants over and over.

Later, at the concert, the girls are touched by a sort of wild enchantment that spirals into near perfection as the evening slides into night. Dancing in the tight crush of bodies at the front of the Cow Palace auditorium, they are tugged onstage by the band's bass player, where they abandon the final shreds of their inhibition and gyrate like the rock stars they habitually dream about as banks of cameras record their joy.

Back on the ground, panting with uncharacteristic exertion, Raquel feels her feet skid in the manic swirl of sweaty dancers. The alcohol pulsing through her veins—two pre-dinner glasses of Cab, a few rum and Cokes, enough beer to wash down a cheap tapas meal—has rendered her clumsy *and bovine. She struggles against the undertow surge of the crowd. A small flame of fear licks at her gut.*

"Hey, you okay?"

The voice, pleasantly bland and Californian—L.A.? Orange County?—and slightly raspy, wafts from behind her left ear. Her back is pressed against the guy's chest, so tightly she can feel an obstinate ridge of belt buckle against her tailbone. Glancing down, she registers a pair of forearms crossed over her waist. They are tanned, the hair bleached by sun, thick and soft-looking, like animal fur. Their hold on her feels surprisingly comfortable, no more obtrusive than a timeworn cardigan. Her heartbeat slows; her feet are back on the ground.

"You smell good," the guy with the furry arms says, his voice nuzzling her ear. "Like figs." He's wrong—her bath gel is infused with linden—but the fact that a stranger with a big carnal belt and a sexy voice would even try to name her scent astounds and intrigues her. At his words, a tendril of attraction unfurls from her belly up into her core. She has yet to see his face.

The guy's name, he tells her eighty-five minutes later over late-night tamales and beers at the taqueria, is Phil. He has just returned to California after two years in the Peace Corps teaching English to traumatized Hutus and Tutsis who carry machetes in their back pockets like driver's licenses. The abundance of sound, food, unnatural light, expectations here at home unnerves him. He is still reeling from the plunge back into modern life. He is not used to talking to white people; they are so aggressive. Greedy. Coarse.

"I'm in a Ph.D. program at Cal," he offers, putting down the bulk of his burrito uneaten. "Artificial intelligence. What are you working on?" he goes on, as if he finds the standard-format career question distasteful.

"I'm an artist." For the first time ever, Raquel says it without flinching.

Later, their naked bodies dappled in neon light from the taqueria sign, Raquel feels herself kiss the scar that curves above Phil's green eyes. It is bumpy and fresh. She knows the kiss is too tender. Raquel wants him to leave so she can start planning distractions for when he doesn't call her.

"Africa?" she says, tracing it with her finger. She conjures emaciated children rioting in the streets with blood dripping from moon-shaped blades, acid shouts rising like dust from Jeep wheels.

He grimaces. "Garage door."

They laugh together.

"Raquel?"

The image of Phil BCE (Before the Collapse of Expectations) dissolves and is replaced by something infinitely more photogenic: Duke the Surfer grinning at me from under a fringe of unkempt bangs. He plunks himself down on a bar stool. I wonder what he'd say if I told him the truth: I love my kids and I love my husband. It's just that they, not cancer, are killing me.

"How did you decide to get into surfing?" I say, and immediately feel foolish. Pretending it constitutes a thoughtful career change is not going to make the boy any older.

Duke humors me. "I grew up in Kansas City. But once I came out here and got into it, I knew it was the right thing. I'll never live inland again."

"The girls think you're a good instructor."

"Girls usually do."

"Modest, I see."

He looks pained. "No, I just mean it's easy to impress little girls here, if that's what you want. I'm not into them, myself."

The motive for his attention becomes clear. God, what an

idiot I am. One person's flirtation is another's pity party, I suppose.

"So, does your boyfriend surf, too?"

"My boyfriend?" His lips pause at the neck of his Bohemia.

"Oh, I just thought because of what you said—"

Duke laughs. "You thought I was gay because I don't date high school girls?"

"Well, I couldn't think of any other reason...you know."

"What?"

"Why you're, you know, always talking to me." I feel my cheeks redden and wonder briefly if my bald head blushes, too.

Duke scooches his stool closer to mine. His non-beer-holding hand drops to my thigh, shooting a dart of terrified lust through my body. "I like talking to you. You're smart. You're weird. You make me laugh."

My eyes begin that weird guilty darting dance that eyes do when you are doing something the morals police would not approve of. I pray that the girls are still waiting for the check at their final unchaperoned Mexican dinner. The mere idea of my daughter and her friends absorbing the sordid snapshot of me, Taylor's fat bald mother, with her leg trembling under the hand of a surfing instructor, is enough to send my blood pressure soaring.

"I've always liked older women," Duke says under the buzz. "You're so real. You've got experience. I can tell"—the hand emigrates to the nape of my neck, rubbing—"the way you look at me...you remind me of Diane Lane in that movie where she cheats on her husband with the Russian guy."

I don't bother to correct Olivier Martinez's nationality. We both know what Duke's talking about, and it's not perestroika.

"What about my hair?" I say stupidly, which is not, in all likelihood, what Diane Lane would have said. Something has shifted; I relegated this person to kindergarten, and all of a sudden he has matriculated.

Duke the Demented leans back and studies me for a second. "I like it. Makes you look insane. Tall. Like an Amazon. Hey"—he nuzzles my neck—"do you read *The New Yorker?*"

"The second it hits my mailbox," I tell him, though my subscription has lapsed. The statement provides relief; it is almost true.

I slide *Teen People* out from under a sleeping Taylor's hand and slip it inside the copy of *The New Yorker* I bought for the equivalent of twelve dollars at the Puerto Vallarta airport. Now I can brush up on Hilary Duff's methods of applying self-tanner in a taxicab while the rest of the plane thinks I'm contemplating Alan Greenspan's position on third-world debt relief.

However, instead of reading, I gaze out the window as we bank upward through strings of jet stream. I've done nothing wrong. This I'm quite confident about. Infidelity involves certain transgressions. Hands on thighs don't qualify. Fantasies don't qualify. Flirtations on pristine beaches don't qualify. If there were an entry exam for adultery, I would have failed it. There's just one thing I don't understand: If I've done nothing wrong, why, as I stare blindly out the smooth oval of airplane window, is my soul painted over with what seems to be regret?

CHAPTER 9

It's Fakakta, Is What It Is

For a second the naked woman's large, dark eyes meet mine, and I feel myself plummet into her pain as if shoved off a cliff. Then I wrest my gaze away and continue wrapping the dripping sheet of plastered fabric around her bare torso.

"It's cold," she says. "I'm always cold now."

She is waiting for my commiseration. This is how it works: tit for tat. Or, as the case may be, tit for no tit.

"I used to wear flip-flops all winter. Now I have to bundle up just to go shopping. And I hate the frozen-food aisle," I say. I tuck the end of the wrap under itself.

The woman, a Pacifica mother of two who clerks in a dentist's office, nods her cueball head. Her skin, a tawny coffee, has yellowed a bit from chemo. My fraudulence must glow off my skin like nuclear offal, I think. But perhaps to others, expecting cancer, it just looks real?

I say, "There. Now we just wait for it to dry. Do you want a drink? I have some cookies here." Sue keeps my makeshift studio in her backyard cottage filled with goodies for my subjects and, unwisely, me.

"Do you have some—"

"—wine?" I finish for her, prompting a laugh. I pull a chilled bottle of buttery Chardonnay out of the mini-fridge and pour two ample glasses. I've always worked better with a drink or two in me, and work is what I need to do if I'm to make Saskia Waxman's July deadline for my show.

"This is kind of embarrassing, but would you mind if we turn on the TV?" my subject asks. "There's this show I always watch at ten A.M."

I gesture toward the remote and busy myself cleaning up my tools. I need to get out of here by eleven o'clock if I am to get home in time to pick up the food for tonight's party.

A few seconds later, my sister's dulcet tones fill the room. I feel my eyes pull toward the television. During Laurie's tenure as the queen of local talk shows, I have learned that you cannot *not* watch someone you know on the box: It's not humanly possible.

Laurie has on a screamingly expensive creamy pantsuit with strappy medium-heeled pumps. Her lapel is pierced by an apple-green ribbon. I try to recall what cause that color signifies but am distracted by a flash from one of my sister's ears. Diamond studs. Big ones. I wonder if they are a gift from Ren. As the years have gone by without any children, and Laurie's otherwise flawless smile has gotten incrementally tighter—though no less dazzling—the baubles have gotten bigger.

"I'm addicted to it," the Pacifica woman says apologetically. "Have you ever watched? She's so great. So inspiring. She always finds a way to talk about people's problems without making them feel bad about themselves."

True, I think but don't say as I slide spatulas under water, *she left that part to Ma.*

* * *

"...happy birthday to YOU!" we shout. I raise my voice so as not to be accused of being one of those birthday-song stragglers. Ma sits stoically throughout, peering at us from behind her reading glasses, which she habitually keeps on to read food nutrition labels.

"Yeah, yeah, all right," she says, waving her hand at us. "Thanks, kids. Now you"—she tugs Micah's ear, which pokes out from under his tumble of shaggy light brown Phil hair—"tell me about that soccer tournament in Pleasanton. Your mom said you scored on a corner."

After a quick survey to make sure the food and drink platters are fully stocked, I escape to the kitchen. Sue follows me.

"So, tell me about this surfer," my best friend says after she grabs a deviled egg and pops it in her mouth. She says it several (dozen) notches too loudly.

I shush her and slide a tray of homemade—by Draeggers's pastry chefs, but so what?—brownies in the oven to warm. The punch needs to be refreshed, so I start slicing oranges and lemons on the cutting board.

"Didn't I tell you about Duke already?" All the lying I am doing has my internal information-tracking software in a dither.

Sue widens her gray eyes toward the heavens. "Duke? Oh my God. She slept with an underage dog's name."

"I didn't sleep with him!" I recall the smooth feel of young hand against my own increasingly withered flesh and unsuccessfully suppress a smile. "We just made out. Not even that, really. It was more like, you know, an innocent kiss."

"Oh my God," Sue moans. "Innocent, my ass! Tell me everything. I want details!"

In a hushed torrent, I relay the minutiae of our last night

in Mexico: how, at the bar, Duke's hand migrated leisurely across mostly visible parts of my body while we discussed the whimsical logic of Malcolm Gladwell; the terror of being spotted that did wonderful things to my already panicky state of lust; the drunken high-school-girl moment when I swayed against the boy on his salt-cured doorstep, refusing his unspoken physical entreaty to join him in bed; the cool relief of starched sheets rising up with each of Taylor's inhalations as I slipped, too awake for sleep, into our shared bed. Sue took it all in with bright, enthusiastic, scandalized eyes. The intimacy and lava-flow urgency of the conversation make me feel even younger than Duke's good-night kiss, which, as kisses go, was relatively chaste.

"So you didn't do *anything* with him? What a waste." Sue sighs.

"For God's sake, Sue, give me some credit." I open the oven and press a toothpick into the brownies. It sticks. Fuck. Overdone.

"I know. I know. I just wanted to wallow in something fabulous and lurid. It's been so goddamn long. I'm between books," she explains. Sue's literary taste runs toward the pornographic and bodice-ripping.

My stepfather pops his head in. "Rachel? What are you doing in here?" He frowns at the picked-over spread of brownie crumbs and shakes his head. "Those carbs'll kill you. I hope you used whole-grain flour. *Oy,* they think they're going to live forever! Ren's looking for you. He's out back." Eliot darts out again.

I make a horrible face at his departing back, as much to seal my gossip session with Sue as to make a deposit to my High-Yield Eliot Irritation Account. My elderly stepfather is fond of wearing the sort of tight, stretchy T-shirts favored by gays and Jack LaLanne. I guess he wants the world to enjoy the fruits of his daily weight-lifting sessions and Dean Ornish–approved, prostate-cancer-delaying diet.

Then I mainline about a liter of Chardonnay and go in search of my brother-in-law. I cannot imagine what Ren wants to talk to me about. In the two-plus decades since he dumped me for Laurie, our conversations have focused mainly on the weather, his clients' liposuction addictions, and my children's athletic prowess.

I find Ren in the backyard, cornered by three members of Ma's Humanitarian Judaism/bridge/birding/whining group.

"So, tell me something. I always wondered, what do you do with the fat you suck out?" Estelle Gilden is saying as I walk up.

"They save it for boobs. Right, Loren?" Coco Stein slides a toothpick into her bridge.

"Maybe we can donate some to Raquel for when she has the mastectomy." Edith del Toro shakes her neat, birdlike head in sympathy, the crisp black waves bisected by zebra-like gray streaks. I feel a flush of heat shriek through my neck and chest at her words. It is so embarrassing, this blithe focus on your body parts. It's as if cancer annexes what used to be private and makes it public: RAQUEL'S BREASTS: OPEN 10 A.M.–5 P.M. MONDAY–SATURDAY, CLOSED SUNDAYS FOR MAINTENANCE. PLEASE PICK UP YOUR DOG FECES.

"Actually," Ren begins. He looks pained. While his generosity extends to melding the palates of the less fortunate, coping with the fervor of Jewish mothers is not his strong suit.

"Hi!" I say, glad for the opportunity to save him. Ren's face brightens. Sad sack that I am, I take a millisecond to enjoy the sweet kiss of happiness his approval has always spawned in me.

Estelle Gilden grasps my arm. "Raquel, dear, how *are* you?

How. Are. *You.* Your mother told us all about it. It's *fakakta,* is what it is."

"Too young!" Coco Stein.

"Too healthy! Look at this girl. Strapping!" Edith del Toro.

"It's the hormones in milk. Ask Eliot about it." Estelle.

"So, honey, listen: My sister-in-law's sister survived it *twice.* Imelda, that's her name. Like the dictator." Coco is already digging in her bag for her address book. "I think you two would get on like a house on fire. You know what she did after the cancer? Dropped fifty pounds and became a life coach, that's what! You're going to call her."

This is part of the Great Fraud I never anticipated: Whereas in the past, I was at pains to deflect Jewish-mother-initiated offers of dates and potential husbands, now I have to deal with an army of well-intentioned yentas who want to set me up with my breast-cancer soul mate.

"She sounds wonderful," I lie. *Like hell. She sounds like an anorexic tyrant with a closet full of Manolos.*

"I must have left it in my other purse. It's okay, I'll call you," Coco promises, nodding. I can see the onslaught now; in a matter of days, I will have to change my number or take a turn for the worse.

I force a smile. "I'm sorry, ladies, but I've got to borrow this guy for a minute." Taking Ren by the elbow, I steer him toward the gazebo, a contrivance whose only contribution to the family history is having served as a whelping box for our basset Stella's second litter.

Ren tilts his head toward the knot of ladies. "They scare me."

"They scare everyone."

We laugh. It feels too good, so I think of my credit-card bill. There. Balance restored.

"Eliot told me you wanted to ask me something." I try not to study his hazel eyes too deeply, instead scanning

the crowd for disgruntled guests the way a properly indifferent sister-in-law might. On the far side of the pool, I see
Taylor chatting with Ronnie Greenblatt. Her head, with its
spaniel-like sheaves of highlighted chestnut hair, is tilted in
a coquettish way that does not say talking-to-boring-old-
big-brother's-friend. I make a mental note to send her to
military school forthwith if the look graduates to outright
flirtation.

"How are you feeling?" Ren says.

"Pretty good, considering." This is basically true.

He nods, pleased. "You look great. Better than I could have
hoped. So how long does Meissner want you on chemo?"

"Four rounds." I've done my research: I've talked to my
sculpture subjects. I've interrogated strange women in doctors' waiting rooms. For the most part, I've tried to maintain
an aura of mystery and obliqueness around my (not-)cancer
treatment, deflecting probing inquiries with vague mentions
of catheters and stool softeners. Obviously, this is much more
challenging with an actual doctor. Among my other para-
noias, I live in fear that Ren will stumble upon Meissner in the
hospital cafeteria or on the golf course and find me out. I pray
regularly that Wendy Yen is hot enough in the sack that Doctor Boy Meissner has no energy left for anything but surgical
pursuits.

"How are you handling the Taxol?"

"Pretty well. They administered the first dose in the ICU,
but I was okay." So many people have allergic reactions to
the highly toxic drug that they first give it under the watchful
plink of cardiac monitors and trauma physicians. Just reading
about it made my stomach ache in sympathy and guilty terror,
so I did what I always do now when regret overrules stead-
fastness—think of the number $245,325.

Ren clears his throat. "I know the timing is somewhat off,

but I need to ask you a favor. I wouldn't ask unless it was important."

Well, I hate to say "I told you so"...I'm sure Phil won't mind a little swappy-swap now and again...

"Uh-huh." I try to look grave instead of hopeful.

"You know that Laurie and I have been trying for a family for many years now. It's been really hard on her, primarily because they were never able to identify the cause, or causes, of our infertility." Ren glances away, toying with his keys. His plastic surgeon's hands are long and lean and ageless. I wonder if he applies chemical peels to them between patient appointments. For research purposes, naturally.

"One of the things that's been a sticking point for us is whether to keep trying IVF or start thinking about other options. Laurie was—*is*—very invested in the idea of us having our own biological child. Me, less so, though I empathize with her position." Ren looks straight at me for the first time. His pure hazel eyes are warm and steady. I have the horrifying sense he is going to violate the twenty-three-year covenant and suggest we repeat the act of our sixth date, twelve days before the Thanksgiving visit that changed all our lives.

He veers in an unexpected direction. "We made a decision to start the adoption process. It's quite rigorous. One of the components is character references. Laurie and I—that is, we'd like to ask you if you'd write one for us."

Relief engulfs me. Among the favors he could have asked for, this one rates high on the comfort scale. My mind flits through complimentary things I could say about my sister to make them give her a baby: *Thin genes. Cleans grout on a regular basis. Speaks Mandarin like a native. Never actually asked if I screwed her husband.*

"Oh, Ren, of course I'd be glad to do it. You didn't have to worry about that. I want to do anything I can to help," I say instead.

"I knew you'd be okay with it. I know you and Laurie don't always see eye to eye on things, Quel, but I didn't think that would matter when push came to shove." Ren takes a sip of his gin and tonic, easygoing now. He shifts his fine body closer to my less fine one, near enough that I can see the individual hairs comprising his thick brush of eyelashes.

"If you hadn't gotten the cancer, things might have been different, you know," he says, his tone thoughtfully conspiratorial. "If you weren't undergoing chemo right now, I'm pretty sure Laurie would have asked you for some eggs."

This warms me. *Raquel Rose: fertility goddess, maker of eggs, breeder extraordinaire.*

I am about to offer Ren my eggs any way he wants them when Phil ambles over and plants a sloppy kiss on my head. "Stop hitting on my wife," he says to Ren with easy bonhomie. He could be talking about his love of beets.

Phil and Ren do one of those manly handshakes where one grasps the other by the forearm and squeezes at the same time. Everything is right in the land of brothers-in-law! This is precisely the problem. What is it about me that gives my husband complete confidence that I would never flirt with an attractive man who used to be my boyfriend? Or is it complete confidence one would never flirt with me?

"Hey, buddy. I had to schedule an otoplasty for late Wednesday. Can we move the game to Thursday?" Ren says.

Phil says sure, and they launch into a discussion of major-league sports that would have made me whimper with ennui if not for the way the afternoon light is falling on Ren's fair hair (like Robert Redford's in *The Way We Were,* if you want to know).

Sometimes I hate myself.

Of all the things that bug me about the way Ren has acted with me since the fateful moment he shook Laurie's hand in my parents' avocado-colored kitchen, it's the way he is with Phil that bothers me most. In the twenty years that have elapsed since my date fell in love at first sight with my sister, Loren White has never shown the slightest subtlest inkling that he begrudges my husband his catch.

CHAPTER 10

Good Like Back Fat

Lies don't spring fully formed from nowhere. Like parasites, they hunt for a welcoming environment, a warm, moist haven of subterfuge in which to burrow.

Also: Years of hands-on research have led me to believe in a connection between lies and fighting. Shocking, I know.

Phil and I fight about money. Not so original. However, we also lie about money. What I should say is, *I* lie about money. This, it turns out, is infinitely worse than the fighting part.

I know what you're thinking: Who doesn't allow the occasional financial fib to sully the otherwise sparkling web of honesty between herself and her husband? Perhaps it's that daily trip to Starbucks you leave out of the monthly food budget, or the oxygen facial you passed off as a teeth cleaning. So what if you bury your *Star* magazine addiction under a mound of property-value-enhancing perennials?

That's not what I'm talking about here.

What I'm talking about is that for the past eight years, I have accepted a monthly check from my rich stepfather that funds, among other things, our children's education, the occasional family vacation, and a large chunk of our mortgage. Since money doesn't grow on trees—or pool algae; we've tried—I allow my husband to believe the allowance comes from a stipend from my own father's trust. In conversation, I have even called it that: The Stuart Myron Schultz Family Trust. Six words that, together, represent an entity about as real as the Bermuda Triangle Neighborhood Association. Not real, but so unimpugnable. Who, after all, would deny a dead father the privilege of gifting his beloved daughter with a monetary bridge between ends meeting and financial ruin? A scrooge, that's who.

Part of me wishes I had told Phil the truth about why our perennial beyond-our-means existence—not uncommon or particularly stigmatizing in the ridiculously expensive Bay Area—stresses me out so much. Because Eliot's checks don't come for free: The little string-trussed albatrosses are the monetary equivalent of a leash. On me. I feel the tug every time I argue with Ma and meet Eliot's godfatherish eyes across the table, reminding me of my promise to make nice. Every time Phil and I charge something massive and fever- ishly desired—competitive soccer camp, weekends in Tahoe, bathroom renovation—and Phil says, "Here's to Stu! God bless dinette sets." (Dad was in the furniture business.)

I feel the tug. Yet I continue to cash those checks. So, you see, my career in deception, self and otherwise, began long before a cancer misdiagnosis.

But back to the fight.

"Let me put this in a way you can understand," Phil says to me now as I tremble with anger and shame, a thick spray of ugly sympathy daisies separating us on the counter. "No French immersion class. No Spanish. No Italian or Greek or fucking Tagalog. Because. There's. No. Money."

I feel the chasm open in front of me, yawning wide. *I should leap it,* I think. *Leap it. Then run. Run fast.*

I fall in.

"If you'd stuck with the program, you'd have tenure and a

patent by now, and we wouldn't be having this conversation!"
My voice is thin, shrill, hateful. I detest the words the minute
I release them into the atmosphere, but none of it matters,
because I'm sliding down the cliff wall, frantic heels scudding grooves into dirt, sending plumes of shale and stones
raining around us. Like all fights, this one has a surface topic
and a deeper, truer subtext; a twisted little part of me knows
I've been mad at Phil ever since he diminished me by marrying me, thus setting me on the path toward disgruntled
housewifedom.

Phil thrums his fingers on the chair back. "Oh yeah, you'd
have loved that. Years of dinky apartments until the great
Ph.D. ship came in. And no control over where we lived.
Being the little academic wife. Kissing department-head ass
while I developed something market-ready—"

"That's not true! You're the one who decided for us, Philly!
If I'd had a say, we'd have stayed in the city and rented a one-
bedroom in the Sunset! I could have stayed at the museum.
The kids could have gone to public school. We'd have been
fine. You're the one who said, 'Stay home with the kids, Quel.
I'll take care of it.' What'd you say? 'Kids need their mother
at home.' Isn't that what you said? *'Kids need their mother!'*
Not this...this McMansion!" This is true, isn't it? Phil likes the
house in the suburbs, relishes the deeply sunk fence posts
and sturdy convention of the French doors and brick facade,
even as I find the house and its environs square, spirit-killing,
provincial, and deeply, humorlessly unimaginative.

I need to believe this—that it is to satisfy Phil's and the kids'
aspirations, not mine—that I swallow my pride each month
and let the many zeros on Eliot's checks stain my clammy
fingers. It's the dank, abiding shame inside me that blots out
what I know to be true, even as I deny it: I, too, want the
McMansion. Maybe not the fussy doors and the bourgeois

landscaping and the many miles between us and the nearest decent cappuccino, but certainly the idea of it. The ethos. The illusion of strength it projects to the outside world, as if to say, *Don't fuck with those who reside herein; they are solid. They are successful. They have* pillars.

Weighing my accusations, my husband's shoulders stiffen. "You're crazy. You are just…You're so fucking nuts, Quel. Don't think I'm going to put up with this shit because you have fucking…because you're sick."

"*Say it!*" I scream, more enraged than I've possibly ever been. I'm not even sure what I want him to say. What I know is, the cancer is a test, and he is in danger of failing. What if I'd really had it? Would he have risen to the occasion or smothered me in useless euphemisms that did fuck-all to show me real devotion?

"*I'm so over this!*" I scream again. The "this" goes on and on, a grim echo against the sanitary confines of our stainless-steel appliance-heavy kitchen, which has recently begun to emit the self-important stench of the early nineties.

For a long, agonizing fracture in time, Phil says nothing, just stares at me, his green eyes stewing anger, resentment, hurt, disgust. Then he turns and moves toward the door. His calves are muscular from all that supposedly noncompetitive racquetball with Ren. His gait is stiff. Phil has problems with tendons, ligaments, parts that hold things together. I wonder if he is doing his stretches or simply taking lots of ibuprofen and shark cartilage supplements.

"I'll get dinner out," he says to the wall on his way out.

She sees me first.

Later, I'll wish I had been paying attention. I'll wish I had swung the Sienna into the Nordy's lot instead of Neiman's, stayed home and sucked down a gin and tonic instead of barreling through In-N-Out blindly hunting the tried-and-true post-combat comfort of ground beef and fries.

Still reeling from my fight with Phil, I lurch blindly from makeup counter to jewelry rack, seeing nothing but the dim glow of shrink-wrapped packaging and candy-colored jewels. Our arguments about finances, not an original thing to wrangle over by any means, nevertheless leave me feeling empty and remorseful and terribly alone. Shopping helps.

"Raquel? I didn't recognize you for a second. What did you do to your—"

"Oh, hi!" I yelp. I don't recognize the goofy teenage squeak I produce. All I know is, I'm staring into the wan face of Wendy Yen, she of the (real) cancer, shelved medical degree, and petites wardrobe.

"You're Raquel Rose, right? I think we met once at a charity event. But your hair..." Wendy begins, allowing a dainty frown to crease her otherwise flawless forehead. I ransack my brain for awareness of how far the grapevine could have stretched vis-à-vis my not-cancer, arcing from Annunciata Milk to Rochelle Schitzfelder—who may never forgive me for not telling her first—to Robin Golden to Mimi LeMaitre like a thick spine of Napa Valley fruit. Wendy and I barely know each other. But if Wendy knows, she may tell her boy toy and my would-be doctor, Babyface Meissner.

As I sweat this revelation, a small nudge of memory tells me Mimi is out of town. I pray that my analysis is accurate—and that the gossip train creaked to a halt before it reached Wendy—and plunge into the game.

"I know," I say. "Isn't it horrors? I was getting a double process over at the salon and, well, Jesus, they just fried me. Everything fell out. They said they'd never seen anything like it. I'm considering a lawsuit."

Wendy is looking at me, her smart, penetrating almond eyes searching for something fishy about my bald, lying, demented person. If I allow further assessment, she will guess. I know it. This is someone who is legally entrusted with applying glycolic acid to people's faces, after all.

I glance at my watch. "I've got to go. Picking up Taylor." I lay my hand quickly on Wendy's pale olive arm, which, I realize with another kind of horror, is itself weirdly yet predictably hairless, unlike her head, on which, I recognize now, she must be wearing a wig, so thick and silky-black is her hair, even after chemo.

"You look great," I nearly yell at her as I leave, knocking over a pyramid of anti-aging creams that shower the aisle like chunks of Sheetrock upset by earthquake.

This has to stop.

The words visit me in the studio, silently deafening, uncomfortably vibrato against the inside of my skull. My hands, which I like to think are gentle, soothing, on my subjects' tortured flesh, halt midwrap, sticky with mâché. The subject, a heavyset black woman in her fifties—an attorney at a nonprofit before she had to quit her job to get on Medicaid—glances at me quizzically.

"Need a break?" she says to me. The lawyer's kiwi-green eyes are less a surprise than a bonus, knowing and clear and pitiless in the way only the most striking eyes can be.

"I'm supposed to be asking you that."

She laughs, a chortle rich as ground coffee. "And I'm supposed to be litigating *Hough v. Grossman* before the California Supremes. And if we had national fucking health care, I would be." The large woman slides off the neat podium, an unheralded gift from Arlo that had brought tears to my eyes. "Not that I'm complaining, mind you. Not that I'm complaining," she repeats, shrugging unself-consciously into a hibiscus-covered silk robe. Her hefty remaining breast flows toward the rolls of flesh at her stomach like a chunk of lava, puckered from surgery. With one breast, I've learned, there is no cleavage—just a soft, lone outcropping, jutting or drooping into space.

I excuse myself, quickly rinse my hands at the work tub, go to the toilet, then sip cold unsweetened green tea from the jug Sue leaves for me each morning before she heads for the restaurant. My hands are shaking slightly.

The lie is getting to me. Lies, I should say. That's something I suppose I should have predicted, how lies multiply. Like cancer itself—how can I not make the tired metaphor?—the original deception clones itself madly until one's life is littered with potholes, mines, no-go zones, potential missteps.

Lies.

"Jean, what's your day looking like tomorrow?" I ask.

"Just not feeling it today, huh? Well, tell me about it. I haven't felt it since Goddess knows when"—she clicks rapidly through her BlackBerry—"let's see. Radiation at ten A.M. Survivors' group at noon. Lunch with my partner's daughter at one-fifteen. And I have to buy shoes." A smile. "I can deal with the cancer and the surgery and the insurance bullshit and the rest, but damned if I'm going to wear nurse shoes."

I think I might love this woman. "Can you fit in another casting?"

She snorts. "Are you kidding? This is the highlight of my week. Maybe my month. Who else is brave enough to put these girls in bronze for posterity? Girl, I should say," she finishes, hefting her monoboob in a way that is more tender than lewd.

"Thanks, Jean. We'll finish you up tomorrow."

"No problem." She turns around before heading for the dressing area. "You in a survivors' support group yet?"

"Uh—"

"No? Honey, you're going to need people to talk to about this. People who know what the hell they're talking about. This is not something you do alone. Why don't you come with me? We could use some new blood, bunch of old battle-axes with anger-management problems and bad brassieres." She laughs at her own joke.

"Oh. Well, tomorrow..."

Jean holds up her palm. "Doesn't have to be tomorrow. No pressure. You'll come. Whenever you want in, you just let me know. But I'll be after you, girl, make no mistake." She wags her finger at me in what I want to believe is a fond way. I hear her muttering to herself behind the modesty screen. When she leaves, she hugs me.

Phil and I are tucked into his car, heading toward Taylor's volleyball game to offer parental support, money for post-match pizza, and a lap in which to deposit unwanted clothing.

Phil covers my hand with his—but not by much. My dad used to call them "Rachel's mitts."

"You look nice," he says.

"Thanks. You don't think this shirt is too boobyish for school?" I push my chest out. Phil thinks I am having surgery next week. Perhaps he will have a wake. For the Twins, I mean.

The car slides off course, straddling the divider bumps. "No, no. It's fine."

Okay, that was cruel.

Lately—since what I've come to think of as the Fight About Money and Infrequent Lukewarm Sex and Everything Else

That Is Fucked Up in Our Lives—Phil and I have tiptoed around each other. Our calls are subdued, dinners mechanically respectful. We leave notes for each other, terse, bloodless communiqués that exude a faint whiff of unhappy shame at our marital performance. During his last conjugal visit, Phil went down on me, not realizing such atypical enthusiasm would be interpreted as ominous—the sexual equivalent of an overzealous friend who wants only to hang out with you so she can sleep with your husband.

"Do you think she'll get to play?" Taylor has been bumped up to varsity from JV this season, one year early.

Phil snorts. "With that serve? McLeod would have to be crazy to keep her on the bench. With Savannah injured and that Spelling girl suspended, for pot, I think Tay's going to start." He slots the Accord neatly between a couple of Subarus. We can hear people shouting encouragement from inside the gym. Phil doesn't leap out, and neither do I. His hands grip the steering wheel.

"We're going to get through this," he says. It sounds like a question.

I study the creases around his eyes. For the first time in a long while, I sense something frightened and fervent behind his words. I can't help it; it feels good.

What have I done?

"You're my wife." This time Phil looks directly at me.

Tenure in someone's heart—isn't that what I've always wanted?

"You're *my* wife," he says again.

The game is five minutes under way as we climb the bleachers toward an empty spot. I spot Rochelle Schitzfelder and Robin Golden three rows away. Robin is wearing a cheerleader outfit. I shit you not. It is white and gold and cropped in all sorts of ill-advised places for anyone over, say, fifteen. Robin's stomach is the hard, unrelenting brown of parched earth, so maybe she thinks that makes it okay. Rochelle is knitting, with a big pile of white and gold yarn on her lap. She has been working on Tater-pride sweaters as long as I can remember, spinning them out, machinelike, for any man, woman, child, or dog who will wear one. They are ugly, but Rochelle's intimidation tactics are uglier; I notice a few of her masterpieces in the crowd.

I waggle my fingers at Rochelle and Robin and a couple of other parents and plant myself on one of our foam butt pro-tectors. Phil orders these sorts of things from weird places—SkyMall catalogs or Sharper Image or God knows where. Once in a long while, he buys something that actually comes in handy.

We watch and doze and cheer and fantasize our way through the first quarter. Taylor comes off the bench to score three points in a row. We bask. Then Phil—aka Mr. Attentive—goes to get me a drink and nachos with extra jalapeños.

Robin sits down next to me. Her skinny thighs under the cheerleader mini look like tongue depressors slathered in yams. She grabs my arm. "Taylor's doing *great*. You must be so *proud* of her. We're all *so proud of her*." She narrows her eyes at Coach McLeod, who has committed the unpardon-able sin of letting jumpy little Ginnifer Golden languish on the sidelines for longer than three seconds. Then Robin turns to me and slides her elbow through mine. "So, Raquel, I hear you're *famous*!"

Yes, I plan on taking an entire Denny's with me when I finally end it all, Robin. It should make the eleven o'clock news.

"Oh, you mean the show?" I say with just the right amount of timorous modesty.

Robin slaps my hand playfully, then recoils. This is something I've noticed: People of otherwise average intelligence think it's contagious.

"*Yes,* I mean the show! Rochelle told me she ran into Lauren at Whole Foods, and she said you went on TV to talk about, you know"—Robin interrupts herself to get up and scream, "*Golden!*" as Ginnifer trots onto the court, wincing at her mother—"anyway, what was I...Oh yeah. Lauren said you raised a bunch of money for, uh, breast cancer?" Robin forces out the words behind a bright smile.

"Yes." I tell her the six-digit number, drawing it out. I can tell Robin is surprised. I am pleased. I may be a big fat liar, but I am also a beacon of hope. No shit. That's what Laurie's producer called me: *a beacon of hope for other women battling the cruel forces of nature.*

"Well, I think it's great. I think it's very brave. I couldn't get up there and tell my story, that's for sure. I'd be so nervous."

Hmm. Since Robin's story goes something like: Graduate Pepperdine, marry rich guy, quit flight-attendant job, pop out kid, get plastic surgery, I'd think she might have risen to the occasion.

"Oh, I'm nervous," I echo. We watch as Phil negotiates the stairs with his suitcase-sized box of food.

Robin watches enviously as Phil hands me my nachos. "Chemo must burn *so* many calories," she says (she really says this).

"With most treatments, but not breast cancer. Sometimes your face swells up and you gain weight between your shoulder blades." This juicy tidbit courtesy of a pamphlet from Dr. Ruiz-Milligan's office.

"Like...back fat?" Hushed horror.

"Yep. Back fat." I scoop out a gigantic, dripping chipful of cheese and swallow it whole. "I don't know what's worse, that bulge over my bra or the diarrhea. But the acupuncture's really helping."

Robin stands up. "Oh. Yes, well, I'd better get back. I don't think Ginnifer can hear me up here. *So* good to see you looking so *well*, Raquel. We'll definitely tune in to see you on the show next time." She flees toward the relative safety of Rochelle Schitzfelder and her knitting needles.

I can feel Phil's attention pulsing against my neck. "What?" I ask.

"I was just going to see if you wanted the other hot dog," he says.

Taylor scores again. We stand up and scream. We sit down.

"Gimme that," I say.

Phil hands me the dog. It has about three inches of sauerkraut on it. I munch it hungrily, relishing every dripping bite. A wad of the stuff sticks to my chin. The beautiful raw comfort of it is like a mother's kiss.

I nod at Robin and Rochelle. "You'd think they never saw a woman eat before."

Phil rewards me with a laugh.

CHAPTER 11

You Make It Up, It Might Come True

Ma always says woe will befall anyone who buys her own bullshit. Frankly, if this is the flavor of woe, I'll have another scoop, thank you very much.

My arms rise into the climate-controlled studio air of their own accord, fists punching upward in the universal sign of "personal triumph of the human spirit just waiting to be optioned by Hallmark Presents." Laurie, great as she may be, is still Laurie, but I am Tom Cruise, leaping over social constraints in a single bound, declaring my love before Oprah and the world. For women. For my sisters in suffering. For myself.

The studio audience cheers.

God help me, I do it again.

Laurie hides her ambivalence at my awe-inspiring performance under a ghost of a smile. "My sister, everybody! My sister the survivor!" she announces.

Up close, Laurie's television makeup looks like a mask, its adobe thickness obscuring her natural sunny glow. It really does not look normal. Is it possible that dour, foundation-wielding Cleo dislikes my sister? Is it possible that I, Raquel

Rose, am on television being interviewed by *Living with Lauren!*, talking with great sensitivity and depth about surviving breast cancer while the eerie glow of the pledge tracker lights up the stage and, somewhere in Sayulita, Mexico, a surf god named Duke recalls me fondly as the one who got away?

Something is seriously wrong here, folks.

Laurie gives me a nudge and I am standing, gazing blindly into the sea of faces. A woman in the front row, thick-ankled and abject in a matronly linen skirt suit, wipes tears from her cheeks. Her friends, a study in frosted wedge haircuts and sweats masquerading as pants, applaud my courage. Offstage, beyond the cameras, I spot Cleo and Jonesie in the kind of sodden embrace normally reserved for young mothers' funerals and special-ed graduations.

"I just want you to know..." I begin. The cacophony continues. Someone in the audience actually yells at the crowd to shut up.

"I just want you to know," I say again, "that if you're facing cancer, facing struggles—and who isn't, right?—if you're up against something too big, too scary, too *much* for you to handle..." Against all probability, my eyes land on a golden head in the back row. Instantly, I lose my train of thought. Ren? Can it really be Ren White watching my Susan Lucci–esque performance with hazel eyes bright with unshed tears? Ripping my eyes away from the shadowed figure, I try to focus on what I was saying. Something about big struggles and scary...um, love handles?

"Look inside yourself," I whisper conspiratorially, the sweet-ass tiny mike throwing my words against the walls of the studio and back again. "All I want to say is, look inside yourselves, my friends, because whatever you need in order to deliver yourself from the fear—and make no mistake, it's fear you face, not the problem itself but the *fear*—you've got it. Oh, you've got it. I didn't think I had it in me, either, but when life takes a turn you never anticipated, when life *betrays* your trust"—I'm not talking about my fictitious cancer anymore but remembering the crude terror of those early weeks, before my fate was reversed—"and you think, *Well, okay, I give up, I'm just going to crumple up and disappear, bye, bye!* Well, here's the thing: When you think you can't take it anymore, something happens. Maybe you meet someone. Someone who has that little spark that lights up your own little spark. And you feel...hopeful again. You feel like this whole life thing might be worth sticking around for. You feel *right.* Or maybe you come across the most perfect pair of shoes"—Jean, my monoboobed model, resplendent in a dashiki and uppity stilettos that would have crippled a lesser woman, acknowledges me with glowing eyes and a deep nod—"and you stop feeling sorry for yourself for half a second. And that half a second is all it takes. To. Change. The World."

I finish strong. So strong that applause rings out, crescendos over me in delicious waves. For a second I'm actually glad Phil harassed me into getting TiVo. Next time Ma accuses me of being a quitter, I'll hand her the DVD of my second appearance on *Living with Lauren!*

Rational voice: *But it's all a lie, Quel.*

Self-aggrandizing voice: *So what? I'm really helping people.*

Rational voice: *On the basis of lies.*

Self-aggrandizing voice: *You think that gal with one leg who married Paul McCartney really stepped on a land mine?*

Rational voice: *I think it was a motorcycle accident. Besides, they're getting divorced.*

Self-aggrandizing voice: *Whatever.*

Rational voice: *If you're doing this to impress your mother, it's not worth it.*

Self-aggrandizing voice: *Can you say $245,325?*

I open my eyes, heart pounding, seeking the answer of Ren's golden face in the shadows. But when I scour the back row, there's nothing there but an abandoned seat, not even quivering, as jarring as a missing tooth.

Something miraculous happens after my second appearance on *Living with Lauren!* Something, I realize with the smallest flutter of shame, that I have secretly wanted, fantasized about, for years.

I am famous.

Not the sort of famous that makes paparazzi camp out at your back door, hoping to catch you in sweats and no bra, emptying the trash, with a forlorn cigarette hanging out of your lipstickless mouth.

No, it's more like a low-grade flu. A continuous stream of minor attention that makes me run a little bit hotter than I would otherwise. People I haven't spoken to in years call me out of the blue, follow me in shopping carts at the market to say they've heard about my work, seen my guest spot on Laurie's TV show, read my column in the *Peninsula Weekly,* you know, the one about coping with cancer while managing a career as a successful artist and raising two great kids with a loving husband. They tell me they support my cause. They always use that word: "cause."

Without meaning to—in fact, with constant worry nipping at my heels—I nonetheless begin to bask in the glory of it. I get up fifteen minutes earlier, mindful of needing time to apply lipstick and the occasional herbal peel (wouldn't want to disappoint my fans by looking washed out or sundamaged). I buy new clothes, trendy ones that prompt me to ask Sue if they're too young for me (great good friend that she is, she always says no). The clothes are the type of trendy that, in the past, would have earned me a flurry of rolled eyes from Taylor if I so much as fingered them on the rack. Now my daughter shops with me almost willingly, or at least without visible sullenness. One bright Saturday afternoon, Taylor actually seeks me out in the backyard—where I am ostensibly planting goldenrod but am in actuality devouring a copy of *In Touch* that the cleaning lady abandoned—and asks me (this is a quote) "to help her find a dress for the dance." Nothing "too Britney" (that's a quote, too).

That day I stop doubting my burgeoning cool factor and start shopping for flowy, glittery Indian-inspired tanks and designer jeans that promise to cover my buttcrack while simultaneously whittling my thighs.

What else? I spend so much time shuttling back and forth to Sue's house, to my San Francisco studio, and working, that I forget to eat. Literally forget. In a matter of months, my pants bag out, fall gracefully down my hips in the manner I have always envied in the young and boy-bodied. And the ass! Still full but not—okay, I'll admit it now—fat. Now I am merely padded, womanly. Stepping on the scale in late June, I am shocked to discover that I have, for the first time in my life and without effort, lost twelve pounds. Like the movie stars, it seems, I have entered an alternate orbit, one where everybody has a hummingbird metabolism and Pilates actually counts as real exercise.

Saskia Waxman phones. My upcoming show has gotten too much editorial coverage for her to handle. She has hired a publicist. Can I send her a bio? Do I have a professional head shot? "No," I say, for once telling the truth. "But I'll get one. Tell me, does it have to be my own head?" "You kill me," she says before hanging up on me, a habitual move I used to find uncharming—before I, too, joined the ranks of high-velocity people who don't have time to say good-bye.

Annunciata Milk phones. She is organizing a benefit to raise money for the impoverished gang children of East Palo Alto. To buy them a new play structure at the playground. She needs me. I am irreplaceable. I have credibility. Moxie. Edge. Edgy moxie. And can I please get Laurie to mention it on her show? Oh, and by the way, my post-mastectomy reconstruction looks *amazing*. Gorgeous rack. Doesn't even look like implants. May she ask who did the work? C'mon, I can tell her. Was it my brother-in-law? Was it the guy up in Mill Valley, the one who did Mimi? Sure it was, Annunciata. Sure it was.

Ma phones. I saw your picture in *San Francisco* magazine, she says. In the party section, next to a photo of San Francisco's handsome young mayor riding a dirt bike along the Embarcadero, his sweep of shellacked hair holding fast against the wind. You were with that Getty woman at some museum opening. Tell me something, kiddo: All the money that woman has, and she can't do something about those yellow horse teeth? And that *shmatte* she's wearing? And while I have you on the line, why don't you get rid of the beanie and get yourself a nice printed scarf? The hat makes you look like a hoodlum.

Ross Trimble phones. I am cleaning Taylor's room when the cordless rings. I'm sorting through piles of tank tops and unnervingly sexy panties and the sort of pajama bottoms mothers actually approve of—floppy and chastity-promoting and covered with monkey faces. We have an arrangement, Taylor and I: Anything incriminating must be removed from her room prior to Thursday morning, when I clean up for the maid service so the maid will not think I am derelict and call Child Protective Services.

"Hello?" I say, scraping a crusted bowl of something rust-colored out from under the bed.

"Raquel? This is Ross." Like Madonna, my husband's boss does not deign to use a last name.

"Hi."

We exchange pleasantries. All in all, the conversation is meaningless and agreeable, which sends stalactites of anxiety through my body. For a black second I imagine he is calling to warn me that he's going to fire Phil.

"I'm actually calling to see if you're free a week from Saturday," Ross says.

"Well, uh"—I rack my brain, trying to recollect soccer parties and school plays and the *Desperate Housewives* schedule—"I think so."

"I'm hosting a little dinner at..." He names a swanky restaurant in Burlingame, the sort of place where the servers dress better than you do and everything is bathed in a reduction. "Just getting a few of our artist friends together." In quick succession, he names an architect of some renown; a painter who's recently become quite successful with her studies of the Stinson Beach snack bar; someone whose name I recognize from the SFMOMA board; an Academy of Art college professor; and a transsexual found-object artist living in a squat, whom he refers to as "subversively brilliant."

"Well, let me talk to Phil, and I'll let you know," I say.

"Oh, I doubt Phil would be interested, though he's very welcome," Ross says smoothly. "Tate's not even coming. I was really hoping to talk art with serious artists. I have some ideas I want to bounce off you."

I lug Taylor's laundry hamper into the hallway. Something mushy squishes up between my toes, tangled with grass. I peer at it, sniffing. Fuck. Dog barf.

"I'm sure I can make it," I hear myself say.

* * *

That night, driving home from the studio down the 280 freeway, enjoying the gentle hug of low green hills to my right
and sparkling bay to my left, I find myself swinging the Sienna
toward the Millbrae exit. I pick up my cell to tell Phil I'll be
late, but the small window says NO SERVICE.

Just as well.

I steer the car into the cemetery. Dad's grave is on a nub
of hill a half mile or so in. I remember feeling relieved at the
burial that he was on the edge, away from the crowds, the
way he liked it. In my addled state, I hadn't thought about
the people who would die after him, keeling over in bedrooms and hospitals and convalescent homes, swarming the
morgues, filling the open green space with their crass spirits.

Ruining the neighborhood, as it were.

I park and get out, inhaling clean, green-smelling air. Stum-
bling a little in the moonlight, I grab a smooth stone from the
ground.

"Hi, Dad. It's Rachel." I place the stone on his tombstone.
When Dad used my real name, it sounded strong and ancient,
not plain and boring. He was the only one I hadn't made call
me Raquel, and when he died, he took any affection I har-
bored for my real name with him.

"I miss you so much, Dad," I announce to the speckled
marble. It's so quiet; even the birds have retired for the night.

I tell him about Ma's birthday party, about Ren asking me
for an adoption character reference because things were too
weird between me and Laurie for her to ask me herself. I tell
him how much money we raised on Laurie's show. I tell
him that things are not good between Phil and me, that I resent
my husband for things that are technically not completely his

fault. Things like the fact that until recently, I had no career to speak of, we live in a glorified Stepford subdivision, and I feel about as attractive as Mrs. Doubtfire. That I feel bad about it, but I cannot seem to stop, because something in the thin thread of anger I cling to makes me feel anticipatory, human, *alive*. I tell him that I bought a slinky black negligee at Victoria's Secret but can't bring myself to wear it, for fear of not seeing the answering spark of interest in Phil's green eyes, and because it seals my fate as a middle-aged cliché. I tell Dad about Micah's soccer victories, about my son's acceptance letters from UCLA and Michigan and Princeton, the last of which is so viscerally thrilling yet constitutes a monetary problem I don't even want to think about. I tell him about Taylor's supposedly secret late-night calls with a boy who goes by the unnerving name of Biter. I tell him Micah knew what Tamoxifen was and hasn't wrecked the car since last year's incident. I speculate that some random nugget of mothering instinct is telling me that Micah is lying about something of consequence, but I don't know what. I describe my upcoming art show at Saskia Waxman's gallery in detail, from the intriguing lives of the women I'm casting to the exhilarating results of my efforts to the sweet rediscovery of a San Francisco I thought I'd lost. I tell him about my latest appearance on Laurie's show, how fan e-mail came in such record numbers that the show's server went down. I tell him that a book editor approached me about writing a self-help memoir. I tell him how Sue's restaurant is thriving, as is her relationship with Arlo, and that Arlo finally got my friend on a motorcycle. (Sue declared the ride exhilarating and promptly destroyed the girlie-pink helmet Arlo had purchased with a hammer, so she wouldn't be tempted to do something so dangerous again.)

What I don't tell Dad: that I think a little too often about surfer boy Duke's salty brown hand on my thigh. That I'm pretty sure Taylor is having sex with somebody (my mind halts and spins at whether the perpetrator is indeed Biter, or some other crudely designated creature). That I asked Eliot for an increase in our monthly stipend to finance Taylor's language classes. That I begged Eliot not to tell Ma. Or, God forbid, Phil. That I have never told Phil about the stipend but, rather, allowed my husband to think the gap between our income—Phil's income—and our financial outlay is filled by a trust fund from him (Dad), a gift that has about it all the beneficence of a father's love and none of the smug control of a domineering stepfather. I don't tell him that I suspect I'm enjoying my fifteen minutes of fame a little too much, that the return of the sidelong male glance to my life has done more for me than five years of therapy ever did, that the idea of "She Who Has Everything and if She Doesn't Buys It" Laurie yearning after my weary forty-three-year-old eggs gives me a creamy jolt of pride (followed speedily by guilt, but I don't tell him that, either).

I tell him none of these things. Although I'm fairly sure our hereafter privileges don't extend to bilateral conversations with loved ones, the mere idea of imagining Dad's kind, concerned face crumpling if confronted with the vagaries of my family's—*my*—moral decrepitude holds me back.

I redeem myself somewhat by leaking the whopper. "Dad, I did something really, really shitty, and I don't know how to make it right."

Stern silence from the cold marble.

"I found a lump in my breast three months ago, and I went to the doctor, and he told me I had cancer, and I was sure I was going to, you know, die, and then it turned out they were wrong, and instead of being over the moon, I was"—an image of Babyface Meissner chastising me for being an ingrate pops into my mind—"I was sort of…stunned, I guess. What I'm trying to say is…"—another image, of Ma's small, pert nose quivering as she held back tears when I delivered my bad news—"I let everybody think I still had it. Have it, I mean. Cancer," I whisper, for, not surprisingly, the word has assumed the incantatory power of a witch's curse for me. "Except Sue. I told her the truth from the beginning. She tried to help me, but"—a vision of my newfound life swirls before my eyes, a kaleidoscope of adventure, accomplishment, *promise*—"I was so happy, Dad. I felt like I had a chance to do something worthwhile, something the kids and Ma would be proud of, to do some of the things you always encouraged me at. I just didn't know how to start, but now I do, you see? I know I have to tell them, I do, it's just now, I…It has to be the right time." I try the concept on for size. "I'm going to tell my family I don't have cancer as soon as the show's over," I say out loud. "I promise, Dad. I'll make it right just as soon as I have a chance to—"

The menacing clank of metal on metal sends my denial-perpetuating speech to a shrieking halt.

I spin toward the sound in a kind of exquisite terror, conscious that I fulfill every characteristic of a stereotypical slasher-movie victim: dumb, white, female, arrogant, morally reprehensible—

In front of me, looming in the darkness, is a very old, very bent man of indiscriminate origin. I register four things simultaneously: His fly is undone, he is going commando, and not only can I take him in hand-to-hand combat, he will likely die of a heart attack before I can get him to a hospital.

"You pretending you got the cancer, girl? That really sick.

Lie like that is always bad idea." The wizened man shakes his woolly head despairingly, as if he is Bill Clinton's chief of staff and I am a bottom-heavy intern caught under the head of state's desk yet again. "You make it up, it might to come true," he says, already shooing me toward my car with his jangling keys in hand.

CHAPTER 12

What to Expect When You're Defecting

This is so much fun. So perfectly, thrillingly, uncomplicatedly fun.

I take a dainty sip of wine, something red and rich and flutter-inducing that Ross and Rae, the transsexual found-object artist—who has quite refined tastes for someone so poverty-stricken and subversive—labored over for at least fifteen minutes.

"Kelly, what do you think?" The frizzy-haired Academy of Art professor leans toward me, almost falling into my entrée, as if my response is weighty and precious, a veritable gold Incan mask of insight. The fact that she gets my name wrong—indeed, has gotten it wrong since the evening commenced—doesn't detract from her respect for me or my opinions in the slightest.

I pretend to ponder, sipping my wine. A man in a navy overcoat with a broad, sunburned face and a shock of strawberry-blond hair pushes past us toward the bathroom. He looks remarkably like Connor Welch—poor, cuckolded, gazillionaire Connor Welch—but it couldn't be, because Connor Welch doesn't go out now that his wife has left him for young, unintimidated Dr. Sam Meissner, and now that the latest in a string of bedraggled nannies has, according to Rochelle Schitzfelder, up and quit.

"I find his work very compelling," I say gravely, as if reluctant to offer such high praise. I have never heard of the artist we are discussing, let alone seen his floating Scotch-tape matrices, but like everything else about this airy evening, the question does not require a serious response.

"Really? I thought it was sort of…derivative," the Stinson Beach snack-bar painter mumbles. I glance at her sharply. She disappears back into her Scotch, obviously no stranger to the bottle. We both know that Ross is sorry he invited her, apparently not aware that extreme lactose, gluten, and perfume intolerances would make eating out with the woman akin to being rolfed on a bed of flaming nails.

"Excuse me," I say, careful not to knock over my chair as I head for the bathroom. As I leave, it seems that Ross Trimble smiles at me slyly, confidingly, the secretive sort of smile that burns like summer sunshine, as if this whole shindig is a ruse so we can be together. Then again, it could be a trick of light.

Or I could just be drunk.

When I get back to the table, fortunately without mishap, the bill has been paid—by Ross—and everyone is getting ready to leave. Suddenly, that urge toward home—you know, the one that makes every second between you and your rattiest gray sweatpants seem like a travesty—shoots through me, and I thank my husband's boss almost abruptly and head out to the parking lot.

The asphalt tilts, and I recall the countless times I have counseled—begged—Taylor and Micah to call me if they need a ride home from a party. The situation in which I currently find myself, unfortunately, was not covered in *The Minds of Boys, What to Expect When You're Expecting, The Out-of-Sync Child, Revised Edition,* or any of the other parenting tomes I've scoured over the years in a futile attempt to achieve parental competence. I suppose I could call Phil, but then I'd have to talk to Phil, which, lately, has not produced the desired outcome, in this case surviving the ride home.

I decide to drive myself home. I'll go slowly, no more than ten miles an hour. It will be okay. (At this point my rationalizations are becoming so robust they could drive me home themselves.)

I turn the key.

Dead battery.

I wonder if Ross Trimble arranged this—perhaps his earlier potty break wasn't really nature calling but a quick undercarriage journey into my van's innards—and just as quickly, I dismiss the thought. The idea of such treachery—both the cynical sordidness of it and the paranoia/self-aggrandizement that must be present to produce the absurd suggestion—immediately cause the sea bass and sake tiramisu in my stomach to tussle. Ross Trimble has not crawled under my car and detached the battery cables in order to trap me into a ride home on which he'll issue a smooth pass because, well, he is Ross Trimble and I am—updated Social Security records to the contrary—Rachel Schultz.

"Car trouble?" With perfect paranoia-validating timing, Ross's face appears at my window. In spite of the rich food and the lateness of the hour, he looks as clean and sleek as he did three hours ago—his smooth tanned skin has a reptilian quality that suggests the absence of sweat glands entirely.

"Um, yeah," I say, mirroring his impassive tone. "Battery, I think."

He glances at his watch. "Let me give you a lift. You don't want to be out here waiting for Triple A, this time of night."

I lock the minivan and wander toward his car as if drugged, trying to decide if my incipient ravishment is a foregone conclusion, a delightful assignation, or a Big Mistake. Am I already lying on some figurative casting couch, Phil's career—and possibly my own—riding on my acquiescence, or is this some sort of weird test of my virtue as both a woman and a Serious Artist? The idea that Ross Trimble, he of the defense budget–sized trust fund and Hilary Swank–bootied wife, would want to sleep with me due to mad lust enters my mind briefly and flies out again, soundly rejected. There is clearly more—or less—going on here than meets the eye.

Before I know it, I am enveloped in Ross Trimble's bullet-colored BMW, a low-slung sports car that seems to float above the potholed streets like something from *Star Wars*. I fight the urge to stare at his hand caressing the succulent leather-swaddled gearshift, for fear Ross will interpret my interest as permission to migrate the hand to my thigh. Having inhabited the automatic-transmission minivan world for so many years, I try to remember if it is really necessary to fondle the stick shift that way.

"Good Lord, that woman was tiresome," Ross says, smoothly navigating the tree-lined residential streets between the restaurant and my house.

"I'm sure she enjoyed her soup." Near to implosion, the waiter had offered to bring Stinson Beach Lady a bowl of plain chicken broth.

Ross laughs, glances at me. "The Miró came. It's been framed and hung. You want to see it?"

"Oh…" *But is it well hung?* "Okay," I finally say.

Ross veers off toward his Hillsborough estate. It actually has gates. And a guard booth. Tonight there is nobody there—to take my photo and sell it to the *National Enquirer?*—just an alarm touch pad that scans in Ross's palm print as if we are entering Los Alamos National Laboratory.

As soon as we enter the mammoth house, Ross goes to the bar to prepare drinks. Apparently, I am such a good judge of fine art, I can even do it shitfaced. I excuse myself and stagger into the bathroom, a gallery of marble and soundless, weighty fixtures. With great relief, I release a hot stream of wine/pee into the commode. Since the children, bladder control has been something like a recalcitrant handyman, reasonably talented but never exactly there when you need him.

I snap open my cell and ring Sue. I get Sarafina. "What are you doing up?"

"Mom and Arlo said I could watch C-SPAN." She giggles. City kids are so precocious.

"Is your mom there?"

"Yeah."

"Can you get her?" I press out a little more pee, anxious to hide the sound of the call.

"Quel? Hey," Sue says.

"I am about to have an affair with Ross Trimble," I hiss, feeling nauseated.

"Where are you?"

"The toilet."

"Whose toilet?" Sue says it very slowly, as if to a non-potty-trained three-year-old.

"Ross's."

She ruminates on this. "Do you have a condom? He's pretty old. He might not, you know, be up on that sort of thing."

"Sue, for God's sake, help me out here."

"What am I supposed to do, hold your hand?"

"No, you're supposed to talk me out of it."

"Okay, don't do it."

"I think it's a test," I say. "What if he fires Phil?"

"I don't think that'll happen. I think if you reject him, he'll have his driver take you home instead of driving you himself. He'll be very gracious about it and act completely normal to you in the future, so you'll always wonder if you imagined it. If you do sleep with him, he'll probably want to continue it for a while, unless you start acting clingy or something, or fall in love, or gain weight. Then he'll tell you how great it's been, how important you are to him, and how he has to end it because he loves his wife."

Sue is so smart about these things, it scares me.

"I see," I say evenly.

I hang up and creep back to the living room. Ross hands me a drink. His beige eyes gleam with what I think must be ardor, WASP-style. He is very slim. I might crush him to death in the impending tussle. I will have to kick off my heels before he tries to kiss me, or he might hit my chin.

Just as I'm about to begin (discreetly) removing my (ill-chosen) thong from the depths of my rear end, the door opens to the sound of a woman's laughter.

Tate Trimble prances in, her stretchy butt-cupping deep blue gown an exact replica—I kid you not!—of Hilary Swank's 2004 Oscars ensemble. In spite of the fact that none of the woman's fleshly parts dares jiggle, I can tell she does not have on undergarments of any kind underneath the dress. What she does have on is Connor Welch—am I psychic or what?—who is draped around the woman like a big furry blond coat.

"Hiya, Ross." Connor regains his Silicon Valley executive aplomb, which is somehow enhanced by the dorky frat-boy greeting.

"Hi, hon." Tate Trimble kisses her husband on the cheek. There is lipstick, red and smeared, staining her cheek, which nobody acknowledges.

Ross turns back to the bar. "Would you like a drink? Raquel and I were just having one."

This is getting too weird for the likes of straitlaced old me.

"I'm going to catch a cab," I hear myself say, and *as per usual,* nobody stops me.

"You're such a bitch!" Taylor screams at me.

The windows to the front yard are open. The Bonafacios, observant Catholics, operate, as far as I can tell, a curse-free home. Maybe they will move, find some neighbors who don't drop F-bombs on them and will remember to water their hydrangeas.

I am too stunned to reply. Four months ago, this response would not have shocked me. Today, in the general sea of deference and adulation in which I swim, it is an unexpected, even horrible, oddity. A mutation, if you will.

A comment sparks in my memory: a woman at the hospital with the unlikely designation of "patient navigator." She'd seen Dr. Ruiz-Milligan's pamphlets in my hands—"The Case Against Underwire"; "Fighting Chemo Brain, One To-Do List at a Time"; "Knit for the Cause!"—and cornered me outside the elevator. When I told her how stellar my family's BC performance had been thus far, she laughed sharply.

"Just wait till you're done with chemo. Everybody starts out taking you to appointments, taking you shopping for bras and wigs, holding your hand. You've got casseroles coming out of your ears, right? Uh-huh. Then they start thinking, *When's she going to get over it? Couldn't we have just one day without this* thing *hanging over us? Why does she always have to talk about it?*" The woman handed me yet another pamphlet: "30 Ways to Cope When Your Friends Disappear," or something like that. I smiled sickly—and convincingly—and ran for the exit.

Still.

Taylor has broken the rules, forgotten how sick I am, how I cling to life like a poisoned frog gasping on a lily pad. I have done too good a job at making things seem normal, it seems. My daughter is about to see how not normal things really are.

"You're grounded." I'm pleased with my tone, which falls somewhere between *Nanny 911* and godfather consigliere. Discipline is normally not my strong suit. Now that I am sick, my dicta have so much more *heft*.

"I'm not grounded. You don't ground us!" Taylor shrieks.

"You're grounded," I say again, this time with index finger extended.

"Bullshit."

"Stop cursing!"

"Fuck you." Her voice is low, menacing. Uncertainty approaching fear gels in my gut. Is my daughter's hostility a symptom of her newfound love for the wretched Biter or—bear with the psycho-mumbo-jumbo, here—is she afraid I'm going to die, so she's trying to alienate me to minimize the incipient sense of loss?

"Tay," I say, trying futilely to grasp my daughter's hand and make amends. "I know you didn't mean that, but it would be nice to hear you say it."

Her eyes—so clear, so greeny-gold—which I used to regard as innocent but now resemble Zsa Zsa's hard-earned emeralds, brim with tears. "You don't understand *anything*. Biter's right, you just want me to be a *loser*."

"Explain it to me." I ignore the Biter remark, certain that the next time I see the stringy criminal, I'll strangle him dead with his iPod cord. Right now I'm going to take the high road. Isn't that what you're supposed to do in these situations? Listen? And take the high road? After the Valium kicks in, of course.

"As if." Taylor is sullen.

"Well, unless you can convince me why it makes sense for you to spend the night away with a boy we have met exactly once and who didn't even find time in his busy schedule to have dinner with us, you're not going."

"I'm going over to Grandma's. You're crazy!"

My long-legged daughter zigzags toward the door, coltish and wild as an unbroken filly. In a heartbreaking act of self-control, she restrains herself from stealing my car keys and stalks off down the street, presumably to see her best friend, Lindsay. Lindsay, an overripe sixteen, recently got her driver's license and can transport my wronged daughter to a sympathy outpost in the manner to which she is accustomed.

I tell myself it doesn't matter, that this is one mistake among thousands of moments I got right, but the rationalization doesn't make me feel any better. At this precise second in time, I am conscious of nothing more than the desire to make my daughter—beloved, cherished, precious girl—like me again. I know you're not supposed to think about that. You're supposed to focus on things like inherent self-esteem and ego boundaries and setting limits, all the fizzy catchphrases the parenting books throw around so blithely, but in the end, don't we all just want the little shits to love us?

I stagger to the sink and pour a glass of water. It is milky-looking (number 384 on my list of domestic insults). I choke it down anyway. Hypercritical. Is that what I am? The one thing I have tried not to be with my children. The thing that leaves the sourest taste from my own childhood. Also: mistrustful. Another bad one. When they were little, before the grim specter of sex with bad people bared its reaper smirk, trust was easy to forecast. *Our relationship,* I'd think—oh, so naively—*will be based on trust. I'll trust them to make the right decisions and to come to me when they need guidance.*

Because they know I'll never judge them. I won't need to. Because they will make the right…

Yeah, right.

I sag into a kitchen chair. A thought curdles: *I have become my mother.*

A vision. Of Laurie and me arguing with Ma. The memory is old—so old it has the stale, musty air of a story discovered in an unpopular waiting-room magazine, a tale that is as likely to have sprouted from somebody else's life as your own.

Set the scene: I know it is not yet 1980, because the kitchen is still the buttery avocado Ma layered on in the sixties, a merciless shade that renders all but the peachiest complexions sallow and makes everything but hard-boiled eggs inedible. Through the window, I can see Dad working in the yard, fumbling with the lawn mower, which is the old-fashioned kind that relies on lots of coddling and an unruly pull cord. That year, while the rest of America watches the Iran hostage crisis with bated breath, Dad obsesses over loose rocks, finally wresting lawn-mowing duties away from me and Laurie after he is forced to replace the mower blade a third time in as many months.

Laurie is sitting at the table. Having avoided the trendy pitfalls to which teenage girls routinely fall prey, her hair hangs long and thick and golden down her back, aided only by a squirt of Sun-In she consistently denies using. (Later that summer, I find the bottle in the trash, stuffed inside a Tampax box, and am fleetingly content, a feeling so rare in those days that I am briefly tempted to renounce my great passion for the nihilistic poetry of the Sex Pistols and take up something less atonal.)

My sister is one of those rare teenagers who manage to walk the swaying tightrope between peer popularity and parental obeisance without regret, error, or misgiving. Smart, active, and prettier than the Bionic Woman—indeed, two years later, as a senior, she is voted Most Likely to Be Cast Opposite Lee Majors in a Hit TV Show—Laurie has no need to strain at the leash our parents place on her. Hers, unlike mine, is kept fairly loose and never yanked; it is merely there for show. Why would Lauren Jessica Schultz, cheerleader, National Honor Society member, varsity track star, girlfriend of brown-haired Andy Gibb look-alike Greg Meyers, want to do anything untoward? Anything that would damage her perfect record, which seems to be leading directly toward a coveted spot at a prestigious— and, ideally, fun—university?

"This . . . what is this?" Ma is so upset she can barely speak. She is gripping a medicinal-looking white box. Reared in the pill-popping seventies and intimately familiar with the popular girls' preferred methods of weight management, I immediately absorb the graphic design and call it—correctly—as the diet drug Dexatrim.

Laurie tilts her head to the side and watches Ma carefully. I have seen my little sister use this look before, like the time Christie Mueller asked if Laurie thought giving a guy a blow job counted as sex. I am pretty sure the wide eyes and swish of judgment-obscuring hair are Laurie's idea of diplomacy. I lean against the door frame, conscious of the fact that I am witnessing something both provocative and deviant.

"It looks like cold medicine or something," Laurie says.

"It's a dangerous diet drug, is what it is," Ma says with enough menace to send me backward a step into the shadows.

Laurie says nothing. Her ability to maintain composure in the face of Ma's wrath is nothing short of legendary, a talking point among our shared friends since elementary school.

"I found it in your underwear drawer when I was putting your laundry away." Ma grips the back of a chair with her other hand. Dad, blissfully unaware of his younger daughter's *impending demotion from princess status, kicks the mower and yells, causing the blue jays at the bird feeder to flee.*

"Lauren, tell me you aren't taking this stuff," Ma says. At that moment, drawn by the nauseated disappointment in Ma's voice, I move into the kitchen and meet Laurie's eyes. I know I should feel vindicated, but strangely, I am only sorry for Laurie, the way you'd feel if you were forced to watch a beautiful yet damaged historical landmark come under the wrecking ball.

Laurie's gaze follows mine as I stand in the doorway, the afternoon sun highlighting the thick, hated filaments of espresso hair on my forearms. I am afraid to shave them for fear the hair will redouble its efforts to take over my body. More sophisticated hair-removal methods are beyond me.

Before I can stop myself, I open my mouth. "It's mine," I say.

Even as I hear myself enter the fray so foolishly, I understand exactly what I am doing: tendering a test. I am waiting for Ma's dubious reaction, the flash of admiring anger when she realizes that I, Misunderstood and Underestimated Daughter, have fearlessly leaped to my sister's defense. How many other times has Laurie the Angel lied and failed her while I plodded on, bearing the Schultz mantle of decency alone?

"Well, that makes sense, I suppose," Ma says.

Ma's perfidy is so horrible, so crushing, that I forget to breathe. When I summon the strength to inhale again, I emit a hiccupy sob not unlike the wet gasps of a stabbing victim. The look of irritation, anger, relief—yes, that's what it is—on Ma's face sends me into a spiral of despair. I want to disintegrate...or explode. Yes, that's better. Something messy, something that will ensure they keep finding things—pieces—to remember me by, later on, when they're sweeping under the fridge or flipping pancakes for Sunday brunch.

Laurie goes to the fridge and removes a can of Mountain Dew, which she cracks open before settling in to watch the show unfold. I can tell she is sympathetic. Maybe even a bit sad on my behalf. At no time do I expect Laurie to correct the misapprehension I have created. She may be to blame for spawning the situation, but I walked into it full tilt, upped the ante. The laws of both sisterhood and teen diplomacy are clear on this point: What's done is done.

Dad slides the glass door aside noisily. "Goddamn lawn mower needs a new blade."

"Rachel has been taking diet pills to lose weight," Ma tells him before he can even open his can of Miller Lite.

Dad looks up at me, surprised that even I, in my chunky misery, would stoop to such stupidity. If the Schultz girls have been taught anything, it's that there's no easy way to earn a buck/get into college/drop ten pounds; life is tough, and you have to be tougher. Looking into Dad's melancholy deep blue eyes—they mirror my own, with the same pale blue ring at the center—I feel a spark of gladness: Dad, at least, is on my side.

His large bony hand falls on my shoulder. "Oh, honey," he says.

Then Dad picks up the Dexatrim box and slides out the sheet inside. Most of the pills have been used, the empty pods torn apart like spent butterfly cocoons.

"Oh, honey," he says again.

Did he know? I think now, sliding the spoon into the jar of unprocessed peanut butter, which somebody—what's new—thoughtlessly placed back in the cabinet instead of the fridge, causing the oil and peanut sludge to separate. *Did Dad suspect?*

I pour off the oil, spoon some, and stick it in my mouth, enjoying the sweet-savory thickness of it. Dad and I relished our peanut-butter habit together, sprinkling mouthfuls of the stuff with M&M's or cookie crumbs or cupcake toppings while Ma wrinkled her nose in disgust.

However much I want to trust Taylor, I know I cannot give away the key to my daughter's chastity—not to wet-haired Biter or Prince William or anyone. The possibility that Taylor has already—or will shortly—deliver her body to some callow, rutting boy in a motel room or friend's poolside cabana in thus a manner does not bear rumination. As it is, I have little experience in such matters as young love, my own teen years having been characterized by a virginity so intractable I finally had to offer myself to an indifferent Ecuadorian bellhop on a family vacation. That Taylor will undoubtedly despise me in the short term for refusing to conspire in her ruination is, I tell myself, inconsequential, a twig crunching underfoot in the forest of life's obstacles. Yet—and this may be the most persuasive evidence of my devastating lack of parental qualification—the knowledge that I cannot impart my greater wisdom to my daughter in a way that causes her to collapse into my arms in grateful tears, well, it rankles. The trust and validation I'd longed for from my own parents, the knowledge that they both knew and liked the real me, never really came. Maybe I expected too much. Maybe, like Dexatrim, trusting your kid to make the right decision has been taken off the market for being dangerous to your health.

CHAPTER 13

A Great Success

"You look too healthy," Sue says.

We are tucked into her gleaming kitchen, our hands shiny with olive oil and free-range chicken broth. Rows of dainty canapés and mysterious tartlets and small towers of succulent heirloom tomatoes and French cheeses and button mushrooms and prosciutto-wrapped melon balls blanket the countertops. Sue has been baking and chopping and sautéing for hours, in preparation for tonight's opening at Saskia's gallery. *My* opening. Without Sue, not only would we be tempting our guests with a hubcap-size wheel of Bulgarian Brie, I'd be a cowering wreck of nerves, paranoia, and bad juju.

"Well, what am I supposed to do, eat somebody's dirty Kleenex?" I say.

"You could drink cod-liver oil or something."

"How about arsenic? I mean just a little bit. Not enough to kill me."

"Food poisoning is always hell on the complexion," Sue muses, glancing at the bowl of sun-dried tomato aioli as if to determine its maximum shelf life.

At some unidentified point, Sue became fully complicit in the farce that has become my life, a condition I have delayed pondering until some unspecified and distant point in time.

In my experience, these sorts of matters don't disappear; they come back at the worst possible moment to haunt and compromise your friendships, your life. I will pay for luring Sue Banicek to the dark side, I know. It's just a question of when. And how.

Before I can up the ante further, Sue carefully sets down an enormous butcher knife she is using to section smoked salmon and moves briskly to the sink. I am expecting her to execute some graceful act of chef's wizardry, a ninja slice-and-dice move or a quickie method of turning water into wine. So I am surprised—no, shocked—when my friend leans over and vomits noisily and violently into the deep stainless-steel basin.

"My God, Sue." I touch her back lightly, feeling the muscles convulse under the purple tissue T-shirt.

Sue finishes, then splashes her mouth with water. Her face is the exact hue of avocado in cream, the rust sprinkling of freckles popping out like specks of mud. I wait while my friend leans against the butcher block, willing her stomach to calm itself. After a moment Sue's gray eyes meet mine, broadcasting what ails her in loud, clear silence.

"How many weeks?" I say, already reaching for a packet of salty table crackers and fizzy soda.

"I can't believe this is happening," I say, scooching away from the toilet. Someone has had too much to drink and overshot the bowl. Instead of grossing me out, the pool of piss is exciting, proof that I have officially abandoned the world of boring seat-cover users and entered the Pee Freely Zone, where anything—fame, fortune, STDs—can happen.

I find refuge against a rattan stand stuffed with rolls of TP and topped with burning incense. Saskia and I click glasses and gulp our wine. The incense sticks out of the fat, happy Buddha's mouth like a joint. No wonder he is happy, in spite of the fact that he is carrying a few extra pounds.

"The *Bay Guardian* sent someone. That woman with the gray bob," Saskia says.

"I can't believe this is happening," I say again. Outside, through the slit of sidewalk-level window, four feet appear and kiss, red stilettos mounting Doc Martens in a rough dance.

Saskia shrugs. "You tapped in to the zeitgeist. Women are tired of being written off as damaged goods because they had their tits lopped off," she says in her customary blunt way.

"It just seems so...I don't know. Sudden, I guess. I never had so many people interested in my work before. I feel like a fraud." Unexpected tears burn my eyes as I fiddle with my fake-pink-diamond breast-cancer-awareness pin. "All those wonderful women, they're the ones who should be getting the attention."

Saskia tilts her head so that her red cap of hair cuts across her cheek, and stares at me. As I watch impatience glisten behind her frosty green eyes, it occurs to me that she knows I am a little frightened of her and dislikes me for it. A not insignificant part of me will be glad, when Shiny Pony informs me that the last check comprising that oh so needed $245,325-plus has cleared, to confess the hospital's ineptitude and my own sins and disappear back into obscurity. (This is my plan, in any case.)

"There's nothing fraudulent about it if the right people think you're good," she says.

The show is a great success.

Not just a success. A *great* success.

Such a difference between the two, don't you think? Success, measured in accolades and glad awareness; in the kind, congratulatory words of friends who spare a moment to stroke your arm in passing or slap your back, to share your pleasure. Success brings you closer to people, real people, at least.

But *great* success, that's a whole different ball game. You can see it not in the inexorable pull of others into your orbit but in the opposite effect: In the face of your accomplishment, affection dissolves into deference, connection into distance, overture into seizure. People you don't know want pieces of you, while people you do know put their need of you in abeyance, preparing themselves for the cold day, not too distant, when you no longer have time for them. The difference between garden-variety success and greatness is the difference between people wanting you for their team and being given the mandate to start your own.

Without having experienced it myself, I know from greatness. Even in high school, Laurie had it. You could hear it in the hushed click of lockers shut respectfully in her wake, their tenants loath to sully her passing with a slam. You could smell it in the sour need that poured off boys, hell, *men,* in her presence, their perspirings shouting the depth of their yearning. You could sense it in the weary tribute of our teachers, who were smart enough to know when a student had surpassed them with innate charm, or intelligence, or diligence, or, in Laurie's case, a devastating combination of the three.

How do I know my show is great? For one, when I am walking around the room, rendering my dramatization of the eccentric yet tantalizing yet insufficiently lithe artiste, I overhear someone saying she is going to buy not one but *two* of my busts because—and this is a quote—"they're great." Okay, so it is Estelle Gilden from Ma's Humanistic Judaism group. So what? I happen to know that Estelle knows a lot about art.

She makes a mean cupcake for the Senior Center Purim party, complete with ebony-and-ivory sprinkles that have about them an almost Pollock-esque flair.

The other way I know is even better.

On the way to the buffet table, a bony woman grasps my arm. She has tawny skin and a cocktail ring you could knock around the green.

"Stunning work, Ms. Rose. Stunning. And scathing. Yes, scathing! And stunning, of course. You must come speak at my club. About your *experience*." She leans over so I get a gander at her matching earrings, which look like asteroids that landed in a field and had to be wrestled onto gold posts by teams of slaves. "Have your person call me." She lurches off, her diamond lighting the way like a tertiary moon.

I am still trying to figure out who my person is when I grasp the identity of the woman with asteroids circling her head. The knowledge expels a thin, oily effluvium from my pores that chills into equal parts thrill and dread. I immediately locate my nearest and dearest, who are clustered awkwardly around the bronze-dipped single-breasted bust of Jean the angry lawyer.

"Katja von Warburg just invited me to her club," I say, not too sotto voce, describing the encounter with San Francisco's leading blue-blooded philanthropist/socialite/De Beers customer.

"That's great, honey." Phil puts the minimum level of oomph into it, successfully avoiding marriage counseling for another week.

"Mom's famous!" Micah, at least, looks proud.

Even Ma is impressed. "She said that? To have your person call her person? Feh." She reaches up and rubs my cheek with her knuckles. "My daughter the celebrity."

"Do you think we'll get to go to their house?" Now that I

am famous, Taylor has apparently forgiven me for not offering her virtue to Biter on a platter of squirming puppies.

"Where's Ren?" Laurie says. "He has an early meeting tomorrow."

"I'll find him. I was going outside anyway," I offer. Laurie is not used to sharing the spotlight. I will forgive her the misstep.

It takes me fifteen minutes to make my way to the terrace. The well-wishing is constant and fawning and exhausting and terrifying. I love every second of it. It is terrifying in a delicious way, like surfing point breaks with Duke the Molester of Stretchmarked Geriatrics.

Once on the deck, I take a look around. No one is watching, so I let my stomach pooch out in my black jersey dress and lean against the railing, inhaling the cool bright downtown night. Two stories below, the street seethes with people. It is nearly eleven P.M., but we are in the theater district, and the shows are ending, people flowing into bars and restaurants for post-entertainment victuals.

"Excuse me. Ms. Rose, I'm Nils Cooper." The man is tall enough to make me feel dainty, with a head of flowing salt-and-pepper hair and disconcerting pale eyes. He wears a grown-up suit and a thick S&M-looking ring in each ear, an arresting combination, in my opinion. He shakes my hand. "May I?" he asks, gesturing toward the settee.

He sits down. A tiny computer comes out of nowhere. He is—anxiety alert!—the senior *San Francisco Chronicle* art critic. I sit down, too. I have no experience with such things. Gray Bob from the *Guardian* didn't ask me anything, just stomped around muttering to herself and left. My pulse is thundering. Can art critics tell when someone is lying about art...and stuff?

"Do you have time to answer a few questions?" Nils Cooper

has already flicked open the purring laptop and started tapping on the keyboard.

"Of course." What am I, an idiot? Besides, if I run away and/or soil myself, Saskia will kill me.

"Did you ever think that you were going to die?" he says.

"What? No! God, I mean…" *Actually, I did. Exhibit A: that first month, before the call from Meissner, when every breath felt like a spoonful of sugar doled out as a war ration. That month I thought about little else, and it was, well, hell. And don't forget it!*

He pats my hand. "Nervous?"

"No, it's just…well, maybe a little." Something about Nils Cooper's demeanor—okay, maybe it's the earrings and the wrinkled, faintly debauched state of his trousers—makes me decide the winningest approach is dominant mistress versus client-baby. Sort of like how I treat Micah and Taylor when they push me past the point of wanting to be liked.

"I can't believe that was your first question," I say in a tone that smacks like a spanking. "Couldn't you ask me something about, you know, impression casting in bronze? Or the theme of self-renewal? Or impressions of renewal…or something?"

Nils Cooper grins. "Those are good ones. I'll put them on the list. Now"—he leans over so that his shirt gapes and I can see a tattoo on his chest of a woman with pointy breasts wielding a hot poker the way the rest of us might brandish a spatula over a griddle—"let's talk about death."

I peek at the open doorway. No help is forthcoming. "Okay."

He leans closer. His smile is white but strange, with jack-o'-lantern spaces at the outer corners. "Do you let your husband touch your breasts?"

My eyes flutter closed involuntarily. Just my luck to be interviewed by the world's leading pervert–art critic. The strangest part of this is that I was just thinking about that very question. Jean the Angry Lawyer told me that breast cancer frees you from self-consciousness. She said that after BC, everyone *wants* other people to see them, to touch them. I was skeptical. Obviously, I had to defer to her greater knowledge of the subject matter.

I open my eyes and stare at Nils Death-and-Sex-Freak Cooper, who looked so innocuous in his thumbnail photograph from the paper, even a little professorial. In my experience, there is only one way to deal with this type of provocateur without going down in self-castigating flames: Give as good as you're getting.

"Do I let him touch them? Of course, Nils. I have nothing to be ashamed of. That's really the point here, isn't it? In addition to promoting BC awareness and early detection." I squeeze his thigh hard. It jumps lightly under the wool crepe. "I'm talking about the fundamental conflict between what a person looks like and who she is, Nils. It's the crux of my work. So I really don't give a shit if my husband or you or Viggo fucking Mortensen"—okay, maybe Viggo—"handles the goods, because I'm more than a set of tits. Get it?"

He nods. The pale, pervy eyes are electric with heat. "This is interesting, Raquel. Go on."

Before I can elaborate further on what I am starting to believe is my own fundamental artistic brilliance—or charge Nils Cooper fifty dollars for the thigh massage—my brother-in-law exits the French doors of the gallery and spots me. He and Nils Cooper size each other up in that roosterish way of men when they aren't sure exactly what the other guy's net worth is, or when he last bedded an extremely hot woman. For a second I feel like a trophy, which, because I am forty-three years old and often attired in stretch pants, is quite nice and certainly not a problem in the way it would be if you were actually married to your objectifier.

"Ren, this is Nils Cooper from the *Chronicle*. Nils, this is my brother-in-law, Loren White. He has a plastic-surgery practice on the Peninsula."

Ren, who looks—perhaps for the first time ever—a bit out of place in his expensive sport blazer and overpleated chinos, grimaces slightly as he shakes Nils Cooper's hand. Ren places his hand on my shoulder. The gesture is heavy and, I fancy, somewhat proprietary. Like a puppy, I feel myself automatically push upward for a charity stroke.

"Laurie and I just wanted to say good-bye," Ren says. Then, producing a neat spin on my sister's earlier assertion: "She has an early meeting tomorrow."

"Oh. Well, okay. Thanks so much for coming." We do the congenial half-hug thing we perfected in 1993.

Ren glances at Nils Cooper, who is—oh my goodness—lighting a big fat joint and smoking merrily away.

"Would you like me to see you inside?" Ren says, I think, rather stuffily.

"No, I'm fine." This is *clearly* the best night of my life.

"All right, then. We'll see you soon. Thanks for the, uh, letter you wrote. It was just what the doctor ordered."

Nils suddenly coughs—or is he laughing?

"Well, bye," I say, watching Ren leave. A week ago, his reluctance to exit would have been a balm to my soul. Now . . . let's just say I am enjoying the night air.

"Friend of yours?" Nils asks.

"Brother-in-law."

"Not your fault, then."

"Completely my fault, but it's a long story."

Nils tilts his head. He has very virile hair, thick and springy. "You can tell me about it later." It is salacious. The way he says it, "later" explodes with dense, succulent promise, the verbal equivalent of being handed a hotel-room key card.

Without waiting for my response, Nils grinds out the joint and slips the roach into his laptop case. The gesture is both roguish and elegant; the bag may as well be a codpiece and Nils Cooper a latter-day Errol Flynn.

"I need a quote," he says, fingers poised.

It is clear that I have one chance to run with this greatness thing.

I draw a breath. "Breast cancer is a curse, and breast cancer is a gift. This is not something you can understand pre-BC. It is something you learn. It changes you. Most of us like ourselves—really like ourselves—better now. I mean that. I guess what I'm saying is, ending BC…it's almost harder than beginning it."

CHAPTER 14

Of Alien Abduction and Adultery

Following my show, three things happen, or, more accurately, begin to happen, with alarming regularity.

The first is that commissions start rolling in. E-mails flood Saskia at the gallery, querying her about my whereabouts, availability, and willingness to sculpt this or that commemorative statue/fountain/play structure/retaining wall. Messages start appearing in Phil's and my voice mail, the unknown voices plummy and obsequious. A napkin-dispenser tycoon wants me to construct a toddler bed shaped like a serviette container. The Contra Costa Unified School District has a grant to fund protective booths for the school guards. Can I design one that doesn't make the school look like a prison? And repels 9-caliber bullets? I get a call from a Mormon sect with bank accounts swollen on tithes: They would love a rendering of Jesus Christ Our Savior wearing the Brigham Young football jersey. Am I so inclined?

The second thing is so unexpected, I am inclined to view it with a mixture of suspicion and hilarity.

Phil is a BC activist.

Runs, walks, lingerie shopping, pin-wearing, placard-waving, knit-ins, doctors' appointments, recuperative yoga—no activity is too womanly or cloying for the new and sensitized Phil Rose.

The first time was even his idea.

"Hey, you," he said a couple of Saturdays ago, spreading the paper out on the kitchen table. "How's the energy today?" He was learning not to take the little things—breakfast on the table, toilet paper in the bathroom, basic civility—for granted.

"Good," I said, promising myself another hour in the hair shirt.

"So there's this walk/run thing up in the city this afternoon, at Crissy Field…the, uh, Breast Cancer Awareness Walk. I was thinking it would be something we could all do together, you know? You, me, the kids…"

"You want to walk for breast cancer?" I couldn't help it; doubt narrowed my eyes.

"Yes," he said simply.

Four hours later, we strode along a sandy causeway toward the Golden Gate Bridge, Phil clad in a hot-pink T-shirt and bandanna, arms linked with two grandmothers from Marin, all of them chanting and beaming while I brooded over the loss of my husband to alien abduction. Don't get me wrong: I liked the change, but there were questions. How long would it last? Would people start to think I didn't deserve *him*? Could I still cash in on his life-insurance policy if he was running on green goo instead of blood?

A challenging situation, you see.

We stopped for a photo op in front of the Warming Hut café dock. News cameras flashed. Pink ribbons glistened. Bald heads shone. Phil was the undisputed star of our cluster, belting out "Hell no, we won't go!" and Joni Mitchell standards with gusto. I knew this kind of enthusiasm was what I signed on for, but honestly.

The node-negative, stage I, divorced orthodontist simultaneously bared her veneers at me and glanced at Phil admiringly. "Hang on to that one, honey, he's a gem!" she hissed at me.

I made sure to stand between them on the walk back. The woman may have had cancer, but she also had one of those swively walks that make a person think of beds and *Kama Sutra* positions and silk scarves. Her auburn hairpiece was top notch.

Phil was communing with the couple of other men in our immediate area like an old pro.

"I'm flying to Taiwan next week to ink a deal for these BC fortune cookies to sell at my restaurant," the thirtyish Asian guy in the expensive tracksuit and fancy Bluetooth headset told him. "They're dipping them in this really sweet pink. It's called 'cow's teat' in Mandarin. No, I'm serious, it is! Anyway, my wife and her support group wrote all the messages. They're inspiring as hell, but there are also practical tips."

"Like not asking the wife if there's any beer in the house right after chemo?" The ponytailed programmer from Berkeley wiped some sweat off his forehead with a tie-dyed hankie.

"Exactly."

The men enjoyed a hearty belly laugh at the expense of their less evolved brethren. It was all they could do not to slap each other's sweaty backs with pride. Phil joined in with the rest of them. Oh, poor Neanderthals who have yet to shed the coarse trappings of common manhood and don the royal cloak of BC-compliant maleness!

One of my subjects, a BC patient advocate who, after twelve years helping others navigate the field, contracted the disease herself, had told me that BC functioned as a marital health barometer.

"It's like, if things were tense before, you may as well sign those divorce papers now, honey," she'd said during a break, rubbing plaster off of herself with a scruffy towel. "Frankly, most of the husbands are a disappointment. It's just the reality. Sure, they're all gung ho the first few weeks. But after she's had her biopsy and her surgery and done a few rounds of chemo and maybe radiation, they're like, can we get back to normal already? Three months. That's the length of time your typical husband can deal. After that, all bets are off. Once in a while, you get a star, the guy who puts everything on hold, quits his job or whatever, and makes it his raison d'être. But those ones are like radiologists who can actually communicate with humans—a once-in-a-lifetime proposition."

Could it be true? Could my Philly, he of the family vacations to obscure railroad museums and the ability to watch six hours of back-to-back *Law & Order,* be a once-in-a-lifetime proposition? (In a good way, not a government-study-of-the-socially-damaged way.)

It boggles the mind.

The third thing that has reared its head since the show is Ma. Or, rather, Ma and me.

Before, our relationship exuded the stale whiff of unreciprocal approval—mine for Ma, her lack for me. It now has about it an almost honeymoonish fervor. Used to her pronounced, lifelong preference for Laurie's poised focus and victorious single-mindedness, I am caught off guard by Ma's attention.

She showed up at my door unannounced a few days after the show. She had on a velour tracksuit, a BC awareness ribbon, and an army jacket that looked like it had been abandoned by Che Guevara out of spite, plus her usual chest-strapped handbag—to foil purse snatchers—and tote stuffed with partially used Kleenex, Sweet'N Low packets, flaxseed caplets, and self-help tomes.

"You need acupuncture," she said.

I staggered back involuntarily due to an insufficiently repressed memory of Dr. Minh and his horrible panoply of engorged digestive organs.

"No way," I said.

Ma unfurled a news clipping from a thick rubber-banded wad. "'While medical experts are unclear as to the physiology of its effects, acupuncture is known to relieve a range of symptoms associated with breast cancer and breast-cancer treatment, including water retention and even the memory loss associated with chemotherapy.'"

"Ma..."

The woman who once made me walk home from a spelling bee because I fucked up "calliope" on the first round took my hand. "Look—you can't blame a mother for wanting her precious daughter to have every chance at making a full recovery, sweetling."

Can alien abduction possibly be epidemic?

"I made an appointment for you already. It'll feel good, like a massage."

I sighed.

Then there was Ma's increasing habit of coming to me—me!—for advice on, well, Laurie. Or, rather, Laurie's problems.

"What do you think about all this adoption *mishegoss?*" she asked me the other day. She'd invited me over to help her wash donated clothes for the battered-women's shelter. The clothes teetered on the dining room table, stacks of frumpy sweaters and depressingly bright toddler outfits. Apparently, Ma thought being reviewed by a sex-and-death-obsessed art critic gave one's opinions on reproductive matters a certain gravitas.

"I think it's probably their only chance to have a kid." I was outwardly calm yet reeling. Laurie and *mishegoss:* two words not paired in normal times.

Ma blinked. "Do you think they'll find, you know, a Jewish one?"

"No, Ma. Jewish girls don't get pregnant unless they're married to Jewish boys. It's in the Torah."

Ma jabbed her finger at me. "Don't poke fun. These things get more important when you get older. You'll see."

Ah, the quality-control issue. Perpetuation of the tribe and all that. Ma had always been comfortable with Ren's WASP pedigree—as long as it was paired with the hallowed genes of Rachel, Sarah, and Esther and left to soak in a nice medical-school-love-of-stinky-fish reduction. Now that we were looking at a potential genealogical wild card, Ma was closing tribal ranks.

We talked a little more. Ma made a few offensive remarks; I countered with a few inanities. Either Ma didn't notice that my responses lacked both insight and originality, or she didn't care, because she sandwiched my face in her hands and whispered something laudatory about my unique ability to understand people. And life. She actually said that: "People in your position understand life." I think, like most people, she believes that, along with tumors and general malfunction, cancer bestows upon its targets a sort of Zen clarity and sage-like wisdom.

That's really what gives me pause these days—her *effusiveness.* And my collusion. There is something almost vaudeville about it. "You're *so* great!" she might be saying. "No," I'd reply. "*You're* great!" "No, *you* are!" and so on and so forth. Was this what her approval felt like to Laurie, you know, before? Did Laurie worry that Ma's pride in her was over-the-top and therefore slightly counterfeit? Or am I simply getting the (slightly tainted) quality of maternal love I deserve, after what I've done?

Which leads me to the worst part about this whole business: When I tell them the truth—and I'm going to tell them *soon,* this month, possibly right after Laurie's job proves secure, the telethon checks finish coming in, a few more commissions roll in, and I've torn Eliot's monthly check into green shards and paid the kids' tuition bill myself—is my treachery going to convince them I am worthy only of how they treated me before, or something substantially worse?

"Hey," Sue says. Her face is thin and wan.

"Hey." We hug, and I strip off the many layers of sweaters and scarves that a typical San Francisco evening requires. Through the stained-glass windows, the insouciant glow of North Beach, with its hole-in-the-wall trattorias, dim bars, independent bookstores, and sex shops, beckons. Sue probably picked Vesuvio's, a classic yet slightly bedraggled haunt, because it matches her mood. "How are you feeling?" I ask.

Sue doesn't respond, just raises her delicate eyebrows as if to say, *Are you nuts?*

"What can I get you?" The barista is sleek and tawny-skinned and tattooed and highly fuckable in that way all of them seem to be these days. It is hard to believe we ever looked—felt—like that, but then again, maybe we didn't.

"Anchor Steam. Sue, do you—?"

"Do you have tea?"

The barista nods.

"Is it organic? Okay, then I'll have mint, tea bag in. Lemon, no sugar. Thanks."

"So," I say when the girl's perky backside disappears behind the bar.

"Yep."

"What are you going to do?" Sue's pregnancy is not a fore-gone conclusion. Besides the fact that she and Arlo, though wholly committed, are not contracted to provide for legiti-mate children in the eyes of the law, Sue has always said she was finished having kids after Sarafina.

"I don't know."

"What about Arlo?" I don't think Sue—or I—could stand it if Arlo Murphy walked out on her the way Sarafina's father did, protractedly and painfully.

Sue mumbles something.

"What?"

"I said he doesn't know yet."

"Oh, Sue."

"I just don't think it's fair to tell him, if I'm only going to… you know."

I take a sip of beer. It is cold and slightly bitter. "You have time. You don't have to decide anything yet, you know? It's not like last time"—I let mention of her college abortion hang there, gnarled and splintered, a broken tree branch of a mem-ory—"you aren't a kid anymore, Sue. It doesn't have to be…" I search for the right word, wanting to give my friend real sol-ace, not blather. "Damaging," I finish inadequately.

"Quel, the thing is…" Sue's gray eyes bead with tears as her words fade out. She fingers her mohair poncho. "Things are so good right now. They're good between me and Arlo, with Fina, at Tamarind. It's the first time I can remember that I actually feel like I can let my guard down for a while. Like I'm not constantly making contingency plans for failure. Or wondering if I can pay the mortgage. Or breaking up with somebody. Or taking Fina into bed with me because she's having nightmares that her dad was in an airplane crash or has another family now." Sue hesitates. "God, listen to me. I

sound like the baby—the pregnancy, I mean—is some incon-
venience, something I have to check off my to-do list like the
goddamn shopping. I know I have to tell Arlo. I know it's his
kid, too. It's just that I've been so sick…" Sue's hand trembles
as she raises the tea to her mouth, and she scalds her hand.
Without a word, she puts the mug back on the table, wincing.
"I'm forty-two years old," she says.

"You don't look it."

"But I feel eighty."

I draw my oldest friend into a deep hug, the kind where
the other person's hair fills your nose with its grassy scent
and boobs press against chests and you both know the hug is
as much for you as it is for her. Sue lets go first.

"Want to know why Arlo left Liesl?" Liesl was Arlo's first
common-law wife, a hard nut of a motorcycle mechanic
whom Sue has no beef with and even serves personally on
the rare occasion when the woman dines at Tamarind.

"Because Liesl wanted to have kids and Arlo didn't. It was
the dealbreaker. Arlo was going to get a vasectomy, but Liesl
got pregnant first, and then he walked out. Wouldn't even
discuss it. She had to terminate in the fifth month because the
baby had Turner syndrome," Sue says with real sorrow.

I try to square this revelation with what I know and love
about Arlo Murphy, and how good the man is with Sarafina,
and conclude that nothing, least of all other people's relationships, is as it seems. For all I know, some confused couple is
right now comparing themselves to me and Phil and finding
their own connubial state wanting.

After that, we order one more round of drinks and leave
them standing while we talk about nothing in particular. At
around eight P.M., Sue says she has to pick up Sarafina from
her dinner playdate and swaths herself in her amber wrap.

"Are you going to be all right?" I ask.

"Are you?" It is our standard exchange, employed loyally since college.

"I'll call you tomorrow." I watch Sue leave, imagining my small, plump friend weaving in and out of tourists toward the bus stop, her little feet landing purposeful and sure on the cracked sidewalk. My beer is tepid, but I take a few more sips anyway.

Seeking relief from the evening's tension, I gaze out the window. The stained glass is blue and purple, littered with tiny flecks of orange, with a clear opening in the center. Across the street, a black-haired man in a white shirt and dark slacks stands forlornly in front of an empty Italian restaurant, summoning tourists halfheartedly with a laminated menu. There is a strip club a few storefronts away, with a gigantic neon blonde pulsating above the entry. She is wearing electric pasties. They flash frantically, like a small dog dry-humping the couch.

A couple pauses in front of the lens of the window, blocking my view. The man is solid in an overcoat, his brown hair fluttering in the wind. The woman has a small firm handful of a butt, like Hilary Swank's. The man kisses the woman— or does she kiss him?—bending her backward violently, as if aiming to fracture.

"Phil," I think I whisper, but he is already gone.

CHAPTER 15

Mousse On the Loose

At the precise moment when I receive confirmation of my husband's affair, I am swallowing a mouthful of the smoothest, downiest chocolate mousse you ever had in your life. It is ironic, really, because not three seconds prior to the crash, I was cautiously sure that I was having the second best day of my life.

Why second best? Ask any mom what her best day was, and she'll tell you—as she peels her newborn off her shredded nipple or locks herself in the bathroom to escape her haranguing teenager—that the number one slot belongs to the day she delivered her children into the waiting arms of her OB. She will be lying. That slot belongs, by rights, to the day she received notification of her acceptance to NYU Law, consumed five flawless piña coladas, and bedded the elusive Trinidadian underwear model on her belly-pierced-flashing roommate's Amish quilt. Nevertheless, she will derive real pleasure from her conviction, reinforcing, as it does, the rightness of her current purpose in life.

In any case, my second best day thus far consisted of the following:

- Finding five dollars on the ground outside Starbucks (tax-free).
- A call from Shiny Pony confirming that, thanks to the success of my guest spots, *Living with Lauren!* ratings were up.
- Lunch with Ren White at a trendy restaurant, enhanced slightly by hard-laboring push-up bra and massively by air kiss from fellow diner.
- Securing three more commissions, none of which will require me to adorn Jesus in a football jersey.
- Taylor breaking up with Biter via text message (kapow!).
- Neither dog peeing or crapping anywhere in the house, mud closet, or foyer.
- Refusing Rochelle Schitzfelder's request to chair the next session of the Hillsborough Native Tree Club.
- Relishing the knowledge that there will be no subtle retribution for said refusal, since Rochelle Schitzfelder now believes I am—don't laugh!—"adorable."

See what I mean? Even with the unnerving reason for the lunch hovering in the back of my mind, this day is tops.

"Sorry," I say to Ren when my cell phone chimes for what seems like the fifth time since we sat down at twelve-thirty P.M. I consider ignoring it, but the call window says "Mic." Duty calls.

"Hon?"

"Hey, Mom."

"What's up? I'm a little tied up right now." I try not to watch too avidly as Ren tucks his silky periwinkle tie back between his shirt buttons. It is possible that Ren, being Ren, knows his tie is periwinkle and not blue or lavender or silver; that's the type of guy Ren is. On the rare occasion Phil dons a tie at all, it is brown, stained, too wide, or all three.

"Ronnie and I are going to a game in Marin tonight, so I'll be home late, okay?" Micah says.

"Late as in?"

"Midnight. Or one."

I have no idea what sort of game my son means, and the steadily weakening Mommy warden inside me sounds a brief alarm at the hour and distant location of the event. Nevertheless, the ever distracting presence of my brother-in-law quiets her.

"Call if you're going to be later, okay?" I tell him.

"I'll just wake you up." Based on my experience, this is what kids say when they already plan on breaking curfew.

"Okay, bye," I singsong and click the phone off.

"Everything okay?" Ren says.

"Yeah. You know, kids."

Ren smiles a bit sadly. We both know he has yet to know what it is like to tolerate children. I'm ashamed to say, I have mixed feelings about the imminent prospect of my sister's adoption of a baby, negating, as it will, the only thing I've ever managed to best Laurie at: the womb war.

"Any news on a baby?" I say.

"There was a fifteen-year-old girl in Kentucky who picked us to adopt, but she decided to keep the baby. There were a couple of others—one of the mothers turned out to be an Oxycontin addict. We've been talking to a Chinese agency. It's hard..." Ren shrugs. Over the years, his face has earned a network of gently trod paths that only makes his cheekbones finer and his smile sexier. I am pretty sure Ren has not had work done—if he has, it is subtle—his restraint no doubt a selling point for his more discriminating cosmetic-surgery clients.

"Ren, can I ask you something?"

He nods. Something about his lack of surprise—he didn't

even question the purpose of the once-in-a-decade lunch invitation when I called him this morning—sends a spike of dread drilling into my stomach. In fact, when his reception-ist sent my call through to Ren's desk line and I heard him say my name in welcome, I was struck with the weird notion that he had been waiting for the call and was relieved it had finally arrived. This would have bothered me more at the time, except that, in the intervening days since Vesuvio's, I have convinced myself it was not my husband who grabbed Tate Trimble's thimble-sized ass and licked the perfume off her throat through the telescopic lens of the bar window but, rather, some other middle-aged Don Juan with a thinning rotunda and dun-colored coat.

It bothers me now. Naturally, I take steps to comfort myself—in this case by spooning large shovelfuls of choco-late mousse into my mouth.

"Um, this is a bit awkward," I mumble, my tongue trapped in a thicket of chocolate. "But I need you to be honest with me, okay? If I had any other option, I wouldn't be asking, and actually, I suppose I'm really just coming to you for confirma-tion that I have, um, imagined something that doesn't, in fact, exist—that is to say, that I'm just being paranoid." Ren lowers his eyes at this disclosure, sparing me his vicarious shame and enabling me to continue past the increasingly dry lump in my throat. "The other day? In San Francisco? I was having drinks with Sue at a bar"—in a flash, I see myself lurching out of Vesuvio's onto the empty sidewalk, hoping (and not hoping) to catch my husband entwined with his boss's wife— "and I saw Phil on the street. At least I think it was Phil. He was with Tate Trimble, and they were hugging. And kissing." I say it very calmly, like those tall, emotionally distant women in Alice Adams novels who are able to maintain composure in the face of death, financial ruin, and bad produce. We all know they don't exist—and we'd hate them if they did—but isn't it nice to pretend just for a second?

"Is Phil having an affair with Tate Trimble?" I say. Quickly now: Get. Chocolate. In. Mouth.

"Not anymore, to my knowledge." Like a normal person, Ren has stopped eating and is concentrating on looking embarrassed. Frankly, I am a bit shocked at his honesty. It hits me that I expected him to prevaricate a little, to deny knowledge or squirm or claim an urgent surgery that required his immediate attention. Also, a part of me, the newly lean, frequently bubbly, tentatively confident part, believed I *was* being paranoid, which, in spite of its psychopathologic implications, is infinitely preferable to actually being cheated on.

"Phil and Tate?" The words are gruesome; I choke on them.

Ren's face darkens with that guardedness we are all familiar with from men-misbehaving movies, the one that indicates guilt over the betrayal of a fellow male's right to poke his penis into anything human, animal, or PVC.

"Raquel," he says. It is clearly a plea.

"What? Wait a minute." I grab at the waiter's sleeve as he rushes past. "Can I get another one—no, two—of these?" I point wildly at the half-eaten chocolate mousse. Tears have already started to blur my vision. The waiter darts away from me, his fluffy blouse escaping my hand like a set of reins trailing a galloping horse.

Ren leans forward and takes my hand. As on the day fifteen years ago when my father's heart convulsed its way into a final infarction and Ren's touch was my sole hope at temporary solace, my heartbeat slows and healing warmth pervades my bones.

"Look, obviously, this is none of my business. You and Phil need to talk, and soon. But our friendship goes back a long

way, and that's why I'm telling you this, Quel. Because I know
you, and I trust you to do the right thing with this information. And because it is your right to have it." Even after all this
time, his touch is silken, narcotic.

"As far as I know, it was a brief, meaningless thing, a blip,
and it ended years ago. Years. I know that's small comfort
now, but you have to concentrate on the big picture. Think
about what you have together, what you've built. A marriage,
kids, a home—there's a lot at stake here. Phil fucked up, I'll
be the first to say it. But if it's any consolation, he was a wreck
afterward. It wasn't just the guilt; he really felt like he'd made
a big mistake. He wasn't even into her. Let's just say she made
it real easy for him. Real easy. Caught him in a weak moment,
I suppose. She may even have gone after him deliberately,
back when she and Ross still gave a shit and were baiting
each other." Ren's controlled voice drones on, drowned out
by the slushy pounding of my own heartbeat. It occurs to
me that Ren may have told Laurie. The idea that *Living with
Lauren!* knew about Phil's affair before I did sends shards of
crazy rage deep into my spine.

"That shit!" I choke back the howl that threatens to explode
out of me. Ren leans back, his hazel eyes brimming with concern, my hand still tucked under his. The fact that his eyes
have yet to start the darting, frantic search for escape adds
another layer of affirmation to my belief, deeply held, that my
life took a potholed, dead-end detour the moment Ren broke
up with me.

"I can't believe Phil would make that mistake again. Are
you absolutely sure it was him?" Ren says.

I think back to that night at the bar, about what I saw
through the diamond of glass. It was a flash, so fleeting I am
not sure even now whether I imagined it. If my neglected
imagination plastered Phil's face on the compact body of

another wayward husband, pasted Phil's overcoat over a pair of gray slacks I have, in actuality, never seen hanging in our closet, between Phil's cracked leather bomber jacket and my too tight cocktail dress.

I don't respond, can't respond, as false nirvana in the form of chocolate delivers me from misery.

What do you do when you've just forced your sister's husband to validate your own husband's treachery and three hours remain until the lout slides his Accord under the garage door?

You go stark-raving apeshit, that's what.

It's not hard. Right now I am pathetic, horror-movie, spittle-flying, crazy-lady mad with hurt. Any minute the lantern-jawed men with pumped arms and fat batons are going to pull up in their paddy wagon, shake their oversize noggins sadly at the hurricane-force destruction that afflicts my living room, truss me up in white straps, and tote me away to drool down my days in a human paddock with a euphemistic name under a canopy of vomit and Lysol. Also, I am plain old pissed. The timing, as ever, is appalling, the latest horror falling on the eve of that most hallowed of events: my twenty-fifth high school reunion.

After lunch with Ren, which leaves me so damaged I cannot even manage to cop a feel when he hugs me good-bye, I sail home on autopilot and continue my eating spree in the tidy confines of my kitchen. Bologna, Brie, Triscuits, leftover refried beans with a scrim of blue fuzz, M&M's, picked-over tri-tip all disappear into my gullet while I alternately gag and sob and curse.

At exactly 5:35 P.M., I hear the automatic garage door groan open.

Some weird melodramatic impulse prompts me to draw the drapes and stow my bloated body in a straight-backed chair. Standing sentry in the darkness, I am simultaneously interrogation subject and executioner, victim and attacker, wife and stranger.

"Quel?" Phil flicks on the kitchen lights and sees me. His face is creased and tired. Nobody, not even naturally gifted—yes, I'll admit it—teachers like Phil can spend eight hours interacting with teenagers and not need a Valium and a sit-com glut to regain the equanimity they've lost.

In the interest of spontaneity, I have planned no speech. It shows.

"Philly, how *could* you? She is so"—my mind rifles through stinging adjectives—"*Fresno.*"

"Wha—"

"Tate."

In the split second that follows my saying her name, a small, girlish part of me curls up and dies, because the rough crumpling of Phil's face under a barrage of guilt, shame, and fear tells me all I need to know.

The phone rings.

We freeze. Because I am standing closer, I peer at the wall unit. The screen says "R. Greenblatt." Ronnie. Who's with Micah. At a game. In Marin. After school. Yet he is calling instead of my son. Visions of highway patrol checkpoints and gnarled wreckage cause my pulse to gush.

"Hello?" I nearly howl into the phone. In this thin slice of existence between ignorance and total devastation, I am very nearly Joan Crawford, and Joan is having a very bad day.

"Hey, Mrs. Rose. This is Ron. I'm really sorry to call so late. Is, uh, Micah there?"

Two questions: When did Ronnie Greenblatt of the washboard abs and after-school lawn-mowing venture graduate to Ron, and why isn't he with my son?

"Um, no, Ronnie. Mike's at a game. In Marin, I think." *With you, asshole,* I want to scream. Like I don't have enough to worry about?

Ronnie Greenblatt's headed-for-Cornell 4.5 GPA brain kicks in. "Duh. Yeah, I was supposed to go with him, but my car battery was dead, so I was just going to meet them after I got a jump. I called his cell, but it went to voice mail, so I thought maybe he cut out early."

"Sure, Ronnie." We both know he is lying like George W. Bush at a press conference.

"Well, okay, bye."

I turn back to Phil without hanging up. Thick smears of Taylor's completely unnecessary concealing foundation stain the receiver. It is gross, and I resolve to make her clean it herself before the maid, Estrella, sees it. With alcohol.

"I want you out," I tell Phil.

He scratches his ear. This enrages me. Doesn't he know how insulting it is to engage in the mundane business of personal grooming when our marriage is imploding?

"No," he says.

"No," I repeat. Behind me, the cuckoo clock, an albatross of a family heirloom courtesy of Phil's penny-squeezing nana Vanderhoeven, chirps out midnight. At a quarter till six. The screechy gong shreds my last nerve.

"Philip, it is customary for the *dickhead* to go to a *hotel* in these situations. I'm sure *Tate* can spot you if you can't afford it. Or you could try that Motel 6 by the freeway. You know, the one where the *crackhead* was gutted with a potato peeler last year." The incident, so bizarrely horrific at the time, now unfolds almost sweetly, like one of Aesop's fables. My eyes dart to the cooking-implement drawer, where our own peeler rests alongside its dangerous friends, spatula and garlic press.

"Get out!" I scream.

This time he does.

CHAPTER 16

Things That Come in Flavors

It is 2:48 A.M., and I am staring blindly into the vacant eye of the computer, e-mailing, propelled by three coffees and a singular desire to grill my husband up nice and crispy on the Weber. Without the outlet Web surfing provides, I was starting to feel a little like the mystery brick I took out of the fridge for dinner last night: frozen, animal in origin, and too many years beyond freshness.

"Mom?"

Taylor is in the doorway, her Paul Frank pajamas slipping down her hips, her face rosy with sleep.

"What are you doing up, hon? Can't sleep?"

"Where's Dad?"

I had expected this, just not at three A.M., and not so soon.

"Dad and I had a little disagreement, and we decided together to give each other some space to cool off. He went to spend the night with a friend."

Taylor's brow puckers. "So you're getting a divorce?"

"What? What makes you say that?" On the computer screen, the name Duke Dunne jumps out at me, causing a sliver of self-recrimination to wiggle its way into my dehydrated little heart. In a fit of desperation, I e-mailed Surfer Boy. I move over a little, hoping to block Tay's view of the monitor.

Taylor shrugs. She has my shoulders, broad and brown as a swimmer's. Unlike me, my daughter is still nubile enough to make shrugging in a camisole pretty. "I don't know," she says. "When Quinn's dad left, her mom said the same thing, that they were giving each other space or whatever. But he never moved back, and then he got an apartment with Zora."

A small spark of horror alights at the back of my neck at being tarred with the same brush as Marlene and Avery McWhorter, delusional social climbers who pretended marital bliss for about thirty seconds sometime in the early eighties. I happen to know that Avery's former-babysitter girlfriend, Zora, is Ukrainian and all of twenty and that Marlene has a pixie-haired girlfriend in the city whom her kids know as Mom's therapist, but I don't tell Taylor that.

Taylor continues, "Besides, Dad doesn't have any friends except Uncle Ren, and I seriously doubt he's going over to Aunt Laurie's if you're divorcing him."

I do not have a ready answer for this. Now that she has dismantled my propaganda as easily as she would a preschool LEGO set, Taylor flops into her father's swivel chair, tucking her legs under herself. Recalling the occasional stealthy hiss and stifled shout of my own parents' thirty-year marriage, fundamentally ideal though it may have been, I dredge up a feeling of panic at being talked down to, of being "protected," that inevitably left me with fears worse than any reality could have been.

"Dad and I had a fight—"

"About Micah?" Taylor says it so quickly I can tell some buried truth has been partially excavated. The haze of alarm that has been hovering over me for weeks thickens perceptibly.

"What about Micah?"

"I don't know. Nothing, really. I just thought…" Taylor glances back at the hallway, as if afraid Micah is going to burst out of his room and put her in a big-brother chokehold. "I just thought you were worried because he didn't meet curfew," she improvises.

"Mike called in earlier, around one o'clock. He's spending the night at Ronnie's." After the call, which calmed my worst death-by-Ecstasy-tab visions but did almost nothing to assuage my longer-term worries, I bit the bullet and called Ronnie back on his home phone to verify my son's story. Barb Greenblatt answered with the same terrified hiss I would have used if awakened in the middle of the night in the same manner. After apologizing, I asked if Micah was indeed safely ensconced in Ronnie's bedroom, without explaining why I wasn't calling him myself. Barb sighed and told me she'd heard them come in after she'd gone to bed, and did I want her to get up and go check? No, I said, I'm sure everything's fine.

"So why did you and Dad fight?" Taylor prods.

I test-think telling my daughter that her father has gotten naked with Ross Trimble's skeletal excuse for a wife. This causes nausea to roil through my gut. The whole lying-to-your-kids-to-protect-them thing makes perfect sense to me. What's so great about the truth, anyway? When I was Taylor's age, I was cloddish, desperate, and hairier than is generally considered attractive outside of a few Kurdish villages. Would having these facts confirmed by an outside source have helped me any?

"It doesn't seem that important now," I fib while shutting

off the computer. "Let's go to bed. Things will be better in the morning."

The breast-cancer support group meets in an Edwardian in the Lower Haight that houses the creepily named Institute for Attitudinal Adjustment. This just bugs me. For one, does a bad attitude really require an entire institute to wrestle it back into compliance? Can't they just send my mother over to deal with it? Plus, aren't there more important matters of personal growth at stake that could benefit from having their own institute—for instance, having a mullet or the inability to look good in low-cut jeans? More significantly, who gets to decide if an attitude is bad or just having, say, a bad day?

All told, there is something self-recriminating about cancer victims meeting here, supporting, as it seems to, the proposition that all one needs to do to increase one's white blood cell count is put on a happy face and think about all the poor wretches out there who have cancer *and* halitosis, for instance. Then again, maybe the sign is a typo and they're just borrowing the basement room from the adenoids people.

"I'll get you a name tag. First names only," Jean says, already scribbling my name on one of those stickers favored by conventioneers.

I pick up a flyer from the table, which features a rainbow of handouts and selected reading, including *Grace and Grit: Spirituality and Healing in the Life of Treya Killam Wilber; Dr. Susan Love's Breast Book; Holding Tight, Letting Go;* and the alarming *Estrogen & Breast Cancer: A Warning to Women.* What, did estrogen go out of favor while I was in Mexico? I wonder if I'm supposed to know who Dr. Susan Love is, and quickly scan the jacket bio before Jean returns.

The support group is called Women Expunging Cancer of

the Breast Because Life Endures. I'm not kidding; it's really called that. The acronym, WE COBBLE, is printed, plain as the knot of spider veins on my left calf, on the upper-right-hand corner of the flyer. Beneath it is a logo of a well-rounded woman with hair flowing in a modesty veil over her womanly parts, raising hopeful arms toward the sky, where, presumably, Dr. Susan Love awaits. Cobbling.

"Raquel? You want some coffee? Tea?" I accept an herbal tea from Jean and follow her to the semicircle of chairs.

So far, the support group is as I imagined it: the rickety card table of reading materials, the hushed chatter, the lovingly baked pastries, the weary ferocity of the women, the mood of mingled reprieve and dread at who may not show up this week. I hope I don't have to stand up and confess my diagnosis, A.A.-style, because even with my newfound flair for storytelling, that would feel seriously wrong.

Part of me wants to be gone from here immediately. Another part wants to stay because, frankly, I deserve the torture. Sick people made me uncomfortable before; now they make me downright agitated. A third part is just plain curious. Call it empathy, voyeurism, or simple inquisitiveness, but after having spent a little time with these brave women, I want to hear more of their stories firsthand. I owe them that much and considerably more. Maybe, when I come out next month—and it *is* next month, I've even calendared it!—they'll remember that I was here. Being supportive. Eating pastries. Holding tight. Letting go.

Cobbling.

A slender, well-dressed woman in front waves her hand. "Can everyone take a seat, please? Don't be afraid—we don't bite. Okay, Sharon bites, but we always stick her in the back near the zucchini bread." A few laughs. "There's plenty of room over here. There we go. So. Welcome. This is the primary-diagnosis support group. We focus on the needs of those facing a recent breast-cancer diagnosis, surgery, and treatment. Some of us are just entering this cycle, and others have transitioned to the other side and offer their wisdom and courage to our sisters." Next to me, Jean squeezes my hand. I squeeze hers back, surprised by the rush of comfort I feel.

"I see some newbies I particularly want to welcome today. The way we do things is, nobody's ever forced to share. If you want to talk, talk. If you want to cry, cry. If you want to run over there and eat every last Rice Krispie bar, go right ahead." Giggles filter through the group. "I'm Kendall Calloway, group moderator. I was diagnosed in late 1998, treated in 1999, and I've been cancer-free since." The assemblage applauds. "Lost and gained a husband along the way, but that's neither here nor there." Kendall looks around the room. "Does anyone want to begin today's session?"

A fiftyish woman with thick faded auburn hair twined in a bun and a supermarket clerk's green apron raises her hand. Kendall nods at her. "Doreen."

"Thanks." Doreen scratches her forearm, which seems to have a bad case of psoriasis. "Hi. I, uh, had an okay week. I'm actually feeling okay now that they've got me on the Zofran. The Compazine wasn't doing a darn thing for my nausea, but the Zofran is great at taking the edge off. Anyway, I was sort of hoping now that I'm feeling better, I'd have a little more energy and Cliff and I might, you know, be able to spend a little more time doing something we like. Together, I mean. I'm at the hospital all the time, and when we're home, most of the housework is falling on him. He never complains, but I can tell he's having a hard time. He seems a little—I don't know what you'd call it—depressed? He's just not himself. The other day I went out to the garage to get some wrapping paper—I keep extra in there, 'cause why buy new when you've got all those nice gift bags from people—and I saw Cliff sitting in the passenger seat of the Taurus. Scared the bejeezus out of me. So, I'm like, 'Cliffie, what are you doing sitting out here in the dark in the garage?' And he starts crying, which I've never seen him do, not even when his father died of an aneurysm or when I was diagnosed or anything." Doreen pauses to wipe a tear from her own eye. "He couldn't stop crying, not even when I brought him back in the house and *CSI: Miami* came on. That's his favorite."

Vigorous discussion and several rounds of hugging ensue. An Asian woman recommends a book called *Breast Cancer Husband,* and Jean observes that maybe Cliff doesn't feel comfortable revealing his grief because he thinks he'll be stealing attention from Doreen. An older woman who can't stop fiddling with an expensive wristwatch suggests that Doreen and Cliff attend another WE COBBLE group just for couples; it helped her a lot, and even though they ultimately divorced, they were able to use a mediator to divide the assets instead of a judge. A girl in braids and a short skirt, far too young to imagine having breast cancer, starts sobbing in a controlled, almost dignified way, and several ladies gather around her, clucking with sympathy.

Overall, I am impressed by the grave consideration given to other people's minutiae and close to awed by the capacity of the women to dissect their experiences in a darkly funny manner. Confessions are made. Jokes are cracked. Topics close and open. One minute someone is crying in abject grief; the next, everyone is laughing the hysterical laughter of those who know enough about temporality to grab at a chance for release and squeeze every last bitter calorie out of it.

"Raquel, you're newly diagnosed. How is your husband coping?"

So much for not forcing newbies to talk. I glance around the room. Several ladies nod encouragingly.

Oh, the usual way: an affair with his boss's wife, lots of televised sports, and prolonged stays in the bathroom with the Sunday crossword.

Instantly, I feel guilty. Phil *has* made an effort. There was the awareness walk. And the knitting circle. And that night he made dinner.

"Phil seems to be holding it together all right," I finally say. An image of the last time we made love pops into my mind. Phil did all the usual things, but with an almost terrified gentleness, as if afraid I would shatter and rain toxic bits of tumor all over the bed. I remember thinking at the time: *If I were really sick, there would be something terrible about this.*

"I can't tell if he's being so solicitous in bed because he's afraid he's going to hurt me or if he finds me repulsive," I say.

Horrors.

"I mean, I know he doesn't think I'm repulsive—I don't know why I said that. What I meant was, I think the only reason he has sex with me since the diagnosis is that he's afraid *I'll* think he *thinks* I'm repulsive, which is not exactly the same as really thinking I'm, you know, repulsive." More horror. "Maybe he's just really tired," I add weakly.

Kendall Calloway is looking at me knowingly. It makes me want to make excuses for Phil. See how competitive I am? I want Phil to win Best Cancer Husband 2005, even though we're separated and I don't even have cancer.

"My girlfriend stopped going down on me when I got it," Jean the monoboobed, high-powered attorney says. "One day we got into it, and I had a complete breakdown and just started accusing her of all kinds of crazy shit—cheating, not taking out the garbage, favoring her daughter over me. We were both out of our minds. She admitted that the chemo made me taste funny, uh, down there." Amazingly, Jean smiles at this, as if the memory brings real amusement. "I actually felt a lot better after she said it. I'd been hospitalized for a real shitty staph infection and was in a blaming phase. It was nice to have it validated."

"Methotrexate and 5-FU should come in flavors!" someone yells.

"Just use chocolate suppositories!"

"We don't have enough problems, now we've got to have sugar-coated pussy?"

"Who wants to have sex, anyway?"

"Me!"

"Not me, but I didn't want to before, either—"

Before I realize I am laughing, I am crying, big, luscious tears that streak my face while I hiccup my way toward inevitable bladder failure. For the first time in months, I forget about everything that frightens or disappoints and revel in the emancipation of a hearty round of belly laughter.

"Oh! Oh, stop...oh God, oh, shit..."

Jean and I look at each other with watery, slitted eyes; it is enough to send us spiraling toward another bout of uncontrollable giggles. In this magical moment, I am convinced that the number—$245,325—is worth the lies if it makes these women's lives any easier. Ain't rationalization grand?

"We don't...we don't cobble, we hobble," I manage to get out.

Jean grabs her giant untethered boob and proffers it in a rude gesture, the female equivalent of Michael Jackson's crotch grab. "And bobble," she says.

CHAPTER 17

And Cocoa Butter Prevents Stretch Marks

We are ostensibly grown-ups, yet anyone reading our communiqués would think Phil and I are estranged junior high sweethearts passing notes during class.

You can come pack your suitcase between eleven and three today. I'll be out. I'd appreciate it if you leave me the green Samsonite in the event that I must travel internationally.

He e-mails back. *Raquel, please give me a chance to explain. I won't lie to you—yes, I made a big mistake with Tate. But that was a long time ago, and I want to make things right between us. I love you and can't imagine being with anybody else.*

I let that one molder for a cruel, satisfying eleven hours before I respond. *I'm sure you can't. Imagination has never been your strong suit, Philly.*

He writes back immediately. *Raquel, let's talk. Please. P.*

In spite of my pledge to remain aloof, I feel myself soften slightly at Phil's apparent passion for reconciliation. (Okay, so I set the bar low, but this is the man who bought me the same chintzy peridot necklace not once, not twice, but *three* times for our anniversary. And let's not forget the time in the not too distant past when I squeezed myself into a black lace teddy complete with thigh-high stockings and feathery thong and presented myself against the backlit walk-in closet for my husband's pleasure, only to have him take a rain check because—this is a quote—"I have papers to grade." That's the sort of crazed ardor we're dealing with here.)

I decide to take the highish road. *Not yet. Need time to think. Did you put the Xanax somewhere?*

In guest bath cabinet, behind flea collars. XXXPhil.

It occurs to me as I read this last message that I am being too hard on Phil. That there is something self-defeating and despotic about my attachment to the idea that I am the smart, sensitive, creative, wronged one. Maybe Phil's right. Maybe our marriage does burn with the white-hot rightness of star-crossed love. Maybe we belong together for all eternity. Maybe we'll die together, sexually satisfied and withered, as we spoon under a quilt patched together from our grandchildren's recycled cloth diapers.

Sure. Maybe I will be recruited as a Hollywood butt double, too.

I quit out of e-mail. Before I can initiate a search for disappointment-numbing meds, the doorbell chimes.

"Rachel? This is your mother. I want you to let me in right now."

Fuck. Ma. Here. As opposed to there. There being anywhere else. Like, for instance, Eliot's House of Culinary Torture, at its flagship Woodside location.

I drag myself to the door and let Ma in without checking my mascara. There are only so many points you can lose for smeared mascara when you haven't changed your underwear for forty-eight hours.

"Hey, Ma."

"What's this about divorce?" Ma says with her usual tact—none—as she muscles past me. Apparently, Taylor got to her before I could do damage control. I wonder if Ma and Laurie have had time to confer and decide upon a rescue strategy for poor beleaguered Raquel/Rachel. I wonder if the strategy in question involves anger-management therapy or—petite flare of hope—a destination spa.

I follow Ma into the kitchen and watch her refill her gigantic urn of water, mildly horrified to see that she is using what appears to be an antifreeze container. Equally driven by fear of weight gain and bladder infection, Ma gulps water by the liter. Apparently, there is no real water bottle big enough to flush the engorged kidneys of Minna Louise Schultz Abramson (which, in spite of their frailty, are mysteriously impervious to antifreeze residue). She pops a handful of Eliot-approved vitamins into her mouth and washes them down.

"So you and Phil had a little tiff, eh?" she says.

"I wouldn't call it little. He cheated on me, Ma." Part of me is ashamed to be the sort of woman men cheat on; the other is happy as pie to prove to my mother that this one, at least, is not my fault.

"Hmm," she says, still managing to sound critical.

"What?" I open the fridge door and survey the remains of the breakup feast. At a loss for goals in the aftermath of Phil's departure, I have decided to regain a mere five of the twelve pounds I've lost—enough to grant me the comfort and privilege of unlimited refined-sugar consumption, but not to demote me back into stretch-waisted mom slacks.

I grab a tub of hummus and a spoon and begin eating it without the interference of vegetable or grain.

"My poor sweetie." Ma reaches up, careful not to break a bone against the marauding shovel of hummus, and strokes my cheek. This sort of empathetic gesture is unusual enough coming from Ma—who adheres to more of the marmot or ferret style of parenting—that I choke. "Do you want to talk about it?" she says.

I am surprised to realize that I do.

In between three-hundred-calorie bites of Dulce de Fat-ass, I detail the incidents that led up to the confrontation with Phil: the arguments, the sexual disinterest, the evasion, the sighting, and finally, the confirmation by Ren that my fears were indeed founded in something besides declining colla-gen production.

"Aren't you going to answer that?" Ma says while I'm await-ing additional commiseration. It takes me a minute to realize the phone is ringing. Certain that it is Phil begging me to consider reconciliation, I let the answering machine pick up. Unfortunately for all concerned, Phil is too cheap to upgrade to voice mail, and Ma hears everything.

"Heeeey, Raquel. *¿Como estás?* This is Duke. From Mexico? Got your e-mail and, uh, I'm actually coming up to NorCal in a couple days. Thought we could go surfing up in Bolinas or something. Call me." He rattles off a Southern California exchange. In the background is the unmistakable gurgle of a water bong.

There is also no mistaking the youthful tenor of Duke's voice or the sexual innuendo behind his words. Briefly, I am glad that Phil and I are splitsville, so I don't have to answer questions about why a child called Duke wants to go surf-ing with me in Bolinas in between bong hits. I realize I must have given the boy the impression that I was single and shop-ping. How could I have done that?

Ma may have the nurturing instincts of a sharp-toothed rodent, but she is no fool. "Who's Duke? Are you seeing someone?" she says.

"What? Of course not." Unwittingly, my mind flings up a mug shot of Viggo Mortensen, and I feel myself blush. (Unfortunately, he is nude.)

Ma reads me like a NOW pamphlet. "So you *are* seeing someone."

"Ma, I would never—"

"I'm not criticizing, hon. I think it's great."

"You do?" The words gush out before I can think.

"Does he have, you know, the skills?"

"Um..." I think Ma might be assessing the vocational pedigree of my lover: doctor, lawyer, or presidential hopeful. Inappropriate hilarity engulfs me and I almost laugh, recalling the many, many dates and a few boyfriends who were found wanting because they weren't, in Ma's words, "exactly MENSA material."

A moment passes before I realize that my mother is actually talking about something much, much worse. She wants to know if he—Fictitious Genius/Lover—is good in bed. If, in between solving artificial intelligence conundra and negotiating world peace, he performs cunnilingus on me without my asking. If he contorts himself into mad pretzels in order to simultaneously stimulate my inner ear and rouse my G-spot, as per the instructions in *Today's Kama Sutra* (to which he subscribes, of course). If I have, for the first time ever, multiple orgasms. Multiple orgasms so multiplicitous I'd have to date a mathematician to keep track of them.

I respond quickly, before she can scar me forever by raising the pressing issue of manual clitoral stimulation or reclaim the word "pussy" for the feminists.

"Ma, I said I'm not—"

"Rachel, don't lie to your mother! I can see it in your complexion! You're absolutely glowing!"

"I'm not—"

Ma grabs my hand. "He treats you right?" Shades of *La Cosa Nostra*.

"Yes, he is extremely competent," I finally lie in the soulless tone of a telephone survey taker, if only to get Ma off my back. This is all quite hilarious, since I am not presently having carnal knowledge of anyone, my husband, self, and Viggo included.

Ma smiles, exposing sharp, yellowing canines. "I'm damn glad to hear it. Damn glad. We didn't burn our bras and fight for equal pay so you kids could lie down like the little wifey and let the man have all the fun."

There are some things that move forward in the face of cancer, adultery, gluttony, pathological lying, and impending divorce. High school reunions are one of them.

"Oh God," Sue says when I call to ask her to be my date for the event. "Why? Like having to go to my own isn't torture enough?"

"It *is* the twenty-fifth. People always go to the twenty-fifth, don't they?"

"Unless they're morbidly obese." Sue coughs discreetly, or maybe it's a delicate dry heave. "That's where you're supposed to look for your second husband."

We examine the unfortunate yet inarguable truth: that it is preferable to attend your reunion having been an executive at Enron or molested a deer than to show up fat. At this point I decide I hate most people.

"I wonder if Scotty Mulgrew's still got hair," I say to cheer myself up. I'd always thought he was cute in a Bigfoot sort of way, with that thick unibrow and big hairy arms. Nice, too.

"They never do," Sue says.

"There's a kid I should have dated. Here's a story about

Scotty: We had this biology teacher, Mr. Barry, who was a big drunk, and he always had this mug, but it had schnapps mixed in with the coffee. Everybody knew it."

"Let me guess: popular?" Sue says.

"Oh yeah. But he was an acquired taste. The brains weren't too keen, but the jocks and the rebels loved him. He was one of those great, anti-authoritarian pervy drunks who you could just tell the principal hated but couldn't get fired. Mr. Barry once threw a penny in the air to show us some scientific principle, and it fell down a girl's shirt. Another time Mr. Barry blew up the lab. But everybody liked the guy, so Scotty hid his drink inside a dissected shark when the cops came. I remember wishing I'd thought of it." Instead, hating myself, I cowered and plucked at my arm hair while the firemen picked through the remains.

"Oh, and there was this other guy..." To my profound dismay, I find I cannot remember the name of one of my most Significant Crushes, a smart, punkish skater who decorated his backpack with safety pins and went to college somewhere elite and arty in the Pacific Northwest.

"Maybe I shouldn't go. It's going to be grotesque. All the popular girls are going to have husbands and disgustingly well-adjusted kids named Britney and Jaden and wear the same size they wore in high school because all they've done since 1985 is go to the gym while their husbands run the international marketing division at Oracle. None of the interesting people are going to come anyway. And it's at some boring country club in Morgan Hill that's basically a retirement community because the class treasurer co-owns it with her third husband, who I hear is ancient and loaded and has pec implants."

"So don't go."

"It's just...part of me wants to go." *Because I'm finally a successful artist. And wear a not-too-sausagey size ten. And have two great kids. And a regular newspaper column. And my own online stalker. And am in negotiations to launch my own TV show aimed at homemakers thirty-five to fifty who have sex with their husbands twice a month and make their own low-glycemic preserves.*

"So go," Sue says.

"You're so helpful. Your advice is so incisive. Maybe you should replace Dear Abby."

"Something tells me Dear Abby wouldn't let herself get knocked up at forty-two and a half."

"Something tells me Dear Abby hasn't gotten laid since 1935." I chew the rim of my nail off. It has white spots on it. I dredge up a memory of a magazine article that mentioned white fingernail spots as a symptom of some heinous disease. Cancer?

"Did you tell him yet?" I ask her.

Sue sighs, a long, earthy exhalation that speaks volumes about her reluctance to talk to Arlo. "We're going out to dinner Saturday. I got a sitter. We're going somewhere busy and bright so he can't freak out on me. I'm going to tell him over dessert."

"Arlo's going to be there for you, Sue. You'll see."

"Yeah, and cocoa butter prevents stretch marks," she says.

CHAPTER 18

Go Jump In a River

Fifteen stories below, the water churns itself into angry hillocks, the tips peaked like frothy meringues. The river looks black and cold and slightly oily, cut with iridescent puddles of sage and purple that shouldn't be there. On the left-hand bank stands a thicket of fans. At the moment most of them are silent or murmuring softly to one another in their puffy parkas, their frivolity tamped by dread.

"Remind me why we're doing this?" I try to sound jokey. Below, an ambulance pulls up. A medic gets out, wrestling with one of those wheeled stretchers, as if death is a foregone conclusion.

Laurie smiles tightly and glances back at the coterie of producers and lackeys who are charging around in a dither, trying to look preoccupied and important. I can only imagine the tactics discussed at the pre-event strategy meeting: *So, it's pretty straightforward: Lauren and Mrs. Rose are going to leap off the bridge into space and hurtle toward the icy water at sixty miles per hour. Camera one—if Lauren is unable to maintain eye contact through the apex, then cut to camera two. And for God's sake, shoot her from the side. We don't want a repeat of the chunky-thighs incident. Now, I want the background music to kick in just as Raquel's screams crescendo.*

No, don't worry about which side you shoot her from, just make sure somebody brings the heavy powder for her T-zone.

I spy Cleo and Jonesie behind the barrier and give them a thumbs-up. Shiny Pony stands off to the side, alone with her trusty clipboard, eyes glistening behind her standard-issue rectangular hipster glasses. I'm sure if something horrible happens—if Laurie's cable snaps and she plummets into the rock-strewn river, floating away like a broken doll—Shiny will plod onward in Laurie's memory. I can see her wielding the microphone—with its untouched commemorative Laurie lipstick marks—like a consummate professional, ascending the dais with the hushed reverence my sister deserves.

"Can't we just use stunt doubles, like on TV?" *Where's my Chardonnay now, Shiny twit?*

"That wouldn't inspire people, would it?" Laurie leans over and allows a slightly homelier Shiny clone to clip a small microphone to her chest. "Just remember, we're doing it for a good cause. I think pledges hit two hundred and fifty thousand dollars this morning. It's a show record. And it's all going to the Bay Area Breast Cancer Alliance." We are into round two of our ongoing BC fund-raising effort.

"What if something goes wrong?" I mutter.

We interrupt this programming to inform you that the celebrated Schultz sisters, TV host Lauren White and artist and breast-cancer activist Raquel Rose, died today from multiple injuries sustained in a bungee-jumping accident. The sisters, who attended Bella Sierra High School in Santa Clara, though only Lauren served on the cheerleading squad, are survived by their mother, Ma; their stepfather and family asshole, Eliot Abramson of Abramson Integrated Foods; their husbands, renowned plastic surgeon and hottie Ren White and cheating Ph.D. dropout Phil Rose; Mr. Rose's mistress, Hilary Swank butt double and Botox addict Tate Trimble; and Mrs. Rose's

*children, number one and number two. Bob "Iceman"
Gundershmoover of Grungy Bungee attributes the tragic accident to human error. "We calibrated their jump cords to the
women's weights," he told us from his office in Dixon's Smitty's
Bar. "Unfortunately, Mrs. Rose underreported her total body
mass by an estimated forty-five pounds, causing catastrophic
equipment failure. It's the saddest day for us here at Grungy.
Our deepest condolences go out to the women's families and
Mrs. Rose's creditors..."*

"Nothing's going to go wrong," Laurie tells me. "Don't be
negative."

Before I can retort that somebody has to be negative to balance out her excessive optimism, the bungee guy, a scrawny
fellow whose John Deere cap and grease-grooved knuckles
convey the impression of a moonlighting farmer, gives our
harnesses a final once-over and goes over procedures with us
again. Laurie asks smart questions while smiling gamely for
the cameras. She looks good in her gray jumpsuit, sexy and
vaguely scientific, like Laura Dern in *Jurassic Park*. Due to the
unfortunate combination of larger proportions and surplus
bronzer, I, on the other hand, resemble a beefy Latino sani-
tation engineer. I twine my legs together and try not to pee
through my panty liner, an accessory I cannot seem to do
without since the last baby popped out in 1989.

"Great," says Bungee Farmer. "Let's rock and roll!"

He leads us to the edge of the bridge. Cameras one and
two follow us. I pray for two things: one, that the cables do
indeed hold; and two, that I, too, benefit from the kindness
of diagonal shooting. If a misdirected camera could make
my sister's Gabrielle Reece legs look chunky, mine could be
declared an endangered tree species under the National Forest Protection and Restoration Act.

Laurie steps out onto the diving platform. My sister closes

her eyes and whispers something in Mandarin. That and the wind ruffling her honey mane with cinematic precision cause the paparazzi to go into a feeding frenzy. She extends her hand to me. Like everything else about Laurie, her manicure is perfect: short, pale pink, and classy. I grasp her hand and feel my ass draw involuntarily back toward land, issuing my own prayer—for a well-timed natural disaster or fan heart attack that requires an immediate cessation of this endeavor.

Laurie leans forward with smile intact. "Quel, come on! We have to jump *now*."

"I think I've changed my mind. I'll just, you know, watch you do—"

Before I finish my thought, I am hurtling toward the water. I don't know if Laurie pulled me off the ledge for ratings or if I tried to run and tripped. What I do know is that somebody's going to have to pay to put my internal organs back in their rightful spots, and it's not going to be me.

"AAAAAAHHHHH!" I think I yell. The world around me is a kaleidoscope of sound and light. I am vaguely conscious of my feet flying above my head, the wrong place for them, in my humble opinion.

Just before my face smashes into the water, a giant hand yanks me back, and I shoot upward. To my horror, a thin stream of vomit flies out of my mouth before I even decide I'm nauseated. Next to me, Laurie is a dark blob with Goldilocks hair, shooting upward like a human javelin. After repeating this exercise five, six, a hundred times, we settle at the bottom, swinging gently over the river, which smells earthy and moist, like the rabbit-pellet-sprinkled mud pies we used to make when we were kids.

"Smile!" Laurie says. "Over there. Look over there!" Being upside down doesn't prevent her from waving cheerfully at her onshore fans. Except for a hint of voluminous bedhead and an excited flush in her cheeks, Laurie looks completely normal. I am sure the same cannot be said for me.

I am about to issue a retort when the bridge breaks.

No fucking shit, people. One minute we're rocking like babies on the bough; the next, a slashing groan emanates from the bridge pillar we're attached to, and we drop precipitously closer to the seething current.

Several things occur in quick succession. A couple of people scream. Bungee Bob starts yelling orders at people. Shiny Pony keens out something that sounds like "Nooooo!" The medic plunges into the river, managing to drop his emergency kit, which bobs once, then twice, before disappearing into a froth of rapids. Defeated handily by Mother Nature, he staggers back to shore, leaving us without a clear savior.

"Oh my God!" Laurie yells.

"Are we still supposed to smile?" Ever the quipper.

The plank of metal holding us up creaks down another foot. Being taller, I hit the water first. The icy cold kisses my forehead, ruining my spiky gelled bangs, which have just grown long enough to style. I have to hunch upward in a curl to keep from going under. All I can say is, I hope I have the abs to show for it when they cut us down.

"Oh my God," Laurie says again, this time a little more plaintively, as if the Supreme Being she is imploring is no longer an intimate.

"We are so fucked. I can't believe this," I manage to grunt as I count off the equivalent of my hundredth crunch.

"They'll get us down in a minute. See? Bob's on it. I know he's on it. That's him on the bridge, right?" Laurie attempts to peer upward at the monstrous jumble of creaking metal from which we are swinging. Bob can actually be seen quite clearly at the top. In a mysterious manifestation of riverside acoustics, we hear him say, "Whaddaya mean they ain't got a crane?"

This development causes Laurie to change her Pollyanna tune. "God, what an idiot! This is outrageous! The station's going to sue Bob's ass!"

The supporting beam busts down another notch. In a flash, regrets pour through my mind, paramount among them that I'll never get to secure proper birth control for Taylor, meet my grandchildren, or sit astride Viggo Mortensen in an abandoned grain elevator.

"This reminds me of *The Crucible*," I say as we dangle. "Don't you think? We're being punished for not knowing our place. I'm Winona Ryder and you're Joan Allen. She was the judgmental one," I add unnecessarily.

"Raquel."

"Yeah?" My abs are really hurting now, and I don't think I can hold myself in the air much longer.

"You have to tell me something."

I turn to look at Laurie, inadvertently working my right oblique, which issues a loud shriek in protest. "What?"

"Did you ever sleep with Ren?"

In the distance, sirens pierce the air. From this unique position, I am able to see that a chunk of vomit is clinging to my shoulder harness. Damn.

"Raquel! Did you? Please, I have to...I just need to know." Laurie, a begging novice, sounds eloquent and human, good at it just as she is everything else.

"Uh..." I swipe at the vomit. It smears.

"Quel, we could die here. I can deal with it if it happened, if you and Ren were together that way. I've *been* working on it. I know it was a long time ago. But I just need to know the truth. I think it would be better for all of us. I'm sure—my therapist is sure—that we'll all feel better afterward. Just tell me what happened, okay?"

It would be simple if I could just say yes. Part of me wants to say yes (yeah, that part). The truth is substantially more embarrassing. The truth—honest to God—is that I don't know if I slept with my brother-in-law. Officially. Perhaps he doesn't, either. Maybe that's why, as we dangle from a bridge, Laurie is asking me instead of tying Ren to a chair at home and threatening his elegant surgeon's hands with a claw hammer.

But let's start at the beginning.

Set the scene. College. Southern California. Early eighties.

The summer of 1982 is giving in to the approaching fall, crisp green leaves slowly crinkling into papery oranges and reds. Like most college campuses, U.C. Santa Barbara pales into an off-season version of itself during summer session, students sprinkling the vast lawns and cavernous lecture halls like ghosts.

Rachel Schultz is nineteen years old. She is taking two classes, Physiology 10 and Rhetoric 1B, both to satisfy general education requirements. Although she has found a social niche with a ragtag group of friends from the dorm (Sue) and class (tattooed, bodacious Tawny Schuessler, who later marries an astonishing series of four minor rock stars), Rachel doesn't want her college experience to spill toward the now standard five years. She has a feeling her life won't begin in earnest until she is living in the city on her own, sculpting. She has a feeling of her life being on hold. Also, the job she planned on at a gallery in San Francisco fell through, and she couldn't imagine herself spending the summer at home in Santa Clara, being dragged around to high school senior Laurie's preseason cheerleading practice or track meets, arguing with Ma about whether frozen yogurt was or wasn't fattening, helping Dad mow the lawn down to pristine lushness. So she enrolled in summer school. And got a cashier gig at the Meat Shanty, where she had to sling burgers only when both Octavio and Martin, the cooks, had the night off.

Then there's the guy.

Loren. That's his name: Loren.

Even though they've never spoken—okay, not exactly true; there was that time he muttered "excuse me" to her in the bustling thicket of students leaving class, his voice sending a shot of lustful terror up her spine—she knows his name because their TA, a waifish yet tyrannical postdoc out of NYU, insists on taking roll every section. By July the guy's name rolls off her tongue like a honey lozenge: Loren. Loren White. White, Loren. L. White. Mr. Loren White. Lor-en-zo the White.

Of course he is beautiful, Loren White. Rachel, with her extensive study of beautiful men based on thousands of hours watching romantic films and reading novels by Kathleen Woodiwiss and Shirlee Busbee, has dissected the source of his beauty. It is important to her, this task, because she doesn't want to be the type of girl who falls in love with surface splendor, much as she appreciates it in her work. So she watches Loren White, catalogs the way he makes deep, prolonged, respectful eye contact with everyone, even the shrill Andrea Dworkin–quoting girl who buries her unhappiness under a veneer of bisexuality and the grumpy engineer with the textbook pustule-pocked cheeks and surprisingly fluid prose. Rachel notes the almost affectionate manner he employs with their bitter hag of a TA, how, by the end of the session, the scrawny nutcase is eating out of his hand. Part of his appeal, she believes, maybe the most important part, is his reluctant inaccessibility. It's as if he wants to be open, believes passionately in the ideal of openness, but ultimately can't breach the boundaries of social entitlement that restrain him. Because what Loren White and everybody who meets him knows is that his gifts—physical, social, familial, financial—drive a wedge between himself and others just as surely as if he spoke ancient Greek instead of English. The fact that Loren White is tall—he

*dwarfs Rachel by at least two inches—handsome in an archi-
tected, pedigreed way, earnest, popular, athletic, and premed
doesn't detract in any way from his essential complexity, she
thinks. The fact that a girlfriend has not presented herself—
some tanned, willowy blonde or aristocratically pale redhead
in sexy sorority sweats with a brand name printed on the but-
tocks—only adds to Rachel's case. Perhaps he is saving himself
for someone more . . . singular?*

*Their first encounter is so magically perfect that Rachel
cries afterward, convinced the gods have finally awakened
from their long sleep and smiled on her.*

*Encounter 1: They are assigned partners for a paper to
be crafted and defended in teams. Rachel's partner—a thin,
jumpy Beverly Hills product whose name Rachel remembers
until at least the mid-nineties due to her role in the ensuing
good fortune—excuses herself from class one brilliantly sunny
day to pee and never returns. Loren's partner, the grumpy
engineer, receives a late acceptance to Berkeley, where he has
been wait-listed for a year, and departs to find housing in a
habitat more suited to his obsessive personality, accepting an
incomplete in the course. With a dreary wave, the TA—who,
they are later to discover, has been stalking the course's professor, a married Cuban rumored to have been with Che in
Bolivia in 1967—sanctions their union. Rachel and Loren
exchange hellos for the first time on August 16, 1982.*

*Encounter 2: Rachel and Loren agree to meet after her
shift at the Meat Shanty. The pimple that was threatening to
erupt on Rachel's nose miraculously recedes, leaving behind
just the barest residue of pink, which she conceals easily
under a layer of Sue's makeup. The extra shirt she brings
with her, a not-trying-too-hard boatnecked sky-blue tee with
strategic tears across the abdomen, is deemed "muy sexy" by
Martin, who, if his own heavily notched track record with the*

opposite sex is any indication, can be trusted to judge a book's cover.

Encounter 3: After dispensing with the business of the paper—whose topic, the case for legalization of marijuana, is to remain close to Rachel's heart in the years to come—Rachel and Loren segue seamlessly into a discussion of Soul Asylum, who they agree is the most underrated band of the era, quite possibly the decade. Expecting some degree of verbal paralysis in the face of such stunning yet sensitive maleness, Rachel is surprised to find that not only do words flow out of her in his presence with the sleek levity of liberated helium balloons, they are—fated miracle!—the right words. Later, when she replays their conversation in her mind, instead of the crushing regret she usually registers after an encounter with a desirable male person, she experiences only a tingly sense of pleasure. See how right they are together, how seamless? How their thoughts slide into one another like keys in a lock?

"What kind of medicine are you going to practice?" she asks him.

They are sitting six inches from each other at Mesa Beach, on a Tahitian blanket. It is their fourth study session. Rachel wants to call it a date—don't the flask of Captain Morgan and the presence of the fat, sensual strawberries warrant it?—but allows herself only occasional forays into that particular fantasy.

Loren nips from the flask. With his gleaming yet untamed forelock and tatty lacrosse jersey, Rachel is reminded—thrillingly—of the delicious Finny from A Separate Peace. *Loren is that beautiful. So what if Rachel cannot match his careless elegance? The clash of them, of distilled beauty against graceless need, is what will enflame his patrician senses.*

Loren takes a moment to let the profundity of his mission sink in before he speaks. "Tropical diseases, maybe. Biostatistics or epidemiology. Did you know that diarrheal diseases have killed more people in sub-Saharan Africa in the last ten years than all war casualties since World War Two? It's a disgrace."

The idea—not the diarrhea but the intended eradication of it—sounds ripe and sexy. Rachel closes her eyes briefly. She is not sure what the African climate will do to her skin, but she is fairly confident that Loren—witty, generous, incandescent Loren—will write her a prescription. She has already read Out of Africa. *Several years later, she will rent the video, watching in a disbelieving swoon as Robert Redford tenderly rinses the soap from Meryl Streep's hair; she is conjuring Loren's hands twined in her own thick brunette locks.*

"Rachel." He says her name with reverence, as if he has been practicing it in the shower. In the intervening seconds, he has moved closer, is looming over her. Loren's eyes, she realizes, are an unpredictable hazel, rimmed in amber, green where one would have forecast blue. His nose is so aquiline and fine, it has to be real. She hopes her slightly nobler version does not injure it in the forthcoming tussle.

They kiss deeply, tongues sliding against teeth, fingers exploring the hot dampness of cleft and crevice. He tastes better than anyone—anything—I have ever tasted, *Rachel finds time to marvel.*

The young lovers roll around on the blanket until the sun abandons them, cooling the horizon with its departing emerald glow. Rachel feels herself grow raw, punch-drunk, with glad yearning. This is it, *she thinks as she stands in the warm breeze, letting sand granules fall like sugar from her damp body while Loren folds the blanket.* I am finally going to fall in love. I am finally going to be fucked senseless. This is my last night as a callow virgin from the suburbs.

Skip ahead two and a half months. School drifts gently by, riding the trough between midterms and finals. Loren has spent the night at Rachel's twice. By some unspoken alchemy, they do not have intercourse. Rachel is frustrated but relieved: She does not want her first time to take place within earshot of her roommates. She does not want witnesses to what she is sure is going to be an explosive mating of mammoth passions. The specialness of it, the rarity, demands restraint. So they simply turn out the lights and spoon, exploring each other in the benevolent glow of the candlelight, leaving their imminent consummation hanging like a bulging Christmas stocking.

"Thad's going home next weekend," Loren says, running his hand across Rachel's forgiving but not too fleshy belly. No roommate means he'll have the pillbox, beachfront one-bedroom to himself. He hooks his fingers under her white cotton bikini underwear, a style Raquel likes to think he imagines her in for years to come.

Rachel presses herself against him, relishing the cocked-gun sensation of him. She does not respond; her answer is the involuntary parting of her legs beneath his hand.

The day in question unfolds unremarkably except, perhaps, for the pulsing glow that envelops Rachel like mist at the bottom of a waterfall. She is vaguely aware of being suddenly, happily more visible *than she has ever been, of men's eyes following the sweet curve of her legs as she skips across the street to buy wine for the evening's dinner, which Loren is preparing in the small but renovated beachside apartment.*

A few facts: The $4.99 bottle of cabernet is drunk. Dinner, however, remains untouched, the mossy aroma of mushroom risotto saturating the drapes so deeply that Loren's roommate Thaddeus Park eventually has to take them down and have them professionally steamed.

"I'm here!" Rachel calls as she lets herself in. For her deflowering, she has modeled herself after Sophia Loren in Two

Women, *all tawny cleavage and thinly smocked abundance awaiting ravishment.*

Here's where things get fuzzy.

Ren must have entered the living room from the kitchen at that point. How else could we have migrated to the bedroom so seamlessly? In the years since that fateful encounter, I have repeatedly gone over the minutes that followed my arrival in my mind, worried them into vacant smoothness, so that I am no longer sure what is real and what is the product of bitter disenchantment. I know we never started our meal. That Ren, correctly forecasting delays in consumption, turned off the oven, I am sure. It is likely we did not exchange a word before Ren stripped off my flowing, cinch-waisted, forties-style dress, the miniature print daisies piling up like dirt on snow. I don't remember if we pulled the covers back or lay down on top of them. Were the upstairs neighbors playing the headachey narco-rock they favored, or were they mercifully out? I can't recall. Where the condom came from is a mystery.

If I close my eyes now, peel back the layers of time and disappointment and peer at Rachel and Loren's first—only—attempt at sex with as much cool detachment as I can muster, I see this: a fumbling hand, shaking as it draws the rubber column down over the reddening shaft of penis (it sticks up higher than Rachel expected, pointing toward the sky as if it were attached upside down). I see a grim stream of yellow light seeping under the door to the bathroom, mingling with the weak glow of streetlamp that slices the venetian blinds. I see Rachel hurrying Loren into bed so that she can conceal herself under his comeliness. I see male shoulders silhouetted against the night, arching over the cradle of a young girl's hips. I see two bodies trying to join, banging against each other futilely while a teakettle screams next door. I see the man's body coming down to rest against the woman's, rigid with thwarted effort. I see the girl turning away as tears snake through her moisturizer, scenting the pillow with the stench of dead flowers. I see them disentangle their bodies and get dressed, maybe already, at that early stage of angst, gravitating toward tertiary existences. I see glasses filled with wine and a young woman walking home on legs not nearly wobbly enough for peace.

Did my brother-in-law's penis pierce my body that night? I don't think so, but I can't be sure. The Gothic taint of virgin's blood I'd expected did not appear, nor did the triumphant soreness chronicled in doctors' pamphlets and romance novels.

Did our incomplete coupling qualify as sex? I don't know. Maybe that makes me a fool, or a denier, or just plain ridiculous, but something makes me unable to apply the label, to boil the ingredients of that night into digestible broth for easy consumption. Also possible: Although I have never completely recovered from the loss of Ren, it is still easier to think I never officially slept with my sister's husband.

"Did you?" Laurie's face is purpling. It seems right somehow that this conversation should take place upside down.

Memory offers no clues. I decide on the answer that matches my current level of culpability. "Yes," I say, the word skipping across the water and plunging like a stone.

CHAPTER 19

You Haven't Changed a Bit

"You've got to be fucking kidding me," Phil says.

How did my life come to this? Yesterday, as per my personal Time Line to Truth, I was explaining the concept of remission to the kids under a fragrant canopy of Nestlé Toll House. Today I find myself defending my moral fiber to my cheating husband before a gaggle of feather-haired, corduroy-flare-clad, Kenny Loggins clones who seem to have been airlifted directly out of 1982. Plus, I have a date, and he's...well, not Phil. Let me be clear: I have a date and *He. Is. Not. Phil.* It is confusing; the girl who was voted Most Likely to Be Mistaken for a Football Player in a Nun's Habit should not be attending her high school reunion with a surf god.

"Give us a minute?" Phil says directly to Duke in his sternest teacher's voice.

"Sure, dude. Whatever." Duke ambles over to the buffet table and is promptly set upon by Misty Hughes, who seems to have kept up with her tenth-grade habits of stealing other people's boyfriends and wearing multitiered teal miniskirts.

Phil looks at me. "Nice, Raquel. Real classy. Did you have to drive, or does he have his learner's permit?"

Ouch.

The thing is, Phil has a point. One I (theoretically) agree with. Bringing your daughter's surfing instructor to your high school reunion? Tacky. Perhaps even a little desperate. Clearly a transparent grab for undeserved attention. Verdict? Downright embarrassing. In my defense, I'd had no intention of bringing Duke Dunne; Sue was my date. But Sue—wimp! flake!—came down with food poisoning, and Duke materialized just as he'd threatened and...let's say the offer was hard to refuse.

The scene played out something like this: Fortysomething woman prepares for twenty-fifth-year high school reunion. Discarded garments litter room, which has started to resemble post-Katrina New Orleans. Medicinal highball teeters on top of serum jar promising to "radically reduce the ruinous ravages of photoradiation." Right. Phone jangles. Woman in question hops toward bed, legs pinned by neck-to-toe body stocking. Plumbs pile. Collapses on pile. Finds phone. Listens with incredulity as best friend relays tale of bad potato salad and gastric misery.

"I can't go alone!" Fortysomething wails. "Everyone will think I'm separated!"

"You *are* separated." Best Friend has annoying habit of sticking to facts.

"Who will I make fun of people with?" Almost a bleat.

Best Friend pauses. "Your mother?"

Before Fortysomething can inveigh against the infinite cruelty of such a suggestion, doorbell rings. Fortysomething tells Best Friend to wait and executes lurching crab scuttle toward sound. Realization settles on Fortysomething that perhaps she should have bought recommended girdle size for weight range, instead of more respectable letter two, okay, three letters lower on alphabetical scale.

Opens door. Absorbs shaggy hair, edible complexion, aquamarine eyes, carved biceps, ragged daypack, impish grin.

"Yes?" Uses door to shield Lycra-sheathed body, which
bears unnerving resemblance to uncooked bockwurst.

"Raquel? Hey!"

Edible launches self at Fortysomething. Bear hug. Awkward
nose bump. Illegal placement of hand on rump. Fortysomething recovers enough to tell Best Friend she'll call her back
and don bathrobe while Edible blithely visits guest toilet.

"Did I miss something, or did you just show up here out of
the blue?" Fortysomething demands upon Edible's return. She
knows she is supposed to sound furious. She finds it hard not
to stare. That ice-cut dip where his waist joins his pelvis...is
it possible that he modified it surgically somehow, to get it to
look like that? Iliac crest—the words float into her mind with
the annihilating gentleness of an anthrax spore alighting on
virgin lung tissue.

Iliac crest.

"Plan change. No bookings this week." The aquamarine
eyes clear-cut a swath down the front of the frumpy robe.
Guiltless smile. Hands cross over unyielding chest in supplication. "I know. My bad."

And this, my friends, is how I reunited with the Class of
1980 on the arm of Duke Dunne instead of Sue Banicek, Phil
Rose, or a down-market male escort with a chest wax and a
signed photo of Ricky Martin at his bedside.

Now: I straighten my spine and give Phil the oh-how-you-
slay-me eyeball. "Duke's just a friend. It's not like we're dating or anything." I pause to enjoy the minute crumpling of
Phil's snarky smile, which begins at the word "friend" and
culminates at the word "dating." "We're married, remember?
We don't date other people." I snap my fingers, which, after
three Screaming Orgasms—apparently the leading alcoholic

beverage circa 1980—is relatively challenging. "Oh yeah. You forgot that one, not me."

Before Phil can respond, the band segues from its rousing cover of Billy Joel's "It's Still Rock and Roll to Me" into an almost painfully reverent rendition of "Biggest Part of Me." That this conversation should take place at the exact moment when David Pack is wailing about the part of himself that is, well, the biggest, is nothing less than I deserve, given my own moral transgressions of the past year.

"What are you doing here, anyway?" I snatch a glass of something frothy from a passing tray and gulp at it.

Phil tugs at the hem of his sweater, a design that would have been passably stylish if not rendered in the same brown worn by San Francisco bus drivers. "The kids," he says without elaborating.

"The kids?" The idea of his students—products of trust-fund perpetuation, all—coming together to save our dodgy marriage is not only disturbing, it's embarrassing.

Oh.

In a flash, I realize that Taylor and Micah have, with Phil's lukewarm acquiescence, engineered this meeting. Our family script has been turned on its head, with me playing the hormone-addled wayward female and Phil taking on the meaty role of wronged husband while our children star as maternal nurturance and paternal discipline, respectively.

"They told you to come here?" Out of the corner of my eye, I see Duke and several of my high school peers flinging back tequila shots. Misty has moved in for the kill, her eggplant mascara fluttering thickly in the ballroom glow like fresh roadkill under a streetlamp.

Phil emits a short stress-relieving burp and pats his tummy. "They told me you'd be here. They said you were embarrassed to come alone and my showing up would make you realize I'm serious about getting back together." My husband glances at Duke, who appears to be slurping another shot, this time out of—oh no, say it isn't so—Misty's belly button. "You do look sort of embarrassed, Quel," he says with a smile so evil, I actually take a step back.

"Attention! Hey, everybody! Hey! *Quiet!*" Class president, field hockey captain, and Desert Storm veteran Carolyn Tibbetts has commandeered the onstage microphone. I swear to God, the bitch looks exactly the same as she did in high school: smooth skin, ramrod posture, swingy hair.

War as anti-aging weapon?

"Thank you all for coming. It's great to see so many familiar faces out there, and so many spouses and, um, partners as well." Everybody titters and stares at Jeremy Bench and his equally buff, well-preserved boyfriend. Even though there were half a dozen out-of-the-closet gays and lesbians in my liberal Bay Area high school class, none of them was the captain of the water polo and baseball teams and master blowjob technician Christie Mueller's steady (a fact that seems less inexplicable now).

"Before we move on to the raffle, there's the little matter of homecoming king and queen, kids. So, we've tallied the votes..."

I tune out Carolyn Tibbetts's bossy contralto and try to focus on my husband, who skulks in an ambiguous position between me and a knot of unfamiliar long-haired women in prairie skirts who may or may not be the first documented Bay Area Mennonites. Part of me wants Phil to go away so I can maintain the illusion that I, like Duke, am still clinging to the clammy residue of high school. The other part wants Phil to take me home so we can catch the tail end of *Saturday Night Live* and finish the last of those brownie bites from Costco together.

"Rachel Schultz, where are you?" Carolyn shields her eyes and peers at the crowd. I feel the crowd of people thickening and pushing at me, clawing at my clothes in a way I'd expect if I were, say, Madonna but, as a normal citizen, only makes me anxious and potentially incontinent. "C'mon, Rach," someone behind me says. "Get up there, homecoming queen!" "She's so much thinner than in high school," I hear someone else whisper. "She probably had plastic surgery," a voice responds. "I read about it in *People*. All the celebs do." "She came with *both* her husbands," says somebody else. "More power to her," says another.

"Rachel Schultz!" Carolyn calls again. "Don't be shy. Come on down." Carolyn peers at the card again. "And the 1980, twenty-five-year class reunion homecoming king is Jeremy Bench!"

I stumble toward the stage in a daze. As I ascend, I am reminded of the scene in *Carrie* where the mean girls, not satisfied with pelting the poor girl with tampons, dump pigs' blood on Sissy Spacek as she accepts the homecoming-queen crown alongside the spiral-permed guy who played the Greatest American Hero. I don't *think* I was that unpopular in high school, but lack of proof or revenge-ready telepathic ability forces me to identify the nearest exit signs.

Carolyn, I see, has a false leg that is made up to look like a real nylon-clad foot and strut, complete with crimson toenails and bulbous field hockey–primed calves. She jams a rhinestone tiara on my head. I make eye contact with Phil, who manages to look proud, appalled, and amused at the same time. I realize with a jolt of intense wretchedness that, along with Sue, Phil is the one I would have liked to share the absurdity of this moment with. He's the only one who would appreciate, for instance, that extremely gone-to-seed 1980 homecoming king Troy Somethingorother is silently weeping behind a ficus plant, his throne having been usurped by a fag investment banker with a $2.3 million condo in the Castro.

Someone clasps my hand. It is Jeremy Bench. His tanned skin has a Marlboro Man patina. He wears a simple titanium wedding band on his left hand and smells clean and powerfully musky, as if he applied eau de goat's pituitary directly to his pulse points. I make a note to ask him about the anti-aging benefits of said.

"You look great, Rachel," he says, doing the Princess Diana wave at the crowd. "I saw your show at the Waxman gallery."

"Well, thanks." Does Duke have to stand so close to Phil, or—gawd—slap him on the back like that?

"How are you doing?" Hushed, awed, "I am blissfully cancer free and you're not" voice.

"Good, actually. I'm in remission." *Liar, liar…hey, what happened to Phil's spare tire?* My (sort of) husband is looking strangely svelte, I realize. Or perhaps it's the onstage angle?

Jeremy raises my hand in mock triumph and grins. "Revenge of the nerds," he murmurs.

"Chinese? Thai? Falafel?" I flip through the envelope of take-out menus that has, as of late, come to comprise our four squares.

"Whatever." Taylor flicks *America's Next Top Model* up another notch so that we can all enjoy Tyra verbally bludgeoning the slightly cross-eyed girl from Wichita.

Micah glances up from his calculus text. "Let's have burritos. I'll pick them up as soon as I finish this."

Taylor ups the volume again. Tyra's gingery weave swirls around her head, which seems to float three feet above everybody else's. Having dipped my toes into the tantalizing pool of televised celebrity, I think it is entirely possible she spends the entire show standing on a box, or the bit players have conceded to having their feet lopped off to enhance her superior image.

Cynicism, the new black.

"Tay, can you turn that down a bit?" I dump Crystal Light into the pitcher.

The volume shoots upward.

"Taylor! What are you doing?"

"Nothing."

I go to the TV and manually lower the volume. My head is splitting, and I still have to design the fund-raiser mailing I promised Kendall, the BC support-group leader. Taylor has been simmering ever since I got home from the reunion last night. Instead of speculating as to the reason(s), I buried myself in household minutiae, hoping her resentment had nothing to do with me and was just garden-variety teen angst.

My daughter tears her gaze away from the TV. "You aren't even trying to work things out with Dad! Why don't you just get a divorce and, like, go have a midlife crisis at Club Med or something?"

So, not the garden variety. Clearly, Taylor's interpretation of remission hews quite closely to meaning number three in my dictionary: "a release from debt, penalty, or obligation." From treating me civilly, I mean.

"Does this have something to do with the reunion?" I say.

"Dad *wants* to make things right. It's *you* who won't listen to *him*!"

"Tay, not to condescend, but there's a little more at stake here than simply *making things right*. Not to mention that this is between me and him." I stir the remaining packet of sugar and chemicals carefully into the water. The crystals sparkle. I seem to recall someone at the last BC support group warning us off artificial red #7. The thing is, how would you even know it's in there? Wouldn't they call it something else, something more wholesome-sounding, so you wouldn't sip it and think, *Cancer*?

Taylor slaps her hand against her leg in frustration. "Why are you *doing* this to us?" she cries.

Micah shakes his head, picks up the car keys, and heads outside. So much for backup.

Taylor continues, "I just want to say, screwing a guy half your age is, like, totally pathetic."

"That's enough," I say sharply. *How does she know I'm considering, uh, screwing anybody? For that matter, how does she know Duke is even in this hemisphere?*

Mindful of my face's usual transparency, I try to radiate indignance and also celibacy. Think: Outraged Bride of God.

"When you talk like that, Tay, you only degrade yourself," I murmur. The nuns would be proud.

"What a bunch of crap," Taylor says. Then, with satisfaction, "Chloe Hughes's mom told her you brought a"—nose wrinkling in disgust—"*date* to the reunion! And he was, like, *nineteen*. And he did shots! And you danced with him right in front of Dad! Chloe said you looked like Big Bird doing the chicken dance!"

It is one thing to be outed as a dater of (young) men. It's yet another to be labeled a bad dancer. This hurts. Damn Misty Hughes and her evil spawn. Damn them.

I try to cover Taylor's hand. "Tay, I know you're worried about me and Dad. And me being sick. I think that's what's really pushing your buttons. The thing is, everything's going to be okay. I've gotten through the worst of the treatment, and I'm doing great and—"

Taylor cuts me off with a great jeer of a guffaw. "Is *that* what you think? For God's sake, Mom, stop *using* it as an excuse. You've been, I don't know, *crazy* ever since you got sick. Your clothes. Your friends. Your job. The things you say to the other moms. Going on dates. Flirting with our friends. It's embarrassing. It's humiliating. It's *immature*."

I feel my eyelids prickle with shocked tears. Is it true? Is it possible that what feels to me like being *alive* is just a youth fantasy with a pitiable ending? Is it possible that, all this while, I've justified my fabrications as part of pursuing my true self, as being for a good cause—money—when, in fact, there's just a pouffy-haired sad sack waiting at the end, arguing homecoming-dance themes at PTA meetings in pilled sweatpants?

"I...I'm sorry if I've embarrassed you in any way, Tay. I didn't mean to—"

"Dad's *lonely,* Mom. He eats, like, Hungry-Man dinners! The kind with the gooey pink dessert in the corner!"

"Maybe I could get him some of those veggie lasagnas at Trader Joe's."

We stare at each other, my daughter and I, Taylor's dismay lapping at me like dirty water. Then her face goes studiously blank, she picks up the remote, and Tyra's latest tirade fills the room.

CHAPTER 20

Southern Exposure

I awaken, take inventory of the body next to me, roll over, and stare out the window of the hotel, trying to discern if the San Francisco skyline has changed since I had sex with a man who isn't Phil.

Nope: There is the Transamerica Pyramid, the gleaming arch of the Bay Bridge, the humorless facade of the Bank of America building, the checkerboard sweep of hooker hotels and shoe stores and Chinese pagodas and overpriced condos that is downtown.

Somehow, in the harshness of day, I expected everything to be different. Not just me or, more accurately, the feverish nugget of sex-stoked mojo glowing inside me, but the sheets and pillows, the office buildings and sidewinder streets, the cable cars and taxis, the cloud-flecked sky. The idea that everything continues on, blissfully impervious to the fact that I, Raquel Rose, have just been ravished by a twenty-six-year-old surfer twenty-eight days into my trial separation, is more comforting than not.

I glance back at the bed, a perfectly innocuous Grand Hyatt jobbie, in its undisheveled state a model of crisp, starched whiteness. (Its undisheveled state being nine hours and five penetrations ago.)

"Quel, babe, get over here." Duke is scratching his chest absently with one hand. The other hand is busy stroking his—okay, I'll just say it—dick, which is pleasantly short and thick, the Bilbo Baggins of penises.

Duke Dunne is gorgeous. And energetic. And sweet. He is also somewhat prosaic and quite possibly dyslexic, but who am I to judge?

I return to his side of the bed and lie down next to him. I am about 35 percent less embarrassed than I thought I would be, facing my juvenile ravisher in the light of day without makeup, clothing, or *New Yorker* subscription as protection.

"Suck me," he says without a touch of petulance.

I automatically try on reasons not to, as I've done with Phil for fifteen of the past nineteen years. Then a small worm of an idea squirms its way into my head: *Why not?*

Indeed.

Nine hours ago, I asked myself the same question. Nine hours ago, I found myself slurping down oysters and Laporte Sancerre with calculated abandon at Hog Island, a charming seaside bar stuck, barnacle-like, on the back of San Francisco's Ferry Building. Lights from barges churning toward the port of Oakland studded the black waters of the bay, merging with the rope of traffic that burned a swath across the Bay Bridge. Conversation tangoed with the dulcet tones of stereophonic jazz. The scene oozed romance; I thought I might vomit into the oyster bucket.

"Do you like beurre blanc?" Duke pronounced it "bear blank."

"I'm not sure. Is that food?"

Duke smiled in that boyish, unself-conscious way that said, *I can charm the pants off a Brazilian supermodel; why should I care if my French is crappy?*

"Raquel," he said.

"Hmm?" I busied myself with the menu. *Perhaps the barbecued—*

"Stop."

"What?"

"Stop being a bitch. If you don't want to be with me, just say so. I'll be disappointed, I'll admit it. But I can handle it. I'm a big boy."

Embarrassing.

Duke leaned over and slowly, sexily plucked my white-knuckled fingers one by one off my clutch, which was lying, fondled into suppleness, on my lap. He pressed his palm against mine and twined our fingers together.

"Estás hermosa, Raquelita."

"Thank you." Since my Spanish ran to restaurant menus and Shakira choruses, I had no idea what he'd said, but it sounded admiring and vaguely horny. His other hand grazed my thigh. Not the tame, clichéd lower part. The part that attaches to the body, known among underwear manufacturers, I believe, as "crotch."

Lust, muggy and gelatinous, stormed my nether regions.

You know those moments in life when you see your options spread out starkly, almost topographically? When you feel the weight of your future resting in the balance of spliced time, daring you to make the wrong choice? That was one of those moments. Nine hours ago, here's what I was thinking: Take the dark path and consign yourself to a life of empty sex, of extramarital clutches in murky bars, of leopard-print miniskirts and shar-pei knees spread against indifferent hands. Take the darker path, and say hello to thirty or forty years of married spinsterhood, to a raft of daily motions so featureless, so sexless, that the face of the microwave starts to resemble a grimace. Say hello to the well-thumbed love scene on page 172 of...whatever, because that's the hottest heat you're ever going to feel. Again.

I didn't want to let my kids down. Or my husband (really!). Or my mother. But most of all, I didn't want to suffer the cold vacancy of fate's fingers slipping through mine. I wanted to be warm again. I wanted to be excited. I wanted to excite someone. I wanted to be *alive*.

Here's the kicker I'm not so proud of: I thought, in that moment, *Who has to know but me?*

It may not be an admirable incentive, but it is an age-old one. And that, my friends, is how I ended up laying a thicket of bills on the table, wrapping myself in Sue's pashmina, and floating the ten or so blocks to the Grand Hyatt in a cloud of apprehension, precipitate guilt, and...that other thing.

Back to present.

Duke Dunne is tumescently awaiting my response, which is—boy, am I getting predictable—*Why not?*

We writhe around on the starchy bed, Duke muttering some mild obscenities. It is all unexpectedly and ambivalently validating—sort of like being named employee of the month at Taco Bell. Even the menu is somewhat Taco Bellish (neither tasty nor repugnant, basically just salty and a teeny bit rancid, like a tortilla chip with a smear of guacamole that has turned).

I know women of a certain age and generation—myself included—are not supposed to find being treated like a porn queen by a near-stranger beneficial to the self-esteem, but dammit, it so is!

Duke withdraws, and I gratefully gulp air and await his next move. It is amazing how easy it is to have sex with other people again once you've crossed the threshold into sin. There is very little guilt and a shockingly low weird factor.

That I am able to view the joining of our bodies with a modicum of detachment is, quite frankly, a huge relief and a significant achievement: Finally, after all those years of failing to meaningfully connect with my spiritual life partner, it is no longer intimacy I crave, but a good old-fashioned screw. It feels almost as if my body has a mind of its own, following the biological imperative toward callow virility like a bee buzzing frantically toward nectar.

Duke turns me over, and I wonder briefly if I should have gotten one of those back facials. Not that I'm broken out or anything, but how much better it would have been to blind him with the dewy glow of my flawless shoulders, rather than the mind-boggling dairy-cow breadth of my hips.

"Oh my God," I breathe as Duke pushes himself inside me from behind. His thrusts are very athletic and rhythmic. Not like Phil's, which, though thankfully not rabbity, tend toward the leisurely and irregular. It's heart-attack paranoia, of course. My personal theory is that men in their forties fear heart attack so ardently they actually view sex as a drain on their mortal resources and the loss of their seed as a bad investment.

Duke smushes my face down into the pillows and speeds up. His self-interest alone is enough to catapult me toward orgasm; the coarseness of his assault licks at my exhilaration like flame.

If sex with Duke Dunne has taught me anything, it's that the deliberate, reverent, tortuous thrumming of the clitoris, so widely employed it must be handed down from father to son like a Willie Mays–inscribed baseball, is a waste of valuable finger strength at best and a travesty of amorous misunderstanding at worst. The truth is, there is not a man alive who does it better than women can do it themselves. Let me clarify: *not one!*

I experience a fleeting urge to call my mother and crow—"Ma, you didn't burn your bra for nothing! I'm fucking a twenty-six-year-old, and it's dope!"—before blank, lovely pleasure explodes out of my pelvis and out into the slightly antiseptic-smelling room.

Duke arches and quivers against me. We are so sweaty his hand slips when he braces it on my back, and he bashes his face against my shoulder blade.

"Are you okay?" I ask. Ever the mom.

"Yeah." Pause. "Are you?"

I ignore him. Why inflate his already healthy self-esteem further by telling him I may require imminent hospitalization for ovary displacement?

"Let's order room service," I say instead.

Like a couple of kids, we page through the book of goodies. Protein and carbs, that's what we need. Replenishment. Visions of fluffy banana-almond pancakes and cheese platters and tangy Caesar salads and pan-fried steaks and…

"I'm dying for some bacon." I bounce a little, feeling quite glad, almost happy. The mattress is very springy, and I don't even have to wash the sheets myself. "Do you have any of that pot left, by any chance?" I ask him.

My house is quiet. So quiet, I feel like I'm at church—I mean synagogue—and I'm most definitely a sinner. I drift through the empty rooms, imagining that I'm a real estate agent assessing the house following the untimely demise of its inhabitants. "Such a shame," I might say. "They were so young. And so attractive! They had everything to—Hey, is that a plasma flatscreen? Is it built in?"

I am not supposed to be here. That's why I had to come home. If I were being honest with myself, I suppose I'd say that something in me, some derelict kernel of wanting, knew this was going to happen. Knew Duke Dunne—or *a* Duke Dunne—was going to stumble his way into the vacuum of my need like a shining inbred stallion, kicking his heels and shaking his silky, comely, brainless mane in my face.

You just want to be home after something like this happens. You know the feeling: Break up with husband, lurk around in robe conjuring visions of women-only book clubs and geriatric singles junkets to Reno, choke down handfuls of antidepressants, sleep with nubile surf god, flee home in terror of own audacity and likelihood of contracting crusty venereal malady, curl up in own bed with nutritionally deficient foodstuff, watch cable ringed by crumbs. You want to surround yourself with the familiar so you can identify exactly what's changed in the aftermath of your Shocking Exploit, skewer it on a pushpin and probe it, searching for tender spots.

I'd told the kids I was spending a spa weekend with Sue, which they'd taken as an opportunity to disappear into the froth of their social lives, Taylor to Lindsay's and Micah to Ronnie's. Phil was not a problem. I'd stopped reporting my whereabouts to The Cheater, oh, around the time he was grappling with Tate Trimble under Ross the Boss's Miró.

I enter Taylor's room, a pretty study in sage and peach plastered with tawdry keepsakes and adulatory images of weak-chinned rock stars. The light in her walk-in closet is on, so I turn it off and fling a few stray shirts and undies into the hamper. I wonder if Biter has been replaced yet. Something about the pink hard-candy scent of my daughter's room makes me think so—or maybe it's just my own tuned-up sexual antennae—and I resolve to ask her about it point-blank and make an appointment for her with my ob-gyn.

I walk down the hallway. Willard the dog is sitting outside

Micah's room, his top-heavy basset body pressed up against the door.

"Hey, guy," I say. I cannot remember if the dog has finished his course of antibiotics, but nothing looks like it's in imminent danger of turning putrid or falling off, so I push by him and go inside.

They are in bed.

The bodies are a study in ivory and peach. Limbs tangle around one another like the branches of saplings, pliant and lithe as only young flesh can be. I simply stand and stare, cognizant only of the extreme beauty of naked youth, of the ardor rising up from them like steam off a racehorse on a frigid day. Then shame washes through me; I am a trespasser, a violator, an uninvited witness to the most private proclamation of love. I have to leave. Now.

My presence might never have been noticed. But as I back through the doorway of my son's bedroom, a soccer cleat springs from nowhere, and I stumble backward over it with a soft, clichéd "oomph."

The bodies still. Faces rise up above the nest of sheets, mouths perfect moues of shock, eyebrows arching bold over strong noses. *Oh God, it can't be—*

"Mom?"

I scurry out, crablike, my mind snatching at thoughts, tossing them aside. The sliding glass door is still open, my favorite chaise spread open against the sun. I hurtle toward it.

"Mom?" My son's voice follows me down the hallway, shades of the demanding baby he used to be. *I can't. I can't because if I do, I'll freak out, and if I freak out, I'll fail him, and if I fail him, I'm lost, lost, lost.*

I slip through the doors into the backyard and—

"Mom!"

Micah is naked save a robe he's holding around his waist.

My son is less hirsute than Phil, his torso carved with lithe muscle. Micah's beauty used to seem harmless, a stroke of mild, benevolent genetic fortune that bypassed me and Phil. Now it is lethal.

"Mom, *please,* hold on a minute, will you? Can't you just stop and *listen?*"

I drop into the chaise, careful to avoid the end that always flips. Micah glances back at the house, back where Ronnie Greenblatt, my son's best friend, is likely pulling on his pants and one of those ugly skater shirts he's always wearing. I fish around in my mind and find, to my surprise, that I want nothing more at this moment than to slap Ronnie very hard in the face.

"I'm sorry that happened, Mom," Micah says. He sounds unrepentant and icily, shockingly adult. I actually feel my heart rate ratchet up a notch, locking into high gear like a runaway train. Who is this person, this man with the body of a dryad and the gaze of a predator? Where is my son, my Micah, he of the dreamy blue eyes and soccer passion?

"Is this...Oh my God, did he seduce you?" This is not the question I want to ask. Why did it come out like that?

Micah's normally receptive face, suntanned and eager and blue-eyed, snaps shut. "Actually, I seduced *him,* if you want to put it that way." My son is enjoying this too much; he is angry with me for something that goes beyond today's discovery.

"I thought you were dating..." In a flash, I realize the extent of the feat that Micah has pulled off, weaving social fact and fiction together so snugly that even I, his mother, cannot be sure where his crushes begin and end. My son's girlfriends are legion, yet I cannot pinpoint a single paramour by name. "What do you want me to say?" I ask him.

"I don't know. Nothing, I guess. What's there to say? I'm a fucking fag. Get over it." Micah hitches up the towel and smiles. For the first time ever, my son's smile is cracked, afraid, grotesque.

"Why Ronnie?" The world has shifted, earthquake-jostled bits settling into new places. Micah gay I can deal with, I think. Sure, there is disappointment there, and fear. A lot of that. But also a trickle of understanding, of floating particles slotting into context, that provides relief: Taylor's comment about Micah's whereabouts the other day—how, how, *how* could my daughter have guessed (or known) and not I?—the gradual yet unmistakable reduction in Micah's willingness to confide, the niggling feeling that my son has been lying to me in small, fractious ways.

Micah's face reddens. "I don't know. It just happened, I guess. We...you know...love each other."

I am simultaneously horrified and proud. See how my son talks openly about his feelings like a sensitive, evolved male? See how I raised him to emote fully? See how, like a woman, he is going to get his heart filleted and broiled alive on a spit?

"You're just a kid. Love? Well, that's...well." With great force of will, I stop myself from expelling that old chestnut: *Love stinks.*

"Mom."

"I'm sorry. I just...I wish you had told me sooner, that's all. I could have helped you."

"With what? You think I don't know what love is because I'm seventeen? Or because I'm queer?"

"Don't say that!" *Why not, Raquel?*

"It's just a word, Mom."

"Look at it from my perspective, okay? I know your feelings are real, honey, but it's my job to protect you. I know this is going to sound harsh, but do you think this is a good idea?" My voice has risen, shrieking upward on a fulcrum of dismay.

"He knew it was going to be like this," Micah says furiously. "That's why we didn't tell anybody. I wanted to, but Ronnie says his parents will freak. I was, like, 'My mom won't—my mom's cool.'" His voice turns shrill as he mimics me. "'Do you think this is a good idea, honey?' It's not an idea, Mom, it's fucking reality! God, you think you're so evolved, jetting around San Francisco like some fucking artist-in-residence, palling around with your little queer society friends, but you don't have a fucking clue what it means to really accept someone, do you?"

Micah gets up off the other lounge chair and knots his robe tighter around his waist. Through the bulky strata of walls, windows, and bad feeling, we hear the unmistakable seal of a car door and the patrician rev of a sports-car engine. We both know it is Ronnie, sailing away from confrontation in his hand-me-down Miata. The emotion leaches out of Micah's face as if through a shower drain.

For a pause, Micah and I stare at each other, the moment etched in dismay. What constitutes best parenting practice for these things? Should I hug my pain-racked child before he wiggles away, or is that insulting? Am I supposed to call Phil sobbing and commiserate about the abrupt decrease in our statistical likelihood of becoming grandparents? Or do I invite Barb and Ron Senior over and play meet-the-inlaws?

"That's not what I meant," I whisper finally, but Micah has already gone.

Unlike your child's vaccination schedule, life does not calendar traumatic events in decently spaced intervals. She is inconsiderate that way.

I am shocked out of sleep shortly after midnight by the doorbell. Heart pounding while my pupils adjust to the smear of darkness, I wait for Phil to get up and do a recon with his trusty Louisville Slugger, only to realize a millisecond later that my husband is not here because I kicked him out. Instead of serving as resident male presence and protector of La Famiglia Rosa, my husband is tucked into bed at Extended Stay America, dozing off to the tail end of *Conan O'Brien*.

I am alone.

Reaching under Phil's side of the bed, I am gratified to feel my hand close around the baseball bat. Without turning on any lights—*Perhaps the sudden sight of my ravaged visage at the door will frighten away the rapist-intruder*—I creep toward the entryway. Stella and Willard, the two bassets, are nowhere to be seen. From day one, when Phil brought them home from the pet shop yowling in a ribboned box, there has been something worthless and louche about these dogs, a sense that, if forced to choose between saving our lives and downing a bowl of kiblets, they'd take the food and munch happily while home invaders cleave our brains and steal the Cuisinart.

I tiptoe down the hall, bat in hand. The threadbare rugby jersey and men's boxers I'm wearing provide scant protection against the probing of rapist penises. Unlike Ma, I have not barricaded myself under a belted jumpsuit and five layers of granny panties in my husband's absence. From this point on, I have only my wits and the Slugger as defenses.

"Aaaah!" I yell, heart hammering as my foot comes into contact with a warm, inert, now snarling body.

At the sound of my scream, Stella grunts and retreats toward the comfort of the kitchen, toenails clacking, where I hear her dig in to her food with gusto.

"Damn dog," I say, and open the door.

Sue and Sarafina stand there. In spite of a mild case of first-trimester bloat, my friend looks waifish and wan. A half-asleep

Sarafina leans against her, a Dora doll clutched in her hand, outgrown baby blanket trailing. Their midnight getaway has conferred on them an appearance of both frailty and homelessness. *The Breakup Diet: Wearing Pajamas Full-time and 100 Other Tried-and-True Ways to Look Thinner Now!*

"It's over," Sue says as she falls into my arms.

CHAPTER 21

You Can't Help
Whom You Love...
or Can You?

"He kept saying 'queer,'" I say to Laurie. "It's like he was trying to shock me. *Queer, queer, queer*"—my hand does a nervous jig around my face—"it *was* kind of shocking, actually."

My sister's finely arched, honey-toned brows are nearly levitating off her face. This is a sign of disapproval. I am fairly sure she is uncomfortable with my choice of venue—Caffè Museo—for this revelation. In fact, Caffè Museo, with its dainty wedges of organic frittata and messenger-bag-made-of-recycled-seat-belt-toting patrons, has probably been suburban-matron-screeching-"queer"-free until now.

Since I told her two weeks ago that I did indeed have carnal (if incomplete) knowledge of her husband, Laurie and I have entered into a Partial Relationship Embargo. The PRE is a handy mechanism that grants you the right to draw on familial resources in the event of a Serious Crisis, even if you are presently in a declared state of war with the other family member. Although what constitutes a Serious Crisis has yet to be clearly defined, there seems to be a general consensus that it could involve such catastrophes as TV-show cancellation, rapid unexplained weight gain, or spousal infidelity. Into this pot I would also throw gay awakenings. Walking in on your underage children in flagrante delicto? Definitely.

"I'm sure he's just venting his frustration," Laurie corrects me. "You were just a convenient target." Laurie pauses to accept a paper menu that a fan is handing her. Smiling brilliantly, as if there is nothing more enjoyable than penning her autograph during a conversation about my son's sexual adventures with his best friend, Laurie signs her name with a flourish and lets the woman grasp her hand reverently before turning back to me. "Have you talked to Micah more about this?"

"We talked," I say slowly, feeling disingenuous, a word I cannot pronounce but seems just right for what I am feeling at the moment.

"About?"

"Being . . . gay?" Is this the right answer?

"And?"

"You know what he told me? Last year, when he wrecked the car with Ronnie, it was because Micah came out to him and Ronnie was so freaked that he dropped his thirty-two-ounce Coke on the shifter and Mikey's hand slipped and that's when he crashed into the 7-Eleven." I wipe my eyes, which are burning. "He told me they were high, Laurie. Instead of telling me he was gay and his best friend couldn't deal with it, he let Phil and me believe he drove stoned. That made me incredibly sad. Are we that bad? Did we fail our son that badly?"

Laurie sips her Chardonnay. "Of course not. You have to put yourself in Micah's position. Everyone has an idea of him as a person, how he should be. The fact that it's somewhat—or largely—at odds with what he knows himself to be must be incredibly pressuring. I can't imagine what he's been going through. There is so much more at stake for him than just disappointing his parents. Coming out means potentially changing his whole world. I think you and Phil are open, nonjudgmental parents, I really do. I think whether Micah learns to trust you with this depends a lot on how you handle the next few conversations. Whatever you do, don't forbid him from seeing Ronnie. It'll backfire, and Micah will gravitate toward him even more. It might make him demonize you. I know he's still your child, but he's seventeen years old, not twelve or thirteen or even fifteen, and he probably feels like you're holding him back from his adult sexuality, even if you aren't. Remember how we felt right before college? Remember how *excruciating* it was to wait for the chance to reinvent yourself?" As she says this, Laurie's focus seems to drift to some faraway, melancholy place, her normally cheery visage replaced by something barren.

For a split second I am sucked into Laurie's vortex. I am one of my sister's disciples—needy, intoxicated, and completely in awe. Her psychosocial prowess—not to mention the fact that she, for the first time *ever,* complimented me on my parenting—blows me away. I am tempted to question her claim of possessing an urge toward self-reinvention—why would popular, athletic, prettier-than-Lindsay-Wagner Lauren Schultz want to be anyone else?—but instead I draw the conversation back to the real matter at hand.

"Phil," I say.

"Phil," she echoes. Laurie and I may not see eye to eye on everything, but there are three areas in which we have achieved real—if unacknowledged—confluence: Ma's madness, Ren's gorgeousness, and Phil's obtuseness in the face of familial drama. There are some things I implicitly trust and defer to my sister on. How to best manage Phil during a reign of terror is one of them.

"Do I tell him?" I ask.

Laurie ponders. "Depends what your goal is. Do you want to use this as a jab at Phil's competence as a parent or really figure out together how to best help Micah?"

"How to best help Micah while jabbing Phil," I say without thinking.

"Why?" Laurie's eyes bore into me. I am nearly squirming.

"I caught our son *having sex* in *our house,* for chrissake. Okay, I was supposed to be gone, but my God...I guess I feel like why should I get stuck holding the ball, like always, just because Phil decided to screw Tate Trimble and decamped to a hotel? I mean, I get that Micah is gay. I can deal with that. But he's so *angry,* Laur. At both of us, I think. Or, oh shit...is it just me?" My thoughts erode into a mist of confusion. What *do* I want? Micah to be happy and safe, right? How do I achieve that? Is Micah supposed to tell Phil himself, or am I obliged to initiate this little sit-down? Am I so angry at Phil that my own judgment is compromised? Why does everything have to be so complicated?

Laurie eats a spoonful of fat-free salad, a meal she professes to like. "We can't help whom we love," she says, her words as bitter as the arugula on her plate.

We can't help whom we love.

Here's the thing: While it's inarguably factual, doesn't it feel a little less true when you are the one abandoned for the One True Love? It's all well and good when you're the object of his affection, but try this nugget of wisdom on for size when your heart hurts so fiercely that the mere act of opening your eyes to daylight seems to have been mandated by the Antichrist. You might think, *Well, perhaps you* can *help it,* or, more succinctly, *He's mine, bitch.* Even if there's no third party involved, no femme fatale in diamond studs and a polo shirt, it hurts. Look at Sue. After her pregnancy and her confrontation with Arlo and his defection, she found herself rootless, homeless, and helpless. Her home, she said, was tainted by betrayal; she couldn't sleep there. So she and Sarafina moved in with me, where she proceeded to drown herself in yogurt-covered raisins, Chinese soap operas—she claims to know what's going on, but I suspect she just likes the boys' genial, sable-haired prettiness—and knitting. In spite of the fact that Arlo Murphy has been a complete cad about the pregnancy— he refused to even discuss her decision to keep the baby— the mere mention of his name sends Sue into black despair laced with tears.

We can't help whom we love.

Laurie's comment sticks with me after I leave the restaurant. It floats, pesky and gnatlike, above my left ear as I storm through the parking garage, memories buzzing. When I hand my nine dollars to the parking attendant, instead of seeing his round Filipino face, I see Ren White's college-age visage, his aristocratic nose and floppy forelock, his broad tan chest dusted with fine white sand as he hoists me onto trembling legs. I grit my teeth and the image dissolves, only to be replaced by one of my parents' house, circa late November 1982.

Ma and Dad are waiting for us in the vestibule with the front door open wide, making it patently obvious that the prospect of their eldest daughter bringing a man home for the holidays is extraordinary enough to warrant a new waxy-leaved potted plant and a receiving line. As we shut off the car, I launch into a lengthy list of warnings about my family that I'd not only written but memorized. Ren interrupts me.

"Quel," he says, reaching for my hand in that loose, teasing way that makes me think of Scott Glenn luring Debra Winger

onto the mechanical bull in Urban Cowboy. *"Stop worrying. It'll be fine. They'll love me." He releases my hand, hops out of the car, and inhales the cool, damp northern California air. "Do all the homes have fenced yards here?" he asks.*

Later. Inside.

Ma has placed a bowl of pistachios and cheap green olives studded with pimentos directly in front of Ren, her idea of sophisticated aperitifs. Ma and I are drinking fizzy water, the kind Dad picks up at Walgreens with the horrible lime-green label that says GENERIC *in large block letters. Ren and Dad have delved into Ren's offering, a bottle of elderly Scotch from Ren's father's liquor cabinet. I take their tacit acceptance of his slightly underage drinking as a sign of approval.*

Ren, I realize, is indeed a parent's dream beau. He reveals enough about himself to appear forthcoming without ever hijacking the conversation. A few choice tidbits about our time together exhibit that he has made a careful study of me. His inquiries, about both Dad's work and Ma's causes, show maturity unusual in one so young. He takes off his jacket, a navy sport coat whose intimidating preppiness is undercut by a frayed charm. He grins rather than smiles. Judging my parents' tolerances correctly, he makes none of the obvious mistakes (flirting with Ma, talking lacrosse with Dad). He just seems himself. Engaging. Lucky. Real.

I sense, rather than see, my sister enter the room. There is something about Laurie's hair that captures scent—light, flowery, cotton-candy scent—and magnifies it so that you are enveloped by her before you meet her. She wafts in on a wave of spring blooms. Laurie is wearing worn jeans and a pale blue polo shirt. Her hair shines, pulled back in a messy half-knot, half-chignon whose effortless chic should, by rights, be beyond the province of a high school girl. The pinprick diamond earrings our parents gave her for her sixteenth birthday glint in her small ears. My hand goes to my own ears, the already long lobes tugged downward by bobbly, vaguely Indian gold hoops that seemed so appealing in the shop on State Street. Now they seem big, gaudy, obvious.

Dad hugs her. "This is Rachel's sister, Lauren. Laurie, meet Rachel's friend Loren White. Ren White."

Ren shakes Laurie's hand gravely. My mouth is full of olives. Later, I find I cannot relive the scene without registering the trenchant sting of brine in my mouth.

Laurie sits down at the table, maybe eats some pistachios. The phone rings six times; after the fifth ring, Laurie sighs and tells Ma to say she'll call them back. Collectively, we bemoan the curse of the insanely popular. We laugh. Conversation shifts to the refugee camp killings in Beirut.

Skip ahead two days.

Laurie, Ren, and I are hiking the Santa Cruz Mountains to escape our parents.

"Have you decided where you're applying?" Ren asks. We have been comparing college notes for the last half hour.

"I'm thinking Smith," Laurie says into the foggy chasm of the deep canyon. The private school tuition will be twenty times that of my public institution, a fact I don't think Laurie finds unjustified, given her potential.

Ren pauses to pluck a pinecone off the loamy ground. "Both my sisters went to Smith."

Fear—red, raw fear—floods my gut. I don't know then (and don't know now) how I know, but something about that exchange, so minute, so encapsulating, terrifies me. I stumble on the brambles that crisscross our path. My lungs fail me so that I have to roll down the window on the way home over Laurie's protests, unable to get enough air. That night I go to bed early and wallow in conscious nightmares, my childhood twin bed groaning under the weight of my thrashing.

In the morning, the day Ren and I are slated to make the long drive back to Santa Barbara, Laurie is conspicuously absent, her nonattendance at breakfast a warning siren that sends my self-assurance plummeting. Present, she might have done something, made some small error, to snuff out the ever brightening stars in Ren's eyes. Absent, her presence is as powerful and devious as a poltergeist. I sag under the weight of it. Ren and I pack the car. I hug Ma and Dad. Ren shifts into neutral. We are two hundred miles away, approaching the seaside town of Santa Maria, when confirmation comes.

"The way you described her, I expected Paulina Porizkova or something. Laurie's pretty but, you know, girl-next-door pretty, not centerfold material," Ren says, as if centerfold material is what the Whites want for their only son.

Ren and I see each other two more times, each date a paler, more anemic version of the last. Then the inevitable unpleasant conversation, conducted by telephone, peppered with words like "space," "bad timing," and "great girl." Ren disappears onto campus. I open my mouth like a motherless baby bird and let Sue feed me jelly beans. On a campus of twenty thousand students, I employ complex measures to make sure I don't see Loren White's face again that year. That summer he transfers to Amherst so that he and pretty-as-the-girl-next-door Laurie can have sex on his varsity lacrosse jacket while the New England leaves fall amber and crisp against their faces. I don't see Ren again until Laurie's wedding day nine years later. That afternoon, despite the efforts that have been taken to spare me needless suffering, I vomit into the azaleas outside the synagogue. Thus, my violet matron of honor gown bears a spray of dark seltzer spots fanned out like blood spatter.

It's true, I think, you can't help whom you love—any more than a diabetic can be blamed for consuming that final candy bar.

*   *   *

Sue clicks the remote, muting her—our—televised morning victuals. In recent days, we have descended from the somewhat justifiable *Good Morning America* to less defensible reruns of *The Nanny*. It's all a time-killer until we get to celebrity chef Rachael Ray at nine A.M., so that I can finally learn how to cook and Sue can vent her life's frustrations on a chef perkier than she.

"So, I'm having it," Sue says.

I put down my to-do list. After work, Duke Dunne and I are heading south on a motorcycle ride along Highway 1. The plan is to sample the view, the artichoke soup at Duarte's Tavern, and maybe, you know, other stuff. In a weird, testy, unanticipated little way, I am addicted to the...other stuff. To call what I feel for Duke—for Duke's body—an addiction is surely to overvalue its importance. Yet I find myself thinking about him—it—in a slightly compulsive, somewhat exhaustive, definitely creative sort of way.

Okay: minor addiction.

Sue's words jar me out of yet another replaying of Duke and me romping around in one or another beachy paradise. I don't have to ask what Sue is talking about. "Are you okay?" I say.

"Yeah."

"Are you relieved?" I press.

"Yeah." Sue scratches her stomach. "It was the weirdest thing, how I decided, I mean. I'd just dropped Fina off at school and was walking to the car, and there were these teenage girls with babies in strollers walking by, and they stopped to talk to these boys. Don't ask me how, but I just knew they were the fathers—what do they call them?"

"Baby daddies."

"Yeah, that's it. Anyway, when I saw those little girls and

their baby daddies and those sweet babies all enveloped in white lace like they were going to their baptisms, and none of them was in school, and God knows how the poor things are getting by. I just had this overwhelming feeling of peace and acceptance, like, if they can do it, I *know* I can. And I knew that even if Arlo doesn't come around, we'll be okay." Sue's eyes shift to the TV screen, which has churned onward into Chef Rachael's realm in silence. "Why are you putting the soy sauce in so early, you idiot!" Sue yells out of nowhere.

"Isn't it good to get it over with?" Personally, I like Rachael Ray's approach, which seems tailored toward culinary bunglers like me whose conception of sauce is limited to that which you can dump on the finished product in the hopes that it will mask whatever damage came before.

Sue's face crumples. "No, no...it'll curdle. It'll burn. It'll all burn straight to hell!"

"You seem full of peace and acceptance," I say.

The rush of wind at my face seems to dispel any inhibitions I may have had about...well, anything. I experiment with singing a Dylan song that pops into my head, but the lyrics are ripped away before the melody ripens. Eyes stinging, I bury my face against Duke's shoulder. It smells of pot, sweat, and a hint of starchy detergent. I like it, the triumph of dirty over clean, nature over artifice.

Naughty over nice.

I slip my hand under his T-shirt. His abs have intervals between them, gullies. I strum them like a guitar, switch to a Rolling Stones standard—

Hot shriek of wheels. Ocean and mountains flip-flopping, crazy ripping yell from person and thing.

Crash.

CHAPTER 22

The Machine That Goes Ping

I awaken to the rustle of my family setting up camp at the foot of my bed.

The last time I spent the night in the hospital, almost sixteen years ago after Taylor was born, the height of excitement was the ice pack the nurse gave me to stuff in my underwear every three or four hours. That and the free cranberry juice.

Things change.

"Oh my God, weird—is that what's-his-name, Dude? Duke?" Taylor asks point-blank about five seconds after she, Micah, Sue, and Sarafina arrived in Sue's much maligned, cloud-covered VW bus.

Sue grimaces and shifts Sarafina off the small swell that's just starting to poke out beneath her shirt. "Guys, your mom's really tired right now. Why don't we wait until after the doctor comes back to nail her to the cross?"

Duke Dunne, whose knack for performing oral sex vastly outweighs his motorcycle-driving acumen, hangs his head and skulks out of the room. Good. I close my eyes. The walloping mallet in my head downgrades to dull throbbing. Better.

"What's he doing here?" Taylor stands, hands on slim hips,

glaring at me, Sue, and Micah. A frightened-looking Sarafina and the licorice-breathed male nurse are the only ones who escape Taylor's wrath. Slowly, the identity of my partner for the high school reunion chicken dance dawns on her, and shock clots her features.

"Oh...gross." Taylor covers her mouth in horror.

"That's enough," I say rather weakly.

"Tay, lay off." Micah stares into my eyes, simultaneously coming to my rescue and putting me on notice that he is, on some level, relishing the irony. Somehow, witnessing my son having sex has peeled back the layers of distance between us. We know each other in a way we never have before. It's as if we can smell the sweet char of sexual depravity blazing on the other.

"Did anyone get hold of your grandma? Or Dr. Meissner? She threatened to, uh, call him," Sue says loudly and elongatedly.

Meissner? Ma? Oh, shit...

"Grandma's on her way," Micah says. "I told her not to bother calling him. I'll go call Dr. Meissner now if someone gives me his—"

"No!" I yelp. Micah stops in his tracks. Too shrill. Take it down a few notches. "Micah, honey, you know I can't eat the hospital food. It will aggravate my heartburn. I think I need...I need you to go get me number eighty-seven," I say with a fine show of calm. My favorite chow fun noodles are at least eighteen miles away from the hospital, plenty of distance to ensure damage control. I shut my eyes again. "Sue will call Meissner."

"I'll call him." Sue.

"Did *he* do this?" Taylor.

This is me in the hospital, banged up but fine, held for overnight observation to rule out possible brain damage (not caused by the accident, but they don't know that). This is also me in the utterly embarrassing situation of having fallen off a motorcycle manned by a lover half my age whom I should have sent packing after our first—and only—encounter. *This is what happens when you get a taste of something rich and decide you want just a few more licks. This* is spelled G-R-E-E-D-Y.

"It was an accident." Nobody has to know where my left hand was when we went down, do they? That's between me, Duke, and Duke's 501s.

"That's why you don't let *us* ride motorcycles," Taylor points out.

"That's true. I doubt I will ride one again," I say slowly, thinking of something else entirely.

"I'll go get you some dinner," Micah says. "I'm just glad you're okay." He pats me on the shoulder and stands up. In spite of my son's newfound toughness and our little fight, his voice cracks. "You promise they're only keeping you overnight to be safe?"

"I promise." My eyes burn. Even Licorice Breath slows his hypodermic reorg and turns a sentimental eye to the proceedings.

Sleep suddenly seems possible. But first I want to do something to make Taylor understand. My head wags from exhaustion. I focus my eyes. There. Daughter. Our eyes meet. I broadcast: *I know I'm a mess, but I love, love, LOVE you, you brat!* Her gaze incendiary, Taylor manages to squeeze my frayed palm. Enough. It is enough. Gripping my girl's strong hand, I let the call to sleep pull me down.

The next time I open my eyes, the room is dim with hushed lights and the spectral feeling of deep night, and Phil is sitting beside me. He is awake. For a second I believe he is watching me with the sort of lovelorn, hard-won relief depicted in romantic movies, in which our hapless heroine is reunited with her chastened husband following terrific trauma. After I squirm into a more upright position, I see that Phil is actually transfixed by a machine to my right that spits out a thin fluorescent blue line accompanied by a spoof-worthy *ping*.

It is not even hooked up to me.

Phil stretches his legs, which are encased in—where the hell does he find these things?—dark brown elastic-bottomed sweatpants.

"The dog needs another course of antibiotics," I hear him say.

"What?"

"So...how's the head?" Phil leans over to inspect my bandages. I brush at the mental cobwebs. Is it my imagination, or did Phil just mention the *dog's* well-being before mine?

I decide to give him a pass. I mean, it *is* late. "It's fine, I guess. A little sore. I'm surprised they made me stay at all. I didn't mean to fall asleep."

"Raquel..." The ice cracks.

"Yeah?"

"This has been a bad week for us, hasn't it?" To my horror— why do women always react to men crying with horror?— it appears that Phil is about to break down. While I watch, awash in a jumble of guilt, pity, repulsion, admiration, and fascination, my husband's hand hovers over his eyes. A deep quaking racks his body, rippling from chest to arms to jaw, before he pulls it together and swallows the spasm whole with a giant snort that harmonizes nicely with the machine's *ping*.

"Remember the trip to Tahoe?" Phil says, not too brokenly.

"Which one?" I know exactly which trip he means, but something small and unyielding inside me refuses to grant him relief.

"The one where the pipes broke."

In spite of everything, a grin tugs at my mouth. "And the car was buried."

"And you got frozen to the toilet—"

"And the neighbors called the manager on us for burning cardboard—"

"We ran out of food on the third day—"

"Because the general store closed early—"

"Your mother called the highway patrol to come look for us—"

"And he came in right when we were doing it on the living room floor—"

"Then there was the sled—"

"Twenty stitches!"

"Thirty. I think it was thirty," Phil gasps. My husband's gaze on me feels thick and warm, a far cry from the flinty terseness that has passed for affinity in our household as of late.

"Move over," he says. "I'm coming in."

"Philly! There's no room. It's a twin—" I start to argue, but Phil has already peeled back the coverlet and inserted himself between the crisp sheets. "Watch out for my head," I say foolishly, causing a fresh round of laughter.

After a minute, the giggles subside and taut silence descends, the kind you can bounce a penny on. Given our recent backstory, it seems unlikely that, even with a few chuckles under our belts, Phil is going to make a play for the goodies, so I try to relax into the narrow channel of bed. For some reason, our proximity has the tense expectancy you'd expect from lying half naked with a stranger, not the person with whom you've shared a hamper and a health insurance plan for the better part of two decades. I can tell he feels the same, and I train my eyes on a point above his head to avoid the clash of awkward eyes. *Oh, trusty* ping *machine...*

"I saw him in the hallway," Phil says. "The kid."

Ick. How in hell could I have violated that most sacrosanct of all Jewish-mother covenants: *Thou shalt not, for any reason, ever, ever, EVER straddle a motorcycle?*

"It's okay. You were right, what you said the other night. I guess this is what separated is." Phil shifts uncomfortably. The sheet slides off, baring my bottom. He tugs the coverings back over me, so as to spare Licorice Breath several years of hard-earned therapy.

"Philly, this thing with the, uh, kid—"

"Don't."

Good advice, that. Except it's too late, 'cause I did.

Lying stiffly next to the object of my separation, I begin to sob uncontrollably. What is wrong with me? More important, why didn't good sex with a handsome stranger fix it? How is it possible to suck as royally at sexual liberation as I did at marriage? Shouldn't I by rights be gifted at one of them?

Phil puts his arms around me. This time he is neither careful nor awkward. A cable of sob-drool connects my mouth to his chest. Our feet tangle. His body feels unexciting but essential, like a part of me I wouldn't want to do without. A heart or a kidney. A lung. Something important. Something you could conceivably replace but that won't function as seamlessly as the original.

I hiccup. Licorice Breath breaches the doorway, intent on measuring my vitals, takes in our middle-aged version of high passion, and beats a speedy retreat. We watch him go. I like the feeling of collusion this lends—so much less exhausting than conquest.

"I guess this means everything's fine now?" I say, only half joking.

Phil sighs. "Couldn't be better."

* * *

Ma and Eliot live five or six towns away from us in Woodside. There was an article recently in the *San Francisco Chronicle* magazine that pointed to the prevalence of larger families there, a recent demographical phenomenon spawned by post-dot-com wealth and nonworking former-executive wives who can afford indefinite IVF. Multiple children are now a status symbol among the upper classes. The syndrome has been termed "Woodside Fours" (as in four kids). As I drive slowly through the town's winding, richly landscaped hills, signs of affluent late-in-life fertility are everywhere, from the gleaming Volvo Cross Country wagons to the Bugaboo strollers skimming proudly down the byways, manned by Latina nannies. In some cases, real mothers trail behind, cell-phone headsets wedged in their ears.

I hate this place. No, wait. Let's be honest, Raquel: I *envy* this place.

Eliot himself earned his money the old-fashioned way: He created a company that made millions supplying cheap, nutritionally meager, pesticide-soaked "food" to public school cafeterias nationwide. Nowadays, at least, my stepfather wouldn't deign to let a nonorganic grape pass his lips, and he throws a few thousand dollars at this or that children's charity every year, but that hasn't stopped him—or, to my continuing shame, me—from living finely off the proceeds of his treachery.

As I turn in to the oak-shrouded drive that welcomes visitors to Casa Abramaschultz, I cannot help but stew about the day when Ma introduced us to Eliot.

Set the scene: It is the summer of 1996. The period in question falls six years after the precipitate death of Minna Louise Schultz's first husband, Stuart Myron Schultz, by lap-swimming.

(Okay, so technically, it was a massive cardiac event—how the hell do they get away with this sort of euphemism?—but Raquel prefers to think of her loss as death by exercise, an idea she embraces and vows to promote for the rest of her life.)

For most of the intervening years, Minna has, at least in Raquel's view, conducted herself in a manner befitting an angry, frumpy, slightly crazy Jewish widow. During the first few years, for instance, she throws herself into the futile malpractice lawsuit against the hospital—who cares if the paramedics pronounced Stu dead before his rapidly cooling body even got there?—segueing smoothly into her volunteer work at the battered-women's shelter and potluck nights with her widow-studded bridge club.

Until she meets Eliot.

Her firstborn daughter, Rachel "Raquel" Schultz Rose, knows nothing of the impending shitstorm. On the day in question, she is consumed with the latest in a series of minor familial setbacks that, if weighed carefully, portend more unfortunate events ahead. Tuition has just gone up at her children's pricey private school, and although the reasonable part of her brain knows her kids will still likely flourish if they transfer to the perfectly acceptable—indeed, enviable—local public school, a louder voice inside her cautions against relying on gumption and merit to help them achieve their life's goals, and sounds an alarm in favor of granting her offspring every possible advantage. That's what the dean called it at the open house, after all: "Our goal—and, presumably, yours—is to offer your child every possible advantage in his ascent to a successful existence." It sounded so gloriously preordained, so unequivocal, so philosophically sound: every possible advantage. A successful existence.

Now their successful existence is being threatened by that scourge of middle-class people everywhere: lack of wealth. It's not that Raquel has the desire for the sort of bonuses affluence brings, per se. At least not for herself. But when she gazes at the wide-open faces of her son and daughter, nearly effervescing with the glorious entitlement of the young and aspirational, she thinks, shockingly, of money—money and the way it lies, stacked and thick and insulating, between them and the forces that would claw away at their existence.

Their successful existence.

The Money Problem, as she's come to think of it, has started to filter into her marriage in ways she didn't predict. Like maple syrup streaming into every crevice of a formerly crisp waffle, it leaves its sticky little trails all over her interactions with Phil. Rare is the conversation they have that stays true to the intended message; often, her ire simmering at what she sees as Phil's eleventh-hour abandonment of his potentially lucrative Ph.D.-cum-artificial-intelligence-patent-owner program, Raquel drops unkind, unplanned comments into Phil's path. True, she despises herself for it, but she can't seem to stop. The release of anger has a short-term cathartic effect, she admits only to herself, like a Band-Aid ripped off quickly, baring fresh skin.

So Raquel is already a little tense when she arrives at what she believes to be a standard if irregular dinner at her mother's Foster City condo, a structure so new and underused that the walls still reek of paint two years after its manufacture. Raquel parks her Nissan Sentra on the street (noting that her sister's late-model Mercedes-Benz is parked diagonally in the driveway, taking two spots) and follows the trail of mushroom-shaped ground lights to the front door.

"Ma?" Raquel says as she walks in, somewhat comforted by the familiar scent of overcooked brisket and soggy vegetables.

They are already drinking wine in Ma's neat, sparkling kitchen. Somebody has obviously said something funny, because they are laughing the pleased, collusive laughter of those who have discovered a small but not entirely unexpected zone of commonality. Ma is tiny and bustling in black polyester pants and a V-necked Peruvian hippie tunic that looks like something Jerry Garcia would have worn onstage. Laurie, washed clean of Living with Lauren! *makeup, is prettier and fresher than someone who wakes up at four-thirty A.M. has any right to be.*

Then there's the man.

A stringy, droopy-eared, bandy-legged little bugger, tall enough to top Minna—not saying much—but pet-rooster small by anyone else's book. He stands in masculine repose with one leg bent up on a chair, a posture Raquel finds intrinsically disturbing, signaling, as it does, a level of confidence and dominion over the gathering that Raquel decides instantly he does not deserve. Perhaps the sinewy rooster of a man is a neighbor, one of Minna's strays lured in from the cold with promises of a bowl of soup and a spirited argument.

"Hi, I'm Eliot," the rooster says, shaking Raquel's hand with a vigor that she finds somewhere between dominating and rude. "You must be Rachel." He turns to Minna and—surely this is a cruel trick of light, perhaps caused by an unfortunate burst of fluorescence bouncing off the brisket pan—pats her on the seat of her polyester pants. "Just like you said, honey, she's a big one!" the rooster clucks.

Before Raquel can fully absorb the horrific implication of the rooster's words and actions, Minna plunks the ladle down in a lily-pad-shaped ceramic dish Taylor made for her for Mother's Day and wipes her hands on a dish rag. Minna reaches up and pulls Raquel down for a kiss, staining her cheek with a jammy smear of tangerine lipstick. Minna's eyes are suspiciously bright, almost feral. Raquel wonders if her mother is on (prescription, of course) drugs.

"Rachela," Minna says in a singsongy manner Raquel has never heard from her mother's lips and which sends a spear of deep fright through her chest. "This is Eliot Abramson. We met at Dr. Kolodnick's office. El, this is my daughter Rachel, mother of those two wonderful kidlets."

Then Minna stands there, smiling broadly and, Raquel realizes, girlishly, while she waits for...what? Because Raquel is accustomed to sussing out her mother's preferences to avoid incurring wrath, she figures out in the next few milliseconds that Minna envisions some sort of physical contact to seal the deal, so Raquel leans forward and allows Eliot—who, by some act of cosmic jokery is wearing a tank top, for God's sake, from which his elderly arms poke, ropy and dotted with age spots—to plant a wet kiss on her cheek. Raquel struggles not to wipe it off.

"So, Eliot," Raquel says, trying to keep the optimism from her voice, "you have a heart condition?"

"Did. Fit as a fiddle now. Just ask your mother." Eliot throws an unsubtle lascivious glance at Minna, who has resumed stirring the soup. Raquel tries to meet Laurie's eyes, hoping to share a moment of mutual disgust, but Laurie is smiling at the two of them, her obvious delight a wall of bulletproof glass, impenetrable.

Impenetrable.

I pull up to the house, which looks like a miniature Tara with its white pillars, brick walls, and sweeping window draperies. Like a lot of things about Ma and Eliot that stymie me, the discrepancy in their aesthetics grabs and shakes me every time I come here. Ma, with her unfashionably flowing fluff of curly gray hair, violet robes, and fondness for anything remotely indigenous and feminist, cannot help but clash with Eliot, who is partial to tracksuits, synthetic fabrics, and eighties-style eternal bachelor decor in shades of charcoal, silver, and old blood.

I bang on the door with the big brass knocker that I always imagine smashing down on Eliot's withered testicles and wait, anxiety churning in my stomach. In terms of my ability to be Zen when disappointing my mother, I am still a kinder-gartner, my personal evolution jammed into permanent park around the time I learned to read.

"Rachie, what are you doing standing there in the cold? Come on in." Ma hustles me into the house, which has the stale, overheated barnyard odor of a veterinary office. "You're okay?" She lays her palm on my forehead, as if a mild case of motorcycle accident has raised my temperature.

"I'm fine."

"I saw the review of your show in the *Chronicle*. See?" Ma has taped the strip of newspaper to the fridge, alongside a veri-table microfiche file of newsprint detailing Laurie's media tri-umphs, and a smattering of health advisories.

"Is Eliot here?" I ask.

"No, he's at yoga."

I allow my head to droop. "Ma, my life is a mess."

Ma grabs my hand. "You have it again." We both know what she means. Guilt, sludgy and viscous, clogs my throat. I already know I am a social deviant. Now I'm officially a mon-ster, destined to join the ranks of Ted Bundy and Ken Lay in a special corner of hell.

"No, no, it's not that, Ma. It's...I had an affair." I watch to see if I'm merely spreading icing on a preexisting awareness.

Relief loosens her gnome's face. "Well, honey, I know. You told me already, remember?"

Me. Ma. Embarrassing conversation. Duke's message. Big misunderstanding.

"No, Ma. I wasn't involved with him then. You just wanted to think I was, because of Phil."

"I see." She doesn't.

"After I found out about Phil, I went a little nuts, I guess. I needed to *do* something, to show myself that I could change things in my life, instead of just waiting for things to happen to me. There was this guy, this"—how possibly to describe Duke Dunne's pedestrian charms to my mother—"this *diversion*. I'm not saying we're involved or anything like that. It's more like a sexual, I mean, animal"—egads—"I mean, basic sort of thing. It's basic," I finish lamely.

"You like screwing him."

Ma, ever illuminating.

"It's, uh...well, yeah."

"But he's not relationship material."

"That's right."

"So you wonder what you're doing," she continues.

"Uh-huh."

"Canoodling with a surfer half your age when it's embarrassing the hell out of your kids and causing you to get in motorcycle accidents." Ma sprinkles some flaxseed on our whole-grain toast and cuts me a glance before dividing the toast into four neat squares. "Taylor and I had coffee at the hospital while you were asleep. I know all about it."

Oh.

"I don't see anything wrong with it, myself. You could be a little more discreet, but I understand where it's coming from."

It dawns on me that she views the accident as a ploy for attention. "You think I crashed on purpose? I wasn't even driving!"

"The subconscious works in mysterious ways."

"Thanks, Obi-wan," I mutter.

"What?"

"Nothing."

Ma thoughtfully munches a wedge of toast. "You were always your own worst enemy, Rachel. Self-doubt—it's a toxic thing. If you want to screw a surfer, screw a surfer, but do it for yourself, not out of pique or boredom. And don't expect your family to be happy about it." Ma's bent pinky—which looks like the result of injury but she was actually born with—pokes my way in emphasis. "You want advice? I'll give you advice. You patch things up with Phil, or take a lover, or go join a convent if that floats your dinghy, sweetie, whatever you want to do. But do it with conviction, because that's what really matters. When you get to my age, you think you'll remember all your little successes and failures? Feh! All you'll remember is how much heart you put into whatever you did. That's all I'm saying." She peers at me over her half-moon glasses. "Now, what else is going on?"

"Ma, Micah is gay." It just comes out. I let it lie there. Ma doesn't react right away except to finger a greenish, grass-textured pill, probably one of Eliot's vitamins, a refugee from his horse stable–sized pillbox.

All at once she snaps her fingers. "I knew it!"

"Knew what?"

"What you just said."

I can tell that Ma, despite her newfound position as a devotee of free love, is finding this hard. "The thing is, Ma, that's really okay, you know? Micah is who he is. We talked about it. It wasn't my best hour, I'll admit it, but I think it's going to be okay. Honestly, at first I was a little…upset about it. But then I thought that people have kids with *cancer,* for chrissake"—Ma's stubborn little chin dips toward me as I say this, absorbing its import—"who gives a rat's ass who he's fucking?" I take a sip of the water Ma drew from the Brita pitcher for me.

"My sweet sonny boy," Ma says. Her eyes are wet. What is it about being a grandparent that takes hearts of anthracite and turns them into oatmeal?

"The thing that might be problematic is"—for God's sake, when did Ma get so fragile-looking, so *old*?—"he seems to be sleeping with somebody—"

"Let me guess, you don't like the boy?"

"He's not a boy."

"A girl?" Ma's face perks up in spite of herself.

"No. Well, of course he is a boy. What I meant is, he's a friend. Ma, Micah is sleeping with Ronnie. Greenblatt," I add, unnecessarily, given the flush in Ma's cheeks.

If I'd been hoping for something dramatic, a bold state-ment of support on the order of "Let's castrate the mother-fucker now. Hand me the cutlery," I would have been sorely disappointed.

"Well, he'll make other friends," Ma says reasonably, validating my own cynicism about the culmination of this relationship.

"I suppose. There's something a little sad about it, that's all. They've been friends since they were five."

Ma shrugs. "Now, Taylor, she's the one you should have your eye on. That girl…" She shakes her head. After all the preceding maternal largesse, I can feel censure coming.

"What do you mean?" I know exactly what she means. Ma may be thoroughly versed in women's lib and finding G-spots, but equal rights to women's lib and finding G-spots have no place in her worldview. Free love is for fortysomething foot-loose housewives with cheating husbands and retired ovaries. Sure, she might give a pass to condom-coated teenage boys. Adolescent girls, however, should be trussed up in chastity belts until their dissertations have been formally accepted.

Ma's mouth thins. "Just that she's *this close* to doing God knows what with that boyfriend of hers."

Boyfriend? I thought she broke up with Biter. Does Ma know something I don't?

"I know. I've been meaning to talk with her about it," I improvise, trying to redeem myself.

"Meaning to talk? If you'd been guiding these children like you're supposed to be, and behaving like a proper role model instead of traipsing around the city like Elizabeth Taylor with your head in the clouds, this never would have happened. *Pffft!* It's *meshuggenah,* is what it is," Ma hisses.

I knew it! All that stuff about screwing surfers was a big fat red herring. Apparently, I'm allowed to have sex only if my children are locked in the cellar, studying for their LSATs. I want to scream at the top of my lungs: *Ma, why do you always do this to me? You can't have it both ways. You can't expect me to compete with Laurie, have a sex life, and have three FDA-recommended servings of fiber, vegetable, and protein on the table every night, too. It's not fair. It's not even possible.*

I bite my tongue.

Ma's criticism of my recent performance as a mother is eerily similar to Micah's. So eerily similar, in fact, that I allow my natural paranoia to take wing and wonder if grandmother and grandson plotted to shock me with this reprimand as punishment for too many Budget Gourmets and not enough support for said son's dalliance with best friend–cum–porn star.

"What are you going to do about it?" she asks.

Truss Taylor up in chastity belts until her dissertation is accepted?

"There's my girls!"

Eliot Abramson emerges from the garage. My stepfather is carrying a cylinder of yoga mat and a wheatgrass drink the size of most people's morning coffee. He pecks Ma on the cheek, and I grin into the sour nausea that always floods my gut at the sight of the man who occupies my father's side of the bed.

"What's new?" he says as he slurps down the wheatgrass and unfurls *The Wall Street Journal*.

Before I can answer, Ma shoots me a warning look. "Rachel just stopped by to say hello. She was passing by. Such an angel."

Passing by? Angel?

"How's the head?" Eliot raps his knuckles against my forehead.

"Fine. Well, it was." *Until you clubbed me, prick.*

"Actually, Rachel was just leaving. To go pick up Micah at practice," Ma says pointedly, already picking up the remote to turn on their afternoon libation, *Judge Judy.*

"Why don't you stay for dinner?" Eliot tosses the cup into the recycling bin, even though it is made of Styrofoam. "I'm making my world-famous seitan stew."

Satan. How appropriate.

"Thanks anyway, Eliot, but Micah needs me to be there," I say with an extra-super eyebrow raise directed at Ma, which she ignores.

Two minutes later, I am easing the Sienna under the mature canopy of trees overhanging the drive, having accomplished nothing but hurting and scaring my mother. It occurs to me as I squint into the metallic sheen of light rain that whichever of Dad's flaws live most vividly in Ma's memory, needing to be protected from the truth isn't one of them.

CHAPTER 23

Separation Anxiety

"Just don't threaten. Every time my parents threatened me, all I wanted to do was pound a bunch of acid and screw bikers." Sue adjusts her sarong over her face, exposing her round belly, and grabs blindly for her virgin mai tai.

It is one of those unseasonably warm days we have sometimes in northern California, the kind that imparts a brief feeling of smugness before the pessimism of winter descends again. We are taking advantage of it by lying out beside the pool, which, due to a combination of insufficient funds and Phil's relocation, has a lily-pad-like layer of foliage in it, along with a healthy helping of slimy-looking algae.

Tonight's intervention was prompted by the latest in a line of clues that my daughter's chastity is, if not a relic of purer times, dangerously imperiled. Also, long experience has taught me that once the anvil of Ma's wrath comes down, it is better to heed the order to act than delay and risk further reproach.

Here's a tip for parents everywhere seeking to pierce the web of secrecy surrounding their teenager's (no doubt sordid) existence: Everyone has to shower eventually. After Taylor had several "study" nights at Lindsay's that required a push-up bra, hoop earrings, and berry-red lip gloss, I simply waited for her to start her shower one evening, sneaked into the bathroom, and snitched her cell phone off the countertop. As it turned out, Tay had not only not broken up with Biter, she was—oh, this hurts—"hawt 2 luv u 2nite."

"Phil's coming over after work," I say to Sue.

"That's good. You shouldn't do this alone."

"If I find out she's actually sleeping with that little shit Biter, I'm going to kill him. And her," I add. The boy's name on my lips feels raw and on the verge of decay, the oral equivalent of steak tartare. It is impossible, *unthinkable,* to imagine the two of them together. His person is so greasy, he is a veritable full-body lubricant.

"I tried to be deflowered by my geometry teacher," Sue offers.

"What?" I can tell she is trying to make me feel better. Universal pain and all that. Biter is too gross; it's not going to work.

"Mr. Morioka. He had the smoothest hands. I just thought he'd be, you know, sensitive. Mature. Honorable. He had that Japanese way with us, kind of distant and formal. He always called me Miss Banicek" Sue fans her face. "God, he was so hot."

"What did you do?"

"I failed a test so I could get after-school tutoring with him. I wore a high-necked ruffled blouse like Laura Ingalls and these white patent pumps that made my feet bleed. I thought he might be attracted to my, you know—"

"Blood?"

Sue grins. "Purity. I wanted him to think about ripping off all those buttons. It was a metaphor."

"What happened?" I adjust my sun hat. Why undo the benefits of all that anti-aging lotion I bought for the reunion?

"I got a C in geometry and didn't get laid till college."

I nod. "I had a thing for the swim coach."

"Isn't it always the swim coach?" Sue rolls toward me slightly to make her point. "Everyone in bathing suits. All that butt slapping and yelling. All the tears after you lose and you need a big sunburned chest to cry on."

Taylor's swim coach is Ms. Orvalli, a redwood of a woman with a whiff of *Xena* about her. She does have a big chest.

"I don't think it's going to be her swim coach." I choke a bit on my mai tai. The automatic pool sweep whines into action, burying itself blindly in a miniature Everglades of green crap. "I'm worried she's going to think we're double-teaming her," I yell over the din.

Sue nods.

"I don't want Taylor to have sex at all." There, I said it. I am not evolved. I am not a cool mom. I am not a liberal realist with a packet of glittering condoms I keep fanned out on the bathroom shelf. I'm just my mother—plus ten inches and a fat wad of insecurity.

"No sex. No. Sex." That's good. Tough. Concise. If I practice saying it out loud now, maybe it will come out right tonight, after Phil and I have had our requisite pre-talk fight and I've downed a couple of Prozacatinis.

"Okay," Sue says too lethargically for my taste.

"What, you think I should let her have sex?" Visions of GED tests and manicurist academies in lieu of college flood my mind.

"I don't see how you're going to stop her."

"Sue!"

My friend uncovers her eyes. "Remember the *thing*?"

I nod.

"I wish my parents had been there for me instead of judging me and fighting over custody of the Peekapoos. I wish they'd really listened to me. I swear, they had absolutely no sense of reality. They'd made it perfectly clear back in high school that they didn't want to hear anything about me and sex, and when I finally started getting some, my birth-control method of choice was basically OYLAP."

"OYLAP?"

"Open your legs and pray."

The *thing* was Sue's college abortion, a mildly traumatic yet lingering event to which I accompanied her and held her hand. The drive home stands out in my memory: me grasping the steering wheel between knobby knees as we shot down the 101 so I could shift with my left hand, my right futilely patting Sue's shoulder while tears saturated her fingerless Madonna mittens. Sue's bitterness over her parents' lack of support has not decreased over the passage of years, merely fermented, like bad wine that has given itself over completely to its mouth-puckering tannins.

"All I'm saying is, just be there for her. Show up and really try to listen to her. Let the conversation take its course. Let her talk. I know it's hard, Quel, but try not to go in with a preconceived idea of what you want to happen. It won't help you. It won't help Phil. And it definitely won't help Taylor." Sue munches on the handful of cheese puffs—baked! all-natural!—that she's been fondling for the better part of an hour.

Sue's right. My friend is the sort of sensitive earth mother who knows what's best for everyone except herself.

"Hey," I say, pressing a damp finger into the crescent of orange cheese dust on the table, licking it. "Why don't I buy one of those ear-wire thingies and you can tell me what to say? Like in the movies."

"Taylor, your father and I want to know if you are sexually active." I actually wince when I say this. It does not come out as planned. Instead of a warm, supportive, sensible mom offering wisdom and guidance, I am a Procter & Gamble research scientist whose closest relationship is with a praying mantis.

Taylor's eyes dart over to Phil for respite, in spite of the fact that *I'm* the one who breast-fed her five months longer than the doctor said I had to. To Phil's credit, he manages to maintain eye contact, though he does swallow visibly.

"I can't believe this," Taylor says. Then, to Phil: "Do I have to answer that?"

We are now officially a *Law & Order* episode.

"Not if you don't want to," Phil says almost automatically. He glances at me. "I mean, yes. Yeah, you sure do, kid."

Taylor slouches into the sofa. "Well, I'm not. I'm too much of a dork for anyone to want to have sex with. I'm probably going to be a virgin for the rest of my natural life. Thanks to you guys."

Great. That's resolved. Now, who wants to go to Baskin-Robbins?

"Are you dating anyone?" I say instead.

"Are you?" Taylor rests her feet on the glass coffee table. She knows I hate that. I may not have standards, per se, but I do have an aversion to sweaty footprints under my Doritos.

Before I can present a defense, Baby Daddy Phil snaps into action. "Goddammit, Taylor, don't talk to your mother like that. She's only trying to help. Nobody's pressuring you. It's our job to know these things. Contrary to what you may think, at sixteen, you don't know everything there is to know about sex. Or life. If you *are* having sex, we need to make sure you're taking the necessary, uh, precautions. You want to get pregnant, or get a social disease? You think that'd be fun?"

Taylor's eyes widen at the rawness of Phil's stump speech.

My daughter may or may not have gotten the condom part right, but she is not stupid. Taylor, too, saw the unflattering Britney photos, watched the flat-bellied pop goddess go lumpish and swollen while the fork-tongued Federpup sharpened its talons inside her.

I grant a silent salute to Phil, who has clearly learned a thing or two during his years in the high school trenches. I study my husband, looking, I suppose, for deep-seated reasons to remain married to him that go beyond second mortgages. His visage is stern yet paternal. His voice is a gravelly font of insight. At this moment, were I a Hollywood casting agent, I would definitely cast him as the Wise Yet Fun Dad Who Just Happened to Do His Boss's Emaciated Wife.

Taylor's tears begin to flow. "I don't know what dating is. Sometimes I think we're, like, together, but then he'll, like, go out with someone else or kind of ignore me at the mall or something."

"Oh, honey. It'll be okay." I pull my daughter to my side. Her skin is downy, almost marsupial. I cannot envision such softness yielding itself to invasion without pain. Bile curdles at the back of my throat.

Taylor hiccups under my arm. "It's just…this stuff with Biter…and you being sick. I mean, even though you're better…you could get sick again. And you and Daddy splitting up…I'm so scared, Mom."

"Mom and I are here to take care of you, sweetheart. We love you. Nothing will ever change that." Phil takes Taylor's hand in his own, confident that he's out of the parental outback and back in the paternal largesse zone. We sit in hiccupy silence for several minutes, focusing on various inanimate objects around the room while our daughter welds us together with tears, the human-emotive version of chemical epoxy. After a while, Tay's strangled sobbing ceases. Nestled on the old slipcovered khaki sofa, I am fairly sure we present like a normal family, soldered together by affection instead of fears of teen pregnancy, adultery, cancer, and lies.

I clear my throat. "Tay, do you want me to take you to the doctor to get some birth control?"

"I don't know."

Phil and I look at each other. With the sort of gunshot telepathy that is possible only after nineteen years of marriage, soccer tryout failures, and family diarrhea, we glean that it is Phil who must deliver the next line.

"Tay, you know we'll support you in whatever you decide is best for you, but we need your promise that you'll use protection when and if you become sexually active"—Phil's and Taylor's matching kiwi-green eyes widen simultaneously at the Maury Povich–ness of these words—"and we both feel strongly that the sooner you choose a course of action, the better. Don't let making no decision *be* your decision." Phil pauses to let the threat fester, a neat trick he has always performed better than yours truly.

Such is Phil's unique gift that he manages to squander all gains with his next comment.

"I personally know of several girls at school who've begun their sexual, uh, explorations and successfully gone to their parents for the proper, um, accoutrements."

This, at least: He does not attempt to say "accoutrements" in French.

Taylor stares brokenly into her vitamin-water bottle, probably wondering how, in the game of genetic chance, she got assigned two notorious overcommunicators as parents.

"Daddy," she says, "will you stay here tonight?"

"Of course." Phil doesn't look at me. We both know that if Taylor had asked for a time-share in the Bahamas, he'd have said yes.

Like a lot of watershed conversations in my life, this one has not gone exactly as planned.

"Unzip me?"

"Hair."

I lift the three inches of wavy regrowth off the nape of my neck while Phil zips me out of my turtleneck. Amazing to me—though why, really, should it be?—it's like Phil never left. Here, in the familiar confines of our bedroom, we glide through the motions of our regular ablutions like ballerinas circling the lid of a music box. If Phil is relieved to discover how little I've done to purge the ancestral digs of his presence, he hides it well. His remote still rests, sleek and fat, on the left-hand nightstand, next to a dusty stack of *Consumer Reports* I am unlikely to consume until long after our divorce decree yellows around the edges. His electric toothbrush stands next to mine on the sink vanity, as if guarding the fort in his absence. There's even a crumpled-up pair of boxers in the otherwise empty dresser drawer, which Estrella must have found in the laundry and slipped optimistically back in their rightful place.

I strip off my black slacks and knee-highs, which have pinched a groove around my calves. Automatically, I reach for the sweatsuit of the day, a pilled gray affair with saggy glutes that is designed to dissuade trespassers. Nighties, a vague, silken filament of a memory, went AWOL around the time Phil and I started procreating. I am not sure what the protocol is for such encounters as this, but I am fairly sure it does not mandate consigning your ex-sandbag to the army cot, which, in addition to smelling like gangrenous leg, sports a stain of unknown, suspicious origin.

The conjugal bed it will have to be.

"Well, that wasn't too bad," I say as an opener.

Phil peers at me over the top of the sports section he plucked at random from the gigantic pile of newspapers he's been collecting since 1981. As with his allegiance to all things turd-colored, something in me rebels at the idea that a person could just start reading about a football game that took place nine years ago, and still be regarded as normal.

"I wish I knew this little fuck. I'd rip his nuts off and feed 'em to Stella," he says.

I glance at Phil appreciatively. This is the side of my erstwhile husband's coarseness that I like. The side that is primitive, tribal, brutish, *manly*. The side that used to make me feel like we were together for a reason. A primal reason that did not involve IRA plans and retirement villas in Florida but, rather, some savage imperative to mate.

Phil stares back at me. As usual, his eyes drop to my legs, which, I believe, are still long and lean enough to command a man's attention, in spite of the fact that they originate in a quasi-girdle. In another telepathic moment, I glean what is simmering on low heat behind my husband's saturnine gaze.

Lust.

Okay, not lust, maybe, but *something* animal and avid. Something that signals a desire that goes beyond Phil's standard cravings for TV and beer.

Without thinking, I drop the sweatpants I am about to pull on over my stomach-compressing white undies. I have no bra on, just a camisole with a shelf bra that proffers my supposedly rebuilt rack like a row of recycled carburetors. Since I hadn't anticipated disrobing, my fake scars—discovered at a gag gift shop in the Haight amid sacks of itching powder and piles of fake poop—are tucked into my lingerie drawer, along with the twenty-three-year-old photo of me and Ren at a Stray

Cats concert and the frilly thong I purchased for Defilement by Duke Dunne Day 2005.

Phil lunges.

We bang together like two atoms in a fission chamber. Phil's hand snakes its way into my granny pants, sliding between the folds of my crotch without hesitation. After a few instrumental plucks at the nub of his former friend, the hand migrates to my back, skirting my chest as if it's ringed by an electric fence.

Call me ungrateful, but this annoys me.

In full battle-ax mode, I wrap my legs around Phil's waist, grab a hank of his hair, and yank his head back. Phil yelps as I capture a nip of man-wattle in my teeth.

"Fuck." His voice is near growling. The green eyes have gone yellow and feral. With great abandon, my husband rips through the buttons on the fly of his Levi's with one hand, probably wishing he'd gone zipper back in 1987, when he could still change his mind about things.

Phil flings me onto the bed and lands on me with a chuff of breath. The underwear is around my knees. Phil's shirt is off. He's lost weight since the eviction, his abdomen firmish instead of packed in layers of excess meat. This pleases me. I may no longer want Phil for myself, but I certainly don't want anybody stuffing him with refined carbs. At least not until his pension matures.

I stroke him in all his familiar places. Phil's face is darkening to that impending-cardiac-event shade of tomato unique to white descendants of northern climes. I suppose he'll have me stop soon because of the whole heart-attack thing. Now, there's a book I could write: *The Joy of Spooning*.

"Was she good?"

In the midst of this glorious marital clit-and-cock jubilee, some idiot blurts out this . . . *monstrosity*.

Oh no, it's me.

"Who?"

"Tate."

Phil groans and rotates away from me, quickly doing those minor adjustments men do when caught in a state of untimely arousal. His shorts tent out in front. Why is it that the same hard-on that makes young men appear virile makes its middle-aged bearers look ridiculous?

"That's real nice, Quel."

"I'm sorry." Strangely, I am.

Phil levels me with a glare, as if I suggested we ask a Cub Scout to join us.

"I didn't mean it. Honestly, Philly. It just came out. I don't really want to know. I mean, of course she was. Otherwise why would you have bothered?"

Phil adjusts himself down to pup-tent dimensions. "She wasn't. *It* wasn't, okay? I can barely remember, anyway. It was ten fucking years ago, for chrissake."

"Gimme a break! I saw you in North Beach!"

"I told you. That wasn't me."

Since I first confronted him, Phil has maintained his innocence on this point. For the first time in a long while, I stare directly into my husband's eyes. His are puffy and mean and intelligent and weary. Not for the first time, gazing at them makes me think of a wolf forced out of his habitat, a formerly sleek animal made to survive on fast-food remnants and beer dregs abandoned in alleys bordering tract homes. It strikes me that he might be telling the truth. For some reason, this idea sends a rush of shame to my head and a bolus of blood to my crotch. I really do hope it is not too late for Phil to raise the jib, as it were.

"Come back," I say. Aiming for Bacall, I deliver a perfect Harvey Fierstein.

Phil inches toward me on the bed. He looks a bit wary, but who can blame him? I did, after all, subscribe him to *Titty Titty Bang Bang* magazine and have it delivered to his school office without discretion wrapping.

I put my arms around his neck. He smells...like Phil. Not objectionable. Not great. Well rounded. Like whole-grain toast sprinkled with yeast.

"At least we have two lovely children." I slide my hand into the pup tent, which is rapidly ballooning to a ten-man.

"Yeah. I was going to nominate you for mother of the year," Phil gasps.

"Funny, me, too."

This cracks us both up. Phil gently removes my hand from his shorts and eases off my remaining clothes. I halt him at the camisole with a shy glance borrowed straight from Tatum O'Neal in *Little Darlings;* he acquiesces. As my sort-of husband begins the next stage of his ministrations, I wonder if he can sense the opening of my body to another and, if so, whether it is as clear to him as it is to me that we have Duke Dunne to thank for relighting the oil-lamp glow of libido inside me.

"You know what I've missed?" Phil says into the dimness, inhaling. "Your skin."

CHAPTER 24

Assume the Position
on Memory Lane

I run into Tate Trimble at yoga several days after Phil and I advised Taylor on the dangers of penile penetration and had—for the first time in a while—pretty hot sex (hoping the two aren't related, obviously).

Facing my husband's lover would have been a lot harder before I became a BC superstar and started selling my work. I know it is appalling, but for me, success has put a neat spin on the typical wronged-woman scenario. It's almost as if I am the victor and she the victim, being saddled, as it were, with the immensely past-its-sell-by-date spoils of battle, Phil.

This is not to say I don't experience the sickly trickle of nerves that begins in my stomach and branches out across my lower region like forked lightning. I do. I just don't immediately vomit and collapse in a paroxysm of inferiority, that's all.

"Hello, Tate," I say gamely. Out of the corner of my eye, I see Annunciata Milk whisper furiously to Rochelle Schitzfelder. The rest of the class has gone rumps up, assuming the position of downward-facing dogs, but several women in our circle are simply staring, tights straining at crossed thighs, watching the spectacle unfold, awaiting action. "How are you? How's Ross?" I say.

The woman who would be my nemesis if my life ran to such luxuries stares blankly at me, her pert nose wrinkling above unnaturally pillowy lips. I realize with a frisson of horror that she does not know who I am.

"Fine! Fine," Tate says, not even bothering to whisper (the bitch). The instructor never chastises anyone who has the balls—and butt—to go thong-'n'-tights in lieu of sweats. One of those squirming, sweaty-armpitted hippie-whippet types who populate the ranks of yoga teachers like worms on organic compost, Ms. LaRaza McGuire—no joke—is thoroughly cowed by the vulpine and entitled among us.

"Your husband bought one of my sculptures," I say, increasingly frustrated with the situation. I mean, for God's sake—I'm big, muscular, cuckolded and reputed to be psycho. Why isn't she scared of me? "I'm an *artist,*" I add with as much contempt as I can muster.

Comprehension dawns in the prescription-drug-infested land that is Tate Trimble's mind. The woman really does have enormous lips. I wonder if she gave Phil head. Imagining those collagen-fattened kielbasas wrapped around Phil's cock is actually quite unsettling.

"Of course," she says. "How do you do?"

"I do fine, Tate. The thing is, I try not to do it with other people's husbands." I turn around. "Hey, Rochelle. Your leotard's up your ass, just so you know. Oh, and while I have you here, I resign from the committee."

"Which committee?" Rochelle's eyes are not just slits; they're hermetically sealed.

"All of them."

*   *   *

When I get home from yoga—or, more accurately, from Target, which has this lovely new collection of Belgian chocolate called (ludicrously) Choxie just loaded with partially hydrogenated oils—I am surprised to see Ren's car parked on the street. Before exiting the safety of the Sienna, I brush the chocolate flakes from my chin and adjust my underwear so it covers my life preserver.

"Hey, brother-in-law." *For the love of God, Raquel, who besides you needs reminding?*

"Can I come in?"

"Sure."

There is something disconcerting about Ren's appearance. I realize that in all the years we have known each other since he became a practicing plastic surgeon, I have never seen him in green scrubs. I suppose I always imagined the needle as his surgical implement of choice, not the messier knives and suction hoses that the elimination of fat, wrinkles, and age require. If pressed, I guess I might have envisioned a plastic-shellfish-eating-style bib or perhaps an apron. The fact that his hospital-green blouse is paired with gym shorts sounds an alarm.

We go inside. I unload my duffel bag, purse, Nicole Richie–esque shades, and—discreetly—year's supply of Choxie. "Can I get you something to drink?"

"No, no. Well…okay, maybe a Scotch."

Hmm. Scotch. Before three P.M. Something is definitely wrong in Loren/Lauren-land.

I root around in the "wet bar," a holdover from the house's previous owners that the current owners use primarily to house sports trophies and mouse traps. I find something dusty and suitable, pour it in a glass, and press it into Ren's hand. The brief touch ignites the same tremor of yearning in me that it always has, the one I thought would dissipate under the weight of Duke Dunne's ravishment.

"You have to talk to Laurie." Ren raises his stunningly wrought eyebrows. On someone lesser, the expression would look contrived; on him, it looks querulous. And meaningful. My heart beats a bit faster.

"About?"

Ren doesn't say anything. It takes me a second to realize that he is staring, horrified, at something on the countertop. You know the word "aplomb"? The concept has not played a huge role in my life thus far, but I try to channel it nonetheless as I remove the neatly folded leopard and lace teddy and crotchless panty set and note in Phil's handwriting that says BACK AT 10:00. WEAR THIS and drop it into the Tupperware-lid drawer.

"About?" I say again.

Ren snaps out of it. "I don't know what you said to her, but she thinks we slept together. You know, in college."

Carefully, I ease the Scotch out of Ren White's hand. The magic tingly thing happens again. Then I drink it in one gulp. I do not gag. I do not wince. There are things that need to be said here, but they don't need to be said sober.

"We did sleep together," I manage.

Don't tell me you don't relive the magic daily, brother-in-law.

"Quel, you know we didn't."

You bastard. You goddamn gorgeous life-ruining bastard.

Gazing hard into Ren's eyes, I search for duplicity and madness but see nothing but garden-variety regret and dread. In spite of the suddenness of the encounter and Ren's spontaneously odd getup, it occurs to me that I have expected this reckoning for decades. *Did we or didn't we,* if not the central question of my life, has provided a sturdy container in which to store my fears, regrets, and neuroses.

"We dated," I begin slowly, praying for rescue but not without a measure of relief that the unutterable is being uttered at last. "We went out to dinner and to the beach and the library and class, and then we went to bed together, and we were...well, we were naked, Ren. We slept together." I am sure of it. Surer than I am of the shark tattoo on Duke Dunne's backside. Surer than I am of the fact that, if I die before him, Phil will wear brown slacks to my funeral.

"I don't know if actual *clinical* penetration happened"—a slightly hysterical dart of laughter bursts out of me—"but we sure did have sex! Oh yeah, we sure did." I pause to refill Ren's Scotch glass, which, rudely, I have yet to return. You know what gets me? Having to use the word "penetration" in conversation with Ren White without having actually been penetrated by him.

Oh, the injustice.

"The thing is, Ren, I didn't go around bragging about it. In fact, I've pretty much sat on it all these years. Done my duty. Been the veritable *soul* of discretion. But when Laurie and I were hanging from that bridge and things were looking a little dire, and Laurie asked me point-blank if it happened—no, what she did is *beg* me to tell her the truth—I couldn't lie."

Couldn't I have?

Nausea siphons through my gut.

"Ren, could you excuse me for one moment?"

He nods. I trot briskly to the hall bathroom, fling back the toilet lid, and heave for a few seconds. Nothing comes out. Typical.

I gargle with water anyway to wash away the bitterness of the Scotch, and I try to regroup. *This is not about you, Quel. This is about Ren and Laurie and whatever demons they need*

*to exorcise before they begin the endless trail of sleepless nights
and savage love/fear that is child-rearing. So step up to the
fucking plate, okay?*

I return to the kitchen. Ren stands where I left him, his
eyes as stagnant as my pool.

"So what do you want me to do?" I ask him.

"I don't *know*. This is not good. We're about to adopt. We
took out a second mortgage on the house. Your sister's on the
warpath. *This is not good.*"

Poor Ren, who thinks everything is supposed to sort itself
out with a golden eyebrow raise, cannot handle the deviation
from life plan that has occurred.

"Look, I'm sorry. I really am. But maybe you should have
told her yourself, instead of letting her wonder all these years,
which, if you really want to know, is actually crueler than—"

"We did not sleep together!"

In spite of my brother-in-law's state of ire, his face is not
the mottled red or purple you would expect from such an
outburst. Rather, he has paled to a creamy ivory, an inoffen-
sive hue that Martha Stewart might choose to paint her bathroom. Before I can lecture him again on our appalling state
of nudity twenty-three years ago—which I am almost sure I
can provide proof of in the form of birthmark recognition—I
hear a van pull up outside. Ren, apparently lost in the unique
world of regret that can come only from having dated two
sisters in the wrong order, seems untroubled by the possibility of intrusion.

I dart over to the window in time to see the UPS man jog
up the steps to the Bonafacios' house. Carla opens the door
and, instead of signing for the package, smiles and motions
him inside. I file away this observation in a mental cabinet
marked HOT DELIVERY MEN AND THE DUMPY REGIONAL BANK MAN-
AGERS WHO SCREW THEM.

Relief.

I turn back to Ren. "What is going on with you and Laurie, exactly?"

"I don't *know*. She's gone ballistic. She called me at work today, told my assistant it was an emergency, got me out of surgery to ask me if I think she's *pretty*. Married sixteen years, and she wants to know if I think she's attractive, if her…damm it, if her *hips* are wider than they used to be. This is not the woman I married. This is not Laurie. I'm worried about her, Quel. And I'll tell you something else: The woman's in no state to adopt a child."

There is no other way to describe it: I am floored. The idea that *Living with Lauren!* and I could share the emotions of blind jealousy and diffidence is astounding. Contrary to my usual ungenerous nature when it comes to this sort of thing, I do not feel glad or humbled by my role in Laurie's descent into insecurity. For one, it is too weird. For another, I suspect that, like Ren's nascent love for me, it will not last the season.

"God, Ren. I'm sorry." Empathetic sister-in-law.

"I'm under a lot of pressure right now. My partner's leaving the practice, moving, setting up in Las Vegas. We took out a second mortgage against the house to expand the practice. We already signed the lease on the building. But Rick's wife has to go to Vegas. Because the desert air is good for her chakras or something. Goddamn hippies." Ren dabs at his brow, which is as beautiful and dignified as the rest of him, even when damp.

"Whatever you want me to do, I'll do it." Delusional sister-in-law.

"I don't know. Look, I'm sorry I got a little hot there. It's not your fault. All you did was speak your mind, just like you always have." Ren smiles, the same golden-boy grin that first transfixed me in rhetoric class, and looks me straight in the eye. "Did we really sleep together?" he says.

"Not really. It was more like a doctor-patient thing."

Ren takes a deep swallow of the Scotch I coopted and leans his golden-haired elbows on the table. "It's not like I don't think about it sometimes," he says.

At once the world, with its kaleidoscope of colors, clamors, and pungencies, grinds to a halt, rotating backward blindly like a carousel gone berserk. Beneath my fingertips, the polished oak of my kitchen table explodes into sensual tendrils of sea grass, transformed by rapture...

I am twenty years old, Ren is twenty-one, and we are rolling on an empty beach, the planet tilting wildly around us. I can almost taste the mulchy tang of seaweed in the air...

"Probably more than I should," Ren adds.

The magic words flow over and through me, a river of clear blue relief after a blistering two decades. For years I have operated under the assumption that I was, to Ren, a blip. A trivial bump in the road toward romance that snaked its way into my sister's embrace. The inequity of our feelings for each other, the protracted state of my pain, always seemed to be lodged in my throat like a wad of undercooked steak. I don't know why it never occurred to me that Ren might feel the same. That he, too, might wake up some nights, his heart pounding a terrified cacophony of remorse into the blackness. That he might sometimes feel his universe shift toward hopefulness at the mere sight of me, the mundane shards of our lives refracting banal certainties around him, a vortex of ill fit.

I close my eyes. My mind takes over.

We tumble into each other's arms. We fit, if not like a glove, like a pair of well-worn bicycle shorts—flattering still, and clingy in the right spots. Truly, it is a marvel. Nothing has changed. His cut-grass smell, the gently crinkled skin at his temples, the hard dance of bone and sinew beneath my hands—they send a sweet rush of rightness through me, like they always have. He raises my hand to his lips and kisses my wrist. Slowly. Achingly.

The car door echoes outside again. UPS guy, having finished delivering his package to Carla.

My eyes snap open. Ren is looking at me with—can it be?—longing.

And I feel...icky.

Icky?

"I have laundry to do," I blurt. A glutinous brown spot mars my leggings; I've been Choxied.

Ren jumps up awkwardly, flopping a little, like, well, an old guy. "Of course."

There is no "of course" when it comes to me and laundry (of course). Ren flees to the safety of the kitchen counter, keys jangling. Once again we have skipped ahead of the ritual, embarked on the breakup without the preceding payoff. Who knew the end of rapture could be so simple?

"Right," I say. That sensation pulsing in my chest—can it possibly be pity?

"Thanks for the drink. And the ear," he says.

"Anytime." I check the clock; I can still catch the tail end of *Maury*.

"Well, bye."

After a reasonable thirty seconds spent wallowing in that particular lagoon called immense relief, I get up and start separating whites from colors.

After all, if I'm going to celebrate the end of the affair that never was, I may as well do it in clean clothes.

CHAPTER 25

Call of the Booty

Phil rubs a window into the frost on the windshield and blasts the defogger. "So...what are you doing tonight?"

I wrap my woolly robe tighter. I have on Taylor's imitation UGGS and a fleece cap, but warmth is a pipe dream when you're outside at five A.M., mere minutes away from your downy bed. The Accord's engine, normally melodious, rumbles impossibly loudly. The neighbors' windows are dark, as are the kids'. What will I do if the lights come on, leap into the shrubbery?

"Nothing," I say, too drowsy to lie. "Same routine?"

"Call me when they've gone to bed."

I lean over and peck Phil on the lips, a facsimile of a wife kissing her beloved husband off to work. He looks at me hard and hot—Interested Wolf—and pulls away down our street, until all that's left of our liaison is a stream of carbon-monoxide vapor.

Feeling a little too close to Carla Bonafacio for comfort, I scurry back into the house and down the hall to our room, relieved to discover that the bed is still warm.

I suppose it is obvious, what's happened. Yes, Phil and I are sleeping together. I know, you want me to say "again," but that would sort of discount the many moons we spent ravishing each other on alternate leap years.

I'm not sure how it all came about. There was that night ten days ago, after we "helped" Taylor. And the day Ren came over, when I called Phil and demanded to know what the hell he was doing, leaving a Frederick's of Hollywood number lying in the fruit bowl. And expecting me to wear it. And expecting me to wear it for *him*. There's a name for what happened later, when I was awakened at 1:32 A.M. by the tinny drumroll of pebbles against my window.

Booty call.

"Yes?" I called out the window, rather primly (I'd like to think).

"Sorry I'm late." Phil withdrew one sneakered foot from the tangle of impatiens. "I fell asleep during the fourth quarter."

"Oh. Gee, that's too bad."

"Door has the chain on. Can you...you know?"

"What?"

Phil winced as he collided with a rosebush. "Let me in, goddammit."

The chain slid off without a hitch. One thing led to another and—presto!—I had myself a part-time sandbag. Again.

For some reason—unspoken yet fully endorsed by both of us—we do not want the kids to know about this development. Still trying to lead by example in this great game called life, I suppose. The situation requires no small amount of ingenuity. Generally, I call Phil from my cell phone after the lights have gone out in Micah's, Taylor's, and Sue's rooms. A stealthy hallway check, a brief glance at the thin strip of shadow under the door, a quick shower if I haven't already had one—and I'm back to my room, speed-dialing. Phil drives over from Extended Stay America and parks a block away. Under the cover of darkness, my estranged husband pushes open the strategically unlatched side gate farthest from the kids' bedrooms and sneaks through the yard, entering the house through the master-bedroom sliding doors. The first night the dogs backed Phil into the tool shed—until they figured out who he was and their baying dissolved into joyful slobbering—so now I lock them in the laundry room after all Casa Rosa inhabitants fall asleep, ignoring the accusation in the two sets of doleful basset eyes.

I finally confide in Sue about the affair over lunch at the Ramp. "I can't believe how much more effort he puts into the sex now that we're separated."

"Heh," Sue says.

"It's like now that he has to jump a fence and wear black slacks and a camouflage jacket to get some nookie, he thinks he's some kind of Casanova. He thinks he's George Clooney. I can tell. I caught him reading my *GQ*. And putting gel on his hair." I dip the corner of one of the restaurant's signature burgers into a side of ranch dressing.

Sue nods. "You're the other woman now. Men always want what they can't have. And what other men want. They are such lemmings. If I ever meet one who has an original thought, I'll sell the restaurant and join him at the ashram in a heartbeat."

This misapprehension explains a lot about why Sue's relationships always end like criminals on cop shows, panting their way to their futile, undignified, often drugged end.

"Why are we so much more desirable when they're not married to us?" I slip off my clogs and massage my unpedicured heels against the table leg.

"Because kids and mortgages and bills and seeing you in your Nair mustache aren't turn-ons," Sue says. "Reality is not a turn-on. Fantasy is. As long as you're not doing the daily grind together, you maintain some sense of mystery for them. Stupid bastards."

Duke Dunne's face pops into my mind. If he is a lemming, he is a baby one, not yet fully developed in his lemming habits. Why he is attracted to me, I can't really figure. Maybe in his world, my type of boring is exotic. Once, after one of my high-school-senior-year Will No Man Breach the Fortress of My Chastity crying jags, Ma told me that everybody has a person out there who sees her—the homely person—as an exotic bird; all the idiosyncrasies that make her unique are like plumage. Maybe Duke Dunne doesn't care about my terminal insecurity, my stretch marks, and my extremely long-lived case of sibling rivalry. Maybe he thinks they're cute, like robin's feathers.

"So, I read Tay's diary," Sue says.

"What?"

She pops a fry in her mouth. "I know it's shitty. But... What are you looking at me like that for? I did it for you, ingrate."

"Me?" I think of the shiny notebook with Hello Kitty grinning blankly on the cover, of all the goodies inside that I would love—*love*—to get my hands on, to fondle like pirates' booty dripping through my fingers. Truthfully, ethics haven't stopped me from plundering the pages of my daughter's journal; it is the fear of learning something nasty—and quite possibly true—about me or Phil that gives me pause.

Sue continues, "Yeah. I was just thinking about your conversation with Tay, and I got this feeling like Tay wasn't telling you everything. You know, a *feeling*. So I read it after she went to school this morning. She keeps it inside the leg of her snowboard pants, up on the top shelf of the closet, just so you know. It was the third place I looked, after the mattress and the sock drawer. Anyway, girlfriend's not a virgin."

"Not...?"

"...a virgin. Nope. Fortress breached, I'm afraid." Sue drags her grilled-cheese sandwich through the puddle of ranch and gnaws the edge. "Do you know a kid named Lindsay?"

"She's Tay's best friend."

"Well, best friend and Taylor have been plotting to get you and Phil back together."

"What?" My eyes drop to the dessert menu and soak up two words: banana split.

"They thought that if Taylor had a crisis, you and Phil would have to spend more time together. And that would, you know, reignite things between you. And he'd move back in. Boom—marriage saved. Mom's happy, Dad's happy, kids don't have to move in with Grandma and Grandpa Wheatgrass while Mom cracks up."

"What kind of crisis?"

"They were considering a bunch of stuff, but pregnancy, drug overdose, and shoplifting addiction were the leading contenders."

My mind dredges up a snapshot of my son and Ronnie Greenblatt carving a trough in Micah's bed. "Did they make up the stuff about Micah, too?" I say, trying not to be too hopeful.

Sue smiles and strokes her tummy. "No, that's real. And she did steal a lip gloss from Walgreens a couple months ago, but she felt guilty about it."

"I see." I don't. "Well, isn't this just great."

"Anyway, she's fine. A little hurt over the Biter thing, but she'll get over it. We all did."

Yeah, and it only took me a quarter century.

"Did she say anything about, um, me?" My throat shrinks to about the diameter of a cigarette. I don't expect reverence or even understanding after my recent performance.

Sue nods gravely, which I take to mean I should halt this line of inquiry. I immediately imagine the worst: *Mom is such*

a dork. She has cancer, and she's having an affair with this
guy young enough to be her son. She looks, like, totally huge
next to him. Maybe if she dies, I can have her vintage leather
trench coat.

"She thought you were pretty cool in Mexico," Sue offers.
"And she knows she's been a bitch to you sometimes, and
she's sorry." She taps my hand. "Don't tell her I did it, okay?"

"God, no. I'm planning on you adopting the kids if something happens to me and Phil. I don't want to ruin it." Cut
to an image of Taylor's tear-streaked face, her eyes blinking
fearfully under a layer of blue mascara while she begs Phil
and me to get back together. "In fact, I was thinking of asking you to adopt them now," I say with just the teeniest bit of
truthfulness.

"Anytime," Sue says, finishing off the last chunk of animal
fat on the table. "She could wait tables for me at Tamarind.
It's not a bad career option for an orphan. Pre-orphan," she
amends.

To enter the H. Arnold Tater Academy, you have to drive
through a set of curlicue wrought-iron gates that are better
suited to an Ivy League university or a Hapsburg palace than
a year-round suburban K–12. This show of affluence is meant
to remind *all ye who enter here* that however tempted you
may be to whinge about the tuition, it's all going toward a
good cause: your child's likelihood of befriending a Greek
shipping heir.

I've never felt particularly welcome here, myself. Maybe it's
my Pale of Settlement roots, the ghetto proclivities that incite
me, still, to gnaw the necks of chickens with the hope of
tapping in to marrow, two whole generations after my people fled the Old Country. Maybe it's because of Phil and his

extraordinary ability not to get promoted to dean after four-teen years of teaching tenth-grade math. Or maybe I'm just too plump and swarthy.

Whatever the cause, as I park the car and go in search of my daughter across the vast expanse of putting-quality lawn, I feel the usual frisson of unease that Tater engenders in my gut. The kind you feel when you've sneaked into an extra matinee at the multiplex and are expecting the manager's hand on your shoulder at any moment.

As I enter the administration hall, a passel of first-graders parts around me, shrieking and giggling in that joyful, liberated way only kids can.

Tater tots.

"Hi. I'm Taylor Rose's mother. I'm wondering if you can tell me where she is this period?" I say to the secretary, a hollow-cheeked thirtysomething with narrow shoulders and stylish eyeglasses. "It's not an emergency," I add, wondering if I've inadvertently initiated some sort of security process I'll later regret.

Skinny Shoulders—Ms. Swain, I see by her nametag—taps some keys on her computer and asks for my ID.

"P.E. with McLeod. Do you know where the gym is?"

"I think so."

Ms. Swain releases me, and I wander across the quad toward the barnlike building that is the gym. Since my kids' sports take place mostly on a field and in the pool, the gym is not a place I've visited much over the years.

The locker room smells (appropriately) of sugary perfume and sweat, McDonald's and talcum-sprinkled clove ciga-rettes. I meander around shower puddles, trying to repress the sensory-memory leap back to high school. Inside the gym, it is a flasher's wet dream, replete with teenage girls in half-shirts and hip-baring short shorts, swatting each other's bare flanks as they lope back and forth across the basketball court.

Two of Tay's friends, Madison and Savannah, spot me in the doorway first.

"Hey, Mrs. Rose." Madison Platt has always been my secret favorite, her splash of pimples, too-large nose, and unself-conscious donkey laugh calling cards for lasting friendship.

"Tay, your mom's here!" Savannah Jain calls. Savannah is one of those girls whose popularity is no mystery; the girl is self-obsessed, witty, occasionally mean, and almost eerily good-looking.

Taylor trots over, her grace, athleticism, and general air of entitlement stopping my heart, as always. "Mom, what are you doing here? Is everything okay?"

"Yeah, everything's fine, honey. I just wanted to talk to you for a minute about something."

Taylor climbs up into the bleachers. Together, we ascend to the highest pew. Taylor's steps slow near the top, and not from fatigue. I am pretty sure she understands what's happening. Coming to school, something I haven't had to do since she was, oh, eleven or so, is bound to send a message.

"Are you doing okay?" I say pointedly.

"Um, yeah."

"Is there anything you want to clarify, like about our conversation the other night?" Giving her the chance to fess up on her own, so I don't have to risk accusations of diary violation.

"Not really. Oh, I got an A on my trig midterm."

"That's great, honey. Anything else?" Slightly cooler.

"No?"

"Taylor, the first time is something you remember for the rest of your life. I'm not saying it's always going to be like it was that time, but there it is." I shut my eyes and conjure a young Ren White lying next to me, propped on his elbow, focusing on my face as if it is the best, most compelling face he has ever seen. "There's something about it being your first time that makes the person you do it with more important than he really is. That makes you more vulnerable to his actions."

She turns to me, her foot kicking the bench in front of us. It is not a struggle to summon the feeling reflected on my daughter's face: the one that compels you to relinquish the illusion of adulthood and wallow in being somebody's baby when life begins to seem a little more complex and unmanageable than you'd originally envisioned.

Taylor's eyes fill. "We did it. Me and Bite. It wasn't what I thought it was going to be like, I guess. It didn't hurt that much or anything. It just...I thought it would be easier. More like, you know, *fun*. It wasn't, like, gross or anything, just *nothing*, you know? I didn't know what I was supposed to do. I felt so stupid. I kept thinking about the other girls he had sex with and how I was probably the worst one, because I waited so long and didn't learn how to do it when I was younger."

Waited so long? I don't know whether to scream or laugh or ululate at this revelation. Beneath us, the two half-court games churn on. Somebody gets a ball to the nose, and the action grinds briefly to a halt while the player is escorted off the court with an ice pack on her *shmecker*.

"And the worst part is, the...uh...condom kind of came off, Mom. Um...inside me? It was so disgusting. I was so scared I was pregnant or something. Then I got my period. So I knew I wasn't." My daughter draws a long finger over a crack in the bleacher seat, pokes at it. "Bite called me back once. To ask if he left his iPod headphones at our house." She smiles, and I spot redemption in the grin and feel proud (this in spite of the fact that much of the preceding detail is, according to Hello Kitty, not quite accurate). "I gave them to Sarafina," she says.

"C'mere."

We hug. I envision us thirty years from now, commiserating about pain-in-the-ass teenagers and male treachery. With this vision, I realize that my definition of parenting success has shifted from its original focus on rampant bliss, achievement, and daily phone calls from my brilliant and devoted offspring to survival and any relationship with my kids that is warmer than estrangement.

"He's such a dick, Mom."

"I know." *In two years, when you go to college, you'll start to say "prick."*

"I hate him." Pause. "Everyone knows."

I hug her tighter. *Don't worry. Next week Samantha Mosley will get wasted and give somebody head in the bathroom, and they'll forget all about you and that ass-tart Biter.*

"I'm sorry, Mom. I didn't mean to lie to you and Dad. It just happened."

Tell me about it.

"It takes a lot of courage to tell me now. But I'm not surprised, honey. That's the person you are. I'm proud of you."

Taylor adjusts her gym uniform and wipes her eyes, where half-moons of azure mascara have pooled. I use my finger to wipe a smudge from her cheek; it comes away glittery.

"Can Dad come over early tonight? Can we order pizza?" she says.

CHAPTER 26

Friends of Baron von Münchhausen

Arlo Murphy and I have always had an understanding. The understanding is, he treats Sue Banicek like a goddamn queen, and I allow him to be part of Sue and Sarafina's life. I don't know why he is suddenly finding it hard to uphold his part of the bargain, but I intend to find out.

"Hey." I tap Arlo's shoulder. His wife beater is plastered to his back. He is nearly swallowed by the innards of a motorcycle, which lies dismembered on the floor of his Mission District warehouse.

"What?" Without turning.

Hmm. I sense a distinct reduction in friendliness. "Arlo, come on. I want to talk to you."

"Nothin' to talk about."

I decide to go straight for the big guns. "Sarafina's crying herself to sleep every night, Arlo." Okay, a small exaggeration, but I thought I saw a few tears last week when we rented *Erin Brockovich* (Arlo looks a lot like the Aaron Eckhart character).

Arlo sits back on his boot heels. "Goddammit, Raquel."

"Let me buy you a beer."

Five minutes later, we are holed up in the Phone Booth, a puny dive that caters to anyone seeking the chance to rub up against an unemployed drunk while enjoying her libation. Arlo is working on a Guinness and pretzels; I stick to my usual Sierra Nevada pale ale and Ziploc bag of baby carrots.

"Sue doesn't know I'm here," I say as an opener.

Arlo scratches his beard. I can tell getting him pissed off and sick enough of me to promise things is going to be challenging. He is not Phil. He is not Ren. He is not moved by conventional henpecking. My original plan—to badger and berate him into taking Sue back and raising the baby properly—is not going to work. Foolishly, I have borrowed a strategy from my own tumultuous marriage playbook; Arlo Murphy is going to require a different tactic. I decide on a flattery ambush with a drop of motherly censure.

"You know, even though you have done my best friend wrong, I still like you. I can't help it. I don't think I could say that about any of the others. Not a one." I look him straight in the eye. "That doesn't mean you aren't being a complete asshole."

He looks embarrassed.

"You know you love her, so what in God's name are you doing?"

"She knows I don't want children."

"You're already raising Sarafina. What's one more in the scheme of things?" I lie.

"We had a deal. Woman broke it." He wipes a froth of Guinness off his lip.

"For the love, Arl, listen to yourself. You sound like a refugee from a fifties spaghetti western! She didn't do it on purpose. These things happen. And we deal with it. We don't run away and stick our head in a carburetor. Nobody's perfect. Birth control isn't perfect. Hell, self-control isn't perfect.

You're willing to throw away a whole *relationship* because of a mistake that reveals absolutely nothing about the way you really feel about each other? About how happy you can be while you get old together?"

"Sounds like the pot calling the kettle black," Arlo says simply.

I freeze. *Dear God, he's right.*

This is the first thing I think as I ponder Arlo's observation on the cesspool that is the Rose marriage. The second is: *What if, contrary to popular opinion, there are worse things than a ten-year-old affair when it comes to the survival of a marriage? What if I'm the one throwing the baby out with the bathwater? What if I don't take Phil back and he turns out to be a genius at IRA investment?*

Embarrassment makes me aggressive. "How could you possibly kick her out of her own house? With Fina? At a time like this. That is low."

"I never said she had to get out of the house. Of course it's her friggin' house. I just walked out. I've been sleeping on the floor of the shop." Arlo pulls a bag of chew out of his pocket and looks at it yearningly. I hope no other woman gets to benefit from Sue's housebreaking methods. "Did she tell you that?" He looks pissed.

"Uh, not exactly." She did. Maybe she was just lonely?

"Look," I say, hoping he doesn't resume the habit on my watch. "Let's cut the crap. Do you know what Sue told me when she first met you? She said, 'Arlo is the only man I've ever known who makes me feel like everything that came before was worth it, because it led me to him.'"

"She said that?"

"Yeah." *What's a little paraphrasing among friends?*

Arlo wraps his huge hand around the sweaty stein. "My dad was the biggest shit of a drunk who ever lived. This"—he raises the beer—"is a problem for me sometimes. I like it too much. I don't think I can give it up. I feel like I gave up enough for people, when I was a kid, in 'Nam, in...Fuck it."

"No one's asking you to change. If Sue didn't think you were good father material, you wouldn't have spent a day with Sarafina. You wouldn't have spent a minute with her." Of this, I am sure.

"I just don't want any kid of mine to live with this." He sloshes the beer.

I grab Arlo's mitt of a hand. "Then he won't."

"Munchausen syndrome," Sue says. She picks up the stack of printouts. "'A so-called factitious disorder in which the patient repeatedly reports physical injury or evidence of disease, when in actuality, he has caused the symptoms. The illness is named after Baron von Münchhausen, an eighteenth-century German known for his pathological telling of falsehoods. Although its sufferers may injure or harm themselves, Munchausen originates as a mental illness and must be treated as such by health practitioners.'"

I cross my legs and try to levitate to my happy place. Sue has decided that I am mentally ill. If it is her cause du jour, there is not much I can do about it.

"Faking an attention-getting or chronic disease? *Check*. Engaging in behaviors that perpetuate contact with the medical establishment? *Check*. Going so far as to hurt oneself? *Check*. Reluctance by patient to allow family contact with health-care providers? *Check*. Extensive knowledge of medical terminology, including pharmaceuticals and surgical procedures? *Check*. Eagerness to undergo medical testing? *Check*. Oh my God, listen to this one: 'Identity problems or low self-esteem.' *Check, check, check!*"

"All I did was fake a couple of doctors' appointments and shave my head. I didn't even nick myself," I say.

Sue drops the pile of papers on her dining room table. "I think you have it. You need to see a psychiatrist right away."

"Wouldn't that just aggravate the condition because I'd be going to another doctor?" I tease.

"*Why* can't you take this seriously? I'm just trying to help you."

I lean over and flick off the kitchen TV before Laurie can come on and annoy me further. "Sue, I don't have Munschnauzer, or whatever it's called. Haven't we talked enough about this already? I can't come clean until I know for sure the telethon money's been good and spent and Laurie's job is secure and, you know, other stuff. Besides, I think you have to benefit from the attention you get from the illness itself. The way I see it, I'm benefiting from my own steam, from my own work, and the cancer only indirectly." I inhale a quasi-furious breath. "I can't very well claim to be a breast-cancer advocate and survivor artist if I don't have it!"

"You don't have to yell!" Sue yells.

I take it down a notch, my attempt to locate the happy place abandoned. "Look, I want to tell them the truth, but I can't right now, because then what will happen to Laurie's credibility? And the Breast Cancer Alliance budget for next year? And my gallery pieces? And my guest spot on Laurie's show? And my column? And the book deal? I know this can't go on forever, but a lot of people depend on me because of it. I can't just let them down." I think of Jean, of Doreen, of the other women from the support group, the women who watch me on Laurie's show, and the money from the sale of my bust constructions that has funded, if not breast-cancer research itself, a nice chaise for the support-group lounge and a subsidy for member child care.

Sue pushes back her chair and hoists herself upward. "I can't stand it anymore. I feel so guilty. I can barely look your mom or Phil or the kids in the eye. You're out of your mind, you know that?"

"I tried to tell them! They didn't listen, remember?"

"I never thought it would go this far." Sue's bottom lip quivers.

"This is the thanks I get for fixing things with Arlo and putting your family back together for you? For massaging your disgusting pregnancy bunions and running your baths and shopping for the goddamn black Perigord truffles and Tibetan saffron you want, even though I had to go all the way to Burlingame for it, and driving Fina to school forty-five miles away every damn day while you rail at Rachael Ray just for being cute?" Now that Arlo has agreed to give biological fatherhood a shake, I am here to help Sue move back into her house, I'm not here to get crucified for past sins, and I am pissed.

"Oh, you're going to take credit for fixing my family, too?" She raises her eyes to the sky in appeal. "Thank you, queen of the universe!"

"*I'm* the one who went to talk some sense into Arlo! What were you doing while I was traipsing around fixing things up? Lying on your fat ass eating bonbons and watching soaps, that's what! While Tamarind sinks into obsolescence because *la capitana* has decamped for some poolside moping."

Sue points one of her short, blunt-nailed little fingers at me. "Don't ever say that about Tamarind! I kept you in frittatas for more years than you deserve!"

"Is Tamarind all you care about? Your little"—I point my nose in the air—"hoity-toity rabbit-food palace for the appetite-impaired?" I regret the words as soon as they come out. "Sue," I say immediately. "I'm sorry. I didn't mean that—"

"Of course you did." She clings to the butcher block as if faint.

"No, really, this conversation has gotten totally off track. Sue, *please.*"

"Quel," Sue says tiredly, "we both know we'll be friends tomorrow, and the day after, and probably next month and next year, so I'm not going to waste our time pretending otherwise. But here's the deal: I am going to take a step back for a while. I'm going to grow this baby, and then I'm going to raise it. I wouldn't presume to give you an ultimatum or anything, but this is how I feel: I don't want to be around your family right now. I know what's going on. They don't. It sucks. I can't do it. I don't have the energy."

She shakes her curly head and levels me with her clear gray gaze. "You've changed, Quel, you have. I'm glad you're living your dream and all, I really am, but I'm not sure if the Raquel of your dreams is the one I would have become friends with, if I had met her first."

CHAPTER 27

A See's Candies Moment

I am awakened by pebbles hitting my window at 2:46 A.M. *Goddammit, Phil, can't you just remember what day it is? Is that so hard?*

I roll over and burrow under the blankets, willing the noise to cease. I had a terrible time getting to sleep, what with the fight with Sue and my children's continued unexplained absences, which could point to all manner of scenarios, all of them bad.

Tat. Tat, tat, tat.

Shit.

Phil and I have maintained separate residences since the, well, separation. I think we both like it this way, the safety net of marriage unfastened but not as yet discarded and consigned to the Dumpster. That doesn't preclude our biweekly midnight rendezvous, which are scheduled for Mondays and Wednesdays.

It is Thursday.

Tat. Tat, tat, tat, TAT.

What'd he throw, a boulder? Incensed and bleary-eyed with exhaustion, I extract myself from the tangle of sheets, stub my toe on the bedpost, yelp, and feel my way toward the window.

"Go away," I hiss. "What do you think this is, the Mustang Ranch?" Nevada's most famous legal brothel is, what, a mere three hundred miles away? Dear Hubby can go there to get his fix if he can still afford it.

"I think the feds seized the place a couple years ago," Duke Dunne says. He is standing under my bedroom window, in my rosebushes, looking quite satisfied with himself, if a little out of place. He still looks like Gael García Bernal, but like GGB stuck someplace incongruous and unworthy of his greatness, like Kentucky Fried Chicken.

"What are you *doing* here?" We haven't seen each other since the accident. As far as I'm concerned, the statute of limitations on our relationship expired along with Duke's motorcycle. There are things that aren't meant to be, after all. See how Zen I can be when I am pretty sure what I am doing is illegal in Alabama?

"I have to talk to you," he says.

"How did you get here?"

"Drove."

"A car?" It is strange, but he and his freewheeling persona are so linked to beachcombing in my mind that I cannot imagine him taking conventional modes of transportation.

"It's Freshie's," he says, naming the friend he was staying with in Santa Cruz. "Hey, let me in, will you? I gotta take a leak."

I let him in the front door, not even bothering to tiptoe around or make myself passably attractive. Why bother? Everything is unraveling anyway. Why not give the kids something sordid to tell Phil's lawyer when the time comes? If Duke wants to spirit me south of the border this time, he can do it with me in my robe and night cream, sans support bra.

After showing Duke to the powder room, I lead him to the kitchen. The sight of Duke Dunne surrounded by the mundane trappings of my real life, the soccer schedules and overloaded trash compactor and commemorative plastic cups from McDonald's, almost makes me laugh. Strangely, it does not diminish him; it's the kitchen that looks fake and weird, like someone's ponderous, mocking idea of a kitchen.

"I'm sorry I woke you up." Duke reaches out to touch me and seems to reconsider. "I'm going back to Sayulita tomorrow."

"Do you want some cereal?" He shakes his head, and I pour myself a heaping bowl of peanut-butter puffs and milk and dig in.

"How are you doing?" I say. I have to say, he doesn't look well, sort of flushed, with matted hair and a hint of body odor I don't recall from our earlier adventures. I wonder if he'd consent to a shower. We could take one together, to save water. California often has a drought on, you know. It can't hurt to plan for the future. For the children.

He waves me off. "Whatever. I just wanted to...I came over 'cause we never agreed on"—his eyes rake me up and down—"Christ, I'm so fuckin' into you," he says.

I drop the spoon, which splashes some milk on Duke's sleeve. Impulsively, I brush his arm; I feel it tremble under the worn denim. He grabs my face in his hands. My hands travel involuntarily to his arms again. The knotty ropes of muscle under my fingers make me a little dizzy.

"It's you," he says.

"What's me?" I hope he can't smell my breath. I brushed my teeth before bed, but I did have garlic scampi for dinner. Twice.

"I think I'm in love with you," he says impatiently.

"Duke," I say gently. "You're conflating things. Boredom.

Change. Wanting something different. We don't really know each other, do we? You were ready for something to happen, and I was there. I'm an idea, that's all. A bad one." I am on solid ground when it comes to bad ideas and escapism. In this matter, finally, I am an expert.

Duke kisses me.

As kisses go, it is sloppy and unstudied. Duke's mouth is gamey with the taste of all-nighter and misconceived ideas. My hands slide into his wild thatch of brown-gold hair. It is thick and slippery, like seal coat. Our teeth slap together once, twice, before we gain traction and sink into the kiss. He is a grunter the way I've been told I am a moaner, his every inadvertent utterance a spark that sends flames licking up my belly. This (last) time, I am gratified to discover he is still Duke, still achingly unformed and problematic, not a generic force barging its way into my space with stubble and neediness bared.

"Raquel," he murmurs against my cheek.

He pushes my robe apart. The bar stool wobbles, but his grasp on me is firm. I understand why people invent words like "automagically," because, lo and behold, my legs automagically part and wrap themselves around him. We kiss violently for a while, or it could be minutes. I don't know. Everything is bright and stark and overclarified, even a little bit ugly, like a sex scene in a French movie aiming to shock. It is, I am fully aware, a perfect good-bye.

"I'm not saying good-bye to you," he says, nuzzling my ear and neck and lips. The sound of his breath ragged against my face makes me weak. Duke's palm steals under my cami and around my breast, rough and possessive and deliciously dirty and—do I imagine this?—just a little bit awed. For the first time in memory, I am able to see my ample, prone-to-sagging forty-three-year-old rack through someone else's eyes, and the view is favorable. Under the patchwork Levi's, Duke's crotch is alive and hard. I slide tighter against him, reaching deep for something I didn't think I wanted to find a moment ago. The jeans give a satisfying leap.

It is, without question, the best kiss I have ever had.

The kiss does something instantaneous and irrevocable to memories of all other kisses. Not only do I recall all of them in a moment of instant, beautifully preserved clarity, but I am, perhaps for the first time ever, able to view them with the tenderness and lack of judgment they deserve. It's as if I opened a box of See's Candies, and each one represented a single aspect of myself, from the singularity of dark chocolate to the artless delight of moist caramel. With Ren, I see now, I was toffee brittle, so stratified with girlish passion and unfulfilled need, that to kiss me was to shatter me. The girl who first met Phil Rose was pure milk-chocolate buttercream, primed and velvety, with a drop of rummy sophistication fermented by Ren's injurious abandonment. Later, Mrs. Raquel Rose: bitter nougat, studded with the salty crunch of nuts, coated in complex truffle.

The kiss shatters two notions I have always held dear: first, that you have to be in love with somebody—really, truly, planning-your-future in love—for a kiss to portend a great next thirty minutes. And second, that hellos are always better than good-byes when it comes to sex.

Something falls. It is not me, and I don't think it is Duke, who is wrapped so greedily around me that he may as well be a carnivorous plant.

I look up.

Taylor and Micah stand at the kitchen entrance, looking way too alert for four A.M. Tay stomps her fake-UGG-shod foot again, her face flushed with childlike mutiny. Then she rears back and kicks the wall. It leaves a hole the size of an overturned coffee spill. Unfortunately, it is not big enough for me to crawl into. Tay steps over the crumbs of plaster and takes a few tentative steps into the room.

"Funny, I thought it was past the kids' bedtime," she says.

"Syrup?" I ask.

All three takers sit obediently while I pour a generous amount of Vermont's finest over their pancakes.

"Powdered sugar?"

Duke declines, but Taylor and Micah both nod. The butter has already melted, forming frothy puddles.

"Coffee?"

I have never offered my children caffeine at home, but then neither have they stumbled upon me making out with Taylor's surf instructor on the kitchen island or kicked in a wall with nary a repercussion. Grasping the need to flow with the surreal nature of this encounter, the kids simply hold out their mugs and accept the brew. Truthfully, I am impressed. Children really *are* resilient.

Everyone eats.

I take in the civilized scene and think, *I could get used to this.*

Micah breaks the silence. "Have you ever surfed Mavericks?"

Duke swallows a bite of banana pancake. "Yeah."

"What was it like? Was it insane?" Enthusiastic. One immortal young athlete to another.

"It's like dropping off a thirty-foot ledge into thin air. If you survive the chops on the face—which are bigger than what most people ever ride *ever*—you do it again. And again. The drops are unbelievable. The wave jacks so hard…I'm not sure I'd even try it again. I feel lucky." He looks hard at me as he says this. I blush.

"Are you moving in?" Taylor asks abruptly.

"Nobody's moving in," I answer sharply, glancing at Duke to see if the suggestion has caused apoplexy. Apparently, it is so off-the-charts ridiculous—or he is so deluded by romantic notions of my viability as a MILF—that it causes no distress; he continues to wolf our premature breakfast at a hangover pace.

I do not want to insult my kids' intelligence by dragging out the old chestnut about Duke and me being "just friends." I don't care what anyone else does: I do not nibble the seashell ridge of my friends' ears while they convulse against me, and my friends do not hook their thumbs under the strings of my bikini briefs and massage my hip flexors until I scream. Nor do I intend to apologize for carrying on with Duke Dunne in the middle of the night in our kitchen. It occurs to me that to acknowledge the moral inferiority of your paradigm to your children is to yank the very foundation of life out from under them. The fact that your actions or beliefs may indeed be morally inferior is secondary. They are going to have to trust me on this one.

"I just want to know." Taylor looks at me. Her eyes brim. "So I can get you declared incompetent, get legally emancipated from you and Dad, and go to L.A. to model."

Micah laughs. "She thinks she's Lindsay Lohan or something."

Although I tend to agree, I don't like Micah's tone, which is somewhere between disdainful and downright nasty. Yet I dare not mock Taylor's anger. If I were the one in her position, the foyer mirrors would have come down along with the wall.

"No one is moving in with anyone," I say again. "We can talk about the emancipation of Taylor when everybody's calmed down and had some breakfast."

"I hadn't asked your mother yet," says Duke over a mouthful. "I'm not sure I'm the marrying type. I'm a free spirit, too."

"Duke, for God's sake." But I can't help grinning.

Micah cuts in. "Did you know she drives a minivan?"

"Do you have kids?" Taylor continues the Inquisition, this time flicking the bullwhip at Duke, building her case to take before a mock judge.

"No. I was married for a year after college, but we didn't have any kids. It didn't work out."

The pugnacious Schultz chin sticks out at this newsy nugget. "Sounds like you *are* the marrying type, you just suck at it."

"Taylor!" I scold.

Duke laughs. "You know, she's right. My little sister said the same thing once. She said something to the effect of, if you really want to be a good husband, then don't get married in the first place. I thought it was pretty smart for a twelve-year-old."

"Very observant," Micah notes.

Duke cocks his head. "She's single, if you're interested. Just graduated from UCLA. Brainy, a little bossy, if you ask me. You want her number?"

"I'm gay."

Duke nods. "Oh, yeah, Raquel told me that. Duh." He tugs his goatee. "Dude! This dude I know in Santa Cruz—"

"Guys." My hands grip the table, not white-knuckled, exactly, but close. I may have wanted to flirt with the idea of the blended family, but this is getting ridiculous. Duke as late-night rosebush trampler I can take; Duke as yenta, not so much.

I glance out the window as the sun peeks over the houses across the street, sending them into shadow. Daylight makes me think of reality, which pushes several important things to the forefront of my worry basket: Sue; the pieces I need to finish for Saskia; whether Duke and I have anything resembling a future together; whether Phil and I have anything resembling a future together; what the kids are going to tell Phil; what *I'm* going to tell Phil; how I'm going to end this giant fiasco. Last night doesn't strike me as officially regrettable yet, but I see, now that the moon has descended, it soon will. Maybe it was worth it, though. Maybe my See's Candies moment will flavor things to come.

CHAPTER 28

How to Win a Time Slot Without Even Trying

"Ms. Rose, I saw your new show at San Francisco MOMA, and I have to say, I was so moved." Shiny Pony, Laurie's associate producer, holds her clipboard firmly to her scant chest, as if physically reining in the torrent of sentimentalism that threatens to burst forth, shearing its way through the prim layers of mauve cotton-Lycra button-down and Banana Republic wool crepe. She is staring at me with the fevered admiration formerly reserved for, well, Laurie.

Mindful of not smearing my makeup or mussing my hair, I lean forward and grasp Shiny's blunt-nailed hand, giving it an encouraging squeeze. Also, I give her the thousand-watt smile, baring teeth recently bleached by lasers in the warm-modern office of Dr. Quentin Sloane, who, everyone knows, is the man responsible for the porcelain grins of every news anchor, aspiring starlet, and celebrity artist in town. Gratefully, Shiny returns my squeeze, then slips away with great reluctance, her eyes misty.

Don't laugh. In the months since my first taping, I have

developed a highly functional repertoire of such gestures: the sisterly half-hug, the empathetic shoulder stroke, the prim white-girl power salute, the killer grin. In fact, as Ma observed rather pointedly on a recent family outing, where I was swarmed by well-wishers and fans of the show, my smile was starting to resemble Tom Cruise's in terms of pure eat-your-enemies-with-a-side-of-salsa gusto. I never thought I'd say this, but really, Tom is not *that* bad. I'm sure he's just trying to make his fans feel good. And if it makes them feel good, why not?

With regard to my newfound people skills, I suppose you could say, in addition to channeling my good friend Tom, I have followed the sterling example of someone close to me—modest, successful, unimpugnable Laurie. In this new world of mine, this swirling, tilting, tingling world, collecting accolades is part of the job. The job of being a celebrated role model, that is.

The first time I graced the *Living with Lauren!* set, I was overweight, insecure, and the teeniest bit intoxicated. This time, admittedly with the assistance of clever Jonesie and the divine Cleo, I am svelte(ish), confident (somewhat), and abstemious (perfectly). On this, my fifteenth appearance, I am an old pro with a large and loyal (if slightly insane) following. I no longer cringe when Jonesie squirts volumizer down my esophagus and attacks me with his Mason Pearson blowout brush. I experience no compunction whatsoever when Cleo squeezes filler in my crow's-feet or tamps down my love handles with packing tape. These passive moments—increasingly rare in my overbooked life—allow me to contemplate the purposeful nature of my current existence.

"Excuse me, hon. Can you do me a favor? I could use another one of these. Totally parched." I rattle the cucumber slice around in my empty SmartWater glass. Shiny's new assistant is a sweet-faced Latina with an accent that says barrio and a vocabulary that says Ivy League MBA. The girl's eyes flash with irritation before her thick lashes obscure her thoughts, and she jogs to the canteen to get me another drink. Huh. Well, Sweet Face will have to go. I make a mental note to drop hints—nothing obvious—to Shiny Pony and Boss of Shiny during the next meeting.

Shiny trots over, her well-tended mane flying. "Ms. Rose, there's been a small change in today's panel. I guess Dr. Chen had to cover for a sick colleague who was supposed to be on call, so she can't make the taping. We called around and got another oncologist. I have his name here somewhere"—Shiny leafs through her sheaf of printouts in a rare moment of turbulence—"he's supposed to be excellent," she finishes. Her brow glistens a bit.

"It's okay, sweetie. I'm sure whomever you got is great." It feels so good to throw them a bone. You just can't overdo it, I've noticed, or things get a bit sloppy.

Shiny preens. I pointedly glance down at my notes. Like the Seven Sisters graduate she doubtless is, she gets the hint quickly and scuttles off to kiss some more on-air-talent ass.

Today's show, part of the series I've secretly started thinking of as *Cancer: Reloaded,* is focusing on ways that medical personnel can improve the period immediately following the diagnosis for the patient. As the patient, you're vulnerable, in a state of shock. The docs are anxious to start pumping you with toxic drugs and lop off vital parts of your anatomy. They don't understand why you're being so combative. Don't you know they're your new best friend? Don't you know you don't stand a chance against the Big C without them? The families are reeling. The sickies are keeling. The insurance companies are repealing. All in all, it's pretty touchy stuff. And we all know how much doctors *love* communicating. Laurie and the producers have high hopes for the series, particularly this episode. As in Emmy-winning high hopes.

And to think it was all my idea.

It took three of my guest appearances before Laurie lost her famed composure. Okay, maybe she didn't exactly *lose* it, but it did vacate the premises long enough to produce two medallion-size rosettes on her expertly powdered cheeks.

When Boss of Shiny Pony commented on the unprecedented volume of fan mail and suggested I become a semi-permanent fixture on *Living with Lauren!*, Laurie drew a deep, aggrieved breath and propped her elbows on the conference-room table with her hands resting against her chin. That was when I knew she meant business. You don't pull out the classic Dominance Power Triangle unless you anticipate a serious confrontation over make-you-or-break-you stuff.

"We've only had one other guest on more than twice—Sarah Singer—and she's a Ph.D. who's written twelve international bestsellers, including the definitive text on infant mortality among Christian Scientists of the Pacific Northwest." Laurie's face is redder than I've ever seen it, except perhaps the moment I confessed to sleeping with Ren. Then again, she was upside down at the time.

I looked down at my nails, feigning distress and humility. Sure, I hadn't penned the definitive book on *The Christian Science Monitor* or whatever. But I had something important to say, and I obviously wasn't the only one who thought so.

Boss of Shiny Pony frowned. "Well, Alicia thinks we need to take another look at *LWL*'s key metrics. There's some concern about the third-quarter share decrease."

Everyone knows that Alicia, the station director and Boss of Boss of Shiny Pony, is being cultivated for great things by the network. No one disagrees with Alicia about anything, because everyone wants to go with her when she takes her gigantic pulsing brain and her iced organic no-fat soy chai latté addiction and her framed photo of herself and Oprah at a walkathon for some disease or another and buries herself into the power structure at NBC like a tick in the haunches of a particularly succulent Welsh corgi.

Laurie showed the Schultz aplomb. "Wait a minute. Before we start operating on erroneous assumptions, does anyone have the numbers handy? If I remember correctly, last week we won our time period among adults eighteen to forty-nine *and* twenty-five to fifty-four."

I was vicariously proud of my sister's number-crunching abilities, the gene for which clearly bypassed me, since I can't balance a checkbook or calculate the calories in a triple serving of anything, let alone help the kids with their trig and calculus homework.

"That's one way to spin it," Boss of Shiny Pony said gently, lowering his bifocals toward his notes. "Let's see. We averaged a four-point-one out of ten in adults in the eighteen-to-forty-nine demo...a four-point-nine on top of eleven in adults twenty-five to fifty-four...and a three-point-one out of nine in the eighteen-to-thirty-fours, with a six-point-six in ten households. So yeah, technically we 'won' the slot, but we came in second behind Laqueta in the ten A.M., and KPIW does an infomercial in the ten-thirty, so...Alicia wants us to come up with some ideas that will give us a ratings boost." BOSP looked embarrassed, as if Laurie had just turned up at the weekly strategy meeting in a lace thong. At the mention of Laqueta—Laurie's dashiki-wearing, Kahlil Gibran–quoting, increasingly popular archrival—the room sank into nauseated silence. Laurie had two rules that reign supreme on the set: Remove your outdoor shoes before entering and never mention Laqueta Hacker's name until after Laurie has done her morning asanas.

My sister's quick brain reassessed her power quotient and searched for gold. "I'm sure we can come up with something fresh and exciting that will please Alicia and the viewers. Something fresh but also familiar, so the *viewers,* who rely on the *quality* health information they get here from a *trusted* source, won't think we're abandoning our insistence on *accuracy* for the sake of a few ratings points. Maybe something on how to recharge your marriage? Or stay healthy while traveling? I've come up with some great concepts for a show on homeopathic treatments for attention-deficit disorder that would..."

I tuned out while Laurie grandstanded. Why did she always have to hog the limelight? I wasn't asking for much—only a bit of redress for forty-odd years of unequal footing, sanctioned by God, Ren White, and our sainted mother.

Almost immediately after I thought this, my stalwart friend Guilt piped up: *Laurie's having a bad year, you know. First, all those adoptions falling through. Then the collapse of confidence and the stuff with Ren. And her job being on shaky ground. Maybe you could give her a break this time and back off a little?*

Luckily, my other compadre, Self-preservation, threw a hard-hitting left hook.

What's a bad year compared to a lifetime of anonymity? Okay, so maybe it's gonna hurt a little when the fans clap me out of my seat and she has to maintain the TV-host smile-mask until the commercial break. But let's remember who we're talking about here, folks. This is the girl who was once rejected for a Victoria's Secret job because Tyra felt threatened. This is the girl who stole Ren from me that Thanksgiving without a backward glance, who convinced him to transfer to Amherst so he could be near her at Smith. This is the girl who let me take the fall for the Dexatrim and a thousand other blunders.

Boss of Shiny Pony stroked his wispy goatee. "Alicia's liking Raquel for an ongoing guest slot. Inspiration, recovery, healing, sisterhood, all that jazz."

"Ongoing," Laurie repeated.

"Raquel," BOSP said, acknowledging me for the first time that meeting, "do you have any fresh thoughts on show topics?"

First I panicked. Everyone was looking at me, some defensively, some relieved that the laser beam of accusation had bypassed them, some hopeful, as if, by (supposedly) surviving an oft-fatal disease, I had some sort of revelation at hand. A fresh one. The Massengill douche of ideas, in fact.

Fresh. Fresh like flowers. Like strawberries in summer. Like water from a mountain stream . . .

At that moment, like an intact memory of the best sex you ever had in your life, a delicious nugget of inspiration sprang to the forefront of my fuzzy cranium.

Disease.

Then the voices piped up.

Guilt: *Hasn't this gone too far already? You aiming for* The Guinness Book of World Records *in sack-of-shit lying or something?*

Self-preservation: *Hon, you're in a position to speak for thousands of women who need real help. You've raised $245,325. What's a little fib for the cause?*

Guilt: *Little like her gazoombas are little.*

Self-preservation: *You need this. Without this, you're nothing. Nada. Zilch.*

Guilt: *Try living with yourself after this.*

Self-preservation: *Try living with yourself the way you were before.*

Touché.

"How to do cancer," I said, drawing it out as if plumbing this trough for the first time.

"What do you mean, how to *do* it?" BOSP was handing out no free favors.

"Just…how to do it. I don't mean to sound flip, it's just…Look, when I was diagnosed, I had no idea what to do. I mean, like what to do in the next five minutes, let alone the next few days, weeks, months. I was completely panicked, completely alone. There's no user manual for this stuff. Everybody expects you to deal with it, to accept it and move on, to get a handle on the process and the jargon—but not too much. The doctors hate when you know what you're talking about, you know?" Shiny Pony and Dreadlocked Caucasian Mail Clerk, who had stopped pushing his cart and was eavesdropping outside the door, nodded sympathetically. And enthusiastically.

If I milk this teat any harder, I'll get calluses.

"Consider it a user's guide. The User's Guide to Cancer. *Surviving* Cancer," I added, mindful of Boss of Shiny's emphasis on inspiration. "We could do it like a series. The diagnosis: how to cope. Or how to help someone cope. The treatment phase. What to expect. What are your options? How to talk to doctors. How to talk to *patients.* What to do if you fall in love with your doctor"—around me, the glowing faces dim—"just kidding, people! C'mon, let's have a sense of humor about this stuff, okay? What else? Uh, how to navigate the managed-care and insurance systems. How to find support. What to anticipate when you get better. It's like the primer you need that nobody gives you."

For the next three minutes, I expounded on my fabulous brainchild one crucial point at a time. I was afraid to look at my sister, so I didn't. I was afraid that I'd see a middle-aged woman with crow's-feet and fertility problems, with grown-out roots and a pitying smile that said, *I may be hitting the skids, but at least I don't have to play the cancer card every time I want someone to take me seriously*. Overhead, the clock ticked its way toward lunch. Finally, I ran out of wind and waited for my sentence. *Oh well, at least I have my upcoming show at SFMOMA*. And my television wardrobe, including that teal silk blouse by Chloé that Cleo swore was all the rage and happened to make my chest look almost alert.

"Huh," BOSP said.

"Tacky." Laurie.

"Nobody else has done it." Marketing Lady in White Suit. *White*.

"How?" Extremely Gay Advertising Sales Guy wailed.

"I see a panel." Shiny Pony's pony trembled. With excitement?

"Tacky," Laurie said again.

As if scenting a predator, we all turned toward the door as Alicia, ferret-tongued, statement-sloppy, shark-featured Alicia, entered. Alicia was reputed to have reproduced, but no one at the station had ever seen her children, either in person or captured in laudatory cuteness by digital photography. Perhaps she suspected—justifiably—that she would be taken less seriously if her focus was perceived as split (between the joys of corporate warfare and the rewards of nanny-assisted parenthood). Maybe she ate them at birth. Who knows? We all watched in terror as she flicked back a loose piece of lank graying-brown hair and draw a long slurp from her iced chai. She was fearsome, awesome, loathsome, raw power in a cheap, ill-fitting black suit.

"Brilliant," she said. She was looking directly at me.

I have a song.

No, I mean: *I. Have. A. Song.*

A theme song. That was written for me by real musicians.

Their names are Ned and Arturo. One is short and skinny, and the other one is tall and skinny, and they have a synthesizer with a poster of Gwen Stefani in hot pants over it on which they tap out melodies. They say things like "That so captures her essential optimism, dude" and "Dude, what's with the reverb?"

My song is called "Raquel." Ned, the tall, ruddy, easily embarrassed one, argued for the flashier "Raquel's Song," but stubborn, oversexed little Arturo won out, as is usually the case; he cited the tearjerking film *Brian's Song* as a reference we wanted to avoid (thus my "essential" optimism). Ned explained to me that "Raquel" is contrapuntal, which means it has more than one melody line. Typically—as I'm doing right now—I step through the backstage curtains at the exact moment when the first melody segues into the snazzier second line. Ta-da!

I wave at the studio audience as I stride across the klieg-warm stage to the overstuffed chairs, where Laurie sits half smiling, as if bearing up nobly under the strain of prolonged constipation.

"Hi, everyone! Hi!" I call as I blow kisses. My microphone is wireless. It is attached to the back of my slacks, which are, happily, not mom-ish at all but rather trendy, with a snug high waist and a flattering flare that gives me, for once, a proper waist-to-hip ratio.

Laurie greets me warmly, as if we weren't backstage ten minutes ago, fighting about what to get Ma for her birthday now that Eliot the Snake has sabotaged our plan by buying her season symphony tickets himself.

"For those of you just tuning in, we're thrilled to have my very own sister, Raquel Rose, back with us today for another guest-host appearance. Raquel is an artist, wife, and mother of two teenagers—my delightful niece and nephew, Taylor and

Micah—as well as a survivor of breast cancer, which she was diagnosed with earlier this year." She turns to me. "Raquel, can you tell our viewers what we'll be discussing today?"

"I sure can, Laurie. And I have to say, that color looks fabulous on you!" Laurie is wearing a pumpkin turtleneck. A tiny gold cross twinkles on her chest. Ma's going to *plotz* when she sees it. It is part of Alicia's strategy to win back the Christian Conserva-twats (her words, not mine).

"Why, thank you," Laurie says icily.

"You're welcome." Ever gracious! I arrange my features into a mask of solemnity. "Today, Laurie, with segment four of our ongoing *How to Do Cancer* series, I'm going to moderate a panel on patient-doctor communication. Now, this is a matter that's demanded our attention for many, many years, and it has been sorely neglected by the medical establishment. It's no surprise that patients-rights groups are frustrated; poor communication between physician and patient is the number one cause of patient noncompliance and the second-leading cause of clinical depression among the recently diagnosed. Did you know that, Laurie?"

"No, I didn't, Raquel. But it's utterly fascinating. And certainly revealing." Laurie's swinging heel narrowly misses the leg of my chair.

This is a lot more fun than watching Laurie on TV while manhandling the lettuce spinner in my sweatpants and waiting for Carla's UPS guy to deliver.

I make eye contact with a fiftysomething gay couple in the wings. Alicia says gay men loved me in the focus groups. "It's bad enough getting diagnosed with a dangerous or life-threatening disease. As I'm sure you can imagine, it's even worse when communication between patient and physician is strained or lacking. Today we'll be speaking with some of the Bay Area's leading oncologists and several courageous survivors about how we can improve patient-doctor communication, how we can take a stale or stressed relationship and turn it into a vibrant, healing one. At the end of the show, we'll add our findings to the Cancer Patients' Bill of Rights and petition that we're submitting to the AMA."

I turn to the audience, twisting slightly to allow the V-necked violet blouse Cleo selected to part a little deeper. My bosom performed very well in focus groups among straight men of all ages, nearly as well as my legs.

"Are you ready?" My signature war cry.

"Yes!" they shout.

"I can't hear you!" I used to find this maneuver a bit cheesy. But, over iced chais and spa pedicures with Alicia, we decided it was a crucial part of delivering what Alicia calls "the *Jerry Springer* factor."

Then, as I gaze out at the avid, adoring faces of my constituents, my heart plummets into my Marc Jacobs wedges.

It takes me a second, but, as I count seat by seat, my unease mounting, I realize that the entire front row of the studio audience is filled with my former Peninsula compadres, the power junta of JCC/PTA/MIA (mentally) ladies who lunch that guards the purity of the local social network as devotedly as the Swiss Guard shields the Vatican. In quick succession, I register Annunciata Milk, Rochelle Schitzfelder, Tate Trimble, Mimi LeMaitre, Robin Golden, and Wendy No-Longer-Welch-Yen, along with a couple of other superbly highlighted, chemically peeled, subtly liposuctioned women with lots of disposable income and plenty of time to dream up ways to torture nonbelievers.

As I absorb their intense, almost feral expressions, sleek blowouts, and, oh God, *killer* outfits, alarm begins to cloud my mind, forming a nimbus of foreboding. It is likely that they are not here to cheer me on. They are here for...something else. While I recall, word for word, my confrontation with Tate, then Rochelle, at yoga class last summer, back when I thought Phil was still canoodling Ross's wife and I no longer needed Rochelle's sponsorship to survive among the high-status members of our social set, an icy tongue of dread licks at my heart.

Why are they here?

I realize that Laurie is speaking to me. I turn toward her and smile so big, they can probably see my bleached molars.

"So, should we bring out the panel, Raquel?" If Laurie recognizes these women, all of them several rungs below her on the celebrity meter in spite of their ability to charge purchases in the four figures, she does not let on.

"Absolutely!" I say brightly.

Somebody call in a bomb threat. Somebody call in a bomb threat. Somebody...

The members of the panel—a couple of oncologists, a couple of survivors, a bioethics professor, a patients-rights lady in Birkenstocks—trot onto the stage. They all look suitably enthused to be on TV, a little deer-in-the-headlights, a little nervous, mostly cheerful, except—

Meissner.

Samuel Meissner, aka Jailbait Meissner, aka my supposed doctor, is so surprised to see me that he actually stops in his tracks, causing the professor to stumble on top of Meissner's brown loafers, one of which falls off, clunking on the stage with a soft *thwap*. It is apparent that little Sammy did not make the connection between Lauren White, celebrated host of the station's longest-running local cable-television talk show, and Raquel Rose, stagnated artist, disgruntled wife, and erstwhile cancer patient. Why would he? I'm sure he has better things to do with his time than track the Schultz girls' dramatic tribulations, like screw little Wendy on the hood of the Jag and evade Connor Welch's legal henchmen.

"Whoopsie!" Laurie has risen and is escorting my panelists to their seats, sending me gamma-ray alerts across the jealous-sister spectrum, trying to save her show and her career from my bumbling paralysis. I seem to stick, frozen to the stage, which has about it the air of a man-eating garden, toothy and succubal, drawing me down into the bilge.

Overcoming what must be some sort of undocumented acute post-traumatic stress disorder—future show topic, any-one?—I force my feet to move me to my designated place in the half-circle of chairs.

I cannot believe, out of all the oncologists the Bay Area has to offer—the nest of teaching and university-affiliated hos-pitals in the area is overflowing with the smug bastards—that they happened upon Meissner. Sure, he was recently included in a *San Francisco* magazine roundup of the leading doctors under forty. Yeah, his personal parking spot on the Stanford hospital campus is just three slots away from the head of the department's. And I'll be the first to admit that, with his pup-pyish eyes and hairy Neanderthal forearms, he's minor-league fantasy fodder. But so what? That doesn't make him God's gift to cable-television talk shows. That doesn't make him look skinny on camera. That doesn't make him *God*.

Other things I cannot believe: that I was too lazy to insist on reviewing Shiny's updated panelist list. With a few min-utes' notice, I could have invented something, a family emer-gency or health crisis or spontaneous nosebleed, anything to get out of having to face Meissner, who—oh my God—is looking at me with his brows drawn into a quizzical, near-comprehending grimace.

Oh my God. Oh my shit. Oh my God. Oh my—

"Welcome." In the face of my near-complete collapse, Laurie is back to her brisk, vivacious, accessibly sultry self. She introduces every one of my executioners—panelists, I mean—and turns the mike back to me only when the state of my exhalations indicates that I am neither going to hyperventilate nor soil myself next to the tabletop potpourri.

"So, Raquel," she says in the same grave tone she used to employ when we were teenagers and she wanted to convey the potential consequences of defying her in front of Ma and Dad, "why don't we start with medical school?"

Medical school. Medical. School. That place where people have lots of furtive cot sex and learn how to be doctors. What about it?

With greater force of will than it took to attend Laurie and Ren's wedding, I plaster the fakest smile on my face that has possibly ever been seen outside a presidential campaign, and I address the panel.

Birkenstocks smiles back tentatively. I latch on to her like a suckling wolf pup. "Ms. Johns. Thanks for joining us today. Tell me, do they *teach* communication in med school?" It comes out sounding like an accusation. I realize I am practically yelling. Offstage, Shiny Pony is conferring worriedly with Lecherous Without Cause Producer and Lecherous with Cause Assistant Producer, perhaps deciding whether my condition warrants immediate transfer to a maximum-security psychiatric facility, or if they can get away with a simple roofie and a balaclava.

"I don't know," Birkenstocks stutters. "I'm, uh, a social worker by training. I never went to med school." She looks genuinely sad, as if, by deciding to take Sociology of the Feminist Superego instead of organic chemistry, she failed me in advance.

"Of course," I say, frantically perusing my notes for a name with an M.D. behind it that isn't Meissner. "*Dr.* Keshishian. Abel Keshishian. You're an oncologist. A doctor. A cancer doctor, in fact. What is *your* position on doctor-patient communication?"

Oh God. Am officially the female Bill O'Reilly.

Keshishian raises caterpillar brows. "Uh, it's good?"

"Exactly!" I stand up. "This is *exactly* what I'm talking about, people! How much longer can we put up with pat pro forma answers to this kind of crucial, life-altering question? When are we going to stand up and demand our rights? Our rights as patients, as women, as *human beings?*"

"Hey, that's not fair. I didn't say I didn't think it was important! What the hell is this—" Keshishian mutters a choice expletive, which, because of modern-day sound technology, I later discover after watching the tape for the twenty-seventh time, was easily heard not just in the *Living with Lauren!* back row but also down the hall in Alicia's office and outside the studio by two landscapers who were, at that moment, digging a trench for a perennial ground cover.

Laurie cuts a glance at Boss of Shiny Pony. He flashes his hand: five minutes before we can cut to a commercial break.

A droplet of sweat scuttles down my back, over my tailbone, tickling the groove between my butt cheeks where dumb, gorgeous Duke Dunne lingered longer than was technically necessary.

Laurie gets up and straightens her pumpkin sweater. Her gold cross glints in the light. My sister's eyes glow with the eternal strength of deep ocean, of deciduous forest fleeced with mist. They sweep me and everybody else in the room into a whirlpool of protection. Watching her radiate her unique brand of incandescent, comforting resolve, I acknowledge that there are individuals for whom the reality warrants the hype. Joan of Arc. Oprah Winfrey. Jesus.

Laurie.

Either they really do possess a higher purpose, or they're terrifically adept at making you think they do. Really, at the end of the day, what's the difference? I also think it is unlikely that we—Laurie and I, the savior and the accursed—will be breaking bread together anytime soon.

"Why don't we start taking questions from our studio audience?" she improvises. Immediately, an *LwL!* serf with a microphone darts from backstage, puppyish with resolve, the Wimbledon ball boy of cable talk shows.

Rochelle Schitzfelder raises her hand. Her big slab of lox-fingered hand. Raises it higher than anyone else, her ugly chunky gold wedding bands piled up on her ring finger like dog collars on a Chihuahua. Wimbledon Boy runs to her and holds the mike under her big lox lips. In spite of the circumstances, I can't help thinking, *Christ, somebody should slap a bagel around those motherfuckers.*

"I'm Rochelle Schitzfelder from Los Altos Hills, California. Hi, Heshie! Hi, Bunny!" She flaps her hand at the cameras and slobbers on the mike, causing Wimbledon Boy to wince. "My question is for Ms. Rose. Ms. Rose, how did you react when your oncologist gave you your biopsy results?" Rochelle stares at me, challenge written from her scant forehead to her weak chin. A tic tugs at the corner of her cheek, as if teasing the self-satisfied smile that's waiting impatiently to reveal itself.

In a flash, the truth is out, lying gross and distended between us, a decomposing whale on a windswept beach.

She knows.

I clear my throat. One minute till commercial break. If I can delay her till then, I can "accidentally" sever a finger in the cantina and escape.

"I was in shock, I suppose. Like most people, I was hoping it was a bad dream—that it would just disappear." *Like you, witch-breath . . . poof!*

"That may be true, but you don't really have cancer, do you?"

Rochelle Schitzfelder has extremely small eyes. Unforgiving eyes. How could I not have noticed this before?

A horrible half-burp, half-giggle bursts out of me. "Thankfully, I am in remission," I say.

After this über-lie, I hear Meissner stand up behind me, or at least squirm in his seat. With my back blocking his censorious visage, I imagine him withdrawing a poison-dart gun and shooting me, point-blank, in the head. For the first time since this all started, I want it to end. Just not this way.

"How can you be in remission if you never *had* cancer?" Wimbledon Boy is stunned with horror, but he still manages to hold the mike under Rochelle Schitzfelder's mouth, which is glistening with a vengeful spray of saliva. A buzz of protest starts up from the crowd. Like disciples, the front row falls into worshipful line. Annunciata nods emphatically, as if giving Rochelle's vendetta her papal blessing.

"If nobody else is going to tell them, *I* will," Rochelle says. She turns around. "Raquel Rose is a complete fraud. I have the biopsy results right here! This woman never had cancer. Everything she's told you is a lie. She built a whole career out of her big bad cancer experience." Rochelle is scathing. "The suffering cancer victim, milking it, everyone eating right out of her lying hand. When people, *real* people, mind you, people sitting right here, really have it!" In a stroke of genius, Wendy Yen removes her wig. The effect is as shocking as a vicious slap to the face. All the light of the room seems to coalesce on her bald head, studded with snow-white tufts. Why is Wendy Yen taking part in this piece of horror theater? What did I ever do to her? Besides not have cancer, that is.

Or is that enough?

Rochelle places her hand on Wendy's scrawny shoulder. "Dr. Meissner, you know the truth. *You* tell them."

Meissner scowls. As I watch his ocher eyes crinkle sternly at the corners, it occurs to me that the Boy Doctor is not part of this plot to ruin me. Meissner, operating in a world where lives are rudely snatched by the dread hand of mortality and the innocent suffer for no good reason, finds the whole business distasteful and sullying. No doubt he is sorry he ever met me. It occurs to me that his presence on the panel is one of those blind acts of fate so often interpreted as fortune, good or bad, but in fact an accidental spasm of time and place. While I watch him prepare a response, the faces of my family pass before my eyes: Phil, Taylor, Micah, Laurie, Ma, Ren. I want them, want their arms around me and their hands on mine. I want to go back to that fateful day when Meissner told me the good news, and do nearly everything completely differently.

"The State of California Confidentiality of Medical Records Act prevents me from revealing *facts* about my patients," Meissner says, every word dripping with contempt, "or even whether somebody *is* my patient."

Whatever his intent, the damage is done. The audience erupts in shock and fury. Laurie's hand is at her throat, plucking at the cross. For once, I see, she is out of her depth. For no longer than it takes a lie to take flight, our eyes meet. In hers, I see shock and anger with a pity chaser. Then she looks away. Offstage, Shiny Pony sobs into her script notes.

Boss of Shiny Pony is sliding his hand across his throat. Cameramen flick off their lenses. Technicians cut at last to the planned commercial break. As I sag into my chair, nausea painting my stomach, two words emerge from my parched lips over and over, like a mantra, belying the indictment.

"Not everything's a lie," I say. "Not everything."

CHAPTER 29

When Raquel's Wax Wings Are Revealed to Be . . . Wax

My finger hovers over speed dial: pizza or Chinese?

A black crow, universal harbinger of death, bisects the sky over my head. It feels good to have confirmation. Pizza, then.

After I order the team-size pie with artery-clogging sausage and extra cheese, plus a single Diet Coke—old habits die hard—I let the phone fall onto the blanket and resume staring into the milky bowl of sky overhead.

Ultimate irony: From the minute my family discovered I was not dying, I have deeply, unreservedly wanted to.

It is not the humiliation, per se—although that itself is as jagged and unceasing as a butcher's blade carving through raw sirloin—but, rather, the vile knowledge that no matter what my prior rationalizations were, the experiment in civic activism and self-improvement was not worth the pain I have caused them.

How could I have ever thought that it was?

That I am a monster of some sort is indisputable; whether

monsters are capable of repairing the damage they've caused, let alone clambering past it, is as yet undetermined.

I dip my toe over the edge of the pool for sensual respite before I remember that it is drained. The pale blue-white canyon is vacant and dry, save a rainbow heap of leaves in the shallows and a clot of mud over the drain. Like my conscience, the pool awaits cleansing from unidentified sources. On the advice of our Realtor, we will leave it unfilled until the house is sold, primed for future occupancy.

I feel like a criminal awaiting the firing squad.

Unlike those assembled to eke justice on my criminal brethren, my firing squad delivers the bullets individually and protractedly. The reckoning started four days ago when Rochelle Schitzfelder outed me on *Living with Lauren!* Things show no sign of slowing down.

Remembering is hard, so I try not to think of it. I am not particularly successful. Yesterday I drove over the Dumbarton Bridge to Fremont, an hour away in noxious traffic, to shop for food in a dilapidated Safeway where no one would recognize me. Halfway through, I began to picture the house, empty save me and the two bassets—who, I suspect, would desert me in a heartbeat if they found an alternate food source—and, panicked, abandoned my basket in the middle of the snack aisle. Its contents—two one-liter bottles of Diet Coke, a rainbow of chips (some of which contained the stuff that causes anal leakage), Ho Hos, beef jerky, cold-sore cream, and panty liners—sketched a sad existence. A solitary sad existence.

Alone yet accountable—that pretty much sums it up.

Laurie fired the first shots.

"Are you all right?" Her first words to me, delivered in her off-the-set dressing room after last week's show, were so much kinder than I deserved, they immediately unleashed a wellspring of self-recriminating tears. My downfall had redressed the cosmic imbalance between us. Things were now back to normal, with Laurie operating on high ground while I squirmed in the mud, a swine seeking the throwaway morsels of her mistress.

"Do you have any Kleenex?" I asked.

Laurie handed me a box. Apparently, enough guests required tissue that her show's logo was stamped on the container: *LwL*-approved snot rags. For the discriminating nose-blower. Except for the moral repugnance of my actions, I was not alone in my regrets.

I blew my nose hard. Traces of my lipstick stained the tissue red. A year ago, if somebody had suggested I'd wear red lipstick on an occasion other than Halloween, I'd have laughed.

"Is it true, Rachel?" Laurie looked so beautiful and righteous. She could have boiled in here full of now-you've-done-its and you-make-me-want-to-pukes. Instead, she gave me Kleenex and the benefit of the doubt. For the first time ever, I believed unreservedly that she deserved Ren more than I. She really did.

"Uh-huh." More sobs. "I think I'm hyperventilating."

Laurie cocked her head. "No, if you were, you wouldn't be able to talk."

"Do...Don't you have to go back out there?" How horrible. Maybe I should give her my adoption story, the one I handed out to people like Cleo and Jonesie, so she could distance herself from my ethical decrepitude. For all I knew, she really was born to Scandinavian royalty.

"It's okay. We're re-airing the show about mite-free bedding. Everyone's gone. We gave the studio audience another set of tickets and gift certificates to Jamba Juice."

I pinched my thigh under the beautiful slacks that I'd never wear again. "Do the kids know yet?"

"I don't know. Phil called the studio when you didn't answer your cell. I think he may have told them." Laurie thoughtfully plucked another box of tissues from a cabinet and set it in front of me. "Rach, I think you should call Ma," she said.

We both knew Ma watched *Living with Lauren!* religiously. If I closed my eyes, I could almost see her sitting on the chartreuse sofa, spine straight, one bird leg dangling off the edge, the other tucked under her butt, curly gray head cocked to one side, her small fist curled around a mug of tea.

I didn't answer. I *couldn't* answer. How do you tell your mother you pretended you had cancer because of a telethon? Because you thought your life sucked? Because you wanted to be an exciting person, someone whom others admire, even envy? Someone who has orgasms and sculptures that are reviewed by the *Chronicle* (the sculptures, not the orgasms). Someone who is more to her children and husband than a place to fling coats when they come off the ski lift for lunch. Someone for whom life *thrills*.

I took a deep breath. It had nowhere to go; my diaphragm had been pink-slipped. "Okay. I'll call Ma." I grabbed the phone and pressed the familiar numbers on autopilot. I was 100 percent sure Ma would be sitting by the phone in a confused version of death-watch mode, not even offering a pretense of continuing to thrive by browsing a magazine or going for her daily power walk. I was fairly sure Eliot would be standing by, whispering affirmations of my shittiness in Ma's ear. The image caused sweat to pop out on my forehead.

Laurie placed her hand on mine. Our similarly widow's-peaked foreheads tilted toward each other, met; they were the only physical attribute we shared, courtesy of Dad.

"Will you stay with me?" I said.

"Okay."

Suddenly, the sun winks out.

"Raquel?"

I press pause on the nightmare memory of telling Ma and open my eyes to the (glaring) here and now. A big head looms above me, surrounded by frizzy curls. I want to be dramatic and scream, but since I know it's Sue—I heard the baby, Arlie, shrieking from the front yard during my ruminations—and she knows I know, I fold myself into a sitting position. It is harder than a month ago; I have gained back ten of the twelve pounds. Okay, I have gained back thirteen, but who's counting?

"Hey, you." I get up and hug Sue in what even I can see is an anemic manner not befitting a twenty-five-year friendship. Two-month-old Arlie is strapped across Sue's chest in a fleece sling. She has cradle cap but is still adorable, with a head of strawberry fluff, triangular elfin ears and a wail that says she will give her parents grief when she's fourteen.

"I'm glad to see you're not wallowing in self-pity or anything." Sue glances sharply at the pile of empty processed-food wrappers next to me before pulling out a lawn chair and flopping down in it. "I have come on a mission of mercy," she says. Arlie starts crying again, more lion cub than kitten. Sue whips out a swollen, blue-veined breast and pops the baby on. Her eyes narrow at me. "What's your plan, to just sit here until the house is sold and they come to cart you away?" she says after a minute.

"No, actually, I was thinking I'd leave before the cart part. I was going to ask my only friend if I could rent a room. My supportive, not-into-eviscerating-people-when-they're-down best friend."

"I see." Pause. "Where are the children?" Sue is very stern. It occurs to me that she thinks I might be crazy, that she suspects I have done something even worse than The Great

Lie. She has been this way ever since the Baron von Münchhausen fight.

"They chose to go with their father."

There is no way around it: This hurts. When I had it out with them, Taylor stared at me in shock, revulsion and relief warring on her pretty face as she processed my rationalizations. Her response, when it came, was to stalk to her room and calmly begin packing her overnight bag. Having expected a higher-volume dramatic gesture—flinging herself into Phil's arms and sobbing; coming at me with nails extended—I'd been more than alarmed by my daughter's show of poise. What had made her grow up so quickly? Was it the not-cancer? The not-much-of-an-affair? The not-yet-divorce? Or some combination of the three?

Micah remained true to form, yelling a bit and stomping around, then telling me "You're pathetic and I feel sorry for you" before adding his duffel to the collection of bags at the front door. I felt almost sorry for Phil; his resourcefulness doesn't stretch to providing dinner, especially not with the single frying pan he now uses to heat everything from refried beans to Campbell's Chunky soup.

"And you're just going to roll over for this?" Sue asks.

I shrug. "They're teenagers. I can't force them to stay here. Phil rented a two-bedroom apartment in Redwood City. After we sell the house and the divorce goes through, we'll see what we can afford separately. Micah's been accepted at Michigan. He'll go to Ann Arbor on a partial soccer scholarship. Taylor will stay with Phil through the summer, then decide who she wants to live with for her junior year." Just saying it pains me, but what am I supposed to do? Tay made it clear that the prospect of living with Crazy Cancerless Mom would add significantly to her usual load of teenage angst. I could hardly put her through more trauma simply to salve my own maternal ego, could I?

Sue switches gears. "I ran into Saskia at the corner store. She acted kind of weird."

Weird only if you feel uncomfortable chatting up the best friend of the artist you recently kicked out of your gallery for creating art under false pretenses.

"Maybe she was having a hot flash," I tell Sue. "Or maybe she's just a bitch."

Sue stands up so quickly that Arlie pops off and lets us know it. "What's up your ass?"

I shift and release my sweatpant wedgie in a way that is self-evident.

Sue continues, "Stop being such a snot for once. All I did was drive all the way down here to see if you're okay, and what do I get? A load of smart-ass commentary and evasion. I have some news for you, Quel—they have a right to be angry."

"I know."

"Do you? Because you don't act like it. You act like everyone's being too hard on you or something. Like this is somebody else's fault. Like you didn't—"

"I know! I get it already: I'm a big liar. I'm a terrible mother. I'm a terrible wife. I'm a bad friend. I know! So will you just shut up? Will you please, please just shut up?" My heart is pounding so loudly it blots out the shape of my friend's hurt.

Sue steps back, distress etched into her snub Celt features. "You . . . I can't talk to you," she says. Tears shine all down her face.

"Sue, I'm sorry. I didn't mean—"

"The fuck you didn't. I'm out of here. Man, you are a piece of work." Sue grabs her diaper bag, her poncho, and her assorted babyware, muttering to herself before turning back around with a finger extended toward my chest. "You're such a martyr. You know that? You're so caught up in the idea of your own victimhood that it never occurs to you that *you* could be the one victimizing someone else." With each tear that glosses Sue's pink cheeks, my heart contracts. It's Münchhausenville all over again. Except that this time my record is tarnished by a second strike. In the high-stakes game of friends for life, I'm on my way to prison with no possibility of parole.

"Quel, I'm saying this to you because I am your friend, and I always will be your friend: You wouldn't know a powerless moment if it punched you in the schnozz."

CHAPTER 30

Somewhere Between Great Sex and an Ass Massage

It is Friday night. I am invited to Ma and Eliot's for dinner. My first instinct, honed by many years of reluctance, is to weasel out of it with an excuse. However, as I sponge-bathe my armpits and private parts in front of the bathroom mirror, rub on half a bottle of anti-wrinkle cream in the hopes that more is better, and comb out my tangles so I won't be mistaken for a homeless Rastafarian, it occurs to me that I owe them my presence more than I owe myself another night of bad TV.

Out of all the people whom I wronged, Ma and Eliot are the last ones I would have guessed would extend me a quick and relatively painless pardon. Yet they did. Out of all the people whose feelings I trod on, Ma and Eliot are the last ones I would have guessed would brush themselves off and draw me to their hearth for comfort. Yet they have.

My house is too quiet, with the kids at Phil's. Everything that used to provide comfort—the kid-free master bath, my secret chocolate stash, the now-empty wicker bin for

Phil's newspapers—is a rebuke. Everything that used to be annoying—lights left on, muddy footprints on the rug, crap cluttering the foyer, phones warbling—I sorely miss. Frankly, if we get an offer for the house tomorrow, it will not be too soon. Why is it that the good chapters of our lives are woefully short and the bad ones so long and ponderous?

On the way to Ma's, some chivalrous impulse prompts me to stop at Whole Foods for flowers and dessert. As I pull out of my parking spot with a bouquet of calla lilies and three pints of soy ice cream in the trunk, Mimi and Reggie LeMaitre's Volvo slides into the adjacent slot. Mimi's hand rises to the passenger window in a friendly wave before she remembers my pariah status and quickly morphs the gesture into urgent hair smoothing. I don't see her face redden because I am already waiting at the light, my heart pounding along with the abrasive dance radio station I now listen to because it's the best way to imagine the kids are in the car with me.

I arrive in Woodside without further mishap. Eliot answers the door. He is wearing fluorescent multicolored parachute pants like you see on steroid-freak bodybuilders and a skin-tight black T-shirt with girlish cap sleeves that looks suspiciously like one of Taylor's.

"The Black Sheep's here!" he hollers, presumably to Ma.

I give my stepfather a deliberate once-over. "Nobody told me Hulk Hogan donated his wardrobe to charity for the elderly."

"Heh heh. That's a good one," he says.

For some reason whose source is as yet unclear, I find Eliot a lot less maddening than before. He's still Eliot, but I have started to view his high-flying platitudes as mostly harmless. His comments about my appearance lack sting, and sometimes, when I'm not alert, I catch myself feeling something like happiness when I think of Ma having someone to spend her golden years with. Unlike me, she, at least, will not do the Elderhostel cruise circuit alone.

Ma hands me a ladle when I enter the kitchen. "Stir and simmer!" she commands me before jogging out of the room.

I lift up the pot lid and sniff. The chicken bourguignonne is weak, so I pour in a little more burgundy wine and a snifter of salt before Ma can come back and lecture me about Eliot's sodium intake. One properly salted meal won't kill him, but my mother's cooking might.

While I stir and simmer, I reflect on my relationship with the older generation. It is on level ground at the moment, a position so unprecedented that I can only attribute it to the shock of my unmasking.

When I phoned Ma after the show taping to explain about the misdiagnosis, just one thing about her reaction was predictable.

"You really don't have it?" she said.

"No. I'm so sorry, Ma. I tried—"

"What?"

"I tried to tell you, but"—all reasoning comes up short—"I tried to tell you," I finished weakly.

Ma was silent for a moment, save the slight stressed panting that she sometimes does since she was diagnosed—for real—with early-stage atherosclerosis. I fantasized that she understood how I could have bungled this so severely, and was able to generate compassion.

"Oh," she said. For Ma, gladness was measured in brevity; thus, she was beyond happy. Then: "Make sure you keep all those cancer research links up on your blog."

Check.

Ma returns and takes over the stirring. "I almost forgot I had to tape Terry Gross. She's interviewing Dean Ornish on *Fresh Air.*" Dean Ornish is Ma's version of Brad Pitt. While other women find sexual fulfillment in replaying the bedroom scene in *Thelma & Louise* ad infinitum, Ma pores over low-fat menus and ruminates on the appeal of soy isoflavones, I'm sure with Dean hovering overhead in sinewy splendor.

I pour myself a glass of Ma's crappy Bordeaux and sit down at the table. "I had another fight with Sue. It was my fault."

"What happened?"

"I was bitchy and she was right."

Ma nods. "You always had such conviction about things, even as a child. And backbone. And stubborn? *Oy vey iz mir.* I once had to force you to apologize to Paige Clark's mother for telling her you wouldn't walk to school with Paige because she was too vain to wear her glasses and you didn't want to get run over by a car just because Paige was a stupid fathead. You were very strong-willed. I think you viewed changing your mind about anything as a weakness."

Leave it to my mother to paint her kids' character flaws as virtues. If I turned out to be a serial killer, Ma would have proudly recounted my filleting abilities.

Ma gives the stew another stir and sits down. Her forehead is damp with steam. She takes my hand and rubs it between her strong, squat ones. She can't stop touching me since she found out I'm okay. It's like she was storing up all the handholds she wanted to give me when I was sick, and now they're overflowing.

"Make up with Susie," she says. "Make up with her right away. After we eat, I'll get El out of the office, and you can use his phone."

The subtext is clear: Life is too short to sweat the small stuff. I wonder if she is going to tell me to make up with Phil next. That one is going to be a lot harder.

She attacks from the left flank, so I don't see it coming. "Your father and I split up once."

"What?" I have zero memory of this.

"It was the spring of 1968. I know that because Laurie missed the cutoff for kindergarten that year, and I had to get a babysitter so I could go back to work part-time. Stu didn't want me to work. That was a big part of it. I was so angry. At the time it seemed like he represented everything traditional and paternalistic about men that we were fighting against. I couldn't understand why what he wanted should trump what I wanted. Things were different then."

I try to recast my gentle, patient, loving father with the marauding misogynist Ma is painting, and fail miserably. "What happened?" I ask.

"Well, I went to my parents' for a week, and Grandma Adele came in to cook and clean for him." Ma shakes her head. "She never liked me. She wanted Stuey to marry Joanie Weinberg."

I take a sip of wine. "Would you seriously have left him, or—not to make light of it or anything—was it more a dramatic gesture on your part?"

"Oh, I wouldn't have left Stu over something like that. Work? Feh. I just needed to be angry about something. The sex, maybe. But work? With two beautiful girls to raise? Not a chance. I just wanted him to know that he could take his positions, but there were going to be consequences."

The sex. Ugh. But how bad could it be? They *had* managed to conceive two children.

"What was the, uh, problem?" Delicacy: hopefully contagious.

"Your father, bless his heart, was a bit of a nonstarter in the sex department, I'm afraid." Ma gets up to fluff the brown rice, which she buys at a natural-food store and has the fibrous, swollen texture of a rattan chair thrown into the sea.

"Oh. Okay." In spite of my own recent attempts at sexual

escapades, I think we all know I am a stolid traditionalist at heart (for sure when it comes to knowledge of my own parents' mating rituals).

"He had other qualities," Ma continues. "God knows there's more to marriage than the sex. He was great with you girls. Very hands-on for his time. And a good provider. And smart! We did the crossword together every Sunday. He always got the hard ones. Stuey was good with cars, though not handy generally. And he understood how to balance work and family. So many men at that time never took vacations. But we went somewhere every year, plus the holidays. We had wonderful family trips. Remember the time we went to Rosarita? And stayed in that wonderful casita on the beach?" Ma's almond eyes are warm. I don't remember Rosarita, but it doesn't matter, because seeing Ma melt at a memory of Dad gives me goose bumps. The good kind.

"Eliot knows how to please me," she tacks on with surprising firmness.

"Um..." My comfort zone is receding into the distance, like a city skyline viewed through a jet-plane window.

Ma looks me straight in the eye. "One thing you learn when you're an oldster like me is, things aren't as either/or as you used to think. It *is* possible to love people in different ways. To love them *as much* without loving them the same way or for the same reasons. The young have an obsession with equity. When you age, you come to terms with a different—in a way, clearer—sort of justice. You're all in the same boat, so you don't have the urge to split hairs over what are essentially unimportant things or things you can't control."

I let that sink in. "Are you talking about Dad and Eliot or me and Laurie?"

"What do you think?"

"I think..." What did I think? That Ma always favored Laurie and found me and my accomplishments wanting—and made it perfectly obvious. That it hurt. That, over the years, the hurt accumulated, filming over my innate good sense like a ripening cataract. That a dire fate can leave you feeling weirdly exultant. That although I've been right about some things lately, I've been wrong about a lot more.

Outside, the automatic sprinklers kick into gear, hitting the window every few seconds with a hushed *tat-tat-tat*. The drumroll sensation lends a sense of urgency to the current line of inquiry.

"Why were you always so damn hard on me?" I ask Ma. It is luxuriant, saying it out loud.

"Because you were worth it. Because you *are* worth it."

"Laurie...it was like she could do no wrong. Like everything she did pleased you. And nothing I did." Steamy anger pulses in my chest. It feels good. "It always felt like, to you, we were nothing more than our success, our performance in some game. And Laurie always won the game, because I never knew the rules exactly, or played by them well, in any case—"

Ma is shaking her head before I can even finish. "Laurie has certain gifts. You have other gifts. In a lot of ways, she's not as tough as you. She cares more what people think. She has a more textbook definition of what it is to be successful. You're more like me. Independent. Eccentric. A questioner. A risk-taker."

I laugh. "I'm the most dependent, risk-averse person I've ever known! I can't even go to the bathroom at my high school reunion without taking a friend with me."

"I'm talking about emotional risks, Rachel," Ma says. She waves her hand dismissively. "Do you think I give a damn if you jump out of airplanes or ski down mountains? Your bungee cord's not going to make you chicken soup when you're sick! The biggest pile of fan mail in the world is no substitute for a family who loves you, for kids who trust and rely on you, for a husband who wants to be your equal partner in this big, hard, messy life of yours. I'm saying that you are capable of deep relationships that challenge you, because you are willing to give a lot of yourself. You open yourself up for a million little hurts, but they're worth it, don't you see? Where do you think your talent comes from, your left toe? It's empathy. It's humor. It's *heart*. Do you think Micah would have told you he was gay if you didn't have the emotional depth, the strength, to help him cope?"

"He didn't exactly tell me." My heart fibrillates at the memory.

"That's not the issue."

Hmm. I see holes here, but...

"Let Ren go."

"What?"

"You heard me."

"But I don't—"

"—carry a torch for Ren White. Yes, I know. That's why you've been holding back with Phil all these years, sabotaging your marriage with unrealistic expectations, with visions of romantic perfection in case Ren snaps out of it and realizes he chose the wrong sister."

"Ma..." This is one matter on which I never sought Ma's counsel. It was too dangerous, too fraught. Besides, I used to like hanging on to—what did she call it?—unrealistic expectations and visions of romantic perfection. It had a nice ring to it, sort of like "grilled cheese sandwich with ranch dressing."

"Ma, I think I'm over it." Boy, saying it feels fantastic. And true. True!

Ma peers at me over the moons of her glasses. "Feh. I never understood what you saw in Loren, anyway. He's like those shiksa goddesses in the movies. All blond fluff and social clubs where everyone's got a terminal case of verbal constipation. Redford leading Barbra around by her *yentls*. Corncobs up their hoo-haws. He's a good man, of course he is. He's been very devoted to Laurie. But he was never right for you. You need someone who can stand up to you when you're out of line. Ren's essentially nonconfrontational. He likes things simple, clean. You need a real man. A man who can get his hands dirty. A man with a mouth on him. You need a mensch."

An image of Phil sprawled in our bed after our last round of separated sex fills my mind. His usual postcoital slumber had overtaken him an astonishing eight minutes after the act (compared to the usual four). In the interim, my ex(tracurricular)-husband had managed to don a pair of hideous orange and maroon plaid pajamas and enlighten me as to several points of putting interest from the annals of a three-year-old *Golf Digest*. Oh, and he also gave me a pretty outstanding ass massage. Phil, I can see with the painful clarity of tardy awareness, is *it:* the one, the only, the end of the line, the über-mensch.

My spiritual life partner with a side of sandbag.

"I'm not saying Phil is perfect. I'm saying it's time to get off your *tuchas* and fight. For. Your. Marriage!" Ma waggles her imitation Incan fertility necklace at me.

Laughter bubbles up my throat so sharply that I choke on my wine. Ma slaps me on the back and moves in for the Heimlich, forgetting, in her Red Cross–certified fervor, that there is nothing to dislodge. Phil may not be the antidote to all that ails me, but he is forever Phil, perfect in all aspects of his essential Philness. A vital part of the thing that is Raquel and Phil, the thing that seems to thrive in spite of the abuse we heap on it, a veritable cockroach of a relationship. Phil can be trusted to care about our "usness" long after most men will have frittered away their marital equity on replacement wives and youth-seeking diversions. This fact is not negated by the fact that my husband fucked Tate Trimble a couple of times five, eight, ten years ago. On the contrary: It's proved by it. And this, I know from experience, is a beautiful thing. He has given me a gift—the gift of the impervious marriage.

All these years, I clung to my nineteen-year-old self's notion of Ren White as a talisman against change, a doctor's note excusing me from responsibility for fulfilling my own potential.

And then I tried to do the same with Duke Dunne.

Not that the boy isn't great in the sack. But as Ma once said, marriages are more than great sex. I may amend that: Marriages are more than great sex, but less than a great ass massage.

"I'm going to tell Eliot to stop writing me checks," I hear myself say.

Ma nods. "Good girl."

CHAPTER 31

Maury Would Be Proud

"I think she should look hot but a little unkempt, like Kathleen Turner in *Body Heat* after they find out—"

"—so the viewers know she's guilty of her crimes!" Jonesie actually claps his hands.

"I don't think I can do this," I say. My heart is beating savagely. Perhaps I will have a heart attack onstage. Alicia will be pleased: "Raquel Rose having a heart attack and soiling herself while confessing to her crimes" performed well in focus groups.

Cleo massages my shoulders. "I heard that mail was running two to one in favor of bringing you back to explain what happened. I think people are on your side; they just need to hear it from the horse's mouth. They need to know that you've suffered, then they'll forgive you."

"My mother loves you," Jonesie pipes up.

"I did very well among Asian women forty-five and up," I say dully.

Shiny Pony sticks her head in the dressing room. "Five minutes." Shiny registers my sickly pallor, which no amount of pink foundation has been able to rectify. "Raquel, you're doing the right thing. I think you'll feel better afterward."

"Can someone put a trash can beside the sofa? In case I, uh, puke?"

Shiny sucks it up. "Absolutely." She leaves, and we hear her directing Sweet Face—who never was canned due to my ego trip, which I'm glad about now—toward an appropriate vessel.

Cleo adopts Alicia's brusque Long Island brogue. "Onstage puking is unacceptable! Do you think Laqueta pukes onstage? Do you think Laqueta suffers from 'nerves'? Do you think Laqueta has nerves? I'll tell you: no. Laqueta had her nerves removed, because she wants to host the top Bay Area talk show, and she understands the meaning of personal sacrifice."

I can't help smiling. "You better watch it. She has spies everywhere. She told me when we were getting our salt scrubs."

"I don't care." Cleo thrums her tongue piercing. "Jo, better finish her up. I'm going to need a smoke to get through this one."

Laurie brushes Shiny away and clips the mike to my slacks herself. I interpret this as a gesture of support. Either that or she wants to verify that, indeed, I have ballooned by two pants sizes since my downfall three weeks ago.

"Are you all right?" Laurie rubs lipstick off her teeth without looking in a mirror and swings her sheet of golden hair around so it falls perfectly into place.

"With the right combination of drugs and a one-way ticket to the witness protection program, I could be."

Laurie pats me on the knee. "You'll feel better after this. I promise."

Why does everybody keep saying that? It's as if they planned it at the meeting: *Now, the only way we're going to get her to come on and confess is if we assure her she'll feel better afterward. You and I both know the humiliation's going to be excruciating, but let's paint the picture a little brighter than that for the sake of Raquel's sanity and Alicia's promotion, okay?*

The lights seem brighter than usual. I squint into them, trying to locate a friendly face. Instead, I spot my bust subject, lawyer Jean, looking rancorous, and Dr. Minh with his rat-nest-headed assistant/tart, Karen.

Dr. Minh is snarfing a hot dog.

First, how does he even know my shame? Did the show's producers take out a full-page ad in *Breathivore Digest* or something? Second—and I say this with the utmost humility and compassion—Dr. Minh's fall from dietary grace seems even more reprehensible than him fucking Karen or me pretending I had cancer. Maybe I should text-message Alicia: *Show topic: Breathivore acupressurists who resort to nitrite-laden meat consumption to offset the stress of professional mortification.*

Eliot and Ma are here. Ma is reading *Mother Jones* as if the upcoming affair promises to be no more harrowing than a trip to the dentist. Eliot has chosen to bolster family pride by wearing a T-shirt that says I BELIEVE YOU, RAQUEL. My own husband and kids are absent. I don't know whether to be devastated or grateful. Thankfully, the Peninsula bitch brigade has not deigned to show up for my public lashing.

The crowd warmer-upper passes out the last of the audience freebies, and Boss of Shiny Pony does the countdown. Tactics were discussed, and it was agreed that the cameramen would shoot Laurie in close-up for her intro, in recognition of the gravity of the topic.

My pulse ricochets. "Laur," I hiss, remembering to muffle my mike for once. "I have to tell you something."

"We're about to start." Her smile doesn't waver.

"Ren is your soul mate," I whisper furiously. "I think I had to meet him just so fate would bring him to you."

Laurie stares at me. The countdown ends. She turns to the camera. "Hello, and welcome to *Living with Lauren!* We're glad to have you with us today, as our show promises to be a memorable one.

"We have with us today Raquel Rose. Many of you know Raquel from her many guest appearances on this show. For those of you tuning in for the first time, some history: About a year ago, Raquel was diagnosed with stage four breast cancer. Unbeknownst to her, her biopsy results had been switched with another woman's. Fortunately for her, the error was discovered within the month, and her doctor informed her of the mistake. Raquel did not have cancer at all; her cyst was benign." Laurie shuffles to the next notecard.

"Raquel is a married mother of two teenagers. Before the incident, she was a homemaker in a Bay Area suburb. Following the misdiagnosis, she rediscovered her interest in studio art and jump-started her career as a sculptor. Some of you may recognize her as a regular guest on this show, where she has been instrumental in raising several hundred thousand dollars for breast-cancer support."

Laurie leans forward. "Some things you should know: Raquel did not immediately inform her loved ones of the diagnostic error. She delayed telling them for a total of ten months, and did so only when forced to as a result of statements that were made by studio audience members on an earlier *Living with Lauren!* Also, evidence suggests that she benefited both professionally and personally from the charade.

"We're here today to hear Raquel's story from her perspective. *Why* did she allow her family and friends to believe she was sick? *How* does someone perpetrate a farce of this nature and magnitude? Does what she did qualify as a clinical problem that requires medical intervention, or are there psychological motives at work that fall under the more commonplace rubric of low self-esteem, something I'm sure many of us can relate to? These questions—and more—will be answered today as we explore the fascinating story of how and, perhaps more important, *why* a typical American housewife would pretend to be suffering from a sometimes terminal disease."

I am not surprised to be described this way, by Laurie or anyone, but it still stings.

"In the interest of full disclosure, I should tell you that Raquel Rose is my sister, which makes today's show all the more resonant for me. So, without further ado..." Laurie turns to me and crosses her legs. "Raquel, tell us what happened the day you received your first breast-cancer diagnosis."

Gazing into Laurie's eyes, I am mesmerized. To my surprise, I find that talking is not impossible. "Well, I was devastated. Panicked. All these weird thoughts were running through my head. Nothing made sense. I had so many questions later, but at that moment"—I flash to Meissner tenting his fingers over the papers on his desk and gazing at me with those puppy-dog eyes, and it's almost like I'm back there again—"all I could think was, *No, this can't be.* I felt like I couldn't be, you know, *the one.* I felt too young, too healthy, too *ornery.*" At that, a handful of people in the audience laugh, and my spirits rise fractionally. Maybe I won't be tarred and feathered on a second-rate cable network after all.

"When did you find out they'd given you the wrong test results?"

"A month later. Not a long time, but you have to understand what happens to you, to your life, in the weeks after the diagnosis. It's like everything changes overnight. You go from taking everything for granted to wondering if you'll survive till your next birthday, to see your daughter get married, to watch your son graduate from college. You can't eat—or you eat too much. You can't sleep—or you can't stop sleeping. Everything seems surreal. The fact that everybody else is going about their lives is obscene. It changes you." Out of the corner of my eye, I see Jean nodding. Hope inches further upward inside me.

"Part of me even thought, *What if they're wrong again?* I couldn't bear to go through the assimilation part again. It was too hard. It really fucked me up, actually." Laurie keeps smiling, even as I realize that somebody, somewhere, has had to bleep me big-time. Oops. Still, this faux pas nets me a few more empathetic chuckles. *Things are going somewhere,* I think. "By that point I had come on your show, done the telethon... I don't know how to say this, I was *invested* in it. I was still scared, but in a different way: Could I get in trouble for having raised all that money under false pretenses? Could I get *you* in trouble? Was it better to just keep the train moving and ask questions later?"

Laurie leans forward. "But the truth is, you never told them, did you?"

"I tried. First I thought, *I'll just burst in and tell them. What's so hard about that?* But it never... I could never figure out how to frame it. When that didn't happen, I made a fancy dinner, made sure everyone was coming home early, put on my tunic shirt that hides everything nasty that my friend Sue says looks like Jaclyn Smith for Kmart"—chuckles—"and told them the truth. What happened was, they didn't believe me. I don't really blame them because, frankly, at that point, I didn't believe it myself. It sounded so ridiculous, you know? It sounded a little bit crazy. After that, I kept coming up with these elaborate schemes for doing it gently, but something always got in the way." I dredge up the memory of that night at the dinner table when, *as per usual,* kids and husband were whirring around in a world that seemed just a little bit fuller, a little bit faster, a little bit more important than my own.

"I know it sounds implausible, maybe even ridiculous, but I think the real reason I didn't tell them spontaneously is that I didn't know how to get them to listen to me. It is hard to say this, because I now take full responsibility for my actions, and for my own happiness, but the truth is, my husband and kids and family didn't respect my thoughts or my time. It's not completely their fault, you see, because I hadn't earned that respect. I had no respect for myself, really, and I hadn't in a long time, maybe ever." I catch a sliver of Alicia's pasty moon of a face through the curtain, and my heart freezes in my chest. Maybe I've gone too far?

"I'm oversimplifying. But that is how I felt. This is the kind of insecure and self-recriminating and self-indulgent thinking that got me into this mess. As long as I can remember, I wanted to be special. I never felt good enough. Not to my parents, not to my teachers, to men, to my sister"—I give Laurie's hand a pat, and she nods encouragingly—"so when this happened, I began to see it as an opportunity to change, to make a difference. However, to make it that, I'd have to pretend that I was sick. I just didn't have the courage to reinvent myself without the protective cover the breast cancer provided."

My voice drops. "It wasn't just the money I'd helped raise. I *liked* the attention. I liked that I'd had an idea for a new sculpture series and that a successful gallery owner thought it was promising. I liked the way my kids and husband made time for me and acted like I was a star, not just someone they tolerated. I liked the new me, and I was finding it hard to give her up, even though I knew I had to."

"Tell me what reinvention means to you." Laurie leans

back, as if my answers are sensible and intelligent and therefore relaxing.

"Sex," I say, and this time *everybody* laughs.

"Sex?"

"Having it. Enjoying it. Feeling young again. Feeling exciting. Sexual."

"Go on."

"That's not the only thing. Because this happened, I found my calling again—art. And I did work I'm proud of. Not that I'm not proud of raising my children, or being a wife...it's just that part of me always needed this outlet, this work, and I never had the guts to go after it before, to see if I had what it takes to produce something that moves other people. And it turns out I think I do."—I bite my knuckle. "For the first time, I feel like I'm at the right place at the right time in my own life. I really *own* it. I can be my best self for myself *and* my family. Does that make sense?"

"That makes more sense than a lot of what I hear in this business," Laurie says, then turns toward the camera. "We'll be back after a short commercial break, when we'll talk to some special guests about Raquel's future."

We cut to a commercial.

I tug my blouse away from my pits. It's drenched. "Oh my God."

Cleo sees me and runs out with an identical blouse. "I thought something like this might happen." In front of everyone, she whips me out of the sweaty blouse and replaces it. Jonesie fixes my hair. Cleo fixes my makeup. Laurie gives me a glass of water. I look at the backstage doorway: Alicia is gone. Maybe Laurie will keep her job after all? Or maybe my sister is getting shitcanned as we speak.

"What special guests?" I ask Laurie.

"Oh, just a few experts."

"Therapists?"

"Well, not really."

The first notes of "Raquel" tinkle over us. Laurie ignores me and readies herself to go on-air.

"Hello. I'm Lauren White, and this is *Living with Lauren!* For those of you just tuning in, we're talking to Raquel Rose, a woman who pretended to have breast cancer for almost a year.

"Raquel, what do you want now, more than anything?" Laurie says.

"I wouldn't mind entering the witness protection program." Small redux. Big laughs.

Laurie grins. "Besides that."

"I want to apologize. Not just to my kids and my husband and you and Ma and everyone in our family, but to all the people who supported me during this, uh, misadventure. Jean and Kendall and all the ladies from the awesome support group"—I inhale deeply and pinch my thigh brutally, just in case a nervous giggle tries to emerge—"Women Expunging Cancer of the Breast Because Life Endures. That's WE COB-BLE, and they're wonderful, funny, brave women, and they meet every week in San Francisco. And Saskia Waxman and everybody who bought or reviewed or supported my work in any way. And my friends and neighbors, especially Sue Ban-icek, my best friend, my rock."

I follow Laurie's lead and turn directly to the camera. "Sue, I know you're watching even though you're mad at me—Sue thought I had Munchausen syndrome, but really, I'm just an idiot. Anyway, Sue, I just want to tell you that I love and admire you so very, very much. There aren't many people in this world who inspire us to be our best selves, and you're mine." My head hangs slightly from the weight of the truth. "I abused that trust when I asked you to lie for me, and I know now how very wrong that was. And I'm sorry I said bad things about Tamarind, because anyone with a taste bud knows your apple-stuffed pork loin is to die for"—I turn to the audience—"which is why I once ate four of them, and that was just for lunch!" Laughs. "That's *Tamarind,* people, and it's a hot little restaurant on Potrero Hill.

"And, let's see, my doctors, Dr. Sam Meissner and Dr. Minh, because they were nothing but professional throughout"— why not throw Minh a bone, since he'll be on the crapper for the next three days after that hot dog—"and really, everyone whom my lies touched. And hurt."

I take a deep breath. "Laurie, I'm glad I came on today. It wasn't easy, and it means a lot to me that you were willing to take a chance on me, especially after my actions on your show and how I deceived you."

"Raquel, this seems like a good time to read you a message I have here from the *Living with Lauren!* team, all the producers and technical personnel and stylists and interns who make it happen every day." Laurie smiles at her people. If someone told me to bend down and smooch her butt on alternate cheeks right now, I would.

" 'Dear Raquel. We know how much courage it takes to admit a mistake to so many people, not to mention your loved ones. You are not the same Raquel we admired when we thought you were a cancer survivor: You are so much more than that, even. We believe in second chances, and we know that your example will help others face their personal demons and move their lives forward in more constructive, productive directions. We wish you the best and hope you return to spend time with us again soon.' "

"That's"—I am too choked up to speak—"that's too much…" There's no other way to describe it: I am bawling.

"Raquel, if you're up to it, I'd like to bring out some very special guests who want to talk to you."

I assent through my tears and then nearly faint, because the special guests walking uncertainly through the curtains are Phil, Micah, and Taylor.

The fam.

In an extremely Maury-ish move, I leap to my feet and fling myself into the arms of my exceedingly grown-up-looking children, who—*blessed be me!*—hug me right back in front of everyone. Somehow the microphone attached to my slacks pops off during the melee, and Shiny has to run out and reaffix it. Unfortunately, I am unable to sit still due to the flurry of embracing, and the mike picks up the resounding *rrrrii-iiiipppp* of my butt seam splitting as Shiny, Raquel, and too-snug pants move in three different directions at once.

"Oh my God!" You'd think Shiny Pony had never seen a woman in a pair of tightie whities that say PHIL'S MEAT DEPARTMENT.

I stare into Phil's wolfish green eyes. "It made me miss you less," I explain.

My husband raises my hand to his lips and kisses it perfectly—dryly and full of pent-up passion, no tongue.

Before any of us can react further to the horror, Cleo—who, as far as I know, has never trod the stage during a broadcast—waltzes out like Princess Diana, mincing and waving, and—this has to be one for the books—removes my *pants* on live TV, replacing them with a pair of sweatpants. Upon glancing backstage, I realize that the provenance of the sweats is none other than Boss of Shiny Pony, who is standing there blushing furiously in a pair of faded boxers, his skinny, hairy gams poking out like ectomorphic palm trees.

Laurie digs deep and finds her aplomb. "Well, *that* was exciting, wasn't it? It's not every day we have a guest in her underwear—especially, uh, *those* underwear." Mass hysteria. Laurie speaks loudly and firmly. "I'd like to welcome Raquel's family to the show today to hear their side of the story. Phil Rose, Raquel's husband, is a high school math teacher. Phil and Raquel have been married for twenty years. Phil and Raquel's children, Micah and Taylor, are a freshman in college and a junior in high school, respectively."

Everybody nods. Phil, I realize, is still holding my hand tightly in his, just like the guy on *Maury* who still claimed to love his wife even after she came back from her Florida vacation with FFF breast implants and a new face. Somebody must have helped dress Phil today, because in addition to a very sleek charcoal suit and lavender shirt that brings out the color of his eyes, his shoes are shined, and he's had his salt-and-pepper hair mowed into a youthful spikiness that does not say Mel's barbershop.

There is no mud brown anywhere on his person.

Micah, whom I haven't seen since he left for school at the end of August, is as collegiate and self-assured as I could have dreamed. His hair is a little longer and darker—no surfing in Ann Arbor—and he's wearing his team's soccer sweatshirt. Taylor has not changed since our last biweekly visit, except she has parted her chestnut hair down the middle and let it fall in natural waves, like mine, instead of blowing it fearfully straight. Her legs underneath the modest pencil skirt are long and brown; they will perform well in focus groups with just about everybody except the violently jealous.

"Phil, tell us what those first days were like, when you thought you could lose Raquel," Laurie says.

Phil glances at me and gives my hand another squeeze. "The news was a shock. A brutal shock. It's hard for me to explain how difficult it is to accept something like this at first. It just doesn't seem real. One minute your life is normal, and the next this bomb has dropped. You don't want to accept it, because there's a strong sense that everything else you rely on will start tumbling down. There's a sense that nothing is as it seems, and frankly, that is extremely frightening."

Laurie turns to Micah. "Did you feel conscious of having to support your mom, or were you thinking mostly about yourselves and the effect it would have on you?"

"We were really upset. My mom and I may not always see eye to eye on things"—quick grin, which I lap up like cream-top milk—"but she has always been the center of our family. Despite what she says, she's the one who holds us together. One time she went away to a spa with her friend Sue for the weekend, and we almost burned the house down trying to cook bacon. And nobody could find the checkbook, so the bills were late. And the dogs escaped—one of them ate our neighbors' flowers that had just been treated with weed killer, and almost died—so you see how it is without her. It's terrible. When she told us, I felt sick to my stomach, as if everything was, like, tilted. I was angry, too. I didn't want her to be the one who got it. I wanted it to be somebody else."

Laurie smiles at Taylor. "What about you, Taylor?"

Taylor glances at Phil. "I was scared. What was going to happen to me? How was I going to deal with school and things without my mom? I thought about her being in pain, being bald and sick and getting operated on and everything, and I almost freaked out." Tay starts crying a little, and I reach out my hand. She takes it.

"As we know, Raquel did not have the disease, but she neglected to inform you of this for almost a year. How did you feel when you found out she lied to you?"

I shrink in my seat and start to sweat again. Watching their sweet, worried faces, I cannot believe I really did it. *I am a maniac,* I think. *I should be put down, like a dog with two legs.*

Phil clears his throat. I can tell this is going to be ugly, but something in me seeks the punishment, relishes it. I try to convey this to Phil with my eyes: *Pull no punches.*

He gets it. "I couldn't believe she had done this to our children. It was so far off the scale of what a reasonable person would do, I even wondered if she was mentally ill. I was appalled. I wondered if I really knew my wife at all, or if I'd been sharing a life with a stranger all these years."

"I didn't want to ever see her again," Micah says.

"I thought she hated us." Taylor.

"That's understandable," Laurie says. "Do you feel different now?"

Micah raises his hand. "I do. I guess it's because I, uh, learned some things in the past year. I started to understand what it's like to have a secret eating at you, to hide who you are from people you care about. I thought a lot about Mom and how her life was before this happened. It's not like I'm making excuses for her or anything, or that it justifies what she did, but I understand a little better what it does to a person to feel like you're living a lie. Especially when it started out, you know, innocently—it wasn't her fault they got the test wrong and she went on TV and everything." He gets up and comes over to me. Phil releases my hand. Micah and I hug, a big, comfy, delicious, forgiving hug that does a lot to make me feel like the cells of my body are rejoining, forming a whole again, something I can live with, maybe even happily.

This is really, truly the best day of my life, I think.

Micah places his hand firmly on Phil's shoulder. "I'm gay, Dad. I'm sorry." He turns to the crowd. "I know this show isn't broadcast in Michigan, but I just want my teammates to know

I'll be back for this weekend's game against Northwestern. Go Wolverines!" he howls. Everyone cheers.

I check to see if Phil is going to collapse, but he just sits there, a glazed look on his face.

Taylor raises her hand next. "Nobody's perfect, okay? And anyone who thinks they are is just a douche. Mom, I'm sorry I was so hard on you. I wish I hadn't been. I was really mad at you, but I'm not anymore. You took care of me my whole life, and you're a good mom." She faces the crowd. "I thought about pretending I was pregnant so my dad would come back home to live with us. How lame is that? Although it probably would have worked, since my parents were already sleeping together anyway"—she frowns—"but I don't recommend it or anything. Also, to anyone out there from Tater who's watching, Biter Caldwell has the puniest—"

"Phil," Laurie interrupts quickly, before her show implodes due to profanity and generalized tackiness. "Is there anything else you'd like to add?"

"Uh, I bought some of Raquel's pieces to get her shows moving," he mumbles.

"I'm sorry, can you repeat that?"

"I said I have something to confess, too. I bought a few of Raquel's works anonymously, so that people would start taking her seriously and the galleries would know they'd made the right decision to show her work." I feel my face burn. I can't tell if it's from affection for Phil or consternation that I wasn't the bona fide popular genius I thought I was.

I think it's the affection.

"We're in over our heads financially," he explains. "That's one of the things we always argue about." He squeezes my hand again. "It was just to jump-start things. I only bought two."

"Oh, Philly." I don't know what to say.

From out in the audience, a voice booms. "I knew there was bovine growth hormone in the school milk, but I let 'em put it in anyway, 'cause it was cheaper. I'm Eliot Abramson of Abramson Integrated Foods, Raquel's stepfather. *Proud* stepfather, I should say. I agree with Taylor. Nobody's perfect. Anyway, I'm sorry." Eliot sits down, banging his bony ass on the upright flip chair in the process. His "goddammit" reverberates through the room. I don't think this family will ever grace the *Living with Lauren!* studio again, if Laurie can help it.

Ma stands and peers down her glasses. "I'm Minna Louise Schultz Abramson, Rachel and Lauren's mother," she says in her Bea Arthur rasp. "I'm so proud of both my girls. You carry them inside you all those months, you give them the milk from your breasts"—*oh, Ma, for God's sake*—"you'd lie down on train tracks for them, and still, you have to let them fly free, let them make their own mistakes. It's a mother's curse...What did I want to say? Oh yes: I've always told everyone I met my second husband in the doctor's waiting room—that's Kolodnick, over at Stanford, by the way, the man's a wonderful doctor, and he's single, and he's a *mensch,* ladies!—but anyway, actually, we had an affair years ago, when my first husband—God bless him—Stuart was still alive. It was just the one time, mind you, but I've always felt guilty about it. El and I agreed it was a bad idea to break up our families, but when we met again by chance all those years later, we knew it was fate." She grabs Eliot by the T-shirt. They kiss passionately, two shriveled little Jews in matching black stretch pants. The crowd goes wild. I try to remember if I have a panty liner on under Phil's tightie whities, because I think incontinence is only a giggle away.

Laurie's eyes are closed. For a moment I'm scared *she's* the one having heart failure. She's always been the normal one in our family, and thus the one with the lowest tolerance for Clan Abramaschultz's shenanigans. For perhaps the first time ever, I see what Ma was talking about when she characterized Laurie as more vulnerable than I; with more conventional success to lose, she's always been a little less free to make mistakes. Suddenly, I feel the weight of all that implies for Laurie—along with a surge of gratitude for what was doubtless a lot of heated explaining and convincing on the front end of this deal.

As I'm reaching out to steady my sister, she waves me away and speaks. "Since this seems to be confession day, I'd like to get something off my chest that's been bothering me for years. Everyone: I'm infertile." She glances quickly at the crowd. "That's no secret. I've even done shows about it. But it's my infertility—and my inability to cope with it—that led me to do something terrible to someone I care about very much. Something I've always regretted."

Laurie stands up as if offering herself to her fans as sacrifice. "My secret is, I was so jealous of Raquel's ability to have beautiful children that I once intercepted a letter to her from a foundation informing her that she'd won a grant to serve as a resident visual artist."

"Not the Headlands Center for the Arts?" I'd always had a strange, inexplicable feeling of loss about that one, but the lack of a formal response—even to reject me—had so damaged my confidence that I'd never again applied to another program.

Laurie nods gravely.

"I won that?" I know it's ridiculous, but instead of being furious or sick with betrayal, I feel gratified to have beat out such grand competition for the prized residency. A memory of myself plucking out the smiling newsprint eyes of the winning Stinson Beach snack-bar painter—she of the Scotch habit and laundry list of food allergies from Ross Trimble's dinner party—floods my brain. I am suddenly quite happy.

"It was lying there on the counter when you brought the mail in one day," Laurie explains, sounding miserable. "You went to the bathroom. I read it and stuffed it in the bottom of the recycling." She sniffles softly. "Please, will you forgive me?"

I put my arm around her. "Given that I might or might not have had sex with your husband, I'd say we're even."

Epilogue

(One Year Later)

Have you ever wondered what you'd do if they told you that you weren't dying? Not like, someday you're not going to die. Imminently. As in today.

I used to think about it periodically. Lately, though, I've been too busy. Between the book tour to promote *Sick of It: How Opting Out Can Help You Opt into Success* and my latest show at the LACMA and private commissions and taping new episodes of *Living with Lauren & Raquel!*, I don't have time to watch *Desperate Housewives* on TiVo, let alone brood about big life questions that really don't matter much to me anymore. Also, in spite of the fact that *not* dying certainly qualifies as the less morbid side of death, it's still a relatively gloomy topic, and I'm trying to keep things light and positive for the baby.

Baby?

Yes, baby. What, you thought I was done with all that pro-creation stuff just because I'm forty-four and counting and my kids not only have drivers' licenses but five tickets between them?

You thought wrong.

I'll admit it: Being knocked up at this age is a whole different ball of hemorrhoids. If someone had told me beforehand that the indigestion, swollen ankles, bleeding gums, and pesky zits I endured in my twenties would revisit me in my forties, I'd have run screaming for the nearest empty nest. I've even had restless leg syndrome, if you can believe it. Restless legs! Afflicting me, an avowed believer in death by exercise. The nerve!

I can't complain, though. After all, it *was* my decision. I guess the temptation of having Ren's baby never really fled the coop completely.

What, you say, *Ren's*—gasp!—*baby?*

Get your mind out of the gutter, will you? Of course I'm having Ren's baby. What, you think Phil and I want to go through the corrosive, sanity-eating, soul-stealing fog that is parenting an infant? Fuck no. Excuse me, what I mean to say is, *FUCK NO.*

I'll tell you something in complete confidence: The day I give birth to my and Philly's child and allow the little Morgoth to annihilate the piss-elegant San Francisco condo we moved into last year is the day I rejoin the Peninsula JCC and ask Rochelle Schitzfelder to be my natural-labor coach.

Since I know you're *dying* for the dirt, here's the deal: Meet Raquel Rose, surrogate mom.

Yep, that's it. Surrogate. Before we got deeply into it, when I was still freaking out at the idea and envisioning myself in vomit-stained caftans, I looked it up: *taking the place of somebody or something else.*

After pondering things for a while, I realized how off the mark that definition is. Okay, not off the mark, exactly, but incomplete. A lie by omission. Because one thing I know for sure is that I could *never* replace Laurie in much of anything. Lend her my uterus, yes. Substitute for her? No. What they should have said is: *taking the place of somebody or something in a matter of little cosmic importance that they are unable to address themselves.*

I'll never forget the day it happened. Well, not *happened*—
that rollicking adventure occurred on a paper-coated table
with me on my back, my legs in stirrups, and an embryologist
poking around my cervix while a Muzak version of Jimmy
Cliff's "The Harder They Come" chimed in the background—
but was *conceived.*

Ouch.

It was the strangest thing: One minute I was standing in
front of the magazine rack at Walgreens, sneaking a peek at
an article on celebrity baby nurseries, the next I was speeding
down the freeway to Laurie and Ren's.

I was so excited I left my keys in the convertible MINI
Cooper—I traded in the Sienna when we moved to the city—
and ran up the walkway to my sister's Atherton Tudor. It was
Sunday evening; I knew my sister and brother-in-law would
be home, she knitting or grinding herbs into neatly labeled
jars, he reading medical journals or shining his golf shoes.

"Laurie!" I called as I rapped the door. "Ren!"

Laurie answered. "I didn't know you were coming, Quel. Is
everything all right?"

"It's perfect." I sat down at the kitchen table. The surface was so polished, I could see Ren's worry lines when he
entered from the living room to see what was going on.

"I'm going to have your baby," I said.

"What?"

"We're going to do one of those IVF thingies where they
make a baby out of Ren's sperm and your eggs and plant it
in me. I may be old, but my insides still work. And the baby
would be all yours—"

"Embryo," Ren cut in. He had his arm around Laurie's
shoulders. He often does. When I think of all the years I
spent imagining the glorious good fortune that arm around
me might confer, I am really impatient to get on with things.

"Whatever. Just…I'll do it. Ren, you said it yourself to me once, that it would have been a good idea if only I hadn't had chemo. Well, I haven't had it, and God willing, I won't have it. I'm healthy, I've had my kids, I won't want to raise the baby or anything. I'll do it. Say yes before I change my mind, goddammit!"

Ren and Laurie regarded each other with that expressive shorthand long-married people use when they need to achieve consensus in a hurry and without speaking because other (rude) people are in the room. They didn't exchange a word.

"Yes," Laurie said simply.

"Raquel…" Ren seemed at a loss for words. "Thank you."

I didn't want them to be too grateful or think I wanted them to grovel, so I shifted their attention to the one potential obstacle to this endeavor.

"Now who's going to tell Phil?" I said.

Ah, the memories.

Phil took it like a true mensch. He takes a lot of stuff better than I thought he—or any man—could. That doesn't mean he's a saint. Far from it. The thing with Philip Atticus Rose is, he doesn't play fair—he lets his opponents get overconfident. Just when you think you're home free, *whammo!*, he hits you with the big one. Frankly, I admire his cruelty. Plus, if I *were* married to a saint, it would probably last about as long as my relationship with Duke Dunne, and that's not counting the ride on the motorcycle.

It took exactly forty-two days after we got back together on *Living with Lauren!* for Phil to ask about Duke Dunne. I know this because I marked it off on a wall calendar. I know it's weird, but nobody ever accused me of being normal, right?

We were sitting in the hot tub at his apartment complex

in Redwood City—or Redwood Shitty, as we had taken to calling it when the windows started leaking and black mold overtook the grout. The hot tub was the one plus that the mostly singles-y nest of units had going for it, as long as we snagged it early, before the nightly contingent of swaybacked divorcées and horny Pakistani engineers dropped beneath the beige foam.

Phil filled my plastic water bottle with cheap pinot grigio and stretched out, his back against a jet. "Did you sleep with that piece of shit Dunne?" he said.

I sighed and trotted out the only answer I could reasonably give the man I adored more than any other. "Yeah."

He nodded. "I thought so. You seemed different."

"Yeah, well, sometimes I wish I hadn't. Does that help?"

Phil flicked away a froth of suds. "Yeah, it does, actually. Do me a favor?"

"Sure."

"If I ask you for specifics sometime, don't tell me."

"Okay."

"Especially if I'm impotent or something."

"Like that's going to happen, stud." We laughed. I could tell he wanted to kiss me, but then our neighbor Atiq Some-thingorother walked through the gate, skinny legs brown and shivering, and asked whether we minded if he joined us. We said no, and Phil's long toes with their rough, untended nails scratched my calf underwater, just the way I like it.

Phil never asked about Duke again. I choose to take it as a sign of great affection.

Will passenger Raquel Rose please report to the podium?

The disembodied voice repeats itself several times while I waddle my way to the gate. This is good news: Maybe Philly and I will be able to sit together on the way to Waikiki after all.

I introduce myself to the woman at the gate, a well-groomed Filipina with ash-blond highlights and airline-approved ruby lips.

She frowns. "But *that's* Raquel Rose." She points at somebody a few feet away, a petite woman with a brown bob and two young children weaving around her legs. "She showed me her driver's license. She was waiting for an upgrade, so I put her in business."

As my mind charts the logic from point A to point B and puts together what happened, the woman seems to sense my presence, or maybe she just overhears us and turns around. *She is pretty* is the first (superficial) thing I register. Also: *She looks healthy.* Then: *Where's the husband?*

"Oh," the woman says, unfastening one of her kids' sticky-looking hands from her Bermuda shorts. The boy whines and drops a karate chop in the middle of his sister's back. The girl erupts. "Oh, damn," the woman says, then, absently, "Kids, there's Daddy, run and get him." They charge off, leaving only us, two Raquel Roses in orbit around each other at the United counter.

"Are you...well?" I ask. There is no need to explain; we both know what's going on. Just seeing her solid and actual in front of me—she, the intangible, elusive manifestation of my blunders—is sweet relief.

"Yes. Yes, I am." Her smooth, clear face is serene. "And you?"

I point to my burgeoning stomach. "Pretty good, considering."

"Yes, well." She gestures toward her incoming family, a study in hibiscus patterns and ice-cream stains. "I'd better go."

"Right. Well, have a good time."

"You, too."

I walk ten steps before something turns me around. "Is your name really Raquel?" I call.

She smiles. "Yeah. My mom thought it sounded racy. I've always wanted something classier. Rachel would have been nice."

ABOUT THE AUTHOR

I was born in Hollywood in 1969. That sounds fancy, but all it really means is I played in public parks alongside the children of grips and the occasional transsexual hooker. Throughout the 1970s, I followed the zeitgeist, enjoying *Star Wars,* Judy Blume, Madeleine L'Engle, and recreational soccer under the leadership of various well-intentioned but misinformed dads. For a brief period, I developed an unhealthy interest in the Bermuda Triangle. I read a lot of grown-up books I "borrowed" from my friends' mothers that turned out to be soft-core porn. It was all very *Boogie Nights,* very Southern California!

Then my parents loaded up the station wagon with three kids, a basset hound, and a hillbilly pile of stuff and moved us up to northern California. It was about the same, minus the tans, plus the mullets. The '80s were filled with new-wave music, Boone's Farm wine, and a succession of ill-advised fashion choices. I wrote angry journal entries and a love paean to Duran Duran.

After high school, I left for the big city and U.C. Berkeley, eventually earning my B.A. in political science at U.C. Davis. Flirting with working for an NGO or the diplomatic corps, I got an M.A. in international relations at the University of Amsterdam in the Netherlands, which qualifies me to create exotic settings for my books and little else.

Around this time, I began a successful career in...under-employment. Researching mechanics liens, copyediting reviews of pet-worship Web sites, spoon-feeding psychotropic medication to a clinically psychotic boss...no job was too soul-killing or weird for the likes of me. That's when I decided to take a stab at this writing thing. Really, there was nothing left to fear.

Along the way, I met my wondrous husband, Gabe. (My grandmothers, who never agreed on anything, both deemed him a mensch.) We live in San Francisco with our perpetually curious daughter Lucca and our son Zev, who, at eight months, already smiles like he means it.

FIVE THINGS YOU NEVER THOUGHT YOU'D SAY TO YOUR KIDS:

• • • • • • • • • •

 1. "That's why they call it *medical* marijuana, honey."

2. "Of course surfing is a valid career choice."

 3. "You're sitting on my wig."

4. "Staying together for the children? Who told you that?"

5. "What I did is perfectly legal... in Sweden."